200 HARLEY STREET

Welcome to the luxurious premises of the exclusive
Hunter Clinic, world renowned in plastic and
reconstructive surgery, set right on Harley Street,
the centre of elite clinical excellence,
in the heart of London's glittering West End!

Owned by two very different brothers,
Leo and Ethan Hunter, the Hunter Clinic undertakes
both cosmetic and reconstructive surgery. Playboy Leo
handles the rich and famous clients, enjoying the red
carpet glamour of London's A-list social scene, while
brooding ex-army doc Ethan focuses his time on his
passion—transforming the lives of injured war heroes
and civilian casualties of war.

Emotion and drama abound against the backdrop of
one of Europe's most glamorous cities, as Leo and
Ethan work through their tensions and find women
who will change their lives for ever!

200 HARLEY STREET

*Glamour, intensity, desire—the lives and loves
of London's hottest team of surgeons!*

Conclude your sensational eight-book journey with…

200 HARLEY STREET: THE SHAMELESS MAVERICK
by Louisa George

200 HARLEY  **ERO**

A lifelong reader of most genres, **Louisa George** discovered romance novels later than most, but immediately fell in love with the intensity of emotion, the high drama and the family focus of Mills & Boon® Medical Romance™.

With a Bachelor's Degree in Communication and a nursing qualification under her belt, writing medical romance seemed a natural progression, and the perfect combination of her two interests. And making things up is a great way to spend the day!

An English ex-pat, Louisa now lives north of Auckland, New Zealand, with her husband, two teenage sons and two male cats. Writing romance is her opportunity to covertly inject a hefty dose of pink into her heavily testosterone-dominated household. When she's not writing or researching Louisa loves to spend time with her family and friends, enjoys travelling, and adores great food. She's also hopelessly addicted to Zumba®.

Amy Andrews has always loved writing, and still can't quite believe that she gets to do it for a living. Creating wonderful heroines and gorgeous heroes and telling their stories is an amazing way to pass the day. Sometimes they don't always act as she'd like them to—but then neither do her kids, so she's kind of used to it. Amy lives in the very beautiful Samford Valley, with her husband and aforementioned children, along with six brown chooks and two black dogs. She loves to hear from her readers. Drop her a line at www.amyandrews.com.au

200 HARLEY STREET: THE SHAMELESS MAVERICK

BY
LOUISA GEORGE

All rights reserved including the right of reproduction in whole or in part in any form. This edition is published by arrangement with Harlequin Books S.A.

This ... is ... of ... ..., places, locations ... and incid... ...lationship to any ...al life i... ...ce to any actual places, business estab... ...r incidents. Any resemblance is entir...

This ... is sold subject to the condition that it shall not, by way of trade ... ...nt, resold, hired out or otherwise ci... ...ated with ... ...he prior consent of the ... ...r in any form of bi... ...ng or cove... ...r ... ...t is published and without a si...ilar cond... ...on including this con... ...being imposed on the sub...quent purc...

® ar... ...TM are trade...Es owned ... used by the trademark ... ...wner and/... ...its licensee. Trademarks ...arked with ® are register... ...with the Unit... ...Kingdom Patent Office ... ...r the Office for Harm...isation in the Internal Market and in other countries.

Published in Great Britain 2014
by Mills & Boon, an imprint of Harlequin (UK) Limited,
Eton House, 18-24 Paradise Road, Richmond, Surrey, TW9 1SR

© 2014 Harlequin Books S.A.

Special thanks and acknowledgement are given to Louisa George for her contribution to the *200 Harley Street* series

ISBN: 978 0 263 90775 9

Harlequin (UK) Limited's policy is to use papers that are natural, renewable and recyclable products and made from wood grown in sustainable forests. The logging and manufacturing processes conform to the legal environmental regulations of the country of origin.

Printed and bound in Spain
by Blackprint CPI, Barcelona

MORAY COUNCIL
LIBRARIES &
INFO.SERVICES

20 37 29 85

Askews & Holts

RF

Dear Reader

When I was invited to take part in the *200 Harley Street* continuity I was absolutely thrilled—not only because this is my first ever Mills & Boon® Medical Romance™ continuity contribution, but because it also meant I got the chance to work closely with some amazing authors and some very interesting plotlines. So a big thank you to everyone for taking a newbie under your collective wings!

Declan Underwood and Kara Stephens come from two very different worlds, but both have fled to London to start new lives in their chosen field of Burns and Plastic Medicine. Falling in love is definitely not on the cards for either of them, so it's very inconvenient when a mutual attraction starts to sizzle!

Australian Kara was a joy to write: she's funny and confident and shares my love of shoes. Like many of us, she'll live with pain in exchange for a decent heel and the softest of soft suede! But she also has a history of choosing the wrong men, so staying away from Declan is her preferred course of action.

But who can resist a bad-boy Irishman? Farmboy Declan, with his smoulderingly good looks and an accent that purrs as sexily as his motorbike, has no intention of getting involved with Kara; his life is already too full of commitments to his career and providing for his mother and four sisters. But that's where I come in: plotting ways of getting them together even when they don't want to be anywhere near each other…

I hope you enjoy reading this book as much as I enjoyed writing it.

Drop me a line at louisageorgeauthor@gmail.com or visit me at www.louisageorge.com

Happy reading!

Louisa x

**Praise for
Louisa George:**

'A moving, uplifting and feel-good romance packed with
witty dialogue, intense emotion and sizzling love scenes.'
—*goodreads.com* on
HOW TO RESIST A HEARTBREAKER

'Louisa George is a bright star at Mills & Boon®
and I can highly recommend this book to those that
believe romance rocks the world.'
—*goodreads.com* on
HOW TO RESIST A HEARTBREAKER

'A refreshing, captivating and breathtaking medical romance.'
—*Romance Book Paradise* on
THE LAST DOCTOR SHE SHOULD EVER DATE

'ONE MONTH TO BECOME A MUM is one story
you don't want to miss!'
—*Harlequinjunkie.com*

Recent titles by Louisa George:

HOW TO RESIST A HEARTBREAKER*
THE LAST DOCTOR SHE SHOULD EVER DATE
THE WAR HERO'S LOCKED-AWAY HEART
WAKING UP WITH HIS RUNAWAY BRIDE
ONE MONTH TO BECOME A MUM

The Infamous Maitland Brothers

**Also available in eBook format
from www.millsandboon.co.uk**

Dedication

To Kamy Chetty, thanks for all your support,
positive words and help with the icky medical details
(any errors are totally mine). xx

And to Jane Beckenham, without you I just wouldn't be
here writing this—thank you so much for all your support,
enthusiasm and words of wisdom and for introducing me to
the world of romance books…this one's for you! xx

CHAPTER ONE

'MAKE SURE TO get my best side, won't you now?' Declan Underwood joked to the army of paparazzi camped on the front steps of Princess Catherine's Hospital as he parked his motorbike and removed his helmet.

He smiled towards his clicking, whirring audience, who clearly had nothing better to do than chase ambulances on a sunny summer morning, and tried to hide his growing irritation. The last thing he needed was more unwarranted delays, today of all days. He was not in the mood to be polite.

Making his way up the pale stone steps, he batted away questions like a tennis ace.

'Is Princess Safia here?' someone shouted from behind a long lens. 'Is she going to make a full recovery? Will she be scarred for life?'

'Now, come on, give a guy a break. I can't hear one for the other.' Toeing both the clinic's and his own staunch professional line, Declan exhaled slowly and waited for them to settle. 'As you know, ladies and gents, my hands are tied. There's a young girl's privacy to think of. I just can't make any comment.'

Note: make sure the blinds are closed at all times. Move her to a higher floor. Increase security.

Sure, both the Hunter Clinic and the hospital affectionately known as Kate's relied on positive press to further their reach and their work, but this was way too much interest in a young girl fighting for her life, regardless of her background.

Small wonder the Sheikh's staff had been definitive in their demands to uphold their privacy. If any of Declan's family had been involved in a tragedy such as this he'd want to protect them too.

He shuddered and damped down the tight squeeze in his chest. *Had* protected them, for all the good that had done.

'Come on, Declan, it's no coincidence that you—the country's foremost burns reconstruction surgeon—are here and there's a private flight scheduled to arrive from Aljahar any minute.'

Was that Fi…something—the journalist he'd spent a few dates with not so long ago? Trying to use her inside contacts to get more information? Tut-tut. Declan flashed her a particular smile. Similar to the one he'd given her as he'd left for the last time, whenever it was, that said, *Hey, don't push it.*

With all the smiling his jaw muscles had begun to ache, but he knew that the Hunter Clinic boss, Leo, wouldn't want his second-in-command to jeopardise the clinic's new positive relationship with the media. 'I'm so sorry, but you all know that I'm in no position to confirm or deny any rumours. You all know too that even if I did have any idea as to the whereabouts or condition of Princess Safia I couldn't tell you a thing. The Sheikh, quite rightly, is very keen on confidentiality. But I'm sure he and his family appreciate all the concern and will issue a statement as and when appropriate. Now we need to leave the family alone to recover. And I need to go to work. Thank you so much.'

Closing the door behind him to a barrage of more camera flashes, he exhaled deeply and headed towards the burns unit. Two extensive surgeries, an afternoon clinic and an evening meeting amidst a swirl of media frenzy about a royal with devastating facial burns loomed ahead of him.

It was going to be a very long day.

'You. Yes, you. Stop. Wait.'

A heavily accented raised male voice out in the hospital corridor drew Declan's attention from the notes he was reviewing at his desk over his hastily snatched lunch break.

'What's all that noise on the street? The photographers? Newspapers? His Highness specifically said he wanted Sheikha Safia's arrival to be discreet. His daughter is suffering and she needs peace and quiet. She is devastated about her injuries…'

'Yes, I understand entirely,' an unfamiliar voice with an Antipodean twang replied. 'I have already spoken to Security and they are planning to transfer the Princess through the back door.' Despite the clipped tones the voice was remarkably calm, smoky. Distinctly feminine. Declan put down the papers and listened.

The male voice cut in. 'We understood Mr Underwood himself was going to oversee every detail.'

'Of the surgery and treatment phases, yes, absolutely, but not everything on this list…'

She paused. Declan heard a rustling of paper.

'He's not responsible for the sheet thread count, or the menus or the quality of the glassware… I'll get the services manager to check through all of that…'

'And lilies—we asked for white lilies to decorate her room.'

'Of course. The lilies. Item twenty-two.'

Not an ounce of agitation.

'Unfortunately we don't allow fresh flowers onto the burns unit. It's an infection control issue.'

'No?'

Agitation rippled off the man's voice in streams enough for both of them.

'But for the Sheikha you can do such a thing. She never stays anywhere without lilies. Be warned: His Highness expects high standards and he will get them. His daughter is the very most precious thing to him and he hates her to be upset. I insist you bend the rules.'

'And I insist you leave the medical professionals to *implement* the rules, sir. We have them for a reason. No fresh flowers. The pollen can infect the wounds and make our patients very sick. It's something we're very strict about. No exceptions.'

Declan's interest was piqued. Management had certainly stepped up their game by employing her. He smiled, imagining a stare-off between the mystery woman and the Sheikh's aide.

'Is there anything else? *Sir?*'

'Do not take that tone. The Sheikh is very powerful and can have you removed from your position with just one word.'

The smile was wiped from Declan's face. No one spoke to a member of staff in that way—whoever she was, and however spirited.

He scraped back his chair and walked into the corridor, watching the exchange from a distance, ready to pounce and squash the man if anything got out of hand. He got the feeling the woman wouldn't thank him for interfering and for what that might imply: that she couldn't handle it. When she clearly could. Bringing up his younger sisters had taught him to leave them alone with their arguments and only get involved if things got physical.

'Well, I have a few words I could use too…but I won't.' With a voice so prickly, he hadn't expected the woman to be so young and soft. She had her back to him, but something about her rang bells in Declan's brain. Familiar bells. Warning bells.

The ponytail of light blonde curls, the neat curves in an ice-pink silk blouse and a straight black skirt that skimmed her knees—just. Sky-high black shoes with a razor-sharp heel that surely no one could feasibly walk in but which made her legs look impossibly long and… deeply sexy. A back as straight as a blade, and that voice…smoky…yes…Australian…?

'Let me assure you, sir,' she continued, 'that Safia will receive the finest care in the world here. And if, instead of dealing with your…housekeeping requests, I could finish my preparations for her admission and initial medical assessment, and then actually deal with the injuries she has sustained, we could all make Safia's stay a lot more comfortable.'

The aide stared at her as she rallied.

'I'm sure His Highness would not like to hear that the medical team were held up due to lilies? Glassware? I thought not. We are done here?'

Oh, God. The headache that had bloomed after Declan's sister's early morning phone call threatened to return. This woman was on his medical team? Since when? And why had no one consulted him about it? Declan didn't like surprises. He always liked to know exactly what he was dealing with, and he'd made that damned clear to the powers-that-be.

The Sheikh's aide blanched and bowed slightly.

'Of course. I'm sorry. Of course, Doctor… You know what's best.'

'Yes. Thank you. We do.'

As she turned to watch the aide scuttle away her eyes locked on to Declan's. Her smile slipped completely, and a tinge of pink hit her cheeks. 'Oh.'

The first time she'd shown any hint of bother. But then, within a nanosecond, she'd regained her composure.

'Kiss me.'

A rush of heat and a swirl of memory shook through him. A gold-coloured ballgown that had complemented the colour of the soft curls falling down her back, those startling green eyes commanding his attention, that infuriatingly cocky mouth drawing him in to the most sensual kiss of his life. Only she'd had a sheen of sadness about her too when he'd met her at the bar, knocking back shots. He'd turned it into a game, just to make her smile, which had then turned into something infinitely more interesting.

When was that? Six months ago? The hospital ball? A kiss he'd never found an equal to since, and a woman he'd caught tantalising glimpses of around the surgical unit, at Drake's Bar, and once, possibly, he thought he might have caught a brief whiff of her perfume at the Hunter Clinic. The woman he'd never quite caught up with.

Or even tried to.

And definitely hadn't wanted to.

Because—well…because talking to her, laughing with her, kissing her, had made him want something more. And Declan Underwood never did *more*.

'Good afternoon, Mr Underwood. Adding spying to your list of legendary talents?'

'You are standing right outside my office. It's hardly a covert operation.' Had he ever even known her name?

'Why are you frightening the life out of my esteemed visitors and masquerading as a member of my team? And where the hell is Karen?'

Karen. The timid but efficient junior surgeon who didn't have a bewitching mouth and a dangerous sparkle in her eye.

The woman's mouth twitched. 'White lilies, indeed. If they're all like him we're going to have our work cut out. By all accounts Safia's a little diva. Didn't you hear? Karen's been called away to a family emergency and I've been shifted over to assist until she gets back.'

'Whoa! Slow down. To assist *me*?'

She smiled, but it didn't look as if she was very pleased about the scenario either. He wondered if she was thinking about that kiss too, and how she'd suddenly lost her cool, or her nerve or both, and left him standing on the dance floor trying to work out which tornado had just hit.

Just the thought of it set off a burst of inconvenient heat swimming through his veins.

'Yes, the luck fairies have sprinkled dust on us both today. I'm on your team until Karen gets things sorted.'

Judging by his all too regular experiences of family emergencies she could be away for weeks. His stomach hit his boots. Regardless of what his body might want, mixing work with pleasure was something he avoided at all costs. So he'd be sticking to strictly business.

'And which genius came up with this idea?'

'Ethan Hunter. He called me this morning, said he'd had a call from Karen and was going to run the idea by you, but you were unavailable. He left you a message, apparently. So did she.'

No doubt while Declan's oldest sister had been bending his ear about his middle sister's new boyfriend, the youngest's less than satisfactory university grades and his mother's upcoming birthday plans. He was definitely going to have to set more limits around his personal private time. Sure, hadn't he been trying to do that for the past seventeen years?

'So I miss a call and now I don't get a say about who works with me on one of the most high-profile cases we've had in years?'

'What would you prefer?' Her hands hit her tantalising hips. 'It's me or no one. At least I have a good deal of burns experience. There isn't any other option, with Leo and Lizzie on honeymoon and this place being almost in lockdown with the Sheikh's arrival.'

'No?'

'You could do it all by yourself, but somehow I can't think you'd want to do the junior tasks. Admissions paperwork? Organising bloods?' Her voice rose at the end of every sentence, making it sound as if she was asking an endless list of questions.

'Yes, thank you, I have a full understanding of what is needed. And, it's not that I don't want to do them. I just don't have time.' Stepping up to run the Hunter Clinic in Leo's absence meant he needed more junior staff, not less.

Unbelievable. Declan ran a hand across his neck as he realised he'd been backed into an Antipodean corner. Well, hell, she'd better be as good in surgery as she was at kissing, because he couldn't take any chances—not with his reputation and a young girl's future at stake.

Great. His day had just got a whole lot longer.

'So I hope we don't have a problem here?'

'Absolutely not.'

Oh, but they did. At least Kara did. Declan's Irish lilt curled around her clenched stomach and stroked. Softly. Smoothly. Sexi— *No.* She wasn't allowed to think that.

The man was her boss. And an amazing kisser. *Boss.* Kisser. *Boss.* He tipped his chin to one side and gave her the slightest hint of recognition. A nod, perhaps, to their last…*connection*…?

She felt the blush start at her toes and spread, fast, to the top of her head. If only she'd explained her quick getaway—the reason dancing with him had been such a dumb move. Her surprisingly hot bodily response to the first man to hold her in so long. No—it had been a direct response to him and his strong arms and smooth, deep accent. And then, as reality hit, her suddenly very cold feet.

He leaned against his office doorjamb, folded his arms and eyed her with ill-disguised caution.

Shame, because she'd really, really enjoyed that kiss. However wrong. However badly timed. However just damned stupid. And he clearly hardly even remembered her. But then the man had a following of women who thought they could change his commitment-phobic ways. That kiss was probably not a stand-out for him. Luckily she'd put it far behind her.

She summoned every bit of confidence—or at least the show of confidence she'd learned to wear whenever she was in a difficult situation. Eyes forward, shoulders back. Last time she'd felt the need to summon strength she'd been staring down into a casket. The memory rolled off her in waves.

'It's Kara.'

Just in case he'd forgotten her name. Had she even told him it? She remembered looking up. The sight of him standing there in a tuxedo, his hair a messy nonchalant scruff, had stripped the breath from her lungs. She remembered too the way he'd smelled of something spicy and promising as he'd leaned in, the hot shock of an unexpected desire that had matched hers in his deep brown eyes. The earth tilting slightly as he'd spun her in his arms.

'Kara Stephens?'

'Are you asking me? Because if *you* don't know then we really do have a problem.'

Idiot. She decided to speak slowly just so he could understand. Poor puppy. 'My. Name. Is. Kara. Stephens. Only you don't look very happy about something. And I can only assume it's me.'

Seeing as he was staring right at her. All six-foot-too-much, with his arrogant stance and toned body. Even in scrubs she could see the outline of the sculpted abs she'd pressed against, the biceps she'd held as he'd slow-danced with her. The shoulders she'd wound her arms around as his mouth had covered hers.

Heat skittered through her abdomen like a lit fuse wire.

Boss.

Oh. Yes. The first kiss she'd had in too long and it had been off-limits in so many ways. Alcohol, guilt and lust were a heady combination she'd done her best to avoid ever since. Along with him—Mr Break-Your-Heart Underwood.

And now he would refuse to allow her to join the team. Not just for her handling of a tense situation but because of that damned kiss.

'There's a lot at stake here.' He exhaled sharply. 'What do we know about you? Where did you train? What burns experience do you have?'

'Med School in Melbourne, then Perth, then a stint at the Croftwood Institute, Sydney.'

'The Croftwood? Impressive.'

'Yes. And I aced every exam.' Even so, just thinking

about her last few days there was like a swift punch to her heart.

But she wouldn't look back. London had been a fresh start, and getting onto this rotation had been an absolute dream job—and then the chance to work alongside a world-class reconstructive surgeon. Until one out-of-character misdemeanour came back to bite her.

Well, kissing the boss certainly wouldn't be happening again. Kissing *anyone* wouldn't be happening. Ever.

'So, what *is* this? A corridor interview? I've helped out at the Hunter Clinic before now. If you want a copy of my CV or references just ask.' Irritation tripped up her spine. 'And, besides, Ethan's already arranged everything.'

Declan's eyebrows rose. 'Without consulting me first. Has he ever actually spoken to you? Seen you in full throttle? Because I listened to a lot of that conversation just now, and the way you—'

She jumped in to defend herself. 'Look, I don't believe in taking risks with clients just because someone who has a lot of money or power asks me to. There's not just Safia to think about, but the other patients on the unit too. Money can buy a lot of things, but it won't buy my professional standards.' She studied his face for a reaction but he wore a mask of impartiality. 'Of course I hope I employed more diplomacy than that.'

He nodded and looked at her. Really looked at her, as if trying to work out a puzzle. 'To be honest, I thought you handled him very well—and you stuck to your guns. It's easy to be swayed by people like that and it's rarely for the good.'

Wow, praise from him now? That was surprising. He had a reputation for being a smooth lover and a competent and exacting doctor, leaving his patients satisfied and women always wanting more. Which he steadfastly refused to give.

'If you can handle a skin graft as confidently as you did that aide, then you'll go far.'

The laugh slipped easily from her throat. 'You know, really I just wanted to tell him where to get off.'

'Yes. Me too.' He winked, visibly relaxing. 'But *A*— you didn't. And *B*—you reassured him of your competence and professionalism by not caving in to his demands.'

'I tried my best.'

'Good. I imagine you've more than earned his respect. You need to gain that too when dealing with the Sheikh and the press, which is a necessary role with such a high-profile case. We're a small team with a big responsibility. Are you up to it?'

'Yes. Absolutely.'

'I would suggest you soften a little for the Sheikha, though. Diva or not, she's had a very rough time, she's used to having things her way, and this accident will have knocked her sideways.' Something passed behind those chocolate-coloured eyes and his sharp edges melted away a little. 'Her life has changed forever. She's going to be frightened and in pain and will need a lot of help and reassurance. Not just today but ongoing. Gently.' He eyed her suspiciously. 'You *can* do gently?'

'Of course. Of course.' Hell, she could do roll over and beg if it meant she got to work with someone so talented. Relief flooded through her and she tried to show him her best gentle smile. 'So I'm in, then?'

'For now. It seems I have no choice—and we have to attend to Safia. I'll review your place in my team later.'

'I come highly recommended. Phone the Croftwood and check. I can assure you, you won't be disappointed.'

'No…I doubt that very much.' Declan laughed. 'But, heck, you're a straight talker.'

The same words he'd used at the ball too, when she'd outright demanded he kiss her, right there on the dance floor, when she hadn't been able to stop thinking about how those lips would feel against hers. When she'd wanted something…*him*…to exorcise the past.

She snapped her eyes closed, hoping to goodness he didn't remember that. When she opened them again he was looking at her strangely. Strangely *interested*. The ghost of that kiss hovered between them as his eyes fixed on hers. Yes, he remembered. And if the brief flash of heat was anything to go by he remembered how good it had felt too. That warm glow in her abdomen returned.

She doused it with a quick shot of reality as she began to walk along the corridor towards the burns unit High Dependency ward. The last time she'd got carried away by hearts and flowers and physical desires she'd ended up married. Then endured a swift lesson in a run of all the emotions from *A* to *Z*.

She'd packed a lifetime of hurt into those few years and she had no intention of making the same mistakes again. So much had sent her reeling, trying to work out how something that had started out so pure had ended so damned soiled. Focusing on her career was a lot less painful—but then, that was what had caused all the trouble in the first place.

'It comes from my upbringing, I guess.'

'Oh? What?' He fell into step beside her.

'Forthrightness. I'm an army brat. Always moving around. If you don't say what you think straightaway you'll be packed up and on the move before you get another chance.' There'd been a lot of lost chances before she'd learnt that lesson. 'Although it can get me into trouble.'

'I imagine it can.'

It already has, his look said. On that dance floor.

His dark pupils flared. 'Australian army?'

'Yes. My parents met as new recruits and both followed military careers.'

'Exciting? Interesting?'

'Difficult…for them both, I think. One member of a family in the military is hard enough, but both parents trying to work up the career ladder meant a lot of discussing, juggling, arguing, vying for priority. What their child wanted came at the bottom of the pecking order.'

She'd learnt to speak loudly and fight hard to get heard.

'Constantly moving and growing up on bases makes you grow a thick skin and a quick mouth. But, hey, I can shoot in a straight line and hit a target at a hundred metres.'

'Me too.' At her frown he illuminated, 'Farm boy.'

Now, *that* was a surprise. He oozed class and rubbed easy broad shoulders with a rich and famous clientele. 'Irish farm boy to Harley Street surgeon? That must be an interesting story.'

'Not really.' His smile disappeared and he looked at her as if she'd stepped over some imaginary line. Shoving his hands in his pockets, he quickened his step. She got the message—working together was okay, even kissing wasn't a step too close, but sharing intimate details…? Never. And that suited her just fine. The less she shared about the life she'd left the better too.

As they entered the unit Kara observed an atmosphere of calm chaos—a feeling that matched her stomach. Although being surrounded by busy people was much less intense than being alone with Declan. She knew how to act here. There were protocols and policies, standards and codes. Out there in the real world, the dating world, the rules were far too confusing.

She breathed out and put her professional hat firmly on. 'So, all the staff are up to speed with privacy requests, and everyone has been told not to comment at all to anyone phoning in, regardless of who they say they are.'

'Excellent.' He nodded, walking into the room he'd personally had allocated to Safia. 'This looks perfect, but keep the bed away from the window.' He peered through the blinds down to the road outside. 'No one should be able to see her here on this floor. As soon as she arrives we'll need to check her pain levels and medication. I don't want her to be scared we're going to hurt her when we remove the dressings. Then I'll need an immediate blood screen to make sure she's haemodynamically stable. Then...then we can take a good look and see what we're dealing with.'

'No worries.' She picked up the clipboard on the end of the bed and checked all the correct paperwork was in place.

'So.' Declan glanced around. 'What's her ETA?'

Kara glanced at her watch. 'Ten minutes.'

'Excellent.'

Although this was a devastating case, he looked wired and ready. This was another side of him she'd heard about but hadn't yet encountered: his infectious enthusiasm for his work. It seemed the man had many sides apart from his infamous charm, and yet—as she'd witnessed— a mysterious unwillingness to open up about anything personal.

Which was fine. Because she would not let that kiss get in the way of her job. Or let that body of his distract

her from her purpose. Or those eyes… Her stomach did
a little cartwheel… Those eyes staring at her with playful teasing.

'So, Kara Stephens, it looks like we have just enough
time to check out the sheets.'

'What?' Her pulse rocketed.

The smile he flashed her was nothing less than wicked.
'Thread count?'

'Oh. Yes. Of course.' And she blushed again, because
one mention of sheets and their thread count was the furthest thing from her mind.

CHAPTER TWO

'I SAID, DON'T touch me.' A pair of dark, frightened eyes, trying desperately hard to be brave, peered out through a face covered in bandages. 'Go away.'

Kara leaned in to the bed and lowered her voice. This was getting precisely nowhere, but she could not and would not rush her patient. 'I'm sorry, Safia, but we are going to have to remove the dressings sometime so we can see your burns and then treat them. We just want to help.'

'What part of *go away* don't you understand?' Her muffled voice was thick with the tears the teenager steadfastly refused to allow. 'Leave me alone.'

'Does it hurt? I can give you some more medicine to take the pain away. You must tell me if you need more.'

The girl shook her head.

'I'll do it slowly and carefully. I promise.'

But Safia raised a heavily bandaged arm and pulled the sheet over her head. The spaghetti of tubes reverberated at the swift move. An alarm rang out.

Kara took a moment to compose herself, checked the drips were patent, reset the machines and tried again. And she would continue trying until the poor girl agreed. However long it took. The theatre was booked from eight tomorrow morning. That gave her about eighteen hours. She hoped it would be enough. 'Your Highness…'

'Let me try.' Sheikh El-Zayad of Aljahar, the girl's father, stepped forward. 'For goodness' sake, Safia, do as you're told. We've been waiting for twenty-five minutes for your bandages to come off and it's getting past a joke. The doctors can't do their job and you won't get better.'

'I'm never going to get better. This is it. Scarred for life. So get used to it.'

The Sheikh frowned. 'Do as the doctor says. Stop behaving like a child.'

She is a child. Kara bit that thought back. He had just endured the worst thing any parent could live through—watching his child suffer—and no doubt wanted her full co-operation to get better. But seventeen was barely mature, and the ramifications of such injuries would surely make anyone scared and fractious.

She shot a look over to Declan as he finished his conversation with the Sheikh's wife, psychologically prepping her for the forthcoming procedures and long-term treatment plan. Throughout the long thirty minutes of cajoling and waiting she'd felt Declan's eyes on her, assessing, weighing her up, his playful teasing forgotten, cemented now into something much more serious.

'So to recap—' He leaned forward to speak to Safia's parents. 'We're planning to do a series of operations over the next few weeks. Because Safia's wounds are of differing severity and depth each one will be in its own individual recovery phase. Some wounds, I understand from her notes, are ready for closure or grafting tomorrow. Some will have to wait for closure because they need debriding. I'll keep you fully informed as we proceed.'

Declan's demeanour was one of total calm and efficiency, yet he commanded an authority that stood him apart as he spoke.

'Now, it's getting a bit hot in here. Perhaps Your Highnesses might like a tour of the facility? There's a particularly nice view out over the river from the roof garden. It's very private up there and shouldn't be busy. In fact, I can make sure it isn't. And I can organise some tea for you both.'

Safia's mother nodded and wafted in front of her face with her hand. 'Oh, please. Yes. I need some fresh air.' Leaning in to her daughter, she whispered, 'That is, of course, if you don't mind, darling Safia? We won't stay away for long.'

The sheets moved a little. 'Go. All of you. Leave me here. Forever.'

A quick phone call later and Safia, Kara and Declan were alone.

But now what? Even without her parents in the room it was going to be tough convincing Safia to comply.

Kara was just about to broach the dressings conversation again when Declan laughed. 'Well, would you look at that *eejit*.'

'What? Where?' Kara frowned as she looked over to him. His focus was on a pile of magazines on the table. The latest teen heart-throb was emblazoned on the front cover of *BFF!* magazine, which had been covered in pink glitter hand-drawn hearts. 'Oh, that's Liam from Oblivion.'

'I don't care where he's from,' he continued. 'He looks like he needs a decent feed and a new belt. Are those his grandaddy's trousers he's wearing? Because they don't seem to fit.'

Kara looked up again and noticed he was watching the sheet move down. Just a little.

She joined in. 'How can you say that? Don't break my heart. Liam is hot, hot, *hot*. And what do you know, Mr Fuddy-Duddy? Those baggy trousers are all the rage. Maybe you should get a pair.'

'Maybe I should. D'you think all the girls would come screaming after me then?' He gave a very poor rendition of Oblivion's number one hit. '"That's what makes me looooove you…"'

'Screaming to get away from you, more like. Save our poor ears and stick to the day job.' She leaned closer to the sheet that was now making little noises that sounded a lot like hesitant surprised laughter. 'Great doctor, really, don't let the singing put you off. I heard that Oblivion's doing a tour soon—they're playing in London in a few weeks.' And going to see her favourite singer might well give Safia the motivation she needed to get better.

The girl sighed. 'He played at my sixteenth birthday party. He said I was beautiful.' Safia slowly pulled the sheet back. 'But he wouldn't say that now.'

Declan sat next to the bed and looked at her. Kara wondered what on earth he could say to make her feel better. 'Don't you know you've gorgeous eyes, Safia? Beautiful. A boy could lose himself in there.'

'Once, maybe. But not now.'

'Oh, definitely now.'

Safia met Declan's gaze, still cautious, but she didn't tell them to leave.

Seizing this moment of calm, Declan reached out and began to remove a dressing with painstaking care. When Safia put her hand out to stop him he gave her a quick shake of his head and a reassuring smile. The girl lay back and closed her eyes.

Kara opened another dressing pack and covered the bed as he kept his focus on his patient and smiled softly and gently, as if she was the most beautiful person in the world, the only person in the world. As if the horrendous discolouration and raw melted skin didn't make his heart jerk or his professional eye wonder how in hell they could ever restore her back to her previous beauty.

She'd heard about his slick surgical skills and knew how well respected he was. Heck, the Sheikh had personally requested Declan did the surgery—and judging by his extensive client list both here and at the Hunter Clinic he was well sought after. So she hadn't expected a doctor as talented as Declan to have such grounded humanity.

'There. There. Nearly done now. You're doing grand, sweetheart. Just grand. It's not nearly so bad as I thought it'd be.'

He spoke in a mesmerising, soothing voice that felt as if he was stroking the raw wounds back together again. Kara didn't think she'd ever seen anything so touching.

'I bet you've broken a few hearts already, Safia?'

The girl opened her eyes and gave him a sad smile. 'Yes…you mustn't tell my father.'

'Cross my heart.'

'But I never will again. Who's going to love me with a face like this? Skin like this?' She lifted the arms she'd tried to shield her face with and showed him the skin that had been so damaged. Finally tears began to fall. 'Don't tell me that beauty's skin-deep. Or that scars are sexy. Because they're not. And please don't tell me that looks don't matter—because in my world they do.'

And that was the heart of the matter. A young girl's life was broken and no one could truly fix it.

Kara's throat closed tight.

Declan ran his hand over the girl's hair. 'Ah, now, sweetheart. That's it. That's it. I know. Believe me, I know. Let it out. Just let it go.'

'I'm…so…tired…of being brave,' Safia sobbed. 'Of trying to pretend it's okay when it's not. And all they do is make promises that I'll be back to normal soon. How can I?' She looked up at him, eyes pleading but with a glimpse of trust. 'Can you make me better, Dr Underwood?'

'Call me Declan, please. Actually, call me Dec if you like—my sisters call me that.'

'Okay.' Safia nodded and smiled again. 'Dec.'

'Listen, Safia, I will be honest with you because you deserve that at the very least. I can't ever make it go away completely.' His voice caught a little as he thumbed away the girl's tears.

A few months ago Kara had watched him smooth his way across a dance floor, his charm and flirtatious manner catching her in a moment of weakness. But there was a genuine depth to him that she hadn't imagined.

He cleared his throat. 'But I promise I can make it a whole lot better. Will you let me try?'

'At first glance, Safia's burns are a mix of partial and full thickness—some will need further debridement and then grafting,' Declan said to Kara as they grabbed a coffee en route to the media room.

His head was a whirl of the emotions that always shook through him at this stage of assessment—emotions he had a tight hold of and would never allow to interfere with any professional judgement. Flashbacks from seventeen years ago haunted him each time he removed a dressing, but they made him more determined to improve his skills and techniques.

Another woman damaged. It made him sick to his stomach.

His new junior surgeon took a sip of coffee, oblivious

to what was going on in his head. Which was a damned
fine thing—no one needed to know his motivations, just
his achievements. She smiled and his gut tightened. He
put it down to stress.

'So, Declan, do you prefer autograft or zenograft?'

'It depends entirely on the situation. We can get a better look at the viability of the skin and the underlying bed
tomorrow in Theatre and take it from there.'

Eyebrows peaked. 'We?'

'Yes. Okay, you can scrub in tomorrow. You did well
in there. Teenagers are often the most difficult cases to
deal with. They don't know how to act—they're kids at
heart but trying desperately to be adult. We have to get
the next few days right. How we deal with these burns
will have a huge effect on the rest of that girl's life. Both
physically and psychologically.' From his experience the
mental scarring was often the worst and could change
the very core of an injured person for life.

Kara nodded, eyes alight, blonde curls shivering.
Something unbidden shivered through him too. She'd
been damned good at handling Safia, so he was pleased
to have her on his team. But…really it was more than
that. She was a weird kind of unsettling—and yet settling at the same time.

Her eyes narrowed. 'I can't believe the admitting hospital staff didn't think of offering her some anxiolytics
to help raise her mood. Maybe we could have a chat with
her about that too?'

'I guess they were dealing with her immediate issues,
like keeping her alive.' He held the door open to let her
through. Which was an action he immediately regretted.
The barrage of flashing bulbs that had greeted him that
morning met them as they stepped into the room, catch-

ing her unawares—but he was interested to see just how well she could handle this part of the job.

'Is Princess Safia here now?'

'What can you tell us about her condition?'

Next to him Kara stood tall, her shoulders snapped back, confident. Declan held back a smile as he watched her survey the room with a tilt of her chin. She wore her army upbringing in her stance, and he had no doubt she would answer the press's queries with aplomb and professionalism, but he wasn't game enough to test her with that just yet. In fact he wasn't game enough to do anything that involved any more contact with her than he had to. The woman was mysteriously alluring. So that meant avoiding her at all costs.

No doubt a better man would probably not even allow her to assist him when his hormones were acting as if he was eighteen years old again. But he had stopped being a better man a long time ago—the day he'd lost all faith in love.

Kara's scent wove around him…something exotic that reminded him of brilliant blue skies and endless heat and the tang of flowers on the breeze. His abdomen tightened as seemingly endless heat rippled through him too.

He took a step away and glanced at the floor, trying to take a moment to focus. But all he could see were those ridiculous but sexy shoes, slender tanned ankles leading up to the hem of her skirt, and farther on up to a place where his imagination ran wild.

He ran a hand through his hair and shook that image from his head. *Damn fool.* Since when had he allowed a woman to distract him at work? Since the second he'd seen her firing back at the Sheikh's aide? Or was it that kiss?

He quieted the audience with a raise of his hands and

a smile. Keep them on side and they might actually let him have time free to do his job. 'Thanks for coming to this meeting. We didn't want you getting chilly out there. We're already busy enough without dealing with hypothermic journalists as well. Hope you enjoyed the tea and biscuits.'

Laughter rippled round the room. He waited for it to stop.

'Thank you for your patience, everyone. I have permission from Safia's family to confirm that she is indeed now here at Princess Catherine's Hospital and that I am treating her as an in-patient. I'm sure you are all aware of the car accident she had a few days ago. I can confirm also that, thanks to the great care she received at Aljahar Hospital, she is now in a stable condition, but her injuries mean that she will be under my care for some time. The family again asks for privacy. Thank you.'

'What does the Sheikh think about this?'

'Naturally His Highness is devastated about his daughter's injuries, but he is working with us to get the best possible outcome. Of course we are deeply honoured to have him here.'

'How long will Safia be with you?'

'That depends entirely on her progress and response to treatment. It could be a few weeks.' He paused for effect. 'Okay, I don't think there is anything more we can tell you. Either myself or a member of my team…' He indicated to Kara and she stepped forward and smiled, self-confidence rippling off her. 'This is Ms Stephens, who will be working with me. Either one of us will be updating you on Safia's progress as and when appropriate.'

'They don't teach you that at medical school.' Kara joked as they walked towards the afternoon out-patient clinic. 'They should have "Dealing with the Press" lessons. Confidentiality is such a thorny issue—especially when you're treating someone famous.'

'No one wants to know about you if you're not. But this is a high-profile issue and we have to deal with it— it's just another part of the job. You have to be careful not to give away too much information but just enough to keep the hacks satisfied.'

'It's a bit of a tightrope. I can see I'll have to be careful.'

'I can fix you up with our in-house Head of PR, Lexi, at the Hunter Clinic if you like? She could give you some pointers if you think you might need them.' Why, oh, why was he even thinking of getting further involved in this woman's life? 'But I reckon you'll be fine.'

'Really?' Her smile was genuine. 'Thanks. I'll see how I go.'

That compliment sat between them as they neared the clinic. He'd have to be careful about that—giving her the wrong impression. But something about Kara drew him to her. Even with his internal alarm bells blaring.

As he tried to walk down the narrow corridor without brushing against her and risking an escalation of his already over-excited libido she spoke. 'So, how many sisters do you have?'

'What?' He stopped short, still getting used to her forthrightness. Maybe it was an Aussie thing. No, maybe it was just a Kara thing. 'Sorry?'

'You were telling Safia about your sisters. *"They call me Dec,"* you said, or something.'

'Why do you need to know?'

Her forehead furrowed into a deep V and her eyes sparked with humour and intrigue. 'I don't *need* anything. I was just making conversation. It's what human beings do to fill that very long gap between birth and death. Communication.'

She held his gaze and it felt as if she was throwing down a gauntlet. One he could run with or one he could walk away from.

'Only, I don't have any siblings, and I always thought it'd be nice to have some. It's just a chat, Declan, as we while away the minutes. Not an interrogation.'

She was right. It was just talking. It wasn't exactly baring his soul. And he'd always been a sucker for gauntlets.

'Well, if I were you I'd rejoice in your single-child-dom, Kara—because, trust me, you do *not* need four sisters.'

'Four? Wow.'

'All younger. All a giant pain in the ass…'

She laughed. 'Growing up amongst that must have been busy. But fun, though?'

'It was messy…crazy…loud. Very loud. And awash with wayward hormones.' Remembering the madcap phone call that morning, he shrugged, smiling to himself. They might well be irritating, but they were his. 'Still is.'

'But it explains how you can deal so well with kids like Safia.'

'I don't know about *well*. The way I see it, all girls want to be treated like princesses. It just so happens she *is* one. But underneath they're generally the same. They worry about how they look, who they're becoming, what they want to do with their lives. Love. Boys…yeah, boys mostly, if my lot were anything to go by. Trouble all round.'

He'd had the job of being the man of the house thrust upon him way too young and had had to make sure they somehow had the basics, like enough food to eat, even when they hadn't had the money to buy it. Then as they grew up he'd watched his sisters have their hearts broken and wanted to kill the culprits, but decided not to. He had negotiated conversations about teenage pregnancy and underage sex, about dating rules and bedtimes, had nursed sisters with period pains and migraines and tummy aches of dubious origin. And finally he'd escaped only when he'd known they were all grown up and relatively safe. *Escaped* being a geographical rather than a psychological term.

And yet with all his experience he still couldn't fathom the workings of a woman's brain. Except that he definitely knew when it was time to leave—which was around about the time she started talking about a future.

Kara laughed. 'But I can see the pride in your eyes and hear it in your voice. You love them all, clearly.'

'Yes, I probably do—but don't ever let them know that or they'll take even more advantage. And I chose a job hundreds of miles away from them just to put a good stretch of Irish Sea between us.' He laughed along with her. 'Thankfully none of them are any good at swimming, most of them get seasick, and they can't afford the airfare—otherwise I'm damned sure they'd be here. Making my life hell in England too.'

But in reality he might as well be living back home, seeing as they couldn't or wouldn't make a single damned decision without him. Which was why he kept his tiny slice of private time simple. No getting involved on any kind of scale. His life was already too full of responsibilities and women without taking on another one.

Kara smirked as they entered the out-patients' reception. 'I guess you have to go where the work is.'

'Is that what you did? It's a long way from Sydney to London, and you didn't have four sisters dragging at your heels.'

'I needed a change. Coming here was a good move for lots of reasons.'

The way she said that didn't convince him that her move to London had been a positive choice. She rubbed her thumb around the base of her left-hand ring finger as her eyes darted upwards. She seemed to be searching for an answer. Not the truth, just an answer.

Seemed everyone had their demons. And he was inexplicably intrigued, even though he'd made it his life's purpose never to be drawn into a woman's dramas unless he had a failsafe get-out plan.

She peered up at him and his world tilted a little. He wasn't used to scrutiny, or to someone pushing him for more—or wanting to give it. So why would she have this effect on him?

'And you, Declan? Why choose burns reconstruction when you could have the glory and financial reward of cosmetic surgery? Breast augmentation? Tattoo removal? Enhancement of the rich and famous? Why specialise in burns?'

The way she adeptly deflected the conversation told him she didn't want to delve deeper into her reasons for coming here and he could respect that.

But, hell… His chest tightened by degrees. The questions she was asking. Questions people asked him periodically, but not usually straight after a conversation about his family. Or after a consultation with a badly scarred woman. Questions that he didn't want to answer. Wouldn't answer. Wouldn't no matter how much her sharp green eyes reached down into his soul and tugged.

'Ah, you know…it's just how it worked out.'

And with that he turned and walked away.

CHAPTER THREE

So the great Declan Underwood had walls so high even a simple conversation couldn't penetrate them, Kara mused as she scrubbed up the next morning. She would do well to remember that.

She should have remembered it last night too as she lay in the dark and thought about the way she'd fitted so neatly into his arms on the ballroom floor all those months ago. And the way he'd tasted—of something fresh and new, of an experienced man. Not like the previous kisses she'd experienced from the kid she'd known her whole life. The way Declan's big broad shoulders—a match for any Aussie rugby league player's—looked as if they could carry the weight of a million problems. But she hadn't wanted to share hers. No, she'd had other things on her mind. Nice other things. Naughty other things.

And she should have remembered it too when Declan's face had been the last thing she'd thought of before she'd fallen asleep. Almost the first thing to flash through her brain as her alarm clock blared. The very first thing, as always, had been the thick thud of loss. The reality of how much her life had changed. The tiny slash of almost white skin where her wedding ring used to be.

But this morning the sharp sting of regret hadn't been quite so harsh.

Even so, she still hadn't thought about the barriers Declan had erected, or the way he'd turned his back on her. She'd simply remembered how sweet it had felt when he'd hammered against her barriers with one scorching touch of his mouth.

The same mouth that was now grinning at her as he walked into the scrub room. She put the little heart jig down to excitement at the forthcoming surgery and nothing to do with the sudden scent of soap and spice, or the soft brown eyes, or the way his biceps muscles lengthened as he reached for the tap.

The V neck of his top bared a tantalising amount of suntanned chest and she imagined what might be underneath the navy cotton scrubs… Sometimes a working knowledge of anatomy did a girl nothing but harm. Especially first thing in the morning.

He opened a sterile pack and laid it on a trolley, put on the surgical cap and mask and began washing with the nailbrush, rubbing small circles over his fingers, hands, up his arms.

'Good morning, Ms Stephens. Sleep well?'

'Hi. Um… Yes, thanks.' *Liar.* Sleeping and thoughts of Declan Underwood were not satisfactory bedfellows.

She dried her hands, pulled on her gown and snapped on her gloves. Took a quick check in the mirror and relaxed. There was no way there would be any kind of sexual vibes happening today—hair in a cap and body in oversized scrubs really didn't scream goddess or available. Or any kind of *hot-for-you*. Thank God.

'And shouldn't it be top of the mornin'?'

'A whole millennia of culture reduced to the diddly-diddly. Sure, and we're all leprechauns.' He laughed, his eyes crinkling at the corners.

That tall, broad body was the furthest thing from a leprechaun she could imagine.

'And shouldn't it be g'day?'

'Cobber. If you're going the whole reductive stereo-type, it should be g'day, cobber. Or sheila. And don't forget the cork hat.'

'Same language but not a lot of commonality, eh? That's a shame. A real shame.' He dried his hands, gowned up and smiled. 'Perhaps we should try to forge some middle ground, Kara? There's a whole lot more I could teach you about Irish culture… In the interests of international relations. Obviously.'

'Obviously.' Was that a come on? Or just a joke?

Aaargh. Having been a one-man woman for so long, she didn't understand the language of flirting.

No matter. She didn't have time to compute. At that moment he stepped back, catching her unawares in the tiny airless room. His hip brushed against hers and she turned too quickly, slamming body to body against him. Tingles ran the length of her spine as her heart continued a jig that was *all* diddly-diddly.

'Oh. I'm sorry.'

His gaze met hers and for a split second, maybe two, he watched her. Some weird connection tugged between them. His eyes misted with something akin to confusion, along with an unmistakable heat that seemed to whoosh all the oxygen from her lungs.

His arms were splayed high in front of him, so as not to desterilise them, but that made his face closer to hers. Damn lucky he was wearing a mask or his mouth would have been in frank kissing range.

The heat coming off him was electric, almost palpable. He smiled. Or at least she thought he did—hard to tell under that mask, but his forehead crinkled and laughter lines creased at his temples.

'Nothing to apologise for, Kara. No harm done. In fact…I like it.'

So did she. And, oh, if it wasn't enough just to have that soft accent tug on her heartstrings.

She swallowed through a dry throat, pushed the Theatre door open with her hip and gestured for him to walk through in front of her. How the hell would she spend a morning in surgery staring at those eyes, listening to that voice, looking at that body, and get out whole? He was going to reduce her to a hot mess of unruly hormones.

So she would take a leaf out of his book and refuse to engage in conversation about anything other than the task at hand.

Forcing words out was harder than she'd expected. 'So. How's Safia doing? When I popped up to see her an hour or so ago she didn't say much. I got the impression she was hanging out for you to visit.'

He shrugged. 'She's okay, I suppose. She's scared about the operation. Actually, she's scared about the pain. I did warn her about the initial sting of the graft sites, but we talked about pain relief and I've discussed it with Paul, the anaesthetist, so she should be well covered when she wakes up. I've warned her we can't fix it all today, and that she'll have negative pressure dressings on and to expect lots of tubes.'

'Great. And the parents? They seemed to think you were going to restore her to her former beauty.'

His left shoulder hiked. 'I had a long and honest meeting with them last night and showed them the digital blueprint we mocked up of how we hope Safia will look after the surgeries. They understand that we can only do so much, and that a lot is dependent on how Safia heals, the kind of scarring we get, whether she complies with physio. Although I still think they're a little unrealistic. My main concern is that she maintains function in those hands. But she's here and agreeing to treatment and that's the best we can hope for right now.'

He turned as the technician wheeled Safia in.

'Okay. Let's go. Hands first and then her face. We'll start with debriding.'

It was like watching an artist at work. A study in concentration, he was efficient but thorough. Instead of the brash rock music favoured by a lot of surgeons she'd worked with Declan chose something that was uplifting but gentle. There was a positivity to it, something that soothed yet entranced.

Or was that just him? Kara couldn't tell.

Even though he was the senior member of staff he treated everyone in the room with the same respect and took his time to explain his procedures.

'See here?' He gestured to Safia's damaged cheek. 'If we want to get a good result we have to consider the whole area as a unit, not just the part that's damaged, otherwise the scarring will be ridged. It's a multi-thickness burn—only second degree here, but here, where her face hit the dashboard, it's deeper. So I'm going to have to use a split thickness graft.'

'And attach it with absorbent stitches? Or glue?' She passed him some gauze just as he reached out for it. The third time she'd anticipated his next move.

'In this case, I'd say stitches.' He shook his head, as if trying to get rid of a wayward thought. 'What did you do in Sydney?'

'Oh, this and that. Music concerts, swimming, going out with friends. My husband was away a lot so I was able…to…study…' She slowed right down and noticed all eyes were on her.

Surgery.

That deep, luscious voice was asking about the Croftwood's choice of surgical closure techniques—not about her private life. Her chest tightened. *Duh.* There went her credibility.

'Er…usually stitches. But glue if we thought the dressing wouldn't be knocked or slip easily. Really it depended on the patient and the damaged area.'

She flatly refused to look him in the eye. Flatly. But she knew she was the single beacon of bright red in an otherwise white and sterile environment.

'Husband?'

The accusation hung in the air along with the ghost of that kiss. As she turned to look at him his eyebrows rose.

God. She focused instead on the tube of antibiotic ointment in a dish to her left. Did he really think she'd have kissed him if she'd had a husband? When she'd entered her marriage it had been with an innocent and pure belief in forever. Too bad forever couldn't happen.

'Not any more.'

'Okay.' Declan's voice was impassive. 'Great work, team. Thanks for your help. She's good to go to recovery. I'll head up to have a chat with Mum and Dad after the next surgery.'

The technicians got busy taking Safia out and preparing for the next patient, leaving Kara alone for snatched minutes with Declan. Goddamn, the man stirred a smorgasbord of emotions in her. Right now it was a huge dose of embarrassment.

'Er… About before…'

'Kara…'

He glanced up from the surgery list he was reading. *About what?* his look said. *The kiss? The husband?*

He removed his surgical mask, his mouth tipping up halfway to a wry smile. 'Your life is your life. You don't have to explain.'

'I shouldn't have rabbited on.'

'Oh, no, to the contrary, we were all riveted. Concerts? Swimming?'

The omission of *husband* made her faux pas even more mortifying.

She shrugged. 'What can I say? We're a nation of water babies. Sydney's by the ocean.'

'And it gets very hot and there are snakes and spiders and lots of things that could kill you. I know.' His voice had developed a harder tone now. 'It's also a very long way from here and people can get lonely.'

Was that what he thought? That she'd hooked up with him because she was homesick? Because she missed her husband? Because she regretted everything that had happened?

Well, wasn't it? She didn't know any more.

Four days later Declan was sitting at his desk making a poor show of doing the paperwork, checking staffing levels for the Hunter Clinic and keeping track of patients' results.

He exhaled long and hard as the paper stack wobbled. It had been a very long week so far and tomorrow promised no let up. There were more surgeries booked, no doubt a scuffle through the media camped outside and a report due for Leo when he returned from honeymoon.

So why the hell, when he was supposed to be working, was he daydreaming about soft lips and green eyes? About a junior surgeon who anticipated his every move in Theatre, whose scent he could recognise at fifty paces, who seemed to have a direct line to his brain.

And his groin.

And was married. Or had been. Still, she wore no ring, and she'd been adamant that it was over.

He smiled at the thought of her ill-concealed blushes. She had a cool exterior, and could handle herself very well, but there was an unexpected softness about her too. A vulnerability that she hid, or tried to hide.

So he'd stayed out of her way as much as possible, because she was a heady mix of things that seemed to attract him more than they should. But avoiding contact with her hadn't worked; he couldn't get the damned woman out of his head.

'Hey. Just passing by en route to an emergency surgery. All good here?'

Friend and colleague Ethan Hunter stood in the doorway, his usual reluctant smile playing hooky. Dressed in scrubs, he looked primed for action. And Ethan always took that very seriously.

He'd been offered the position of Hunter Clinic head in his brother's absence but had somehow managed to persuade Declan to take that particular mantle, talking up Declan's silky PR skills. Declan had agreed—it was all good management experience. And, given the trauma Ethan had been through and his fight back to health, Declan hadn't wanted to refuse.

But this was also the guy responsible for Kara invading his thoughts. Declan could either tell him the truth— that she was quietly driving him mad—or get on with it. The very private Ethan wasn't exactly the kind of guy to confide 'deep and meaningful' to.

Declan shuffled some paper. 'All good, I suppose.

Trying to get to grips with the accounts for when Leo gets back.'

At the mention of his brother's name Ethan stiffened. 'I'm sure you'll manage fine. Hey, how's Kara fitting in? I've heard good reports.'

Declan shrugged, trying not to give too much away. If he was struggling with anything he wouldn't let anyone know. And surely Ethan knew about their kiss at the ball? It was public knowledge.

'Okay. But I'll be happy when Karen gets back. She knows the routine—how I like things.' And she didn't pre-empt everything he did.

But the way Kara's eyes had swirled with a zillion different emotions—none of them warm and fuzzy ones—when she'd spoken about her husband had drawn him to her even more. Having nursed his sisters through enough broken hearts to add more than a few grey hairs to his head, he knew better than even to ask Kara what her story was…but for some reason he was beyond intrigued.

'Hmm. I did wonder about allocating her to you, but short-staffed is short-staffed…'

So Ethan must know about the kiss. It was Declan's own stupid fault for mixing work with fun.

Ethan frowned. 'It's not like you to not gel with someone…'

Oh, yes. He gelled okay. Too damned much. Gelling wasn't the problem. *Un*-gelling was. 'Ah, well, you know…'

'I presume you've had the setting the guidelines talk? Taken the "this is how *I* do things" approach?'

'We've been busy. You know what it's like with a media circus on your doorstep.'

'So demarcate some time—take her for a quick coffee, a drink. There's nothing wrong with her medical practice, though?'

'Hell, no. She's an excellent surgeon. But as it's probably only a short rotation with me I don't think we need bother with all that *getting to know you* stuff.'

'No?' Ethan ran a hand over his jaw. He looked tired. And hassled. 'Try to get on with her, Declan. There's been too much bad blood running through this place for too long.' He checked his watch. 'A drink. A coffee. I don't care what you do. Just do it. I want to hear things are going smoothly, right? I could do without the stress of more work-related worries.'

Declan guessed Ethan was referring to the complicated relationship between the Hunter brothers.

'Okay, boss.'

The man must have been a force to be reckoned with in the army. Fighting the urge to salute, Declan slammed the laptop shut and shoved it into his backpack, made his way to the hospital exit and breathed deeply, filling his lungs with disappointingly stuffy city air. What he needed was a good long ride on his bike to clear the cobwebs. A cosy chat be damned. What he needed was a Kara-free life.

Thankfully the car park was devoid of journalists, leaving him a clear path towards his motorbike. He strode ahead, helmet in hand, the evening sunshine glinting off the chrome handlebars.

Out of the corner of his eye he caught a movement. Someone else leaving the hospital, heading quickly—or as quickly as she could in a pair of red satin stilettoes that made his heart stutter—towards the bus stop. Not quick enough, though, as the bus sailed past, leaving her stamping her pretty shoes against the tarmac.

At closer inspection he confirmed it was Kara, her

hair loose down her back, which drew his eye to her slim waist, nipped in by a fitted cardigan and then lower, to her perfectly shaped backside encased in skinny black trousers. A shot of heat fizzed through him as if someone had flicked a switch in his body.

So he should have just ridden away. But before he knew what he was doing he'd strolled right on up to her.

Ethan's orders, right? Taking one for the team for the sake of no bad blood. 'Hey. Dr Down-Under.'

'Watch it!' She jumped round to face him, at the same time lunging at his throat in a well-practised self-defence karate chop move, her palm almost connecting to his chin.

In a knee-jerk reaction he took a step back and grabbed her palm. He didn't think for one minute she'd have a qualm about trying to floor him and using her stiletto as a weapon. 'Hey! Overreaction, much?'

'Oh. It's you. You nearly gave me a heart attack.' She shook her hand free from his grip and frowned.

'Lucky we're outside a hospital, then.' A short, hot kiss of life sprang to the forefront of his mind.

'Do you often jump out at women from dark corners, wearing…'

Her eyes widened as her gaze travelled over his dark grey T-shirt and jeans. A suit and tie were all well and good for an office day, or a riding the underground day, but not for a bike to work day.

Her throat bobbed up and down as she swallowed. 'Wearing…a leather jacket…'

'Only on special occasions.' When she'd stopped staring and had seemed to gather her wits again he grinned. 'You missed the bus.'

'Thank you, Einstein.' A deep V formed along her

forehead. 'He must have been blind not to see me. I was waving enough.'

'Blind, indeed. Any man worth his salt would have stopped just for those shoes. But you were quite a distance from the bus stop—maybe trainers might be a better choice for running next time.'

She looked down, raised an ankle and turned it this way and that to look at her shoes. He followed her every movement, mesmerised. She had damned fine legs.

Purely an objective observation. Obviously.

An eyebrow peaked. 'Ah, come on—never, *ever* compromise fashion for practicality. Oh...' Her eyes toured his body again and landed on his jacket. 'You just did.'

But he could tell from the hunger in those startling green pupils that she liked what she saw. 'Steady, now. This jacket saved me from a skin-to-tarmac pebble-dashing after a collision with a drunk driver. It's my favourite.'

'Ouch. Lucky escape.' She ran her hand up the zipper and regarded the scuffed black fabric. 'By "favourite," I suppose you mean old?'

'Some things you should never get rid of. Now...'

A drink, Ethan had ordered. A chat. Guidelines. He could do that.

'I don't suppose you've time for a quick drink? Coffee? I'd like to have an informal meeting...a chat about our patient list, Safia, the surgery, guidelines...' *And the kiss. And the husband.*

Hell, he knew too much about Kara Stephens, and *so* not enough. And his drama-free night fizzed into nothing under the cynical watchful eye of the sensible part of his brain.

Kara's teeth bit along her bottom lip as she toyed with

his suggestion. 'Maybe I'm already going out some-where? Maybe I have plans?'

Why wouldn't she? A beautiful woman like her was bound to have plans. 'Okay, well, that's fine. Another time.'

'I don't know…' She stared up at him through her long blonde fringe. 'I guess we should have a debrief, at least. Where would we go? Drake's?'

'Ah, no, after the day I've had I feel like taking a spin. A little farther, maybe? Somewhere I can breathe fresh air, away from the city. Blow out the cobwebs.'

'Not too far. I have an early morning start tomorrow, with a hell of a grumpy boss.'

Walking back to his bike, he handed her a helmet from the top box and grinned. It wasn't the early morning he was imagining…it was a late night…

Whoa, his libido was in super-drive. *Getting to know you* had suddenly got interesting.

Which was a pretty damned stupid idea, given she was already infiltrating his every thought. There were some guidelines he needed to be setting for himself too—e.g. a Kara-free life.

'Okay, so how about Hammersmith? There's a little pub there down on the water's edge, just near Furnival Gardens. Not quite Darling Harbour, I guess, but it's a decent spot and shouldn't be too busy.'

She stopped and regarded his bike with a grimace. 'I don't do bikes.'

'You've got to be open to new experiences, Kara. It's how we grow as people. It's just a bit of fun. What have you got to lose?'

'Skin? I know enough about plastic surgery to never go on a motorbike. *Ever.*' Weighing the helmet in her hand, she eyed him suspiciously. 'Do you always carry a spare helmet?'

'Not always. Just so happens the luck fairies have been busy sprinkling again. I'll be careful—and besides, London traffic is so slow we won't get above twelve miles an hour. Come on. Live a little.' Climbing on, he gestured to the back of the bike. 'I promise not to bite...unless you want me to.'

'Oh, no...biting is way off-limits.'

But she held his gaze and he caught that flicker of desire, those green eyes probing deeper into his soul. And he didn't miss the catch in her voice, the breathy sigh. He wondered, briefly, what was within her limits...

'So, are you getting on or not?'

'Seeing as you asked so nicely. Good to see that chivalry's not dead.'

'Wait. Wear this.'

Shrugging out of his jacket gave him a second to rethink this whole scenario. Man, he needed his head looked at—inviting her out when he should have been going through the Hunter Clinic's quarterly accounts instead of pandering to Ethan's demands. But his friend had been right. The least Declan could do was to lay down some ground rules. A quick drink. A work chat. Then make sure she got home safely. That was chivalry. Not giving in to feral instincts.

Unlike his father, who had given in to too many of his own needs, leaving everyone else to deal with the fallout of his selfishness.

And Declan was nothing like his father.

'It can get cold on the bike and wearing this is safer. Like I said—my lucky jacket.'

He wrapped the jacket round her shoulders, held it while she slid her arms into the sleeves. It dwarfed her willowy frame and she looked like a hot rock chick, not a surgeon. An image that zinged straight to his groin, sending ripples of heat shimmying through him. He flicked her hair out from the jacket collar and slipped the helmet over her head, tightening the strap under her chin, drawing on every reserve not to kiss that pouty mouth.

'Okay, you're good to go. Hold tight.'

He held her hand as she lifted one red shoe and straddled the back seat. Held his breath as she slid her hands around his waist.

And he prayed to the luck fairies that she wouldn't hold on too tight. That his body wouldn't betray him again by reacting to her touch. That he could keep control of his libido long enough to get her safely home. Alone.

CHAPTER FOUR

SO MUCH FOR *professional distance*. Kara climbed up behind Declan and placed her hands tentatively on his waist. Then, too close for any kind of sensibility, she let go and held on to the back of the bike.

'Okay,' she shouted as her helmet tapped the back of his. 'Hammersmith!'

'I'll take the scenic route—give you a bit of a tour.'

He grinned, giving her the thumbs-up and gunning the engine. A quick jolt as he accelerated made her inhale sharply and instinctively grasp round his waist again.

Right round.

Now her sharp intake of breath wasn't purely surprise, but was infused with a good dose of fire as her hands slid over cotton that slid over muscle. Beneath her fingers she felt the outline of his abs, lean and taut. Her mouth watered. If she'd been crazy blurting out her stupid answers in Theatre, it was nothing to the foolhardiness of hugging against him as they whizzed through the streets of west London.

At the touch of her breasts against his back awareness flowed through her. Famous city landmarks passed her by in a blur. She thought she might have seen Kensington Gardens ablaze with flowers, the Royal Albert Hall and queues of people waiting outside, the dazzling array of trendy shops in Kensington High Street, but she definitely saw the musculature of Declan's arms as he steered, the tightening of his thigh as they waited at lights, the dips and lines of his shoulderblades.

The traffic flowed remarkably well for rush hour, and he wove the motorbike expertly in and out of the lanes. The warm breeze rushed into her face. The powerful throb and roar of the engine as they sped along gave a power-punch to her chest. Declan was right—this was definitely the way to blow out cobwebs. Her heart thumped and her body ached, but the only thing she knew for sure was that once this ride had ended it would take a lot of convincing for her to get off.

Although not once had she felt any shift in Declan's focus, any kind of reaction to her hands on his body. Maybe she was dreaming that there was a connection between them? Maybe he truly did just want a conversation about their caseload?

In which case she would be fine. She could do professional. She could definitely do hands-off—just as soon as they stopped. For now, though, she was content to hold on tight.

Then, in too few wonderful minutes, they were pulling up outside a beautiful but tiny Tudor-style pub on the banks of the River Thames. Hanging baskets dripped pink and scarlet flowers over mahogany balconies; a smattering of people sat at round tables outside.

He helped her off the bike and unclipped her helmet. 'There we go. Fun, yes?'

'Wow, yes.'

Although not necessarily in the way he was thinking. Her legs felt a little unsteady as she stood, and she didn't think it was all due to the bike.

'I love it. Nothing can beat it. Oh, wait—maybe riding back in the dark, seeing London all lit up.' He secured their helmets in the top boxes, then pointed right along the paved riverfront. 'Should we take a walk first? There's a little pier farther down I like to explore.'

'Oh? Okay.'

She turned to take in the rest of the sights. To their left the green iron latticework of the Hammersmith Bridge dominated the view back towards the city. On the slow-running water members of a rowboat team practised strokes under the watchful eye of their cox. They paused briefly and waved.

Kara waved back. 'Seems like a lot of hard work to me.'

He laughed. 'I prefer rugby myself, but there's a rowing club just down the way. This place gets busy at the weekends, with people hanging out watching boat races and the like.'

'Do you play? Rugby?'

'When I have the time. I play for an Irish club based in Kilburn.'

That explained the toned body she'd run her fingers over. She forced words through a suddenly dry throat. 'What position?'

'You know about rugby?'

How many hours had she stood on the touchline and watched Rob get battered and bruised? How many years of bolstering his flailing ego when they were beaten? Too many to count. It wasn't a memory she wanted to conjure up—or relive.

'Not really.' She changed tack. 'Being a consultant, I thought you'd be more of a wine bar, white tablecloth and fancy grog kind of guy.'

'Grog?'

'Remind me to bring a phrasebook next time. Grog is what we Aussies call beer.'

'I see. It sounded like you had something stuck in your throat.' He laughed. 'I enjoy bars like Drake's, for sure. There's a good crowd in there and it's friendly enough. But sometimes I like a little anonymity—being where everyone knows all your business is like being back home.'

'Or on an army base. Or at boarding school. Both of which I've done.'

'And didn't enjoy, by the look on your face.' He started to wander down the shrub-lined path. Thyme and lavender scented the air. 'I also like to go to places I can pop into wearing my leathers if I see fit. Drake's doesn't really fit that bill.'

'I'm sure they wouldn't mind.' *I wouldn't.*

She sniffed the leather jacket. Got another lungful of Declan. Steadied her heart-rate.

Across the river Kara saw large oak trees, a sports field, people jogging. Next to her Furnival Gardens was in full late-summer bloom, the flowers a little faded now, but bright still, very pretty and so typically English. It was a long way from Sydney's exotic botanical gardens. With no large bats eyeing her suspiciously or flapping their great grey wings over her head. Now, *there* was a bonus.

Ah, Sydney… Her heart stuttered just a little. But she calmed it down again. This new life, so many miles away from the place she'd tried desperately to call home, was going to be stress-free. So long as she kept her heart out of her decision-making.

They walked on towards a cluster of brightly coloured houseboats adorned with a variety of quirky ornaments: gnomes, Buddha statues and pots and pots of flowers. A family of ducks waddled past and slipped into the water.

She breathed the scented air deeply and relaxed her shoulders. 'I can't believe we're still in the middle of London. The air seems fresher here—better than the confines of the city and the hospital's disinfectant smell.'

'It's a good place to clear your head. Sometimes I sneak down here at lunchtime for a run, just to get perspective. It's my guilty secret.' He stopped and turned to face her, looked straight into her eyes. 'What's yours, Kara?'

Oh, God. She forced the still air into her lungs and swallowed deeply. He was looking at her the way he had at the ball. As if he wanted to kiss her. Right now. Suddenly she realised she wanted to be his guilty secret, and him to be hers. To kiss those lips. To curl into his arms.

Dragging her eyes away from his, she glanced downwards. 'Shoes. They're my guilty secret.'

'Ah, yes. Of course. Although there's not a lot secret about that pair. They scream for attention.' He grinned, clearly liking what he saw. 'You sure you can manage a walk in them?'

'Definitely.'

At that moment a jogger ran past and Kara stepped sideways to let him through. Her feet sank into damp grass, ruby-red heels and all. Unless she wanted to hobble across the lawn as if she had some kind of terrible affliction she needed to admit defeat.

'But I think I'll just take them off to save the heels from being ruined.'

He waited as she sat on a bench and unfastened one shoe, then twisted to do the other one. Her hands shook a little as she tried to undo it.

'Damn thing—the strap's caught…'

'Do you need help?'

And there he was, in front of her again, bending down

and peeling the second shoe off, oh, so slowly, his hand on her foot, her ankle, her calf. Her abdomen squeezed at the briefest touch of his fingers on her skin, at the tender way he slid the shoe over her toes, his head dipped in concentration. She almost reached out to run her fingers through that mess of hair. To pull him to her and breathe him in fully. She wondered how the hell someone she barely knew could fire such sensations within her.

Then, as if he'd only just realised the intimacy of such an act, he jumped back and stuffed his hands into his pockets. 'Better now?'

So she'd just discovered that ankles were a definite erogenous zone. Wriggling her toes into the soft lush grass, she smiled. 'Yes. Thank you. Beautiful they may be—but, boy, they feel even better off.'

He laughed, sitting down on the grass opposite her. It seemed the man was at ease wherever he was—operating on complex surgeries in Theatre, in front of the media, roaring through town or sitting peacefully catching the dying rays of sunshine.

'You're as bad as Niamh. She's always buying the most ridiculous shoes—even ones that don't fit properly—just because they're *works of art*, as she calls them.'

'She has good taste, then.'

'Or more money than sense.'

'Niamh?' She knew she was treading on tricky ground here, but she asked anyway. 'Is she one of your sisters?'

'Yes. The oldest of the girls.'

'And then…?'

He shrugged.

She nodded for him to continue.

His smile was hesitant. 'Then there's Aoife, Briana and Roisin.' He counted them off on his fingers.

'I hope there won't be a test, because I'm so going to

fail at remembering them all.' *Efor?* 'There's a lovely musical ring to the names. What do they all do?'

'Apart from get under my feet?'

'There you go again—saying the words, but your face is all soft and filled with affection.'

'Ach, no, I was just squinting because the sun's in my eyes.' He laughed again.

Laughter came easily to him. She liked that. Liked that he found the fun in things. After the past few years she'd struggled to find the fun in anything much, and when Rob had come home all they'd done was argue. But Declan's smile was contagious.

She relaxed into the conversation as he chatted about his family.

'Let me see…you sure you want to hear this?'

'Of course. Like I say, I always wanted to have brothers and sisters.'

'Okay…well, don't say I didn't warn you… Niamh's married and has four kids. Aoife's engaged, for the third time, and has a little one—Declan.' He winced. 'Yes, after me, and not after the hapless idiot who got her pregnant. He disappeared into the ether at the mere mention of a baby. That was a big drama, as you can imagine.'

'Having a baby is always a drama one way or another. And Bri… Bri…?'

'Briana's talking about a wedding next year. Hasn't even met the poor fella yet. And Roisin is causing trouble at Trinity College in Dublin, training to be a doctor.'

Like her big brother. It was all so very different from Kara's life. Declan belonged to something bigger than himself—something full and lively—and he clearly adored them all, regardless of what he said.

A big fist of loneliness curled into her gut. She breathed it away. No point in wishing. All her life she'd tried to fit somewhere—and she'd never found her place, or herself. She'd tried the marriage and profession bit—it hadn't worked because something had had to give and it had ended up being her relationship. Now she just focused on her job, being useful, saving lives, putting people back together again. Taking any further kind of risk with her heart was just not on her horizon.

'How on earth do you keep track of them all?'

'Niamh is an excellent communicator, unfortunately. I think she has me on speed dial.' He rolled his eyes. 'Then there's texts and social media—it doesn't matter where you hide, they can always find you somehow.'

She laughed. 'And your mum and dad? Where are they?'

'Mam still lives on the farm…or rather… Ah, look, never mind.' Dark storms clouded his face. 'My dad… he's gone.'

'I'm sorry.'

'Not dead…just gone.' He offered her his hand and pulled her from the seat, shaking off whatever ghosts flitted at the back of those brown eyes. 'Come on.'

There was more to his family life than he was letting on. Something wasn't quite right. She knew enough about him not to push, but she wanted to ask him about his father. But that would be prying and probably intrusive. She didn't want that in *her* life, so she wouldn't inflict it on someone she hardly knew.

'Now, are you hungry?' He picked up her shoes and put his arms out towards her. 'Shoes or piggyback?'

'Oh, you're really getting the hang of the chivalry thing.'

But she shook her head, imagining how easy it would be to allow some fun into their working relationship. Getting physically close to him again would only make her think or feel something she'd regret. She wouldn't trust her heart to anyone again. So resolutely no piggybacks. The journey home, slammed up against him on the motorbike, would be hard enough.

'Thanks, but I can manage.'

She kept her distance as she walked barefoot into the pub and upstairs to a window seat overlooking the river.

Declan sat opposite her, that sexy mouth teasing her resolve. 'So, Kara, are you planning on staying in Burns and Plastics? Which particular area are you thinking of specialising in?'

'To be honest, I don't know. I love it all, but I'm not sure yet as to exactly where I'd fit.'

'What made you choose it in the first place?'

'I was amazed by the army medics my mother worked with—seeing how they could change someone's life after extensive injury made me want to do the same. So I guess I lean more towards reconstruction than cosmetics.'

'You didn't want to follow your parents into the army?'

She laughed, imagining herself taking orders...and failing. 'God, no, that was never on the cards. I like dealing with clients from all walks of life and different scenarios.'

He took a sip of beer and watched her for a moment, his brown eyes peering deep. 'And has it lived up to your expectations so far?'

'Oh, like all aspects of medicine there's plenty of times when it's devastating and frustrating—'

'When patients don't make it, or don't want to comply? Or when you know the causes of their injuries were avoidable?' He shook his head. 'Believe me, I know.'

'But I still get that mad buzz when someone leaves in a better condition, both physically and mentally, than when they came in. There's not a lot that can beat the high of success.'

'Oh? Really?' Declan put down his beer and leaned across the table. 'Use your imagination, Kara. I can think of a few things.'

She didn't need to ask him what he meant. Those eyes caught on hers again as he smiled, slow and lazy. Sexy too. Very, *very* sexy. An unspoken buzz fizzed between them. Something that was intangible but clear.

Again with the blushing. She couldn't remember Rob ever making her blush, or making her feel this weird mix of fear and excitement just by talking. She wanted to touch Declan. To smooth down that unruly mop of hair. To feel the rough edges of his jaw against her palm, her cheeks, her mouth.

Oh, boy.

'Anyway, am I still on the team, then?' she asked, trying to keep a work focus as the waiter brought their food—a Thai chicken salad for herself and steak for Declan.

In between bites of the most succulent lemongrass-marinated chicken she'd ever tasted she chatted on.

'Do I meet your extremely high standards?'

'I guess I can put up with you. You seem to have exemplary surgical skills and an uncanny knack of knowing what I need even before I do. Which is weird…but I can live with it.' His mouth twitched. 'So we do indeed have an early start tomorrow. I want to check in on Safia before our surgery list starts—make sure she's coping with the pain and the new dressings. Then we're over at the Hunter Clinic to review a couple of private clients in the afternoon. Somewhere in between you can regale the team again with your exploits in Sydney.'

Her cheeks remained heated. 'I'm sorry about that. I

don't usually talk about my private life in the middle of an operation.'

'That's a very good policy to adopt. There's a wicked gossip machine here and it can get you into all kinds of trouble. I find it's best to try to keep a private life well away from work. It stops things getting messy.'

'And who needs messy?'

Messy didn't begin to describe her marriage—it had started out so beautiful, so…naive. Messy had only begun somewhere about the time she'd determined she was going to study full-time, and messy had certainly come to full iridescent bloom at the funeral service.

She gave Declan a tight smile. He was renowned for keeping his relationships clinical. Short. Uncomplicated. And if ever she was going to have sex again that was her game plan too—but he definitely didn't figure in her picture of casual sex partner. Sleeping with the boss would be messy and then some.

She knew better too than to get into a conversation about anything other than work, but she'd muddied things by blurting out details of her life in the middle of an operation. She really did need to make sure he knew that kiss had been fully consensual, and had nothing to do with her memories of Rob or loneliness. And that it wouldn't happen again.

'I like to keep things as uncomplicated as possible. My focus is wholly on my job and I can't see that changing any time soon.' She took a large drink of wine and steadied herself. 'I should tell you, though, just to be clear, that my husband died.'

She could say the whole sentence now without the catch in her voice. She'd come a very long way.

Declan's eyes widened and he put his glass down.

'Oh, God, I never thought… Divorce, perhaps. Separation. What the hell happened?'

'He was killed in action in Afghanistan. Full military honours funeral—quite the hero.' She fought back the rising feelings of guilt, loss and sheer disbelief that had rocked through her for so long. This new start of hers included leaving the sadness behind too. Although that was so much harder to achieve than she'd thought.

'So he was in the army too?'

'Yes. I spent the best part of my teens rebelling against it, but ended up marrying into the firm after all. It was all I ever knew, really. I was very young—too young at eighteen—and I wanted the whole wedding fairytale. Oh, and a career and a family too. Just like every other girl I know.'

She thought back to the struggles they'd both had adjusting to married life, reasserting their individual dreams and trying to mesh them somehow so they could both be fulfilled and happy. She'd wanted a place where she could belong. Finally. Truth was she hadn't found it with Rob either.

Declan's hand covered hers. 'I'm so sorry, Kara. How long ago did he die?'

'Eighteen months.'

He did the maths. 'So the hospital ball must have been close to—?'

'The year anniversary. Yes.' She drew her hand away from his and watched him frown. She didn't want his pity or his sympathy; she just wanted to clear the air. Then she could move on. *Again.* 'But I think I know where you're going with this… Rob dying was devastating, and I'm not sure I'll ever be the same again, but that kiss you and I shared had nothing to do with him. Seriously.'

Declan ran his fingers across his scalp. There were

times when she knew exactly what he was thinking. There were times too when he became closed-off and distant. Right now she wasn't sure what he was thinking at all.

'Yes, Kara, about that kiss…'

CHAPTER FIVE

FINALLY THAT PARTICULAR ghoul was out of its box. Its spectre had hung over them for the best part of twenty-four hours. Or, in reality, six months.

As she put her knife and fork down and sat back in her chair the shadows under Kara's eyes melted away a little. 'It was a mistake,' she asserted.

'Hmm…' Declan disagreed with her. 'Losing your car keys is a mistake. Getting drunk and disorderly is a mistake. Kissing someone like that is no mistake.'

'Well, okay, it was just downright foolish. And it can never happen again.'

'No.'

But, heck, he wanted it to—even now. Even after hearing about the heartbreak she'd been through. She was over the death of her husband? The army hero? *Yeah, right.* Declan knew that loss never left you; the pain dimmed over time, sure, but it still ached in your bones, resurfaced at moments you didn't expect. It snatched clean away the ability to be carefree and left a distrust that life could ever be the same.

But she was clear that their kiss and her mourning her husband's death were separate—perhaps that was what she wanted to believe.

That night at the ball she'd been soft and yet sharp

in his arms, vulnerable and yet defiant as she'd laughed and joked and drunk and danced. And very, *very* sexy. There were layers to her—a fractured beauty about her that intrigued him.

He didn't know how to react to this. Was it wrong to want her after everything she'd been through?

It would be wrong to follow through, he decided—she'd been hurt enough, and he wasn't the kind of man to give her what she needed. But even so he ached to finish what they'd started. The more time he spent with her the more he wanted to kiss her again. And again. To take things to their natural conclusion—bed. Because he could do that very easily.

It was the rest of it—the promises and commitment, the *love* he couldn't do. After the heartbreak he'd seen his mother go through he would never make himself weak and vulnerable—never leave his heart open to such hurt.

So he usually had fun with women who were on the same page as him. Not women who had already had one long-term, this-is-for-life relationship and who clearly deserved another. With the right man. Not him.

'No. You're right. It can't happen again.' That was the right thing to do. The sensible part of his brain cheered from the sidelines.

She flicked her hand nonchalantly. 'We have to work together.'

'Yes.'

'And you're my boss.'

'Yes.'

'And...' Her eyebrows knotted. She obviously couldn't think of another reason why they shouldn't kiss again.

Even though he thought he might be able to persuade her to the contrary, he put his own wants aside. 'And I don't do relationships. And you just came out of one.'

'Hardly. It was a long time ago.'

'You're still hurting. That much is obvious.'

'I'm not. But you don't have to convince me, you know. I *do* get it. We're not doing anything again.'

She looked stung by his words.

'And, yes, Rob's death knocked me for six, that's for sure, but I am in control of my emotions now. I was totally in control back then at the ball too.'

'Knocking back shots was fully in control? Man, I'd love to see you let loose.' She'd been intent on getting wasted and had invited him to join her. Which he had done quite happily, until... 'So why kiss me then run away?'

'Let's just say that in a dim attempt to forget what the occasion was—i.e. the anniversary of Rob's death— I had decided tequila would be the memory-eraser of choice. And I was having a jolly time. Great company.' She winked. 'But suddenly, in a blinding flash of sobriety, I realised that instead of impressing my new bosses I was snogging one of them. And that anything more would be a really bad idea.' Finally her mouth curved into a smile and she pointed at him. '*You* were a bad idea.'

Still no mention of the sizzling static that had crackled between them. The same sizzle that snapped in the air between them now, like a firecracker.

Kiss me.

Oh, yes, he wanted to. '*I* was a bad idea? That's new.'

The smile played along her lips as her eyes brightened. 'Well, you've got to be open to new experiences, Declan. That's how we grow as people.'

'Oh, and we have a comedian in the building. Very clever, Ms Stephens.'

'What's the matter? Is your ego having trouble reconciling that you weren't who I wanted to spend the rest of that night with?'

'My ego is thoroughly intact…' He leaned towards her, unable to resist the allure of that smile. 'Because I don't believe you. You want to know what I think?'

'Not really,' she said

She was smirking in that sarcastic way girls had that was strangely sexy and infuriating at the same time. If she'd been one of his sisters he'd have been hard pushed not to tap her cute ass.

'Oh, do go on. The suspense is killing me.'

'I think you wanted that kiss as much as I did. And that you wonder just what might have happened…'

'I know exactly what would have happened.'

And he could see that she was heading the same way right now too. They both were. Dangerous enough for a fledgling work team. Even more so for a woman whose heart had been shattered and for a man who had no heart left to give. So what the hell his wayward mouth was doing, flirting and teasing, he didn't know.

But he just couldn't help it. 'You never thought about a re-run?'

'Never.'

Her eyes met his and despite her words to the contrary the truth shimmered there in pupils as green as the fields back home.

Home. Reality hit. 'Okay, we should probably be going. Have you finished? Where do you live? I'll give you a lift back.'

'Shepherds Bush.'

She told him the address and for a moment he thought about asking her who else lived there. Did she have flatmates? Was she on her own? Did she need company? He wasn't used to dropping and running. He was used to the sweet magic of commitment-free sex and the unspoken agreement that it was a one-night thing. But not pushing Kara for anything more felt respectful, right… and way out of his comfort zone. It seemed there were a lot of things about this Aussie whirlwind that sent him off-kilter.

He led her out, helped her on with the helmet, watched as she again sheathed her body in his jacket, washing it in her own sweet perfume. He climbed onto his seat and held his breath as she settled in behind him. This time she didn't hesitate to wrap her arms around his waist.

Many times he'd given rides to his sisters and their friends, to colleagues and to dates. Many times a woman had wrapped her hands around his waist but he had never felt so twitchy and so hot. *Damned* hot.

Kara's legs straddled his back. Those shoes either side of his bike were like some goddamned teenage fantasy. Her breathing was sketchy and shallow, her heat fused to his skin and his hormones hit red alert. Gripping the handlebars as if his life depended on them, he accelerated into the night-time traffic, hoping that the brief journey and the night air would cool things down.

No such luck. When he pulled up outside her apartment his gut swirled with a mixture of relief and regret. Laughing, she grabbed his hand and wiggled off the seat, rocking slightly on those take-me-to-bed heels as she straightened up.

So she didn't have to struggle further, he unclipped her helmet and brushed down her hair. The kind of thing he'd do any time for Niamh or Roisin. But the way his groin tightened at Kara's sexy smile of thanks was anything but brotherly.

After he'd removed his own helmet he ventured a question that he hoped she'd refuse. He needed to get away, and fast. 'Do you want me to come up with you, or wait here until you're safely inside?'

'Thanks, Declan, but you go home. I can manage. I'm a big girl now.' She found a key in her bag and paused on the steps up to the grandiose Georgian facade of newly refurbished apartments. 'Thanks heaps for the meal and the bike ride. It was fun.'

'No problem. See you tomorrow. Nice and early.'

He made himself turn around, forced the next few steps away from her, but when he reached his motorbike he felt the soft weight of her hand on his shoulder.

Caught the hitch in her breath.

Heard her whisper once more. 'Kiss me...'

'Kara...'

Her name on his lips sent hot sensations skittering through her abdomen and down her shaking legs. God knew what she was saying or doing, but she couldn't let him go without tasting him again. Could not breathe him in, feel the pressure of his body between her legs on that motorbike, could not hold him tight against her and then *not* feel that mouth on hers.

She'd lied. She'd thought about a re-run of that kiss too many times to count. And now she was going to make it happen. Because if she didn't she might just die. Was it possible to die of desire?

He turned, his look of shock similar to the way he'd reacted to her at the ball. The message in his heated pupils was the same too.

He palmed her cheek and smiled. 'What happened to never again?'

'Never say never.'

Her hands found their way to his jacket collar as she lifted her mouth to his before her courage left her. For a moment she thought he was going to resist or reject her, that maybe she'd read all those signs woefully wrong, but then he pressed his lips against hers, his hands framing her face, his touch heart-meltingly tender.

He tasted of something exciting, of adventure, and of a mysterious heat that seeped into her skin. This was nothing like the kiss they'd shared at the ball—this was deeper, sexier and filled with six months' worth of wishing, of relentless holding back and scorching dreams.

'God, Kara.'

His hands ran down her back as he pressed against her, his heart beating a raging tattoo that matched every beat of hers. And even when she knew this was the most foolish thing to do she pressed harder against him. Even when she knew that this was going nowhere she slid her tongue into his mouth, heard the groan in his throat, smiled as his breathing quickened.

She brushed her foot against his leg and he groaned again, in that deep voice that reached into her insides and stroked. 'Those are the sexiest damned shoes I have ever seen. Whatever happens, do not take them off.'

'Aye-aye, sir.' She wiggled against his hips, leaving him in no doubt as to her intentions.

The energy around them was supercharged. The kiss became hotter and more urgent. It was the kind of kiss that you searched for the whole of your life and rarely did you ever find it. Unexpected, exciting. Perfect.

She ran her fingers over his back, down to the waistband of his jeans, and pulled him closer, arcing her body to fit to his, feeling the swell of hardness between them. His mouth was on her neck now, tracing a soft trail to her shoulder, nibbling, teasing, biting.

Her fingers bunched in that scruffy mop of hair as her breasts pressed against him, her nipples hardening as they brushed against his body. Sensation after sensation rippled through her as his hand swept across her ribs, over her bra. Under her bra. Right there on the city street. And then he was sitting her on the motorbike, steadying himself in front of her, his legs straddling hers.

This was the most sexy, the most alive she'd felt in too long. The most amazing. The most thrilling. And if they didn't stop soon they'd be making love on that black and chrome steel.

Was she crazy?

Yes. She probably was. But she needed this, needed him, needed a night when she could be a sexy woman instead of a grieving widow. When she could feel and be held and be wanted. When she could take what she wanted, be herself instead of trying to fit into someone else's mould. Where she could have Declan Underwood in her bed.

She put some space between them—just enough so she could speak. Her hands didn't leave his body; her eyes didn't leave his face. She barely recognised her own voice, 'Do you want to come upstairs? For...?'

He stilled and closed his eyes for a second, knowing that coffee was not on the menu. When he opened them again she knew his answer before he even said the words.

'I should go.'

No. 'But—' The heat coursing through her veins ran cold with embarrassment and disappointment. He didn't want this after all—didn't want her. And she'd made yet another fool of herself in front of her boss.

His palms stroked over her shoulders. 'Go, Kara. Go now, before we do something we'll both regret.'

'Right. Thanks.' Rubbing a hand across her swollen mouth, she held back the sarcastic laugh. She didn't think she could ever regret spending the night with him.

'You know what I mean. We agreed this would be very unwise. Look, I'm not easy to get on with. I don't answer calls. I don't make promises. I'm not there when I'm needed. Except in my job. I'm always there for my job. The truth is, you don't need me in your life.'

'It was just a kiss, Declan.' Although she got the feeling that their kiss was just the tip of the breath-sapping, heart-stopping, wet and wild iceberg.

'And very nearly something else.'

He gave her a wavering smile. Not a let's-get-naked smile. Not a promising-three-times-a-night kind of smile. The kind of smile, she suspected, he gave his patients before he broke bad news. Or the kind of smile he'd given to one of his sisters when the pet goldfish died. It was not the smile she wanted.

'Go to bed. I'll see you tomorrow. Nice and early.'

And before she could answer he'd pulled on his motorbike helmet and disappeared into the night. Leaving her hot and definitely bothered and with no clue how she was going to face him in the morning.

She needn't have worried. He was far too engrossed in his work to bother about the events of the previous night.

They stood in a large group in Safia's room, trying to get the teenager to vent her feelings. No such luck.

Clean-shaven, hair wrangled into smart submission, and wearing a dark charcoal suit, crisp white shirt and silver-grey tie, Declan looked as if he'd stepped out of the cover of a magazine. Kara remembered how his rough jaw had felt across her cheek, how he'd smelt of leather and heat, the way he'd tasted of adventure, the way he'd whispered her name into the night. How his eyes had blazed with a heat that had threatened to engulf her.

Today, however, he looked rested, calm and perfectly

unaffected. Kara, on the other hand, was well aware she had dark smudges under her eyes from a restless night. From dreams about getting hot and heavy under sheets of a substantially lower thread count than the Sheikha was used to.

His voice was soft as he spoke to their client. 'So, Safia, how are you feeling today?'

Dressed in casual clothes, rather than her country's traditional heavily jewelled dress, the young girl sat in a chair and stared out of the window, her arms elevated for optimum healing. So far this morning she'd refused to speak or even to look at the surgical team. Thick tears ran down her face and she made no attempt to stop them.

Kara relayed what she'd learnt from the nursing staff earlier that morning, 'Safia didn't have a great night. She reports having little pain, but she's…well, she's generally not having the best of days. Temperature's fine, though. Bloods are normal. There's no sign of infection. Physically she's making good progress.'

'Ach, Safi…' Declan drew up a chair and sat next to her. 'Everything is going well. So what's the matter?'

'You wouldn't understand.'

'No? Try me.'

He ushered out the attending nurses, the medical students, the physio and even the Sheikha's parents. Kara waited for an indication of what he wanted her to do— stay or leave. God, a re-run of the night before.

This time nothing flashed behind those eyes that made her feel she should be embarrassed, but there was no reassurance there either. He was nothing but the consummate professional. Heat rose to her cheeks and she picked up her papers and made for the door.

What the hell had she been thinking?

Nothing. She'd thought of nothing past touching her

mouth to his, being wrapped in those arms. Nothing about her responsibilities to the team, to Ethan, to her patients. To her job. To everything she'd sacrificed. She'd been willing to throw all that aside and give in to temptation without a thought for the next minute, never mind the next day, just to have one more kiss with Declan.

Well, it wouldn't happen again.

Out in the corridor a nurse stopped and asked Kara to sign a prescription chart. Then a patient's relative asked for an update. Seemed everyone wanted to talk to her except Declan.

She turned for one quick look back into Safia's room and something about the way he was sitting close to his patient, his voice so gentle, rooted Kara to the spot.

He leaned close and took the girl's hand, looking out across the city and not directly at Safia. A ploy, Kara thought, not to stress the girl out by focusing on her too intently, but to cajole her somehow into talking.

'I see a lot of things in this job, Safia. I see people who have survived terrible accidents, who have lost everything except the ability to haul breath into smoke-damaged lungs. And some are not even capable of that. I see carelessness that leads to injury and I see beautiful people who believe they can't go on but who still have the rest of their lives to live, somehow. And it makes me sad.'

'So why do you do it?' The Princess blinked and wiped her bandaged fist across her eyes, wrestling control over the sobs that had racked her chest. 'Why don't you do something else for a job? Although don't try singing— you do really suck at that.'

'Yeah, I know. Liam's job is safe for now. Truth is, there's nothing else I want to do.' He smiled and turned to her. 'Because when someone can't stay strong for themselves they need someone else to help them along. I kind of see myself as doing that. I stay strong for you until you can find the strength in yourself.' He shrugged. 'Oh, and it just so happens that I'm a genius with a scalpel too. That definitely helps.' He winked at her. 'You're doing fine, Safia. You *will* be fine. This is the hardest bit, you know. Coming to terms with it all.'

'I don't want to come to terms. I want it to have not happened at all.'

He shook his head. 'Ah, sweetheart, I know you do. I know how hard it is. Trust me, I know.'

'How? How do you know? You're a doctor. You're not burned. You don't look like…this.'

Kara squeezed a folder to her chest and watched as emotion bled from his face.

But he didn't shy away from Safia's question. Instead he ran a hand across the back of his neck and nodded. 'Okay…I don't tell everyone this, but it might help you. I hope it does…' He inhaled sharply. 'When I was thirteen we had a fire at our house. I got the little ones out safely, but I just couldn't get to my mammy—my mum— in time…and she got burnt, like you, on her face and her hands…'

Oh, God. Kara's heart thumped and squeezed. She imagined Declan as a young, innocent kid, fighting to save the lives of his family, going back into a burning house to save them. How utterly terrifying.

Blinking back tears, she focused on the blurry piece of paper in front of her. *'Temperature normal. Blood pressure within normal limits…low mood…healing well…'*

Her own reasons for becoming a surgeon paled into the background as she learnt the real reason he fought every day to save people, to try to piece them back together again. And every day the horror of that fire must be somewhere in his mind, spurring him on. She imagined he'd almost lost them in the black smoke and the heat, and realising he hadn't managed to save his mother from being hurt must have bitten deep.

For a man like Declan that would have been a failure. But instead of running away from those demons he forced himself to face them every day.

But he was in London, not back home in Ireland. Had he moved here so he didn't have to face her every day instead? And what about his father? Declan hadn't mentioned him. Hadn't mentioned his dad's role in all of this.

So many questions buzzed around her head.

'So what happened after that?' Safia's voice had lost a little of its self-pity as she stared into Declan's face. 'Is she okay now?'

'She spent a lot of time in hospital and she was very troubled by everything that happened and more. They were hard times, Safia. How she looked on the outside greatly affected how she felt on the inside.'

He waited until the ramifications of that statement settled on Safia's face.

'She wouldn't do her physio, she wouldn't try any more treatments, so her hands and fingers got stiff and sore. She basically lost the strength to carry on. For a long time she let her appearance and her residual pain rule her life.'

Safia's eyebrows rose. 'That's very sad.'

'Yes, it was. She struggled to find that strength within her to make the best of things. That's why I have to be strong, eh?'

He gave her the kindest smile Kara had ever seen.

'But you've got the whole of your life to look forward to. You have very important things to do—I know this— and a happy life to grasp. You *will* get through this, Safia, believe me. You will get through this with dignity and grace and you will make a wonderful life for yourself.'

And until she could he would be there for her...being strong when she couldn't find strength within herself.

Small wonder the young girl looked up at him now with something akin to adoration. 'I'll try.'

'Promise me?'

'Yes. Yes, I promise.' It was a small voice but a big victory.

Kara breathed out slowly. It seemed that the more she learnt about Declan Underwood, the more involved she wanted to become. So she was grateful that he'd stopped talking, because if he was as damaged as she thought he was—and even half as damaged as she was—she could open herself up to a whole new world of hurt.

He turned and caught Kara standing there watching. His mouth opened in surprise, then tightened into a thin line. A torrent of emotion swam across his gaze and solidified into anger.

'Ms Stephens?'

'Yes? Sorry. I...er...' She wanted to tell him she hadn't heard, but he knew she had—knew she'd been listening to him bare his soul. And that, she surmised, was like rubbing his wound raw again.

Then he shook his head and with that swift action flicked the anger off. His shoulders were smoothed down, his features took on their normal ridges and planes.

'Okay, Safia, so we'll be back later to see how you're doing. In the meantime I'll send the physiotherapist in and you can start some gentle exercises to help regain the range of movement in that hand. Now, Ms Stephens, we have a surgery to do.'

'Yes, of course.'

Kara hurried in front of him and headed to the operating theatre, where she could bury herself deeper in her job and forget about the red-hot desire burning through her. Forget about the flash of pain and his subsequent refusal to acknowledge it.

Then, when she was finished for the day, she would work out the best way to stop herself from falling head-long into disaster.

CHAPTER SIX

'YOU WANT TO request a transfer? Are you mad?' Declan exhaled long and hard. Now his day was definitely going to the dogs. His day *never* went to the dogs. Work was the one thing he could control in his life: easy, predictable, calm.

He couldn't help thinking this downward trajectory had all started with the appearance of a certain Kara Stephens. The way she'd looked at him after he'd spoken about his mother... God, such pity in those green eyes. He didn't do this—didn't open up old wounds, didn't want sympathy. Never.

Damn. What was she doing to him? What the hell was *he* doing?

He didn't want drama. And no doubt that was what he'd have got if he'd blathered on any longer. That and memories causing a fist of pain under his ribcage.

He'd been trying to help a young girl, not much younger than his sisters, who reminded him of their feisty spirit, who had got under his skin a little. And along with helping her he'd blown open the secrets of his heart.

Damn. Damn.

So much for escaping to London and putting his troubles behind him.

He glared over the sleek smoky glass desk in his

Hunter Clinic office, barely able to comprehend what Kara was saying. Or to reconcile his rapid tachycardia and the thud in his stomach as she spoke in that cute accent that dipped and rose like the County Dublin hills.

'I know it's going to be difficult and will leave you short-staffed, Declan, but I just thought it might be better if I went back to my old team.'

'You're out of your mind.' But, really, he must have been too, to have kissed her back so completely. So totally and completely. And to be sitting here now, wanting to do it again regardless of the fact she'd seen him raw and open.

He didn't want her to leave. Okay, to be brutally honest, he wanted to have her, here in his plush white and light office. To slowly peel off her cream silky top, to strip off her tight black skirt…leaving the beige heels on, though… Man, his thoughts were X-rated…

He was at *work*, goddamn it.

He leant back in his chair. It had been a long day of holding back and he was reaching the end of his self-control. 'So why do you want to transfer?'

'Because of last night.'

'You want to leave because of one kiss?'

'Two kisses, actually.'

She held up two fingers, as if to ram home the point. A lesser woman would blush or shy away from the subject, but this was Kara and it seemed she always tackled things head-on. He thought he saw a smile waiting in the background there too, in the slight twitch of her mouth and a startling sparkle in her eyes. But then it was gone, replaced by steel.

'Two. Kisses.' She shook her head. 'I kissed you twice.'

'I know. I mastered counting single numbers in reception class. Personally, I thought they were pretty damned good.'

He rested his chin on his hands as his eyes met hers. If this wasn't such a serious conversation he could have some fun here. Hell, it had been hard enough to walk away yesterday and now here she was, trying to make it easier for him, and all he could think of was that he wanted more. A lot more. A lot more of everything. Particularly those slender legs, that tight nip of a waist. That cocky, forthright mouth.

What the hell was happening to him? She made a mockery of his self-control and a challenge to every promise he'd ever made to himself about getting in too deep.

'But a kiss is definitely not something I'd want to leave my job over.'

'I would hardly be leaving my *job*. It's just a sideways move to a different consultant and team. Don't get me wrong, Declan, the kisses were great. But I think we're struggling to draw a line here. This is work, our jobs… we can't stuff that up. If I go and work with someone else then we can put a stop to this…*kissing thing*.'

'Whoa…so, let me get this right. You want to leave me high and dry, with no junior surgeon and a heavy caseload, at the beck and call of a royal family, with a frightened patient who has developed a great rapport with you…' God forgive him for using Safia in this '…just because we had a kiss? In our free time? As consenting adults?'

'Two kisses. And I'm trying to do the right thing. The professional thing. What happens if this…attraction spills over to work? We can't afford to let it distract us.'

It was too late for that. And why he suddenly felt a need to defend their actions he didn't know.

'It won't. People have work liaisons all the time and it doesn't interfere with their ability to do their job.'

'No? Do you want to kiss me now?'

He checked his watch. 'It's after five and we're not technically required to be here... And you're an attractive woman. Any man would want to kiss you.'

'Not helpful. We're supposed to be having a meeting. At work.' She frowned. 'Safia is almost headed in the right direction now, so she doesn't need me, and besides it's you she has the real rapport with anyway. I'm sure they can find a replacement. I'll swap with someone. There are plenty of doctors who'd jump at the chance of working with you.'

'But you're not one of them.'

Her shoulders slumped forward. 'Of course I am, and I've loved every minute of it. But, come on, Declan. We both have jobs to do and this could get in the way. This... this is crazy.'

And the rest. He never spent more than a few minutes thinking about a woman. His life had no space for this. His heart certainly didn't.

Fun, yes—a little playful, harmless fun. But nothing more. And with Kara he had a feeling she wanted more. With what she'd been through she certainly deserved more.

'And if you do leave? Then what?'

She held her hand up. 'I just want to put a huge wedge of space between me and temptation. My life's been stuffed up too many times already.'

Which wasn't exactly a ringing endorsement of his kissing talent. He should have been relieved. He wasn't.

'I have to warn you that my first impulse is to say no. Things aren't going well for Karen's mum and she's requested further time off. If you transfer out it will leave the clinic in difficulty.'

'Oh. I see.'

'Look, I need a good junior surgeon and I have one. Why would I give that up for the sake of temptation? I don't intend to allow my work to be compromised.'

His private desires could go to hell. Was it really because he would be short-staffed? Or was it because he was being selfish? *Gah*, he hated that thought—that he would use his needs to make someone do something they didn't want to.

If that was the case he was no better than his dead-beat father, who had fed his own pathetic needs before putting food in his kids' mouths, forcing a boy to do the work of a man. Who had betrayed the love of his family, his wife. His son.

So, no, he didn't want to be selfish—but he also didn't want to be short-staffed to the point that something had to give. With the desperate needs of his patients and the reputation of the clinic in his hands he had too much at stake right now.

He bit down on the flare of heat as she glared at him. A challenge. But not, he suspected, with the kind of result she was expecting. Because instead of annoying him it fired him.

'Okay, well, leave it with me. I have an urgent report to write in what's left of this evening. I'll see you in the morning. We can talk more then.'

Scraping his chair back, he stood and walked to her side of the desk. She stood too, picked up her bag and slung it across her body—a very chic leather barrier. Slamming down the venetian blinds, he turned to her, watched the steel in her pupils melt into hazy heated green.

She could have left. For that matter so could he. But the only direction his feet moved in was towards her.

He ran his fingers through a loose curl of her hair, reached out and pulled the messy ponytail down until her blonde hair pooled over her shoulders. Then he grasped a handful of it and breathed in the sweet scent of freedom and heat.

He looked into her face, at the smattering of freckles over her nose, her perfect full lips glistening with a pale, barely there lip-gloss, then into those eyes that searched his soul. His thumb ran a trail down her cheek, landed on her mouth, and she bit gently down on the soft pad and smiled. His groin tightened as spasms of heat shimmied through him.

She gasped, but she didn't pull away. 'Two kisses, Declan...'

And both times she'd asked him. Now it was his turn.

He leaned into her neck and whispered, 'Kiss me.'

And he could tell by the way her body softened towards him that she did want that. More than anything. That this buzz between them tugged hard, and that she was struggling to fight it. But he didn't wait—couldn't wait—to do what he'd been aching to do since he'd forced himself to walk away last night. He lowered his mouth onto hers, felt the hesitation, the sharp intake of breath, then felt the heat and the need spiral through her.

She wound her hands around his neck as the kiss deepened. And he should have stopped. He should have allowed her to go, to walk away from his team and to stop this *kissing thing*... But he couldn't. Something about Kara Stephens made him want to hold on and never let go.

A sharp knock at the door had them jumping apart. Kara stepped away from Declan on jelly legs and hung on to the back of a chair, her grip as white as the expensive upholstery. She didn't want to look at him, but she stole a glance to see how he was reacting.

Instead of being in any way embarrassed or flustered, like her, he looked triumphant as he held up three fingers. 'Three. Kisses.'

Kiss number three had *so* not been in her plan.

What was it about him that made her want to kiss him so thoroughly? And so many times?

His story and his humility had touched something deep inside her and that reaction had frightened her. The only logical thing she could do, she'd thought, was to move away…not kiss him again. Every contact she had with him dragged her deeper and deeper under his spell. This wasn't just about a purely physical attraction, and that realisation scared her more than anything.

Her cheeks and body ablaze, she inhaled and searched for inner serenity as Ethan Hunter walked into the room. When all she could find was inner chaos she gave up and threw the head of the Hunter Clinic's charitable arm a wobbly smile, hoping that, if nothing else, she could at least project a semblance of calm. 'Hi, Ethan.'

'Kara, hello. How are you?'

She'd heard rumours about Ethan's temper and mood swings, but so far her dealings with him had been only professional. However, well used to being around army veterans, she could spot the invisible wounds, the need to be treated equally, especially after being damaged both emotionally and physically—as Ethan had been—and the refusal to accept any weakness.

Although he clearly believed he hid them well, Ethan wore the scars in his limp and in his stubborn refusal to use a walking stick, and in his absolute unwavering dedication to his reconstructive work on wounded soldiers and war victims alike.

It had been Ethan's suggestion that she join Declan's team, so now would be a good time to mention that she'd like a transfer…and then start tomorrow as far away from Declan as physically possible. But as she opened her mouth to speak her courage flailed and then collapsed in a puddle.

Was leaving the team the right thing to do? Or should she just wrestle her stupid wayward emotions into some kind of order? Was she just a wobbling mess of overreaction?

'I…er…I'm good, thanks.'

Ethan gave her a small smile. 'Thanks for moving across to work with Declan's team. You helped us out of a big hole there.' He nodded towards Declan. 'He has a lot on his plate, holding the fort here while Leo's away, on top of his workload and other commitments. Lucky for us he knows just how to pander to royals.'

'I like them. They're just as frightened as the rest of us when it comes to surgery, and they all need our help. Besides, Safia can't help her background. Kara's been great with her, though—settled her down…got her to open up…' Declan grinned, fully aware of Kara's discomfort. 'I don't know what I'd do without her if she left. Anyway, what can I do for you, Ethan?'

Declan offered him a seat, which he ignored.

'A drink?'

Ethan glanced over to the decanters but shook his head. 'No, thanks. I just wanted to have a quick chat about cover for Mitchell and Grace's leave… As you know, their wedding's coming up so we'll be two more surgeons down, leaving us short-staffed to cover on-call responsibilities at the clinic. If anyone else goes we'll be in big trouble.'

Declan turned to Kara and raised his eyebrows. 'Actually, Kara was just saying—'

'That I'm more than happy to stay on until Karen gets back.'

She threw Declan a look that she hoped would convey how frustrated she felt. What was the use in arguing? Clearly there was a lot riding on her placement here, and creating personnel issues wouldn't leave them well disposed to writing her a good reference.

And who in their right mind would walk away from working at the glamorous Hunter Clinic? Its client list was a who's-who in movie world cosmetic surgery, and Ethan's charity work brought in heartbreaking yet challenging cases from war-torn areas. As a place to hone her craft it was the very best in the world. It was too good an opportunity to give up just because of a kiss.

Three kisses.

Three kisses going nowhere. She was over trying to save things that were going nowhere. Like her marriage. And as it looked as if she was stuck working with Declan she'd keep her heart well out of it. She could do that.

She could.

A flurry of footsteps tapping on the marble floor out in the corridor had them all turning towards the door. Kara breathed out, grateful for the added distraction.

'Here you all are! Makes a change for me to be crashing into someone else's room.'

The Hunter Clinic head, Leo Hunter, stalked in, wearing a huge grin. Following right behind, her hand firmly in her new husband's grip, came Lizzie.

'Thought you'd all be home by now—it's getting late.'

'Just catching up on things.' Declan strode over and shook his friend's hand warmly. 'Good to see you. Good honeymoon? Or shouldn't I even ask?'

'Great. I think it was France, right? Didn't get out much…far too busy…' Leo winked as he shared the joke with Declan, but then his smile slipped a little as he looked over to his brother, Ethan, who cautiously smiled back. 'Hello, Ethan.'

'Hi, Leo. Lizzie.' Ethan walked over, his face serious and his shoulders hitched. He grazed his sister-in-law's cheek with a hurried kiss, shook his brother's hand quickly, then stepped away.

Kara watched with interest as the family dynamics came in to play. With his broad smile and easy manner Leo was clearly pleased to be back at the clinic he'd worked so hard to salvage from scandal and near ruin. Whereas Ethan's response was…*guarded* to say the least.

Again, the gossip machine had informed her of the rift between the brothers that was slowly healing but was not quite mended yet. For two people so passionately involved in putting lives back together they had resolutely failed to fix their own. There had been difficult scenes, terrible arguments and times when the brothers had clashed spectacularly. But after Ethan had been best man for Leo and Lizzie's wedding there had been some new, more friendly ground covered. Although, as far as Kara could see, the smile Ethan gave them still didn't quite reach his eyes.

Declan stepped forward and kissed Lizzie's cheek too. Warmth emanated from his smile. The contrast between him and Ethan was startling.

'You look great, Lizzie. Tell me, how was Paris?'

'*Très* amazing, thank you. Just…amazing.' She turned

to Leo, her eyes shining brightly. 'Can we tell them? Please?'

Her husband gave her an indulgent smile, his love evident in the protective arm round her shoulder and pride shimmering in his face as he looked only at her but spoke to the room. 'Okay...so, we have news.'

'I'm pregnant!' Lizzie blurted out, running a hand over her still flat stomach. 'We're having a baby.'

Leo kissed the top of her head. 'Yes. And we couldn't be more happy.'

Some people could have it all—work, marriage, love. As flutters of sadness whirled through her gut Kara forced out a smile, feeling, she thought, exactly the way Ethan looked right now: empty. Hollowed out.

But still he stepped forward and again shook his brother's hand, almost as if he was doing what he knew was polite rather than what he deep down wanted to do. 'Congratulations.'

'That's great news!' Declan gave them all a broad grin. 'Really fantastic. Seems it's all weddings and babies at the moment. Do you think there's something in the water?'

'Oh, yes, it's Grace and Mitchell's wedding in a couple of weeks, isn't it? Exciting!' Lizzie positively glowed with happiness. She glanced at her watch. 'Gosh, look, we really should go. We haven't even made it home yet, but Leo wanted to pop in here just to let you know we're back. You know what he's like—this clinic is his baby and he couldn't possibly drive past and not say hi.'

'You mean he wanted to see if the place has managed to survive without him? I think we've coped. Just.' Declan laughed. 'But you must be tired after your travels. Take your wife home, man. You have another baby to think about now. You can play surgeon-in-chief tomorrow.'

'Okay. Okay. I'll be in first thing tomorrow, if you can spare the time for a hand-over?' Leo looked at both Declan and Ethan, who nodded in agreement.

'Of course.'

And with that bombshell Leo walked his new bride out, their excited chatter resonating off the walls as they wandered down the corridor. Ethan followed a moment later, muttering something about a case arriving from Afghanistan in an hour or so and how not everyone needed to wear their hearts on their sleeves. Leaving Kara alone again with Declan, a whirlwind of emotions fluttering through her stomach.

Grateful that it wasn't her own private life in the spotlight, she commented on the scene that had just played out. 'Was it just me or did Ethan not seem particularly thrilled at the prospect of becoming an uncle?'

'He's had a rough ride, Kara. You of all people should understand that.'

Yes, she knew enough about rough times. About loss and grief. About the way dreams didn't become reality. That no matter how hard you tried to love someone, sometimes it wasn't enough. 'I guess…'

'Having seen first-hand how traumatic injuries affect soldiers…'

'Oh, yes. Of course.'

Declan shrugged and walked her towards the door, his hand on the small of her back, its heat sending her mind into a fuzz.

'But I think it's more than that. Between you and me, I think Ethan might be a touch jealous of Leo's happiness. It's something he's not been able to find for himself.'

'I heard they don't have an easy relationship.'

'There were issues between them in the past… That's why he joined the army, apparently—to get away from the messed-up Hunter family dynamic. And that, in turn, is why he's like he is now.'

She thought back to the way Ethan's jaw had tightened at the pregnancy news, the shadows that had formed under his eyes, the hollows in his cheekbones—jealousy? Without a doubt.

But she also knew that you had to dig very deep and get through tough times—find another focus, like work, and bury yourself in it. There was no point dwelling on what you couldn't change. It seemed Ethan, with his devotion to his work, was following the same mantra.

'Hey, are you okay?' Declan touched her arm. 'You seem a little quiet.'

If he'd just move his hand she wouldn't feel like leaning against him. Confiding in him. Asking him to kiss her again, fourth time lucky.

'Is that so strange?'

'Actually, yes. I never thought… All this talk of weddings must hit a raw nerve for you.'

The wedding hadn't been the problem. It had been the marriage. 'My wedding was a long time ago…it was a perfect day, exactly how I'd planned it. It's just a shame everything turned out the way it did in the end. But I'd never begrudge anyone a bit of happiness.'

'Fair play to you, Kara. That's my girl.'

His voice softened as his hand ran up her spine in a tender gesture that made her want to rest her head on those broad shoulders and just stop. Stop fighting this attraction. Stop trying to do the right thing when she wanted so desperately to do the wrong thing—with him.

'And you're staying on the team? No more talk of leaving?'

She pulled herself away from him. She'd managed perfectly well on her own up to now and she could do it again. And again. Unlike his mother and Safia she didn't need Declan's strength. She had enough of her own. She knew not to rely on anyone else because when it came down to it their promises pretty well amounted to nothing. Especially men like Declan—players; men who wanted everything but gave little in return. Well, he could have her one hundred per cent work commitment and that was all.

'I guess you boxed me into a corner there. So, yes, I suppose I'll stay. Even though now Leo's back you won't be so busy.'

'I'm always busy. I like it that way. Besides, he'll need time to catch up.' He gave her a wicked smile that threw her a challenge. 'Think you can keep your hands off me?'

'Oh, don't worry, Declan. I *know* I can.' Even though it would take a huge effort. 'Good night.'

Then she walked out of his office without looking back. Truth was, she had no idea how she was going to get through the next few weeks with any scrap of sanity left.

CHAPTER SEVEN

ALL WENT WELL for the next two weeks. Kara managed to maintain a respectable distance and Declan appeared to be trying too. Not once had they shared another kiss, or even a proximity that might generate one, even in the moments they spent together going over their cases.

Although the heat flickered between them like a smouldering fire—one small, wayward spark and she had no doubt things could get way out of control—she kept a lid on her emotions during the day. Only at night did she allow herself to relive those moments of closeness she'd shared with him.

So it was good to get some perspective now, on a rare day off, on her own out in the fresh air, taking in some of London's famous sights.

Having taken way too many photographs of the magnificent Globe Theatre, she wandered along Queen's Walk by the Thames. Barges glided past, and a cruise tour boat with people hanging out of open windows, cameras snapping, pointing and laughing. The river was as busy as the land on this bright sunny day.

In the distance the iconic sand-coloured Westminster Palace and its famous clock tower, Big Ben, dominated the view. She wandered along the paved walkway, weaving through the clusters of tourists taking photographs, past buskers and living statues, dodging jugglers and Latin American street dancers that added an exotic pulse to the atmosphere. The park was just a little farther along, next to the London Eye Ferris wheel, where somehow Mitchell and Grace had managed to land permission to hold their wedding reception.

Seemed most people from the Hunter Clinic had wrangled a day off to join in the festivities. Thank goodness she hadn't followed through on her request to transfer; she would have missed being here with this group of people who had invited her into their sophisticated yet welcoming world.

Some of her colleagues stood in the corner, laughing, chatting. Kara began to approach, but just at that moment she saw Declan join them.

Heart thudding against her ribcage, she turned away.

With a toned body like his, encased in a dove-grey collared shirt and smart black trousers, he was bordering on illegally sexy.

Oh, please bring back the scrubs.

So much for perspective. How the heck could she get an ounce of that when he was within touching distance?

Keeping her back turned to Declan, she waved at the beaming bride and groom and at Mitchell's adorable daughter, Mia, who was the absolute darling of the piece. And, no, not once did she feel a pang of nostalgia for her own wedding—although she did fight back the sting of tears at the smiling faces, the sweet beauty of the love-conquers-all message.

Because she knew, deep in her heart of hearts, that sometimes love just wasn't enough to keep two people together. Which was so *not* how she should be feeling at a wedding.

She plastered a smile to her face, which wasn't too difficult because Grace and Mitchell's love shone through. 'Congratulations! Happy day! You look gorgeous!'

Voices behind her grew louder. One of them was Declan's. Her back stiffened.

'Oh…er…I'll be off now,' she heard him say. 'Got to go.'

'Wait,' the other male voice said.

Was it Ethan? Leo? She didn't dare turn to take a look.

'Is that Kara on her own? Come and say hi.'

God, no. Her heart dropped.

Declan's voice grew louder. 'No, seriously, I should go. I've got things to sort out.'

So he didn't want to face her either. And why did that not please her as much as it should?

The not-as-smooth-as-Declan's voice shouted, 'Kara! Hey!'

All well and good to avoid proximity in the busyness of work. But out here, in the sunshine, when she'd been caught alone, they were destined to at least talk. Anything less would appear rude.

Drawing a deep breath, she turned. Declan was standing in front of her on his own now, eyes blazing with frustration, his friend having disappeared into a huddle of suited men shaking hands and laughing.

He shrugged and raised his beer bottle. 'Hi.'

'Hi.'

'Nice day for a wedding,' he said politely, picking his words carefully.

The tiny hairs on her arms prickled at the voice. Warm and thick like Irish whiskey, it soothed her to the pit of her stomach. But also, like the strong dark liquor, it made her giddy and excitable.

'Yes.' She drew a breath and steadied her nerves. 'I thought I'd come along and take a sticky beak.'

His smile was breathtaking. 'There you go with that foreign language again. A what?'

'A look. A nosy. My flatmates have gone away for a few days so I was at a loose end. I just took a stroll along the riverfront. I never knew there was so much along here.'

He glanced down at her wedge sandals—honestly, they were only a few inches high...

'Really? Strolling in *those*?'

'Yes, Declan, what else would you do in them?' She held up her hand at the glint in his eye. *Do not take them off.* Suddenly her imagination ran riot with images of him naked...her legs wrapped around his. Heat seeped through her. 'Do not answer that.'

'Don't worry, we're in a public place—I do know how to behave.'

His voice lowered into a growl that simultaneously made her laugh and stoked something hot and needy in her stomach.

'I've been behaving for the past two damned weeks.'

So he was suffering too. That gave her a short blast of something wild and exciting. To have a man have to control himself around her gave her a sense of strength—power too. Something she hadn't had for a while.

'And so you shall continue.' She looked up into his dark brown eyes and thought that out here in broad daylight she was very unlikely to kiss him. Especially when they would be surrounded by people from the clinic. Despite how much she was drawn to that mouth. 'We're going to stick to safe subjects...like work.'

'Really?' His shoulders slumped forward. 'Dull.'

'Safe.'

'Dull.'

'Shut up. Actually, I was wanting to talk to you about

Safia while we have a few minutes. I'm still worried about her.'

Kara had been meaning to catch up with him about the Princess for a couple of days, but an emergency case had taken priority.

He became serious in an instant. 'Me too. She's healing well, but my pep talk didn't really help.'

'Oh, it did. It was exactly what she needed to hear.'

And it had certainly helped Kara get more insight into the workings of his mind. Flirty and funny he might be, but he held people at an emotional distance, carrying baggage almost as big as hers, along with a huge responsibility for a family he tried hard not to care for.

'She's definitely more motivated, but she's still very down. Her parents got her tickets for the Oblivion concert and she didn't even show a flicker of interest.'

'When a girl stops showing interest in a sex god there is something very wrong.' He smirked and held his arms out, puffing his chest and smoothing his fingers through his hair. 'I should know.'

He was a sex god?

Spasms of lust rippled through her as he laughed. Yes. He was a sex god.

He was driving her crazy with his easy nonchalance, his wicked humour, his sexy talk. Crazy and just a little bit sexually frustrated. She took a bottle of water from her handbag and had a long, refreshing drink, hoping the cold might wash some sense into her. It didn't.

His eyes followed the movement in her throat as she swallowed. His gaze was bordering on insatiable. 'You are way too cocky, mate.'

'You just don't know what you're missing.'

Oh, but she did. Knew it with every single second she

spent with him. Knew too that keeping a distance was definitely the only path to take.

She tried to relax and move the conversation to less shaky or sexy ground. 'Funny how life works out. I never thought I'd be working in London, walking alongside the Thames on a day off, visiting places where Shakespeare had been.'

'You had a different life planned?'

'Yes.' Rob was supposed to have left the army. They were supposed to have had a family, settled down. Found somewhere to belong, to fit. 'But here I am, a long way from that.' Making her new life fit around her instead.

He walked her slowly to a patch of grass. Laying his jacket out, he indicated for her to sit. 'Your poor feet need a break. I have about five minutes, then I really do have to go.'

Good, setting out parameters.

Glancing around, she saw that most people had sat down in little huddles, or couples, spreading out in the park. Everyone seemed relaxed, paired off, settled in the sun. To interrupt them by barging into their groups would seem rude. Not to sit down for five minutes would too.

She determined to stay just long enough to be polite. 'What about you, Declan? Did you always want to come here? Where is it you're from again?'

'County Dublin.'

'Do you miss it?'

'Not really. I miss the fresh air, mostly, but you can't beat London for excitement. I love it here. No pressures. I like to be free. No ties.'

No ties. Like her. And yet whereas he clearly wanted to cast his ties off, she'd spent a good deal of time over the years trying to forge them one way or another. It was just that she'd tied herself to the wrong people.

'I've always wanted to visit Ireland—it sounds wonderful. I think somewhere back in our family's past we have people from there.'

'Most folks do.'

His hand brushed against hers and it would have been so easy to grasp it. But instead she shoved her fist in her dress pocket and let herself be carried away by his voice.

'It's a grand place to bring up kids. I can see that now, living in a big city like London where there's noise and pollution and crime, but I couldn't wait to escape. There were times I didn't think I'd ever leave the village I grew up in.'

Was this a good time to broach the subject? Unanswered questions swirled in her head and she felt compelled to know more and more about him. He seemed relaxed, just chatting.

Her heart thumped a little as she asked, 'Was that… because of the fire? Was she badly hurt…your mum?'

'She was close to not making it. Not just physically but emotionally.'

'I can't imagine how bad that was for you all. What about your dad? Was he hurt?'

His eyes clouded like dark storms. But it wasn't grief, it was anger. 'Not badly enough.'

Wow. Bitterness flowed from him. 'What do you mean? What happened?'

'That's a lot of questions, Kara.' He put his hand on her shoulder. 'I prefer to look ahead now, eh? No point in dwelling on all that.'

She looked up into those clouds, saw fear there too, and hurt. She wanted to wrap him in her arms and wipe away that pain. But he would never let her do that—he was too proud, too closed-off.

'You mean, back right off.'

'Yes, I do. Leave it alone.'

At least this time his tone was gentle—but she'd over-stepped the mark. In lots of ways he was right. There was no point dwelling on the past, even if it did tinge every-thing you felt—your dreams, your plans. Taking a long deep breath, she looked ahead.

Adults laughed and chatted, children of all ages played together, teenagers swung toddlers around, made daisy chains, chatted happily alongside each other.

With a sorry heart she thought about Safia in her hos-pital room, so far away from her friends and surrounded by stuffy aides and parents who desperately wanted to make her feel better but were at a loss as to what to do.

But as she watched a thought crystallised.

Declan lay back on his elbow and gave her a lazy smile. His hair kind of flopped over his eyes just a little, and once again she found herself fighting the urge to run her fingers through it. The clouds in his eyes had passed through and she saw only light in them now.

'I have an idea.'

'Oh?' His eyebrows peaked. 'Should I be worried? Scared? Excited?'

'All of the above.' She winked. 'Brace yourself.'

Declan sat up as Kara smoothed her pale yellow linen dress around her. He'd thought he'd been doing quite well, sticking to safe conversations and being on his best be-haviour. And, truth be told, he'd spent two whole weeks reining in his libido to the point of utter frustration—and, man, he'd been good. In Theatre, on the ward rounds, in meetings, he'd maintained a professional distance, had kept his dirty mouth in check, had not touched her. Not once.

And while once upon a time if his libido had been

bouncing like this he'd have gone out and got laid with a like-minded woman, recently he just hadn't had the appetite. But now the sight of those long tanned legs and cute *kiss me* mouth made his heart jump more than a little.

'So...' She gifted him a smile, which turned the heart-flip into a full-scale bungee. 'Now that she's had her second lot of surgery do you think Safia is well enough to be in a shared room?'

'Work, work, work. Of course.' He tipped his head back and laughed.

The woman was either work-obsessed or choosing her conversation topics with absolute care. Judging by the pink tinge to her cheeks, and the resolute way she would not look him fully in the eye, he guessed it was a bit of both.

'Yes, she's healing well, but her parents have specifically requested for her to be on her own. They are very strict on privacy.'

'Yes, I understand that. She might be a princess, but really, as you say, she's just like any other girl. She wants to be with friends, to chat and laugh and squeal over boys. I think she's lonely, and I think she needs normal.'

'And moving her to a shared room would give her company, distract her from her burns. Genius.'

It was a simple idea, but often they were the best ones. He'd been so focused on keeping the girl safe and her parents happy that he'd skipped past Safia's basic needs. Companionship.

Hell, the more he thought about it the more he could apply that logic to himself. But he'd never wanted companionship before—at least not past the bedroom door—so God knew why suddenly he felt as if he'd been missing something...he didn't want to think about what.

'What about the cross-infection risk?'

Kara leaned forward and he caught a flash of pure white lace under the halterneck dress. His mind whizzed into overdrive. The trouble with halternecks was the sheer amount of skin exposed. Her neckline, sun-kissed shoulders, a wide expanse of back that made him want to stroke his fingers down that spine.

But the best bit about halternecks was the amount of skin exposed…the neckline, sun-kissed shoulders…

Yes, he knew exactly what he'd been missing. And looking at those long limbs, that easy smile, the curve of her breasts, he could only guess what else he was missing too.

As if he'd ever dreamt that a loudmouthed Aussie might fill a gap in his life that he didn't even know he had. Confused wasn't the half of it.

He dragged his eyes away and reminded himself of their conversation. *Cross-infection risk.* 'Minimal, I'd say. At least at the moment while she's still on prophylactic antibiotics. She should be fine. We'd just need to keep an eye on her temp and wound sites. I'll talk to her parents and run it by them. I'm not sure they'll be very happy at the prospect of moving her.'

'But we're talking about her mental health here, not just physical. Surely they'll see that?'

'I'll discuss it with them. That's all I can promise.'

His cell phone rang. *Damn.* Not today.

Her eyes flicked to his phone, lying on the grass next to him, but truly he didn't even need to check to see who was calling.

'Aren't you going to answer it?'

'Nah. It's just family stuff.' He'd deal with it later. He took a long slug of his beer. *Later.*

'Then surely you should pick up?'

'Look, I'm having a good time.' The ringing stopped. 'See. She'll leave a message.'

It rang again.

Kara's gaze hooked on to his. 'It might be important.'

'It's Niamh. It won't be.'

Kara's eyes narrowed with suspicion. 'How do you know? How do you even know it's Niamh?'

'She has a special ringtone so I know when to answer. Or rather, when not to answer.' He laughed. 'You know, they're great, but, man, *so* needy. I'm at a friend's wedding, for goodness' sake. This…' He indicated the setting, the weather, his beer. *Her.* 'This is nice.'

Days off were scarce; spending them outdoors with a beautiful woman were rare indeed.

His phone rang again.

'It's okay. Pick up. Seriously, I don't mind.' She reached for the phone and glared at him. But her smile was sweet and she was laughing. 'Declan, come on, it might be important. What if it was and you missed something? Family's important. Just be grateful you have one that cares.'

He saw the flicker of hurt as she flapped a hand in front of her and shook her head. *Don't go there.* But he remembered the bitter words she'd used back in that corridor weeks ago. *What their child wanted came at the bottom of the pecking order.*

She'd clearly had a bad run, with parents who cared more for their careers than for her needs. And her husband had left her a widow so young.

Hell, his family might irritate him but he knew he was loved—even if it was to the point that it felt suffocating.

'Okay. Okay. But I know I'm going to regret this.'

He huffed out a breath and snatched her hand away, grabbing her fingers and holding them. She playfully pulled back, but she didn't wriggle from his grip. Her skin was warm on his. Every single nerve-ending fired into action.

And there…right there…that second…the electricity between them sparked into life again. Need slammed into him. She felt it too, he knew. He could just see the playful teasing in her eyes melt into something dangerous and hot. Her smile wavered into the bite of her teeth on her bottom lip, the reddening of her skin, the quickening of her breath.

She didn't want this. But she did. And, *God*, he wanted her like nothing and no one he'd ever wanted before. He'd held back and held back…

He caught her chin with his hand and tilted her head to his. Her mouth was only inches away. Her tongue darted out and wet her lips as if she was about to eat something delicious.

Kiss me.

And he was going to. As he lowered his mouth towards hers the earth twisted on an axis he couldn't fathom and the breath was stripped from his lungs. And, sure, his whole damned workplace was here, watching again. Like before—that first time on the ballroom floor.

And just like that first time he couldn't stop himself—couldn't stop the pull of her lips, of her fragrance. He just wanted her in his arms. There was a connection—not just a base physical attraction, something more—that drew him to her.

He was going to kiss her once more, just to get her well and truly out of his system. Then he was going to put a stop to these flirting shenanigans and focus on his life and responsibilities.

'Declan?'

She fitted so perfectly into his arms. Her breath was

on his throat like a butterfly kiss. Her voice was hoarse, and he definitely caught the sexy catch.

'Aren't you going to answer it, then?'

The phone. The damned phone.

He exhaled and kept his voice steady—this time not from frustration but from pure, blatant, feral need. Clearly his sister didn't need to hear that.

'Niamh. This had better be important.'

'Hello to you too, Dec. Now, I was just planning ahead awhile… You know Mammy's birthday's coming up…'

Please. Really? Mid-pash? 'Can this not wait?'

'Why? What the hell are you up to on a fine Saturday afternoon?'

He growled. 'You don't want to know.'

'Wrong, Declan. I *do* want to know. What's her name?'

Was nothing private? 'None of your business.'

'Sure, that's an odd name for a girl. Now, tear yourself away and talk to me about Mammy's birthday. She'd love to see you here…'

He listened to his sister blather on and his blood pressure started its usual upward hike as his libido crashed into his boots. 'I'll see what I can do, but you know what it's like. I do have work to do.' He dragged his hand away from Kara, stood and took a few paces away so she wouldn't hear the drama. 'We're fierce short-staffed as it is.'

'It's always work with you, Dec. But I think seeing you would be a real tonic for her.'

'I have to work, for God's sake.' What more did they want from him? He sent home a good amount of money, and it was a far cry from what he'd been forced to do as a kid just to get some food on the table. At least he was on the right side of the law now. 'How the hell else do we pay for the things you all want? Look, I'll see what I can do.'

In reality, he didn't want to face the endless questions that Niamh seemed to think were perfectly acceptable for a girl to ask her brother…and added to five-fold by the rest of his siblings and his mother.

When are you settling down?

What about babies?

Found a nice girl yet?

Despite her own experiences his mother seemed to think that the answer to life, the universe and everything was finding a nice girl. He'd found plenty. He just hadn't loved any of them. And didn't plan to any time this side of the millennia.

'Look, I'll get back to you. I have things to do.'

'Okay, big brother, think about it. Be good. And be careful. And if you can't be careful…you know the drill. Buy a pram.'

Yada. Yada.

He flicked the phone into his pocket and inhaled deeply, trying to find the equilibrium that had been shattered first by a sexy siren and then by his stroppy sister.

Once calm, he turned back, ready to start again with Kara. 'Now, where were we…?'

But she'd disappeared.

He searched the crowd and saw her walking back to the main wedding group, being led by a pair of too-cute little girls in party dresses that reminded him of happier days with his sisters—before the fire had maimed their mother, sent their feckless father running away from his responsibilities and catapulted Declan into being the main breadwinner when there were no jobs for a scrawny kid, no way of earning money to pay for things.

And still, so many years later, they relied on him for everything.

As if she could sense his eyes on her smooth, straight

back, Kara turned and scanned for him. Once she'd found him she shrugged a little, her eyes bright but her smile regretful. Regretful about what? he wondered. That things had nearly got out of control again? Or regretful that they hadn't?

And then, as she wandered through the wedding party, he thought perhaps Kara's feelings were all mixed up with her own past. Did she regret coming to a wedding that would surely bring back memories of her own and of her war hero husband? Was that why he'd felt her tiny shift towards temptation? Did she just need comfort?

And why the hell did he care? Because the last thing he needed was another woman to worry about.

CHAPTER EIGHT

'SAFIA IS PROGRESSING very well indeed, at least physically.'

True to his word, Declan was presenting Kara's idea to Safia's parents in the burns unit family meeting room. Their first meeting since the weekend was going well so far.

No, their first meeting with *Safia's parents* was going well…but Kara was struggling with the near-kiss thing, and how easily she fell under Declan's spell every darned time. A lucky save by that pair of darling girls had put an end to something before it had started, but she was losing self-control with every touch, every look, every minute she spent with him.

Especially when he was dressed, like today, in a smart dark suit and an open-necked camel-coloured shirt. One tiny glimpse of his chest and she was a quivering mess of hormones. And it was way too early in the day for that.

'We have completed phases one to three of her management so far. She is alive and thriving, her burns are now all in a closed healing phase. She is having regular therapy to prevent contractures and she is responding well to that.'

The Sheikh nodded. 'Yes, we are delighted with your care. We are most grateful. She is getting better.'

'Well, yes. Her wounds are healing.' Declan leaned forward and frowned. He seemed to be choosing his approach carefully. 'But I'm concerned about her low mood.'

'She is sad, but she'll feel better soon.' Safia's mother had clucked around her daughter like an anxious mother hen from the minute they'd arrived. And who wouldn't? Who wouldn't fight for their child's life? Love for her daughter shone through, but it was a little…stifling.

'Until a few years ago burns specialists spent a lot of time and emphasis just on treating the burns and keeping the patient alive. Now survival is much more likely that we have to look at how patients like Safia are going to fare in the future, once they've been released from hospital. That's why we've been giving her physiotherapy since the day she arrived.'

'But I don't know what to do with her. She just sits and stares out of the window.'

Declan nodded, his hands clasped in front of him, his eyes soft and gentle. 'I know. I know. And I understand how upsetting it is for you to see her like this. We need to get her interested in things again. What does she like doing?'

'Make-up, clothes, horse-riding. She…you know… *hangs out*. In our country obviously she studies, goes to parties…shopping…friends. But she won't let them come to see her. We'd fly them in, but she refuses to see anyone.' The Sheikha nervously toyed with the edge of her beaded shawl. 'She's always got an opinion on everything. She's a handful at times. But now she doesn't seem interested in anything.'

'Ms Stephens has an idea we want to run by you.'

Declan's eyes fell on Kara, making her pulse jump in a skittering dance. *Damn. Stop it, already.*

'We thought, perhaps, that Safia might benefit from sharing a room with other people her own age?'

'Absolutely not.' Sheikh El-Zayad's voice filled the room. He was a man used to getting his own way, who commanded everyone and everything. 'I appreciate your concern, Mr Underwood, and I'm very grateful for your help in her progress, but my daughter shares a room with no one. She is the Sheikha of Aljahar—a princess. She does not mix with other...ordinary people. We have paid for privacy—it is very important to us.'

Declan shot a quick look over to Kara. No one else would have noticed but his jaw had tightened just a little. He took a deep breath and smiled, his voice now soothing, but with an authoritative edge.

'We could compromise. Perhaps she doesn't necessarily need to share a room—but she does need stimulation. It's very important she has contact with people her own age—not just your aides and...yourselves. The physiotherapist is happy to come and attend to her in her room—but I do think she needs to be occupied for the other hours of the day. At the very least she should come out and join in some activities, eat her meals with the others. Long-term psychological effects on people with burns injuries are well documented. We need to keep her motivated.'

Kara knew he wasn't just talking about his professional experience. So his actions and his words were oceans apart. Because, yes, even though she'd tried hard not to listen in to his private conversation with his sister she'd caught snippets.

He was refusing to go and visit them—and using work as an excuse. Maybe it was easier dealing with someone who wasn't a relative than having to face your own realities at home.

'With all due respect, Your Highnesses…' She smiled to them both, knowing her voice was rising just a little. 'Integration is a huge part of our therapy here. I don't want to alarm you, but I know you appreciate honest talking…' She waited until she'd received a positive response from them. 'Safia won't get better unless she sees some normality in her life—she's had enough of pain and being shut in that room on her own. I'm concerned about the risk of depression. She needs to be engaged. And she needs, really, to be part of this discussion.'

'Thank you, Kara.'

Safia's voice had them all turning quickly to see her standing in the hallway. Dressed in jeans and a baggy sweatshirt, she looked like a regular teenager apart from the left side of her face and her hands which were covered in dressings.

She was pale and unsmiling. 'Talking about me again, Daddy?'

Declan stood and brought Safia into the room, offered her a seat. 'Hey. Thanks for coming by. It's nice to see you out of that room for a change. It must be boring on your own all day?'

'*Duh*. Of course.' Safia shook her head, her black curls bobbing round her shoulders.

As a member of a famous royal family her photos had graced the newspapers from an early age; her face was well known. She'd been a pretty girl—a beautiful teenager. Kara's heart clenched at what the future held for Safia now. She couldn't begin to imagine the grief and loss the girl felt.

She watched as Declan and Safia sat across from each other, saw his generous smile and a concern that went beyond his professional obligation. He pointed through the glass door to the ward where, as luck would have it, a seventeen-year-old boy who'd been brought in after a freak lightning strike had burnt his back, walked past. Wearing teen trademark baggy-bottomed trousers that hung off his hips, and a sideswiped fringe, he stopped and gave Safia a hesitant smile. Then a sort of half-wave before he disappeared into the ward.

Declan watched this with interest, a hint of a smile playing over his lips. 'But I bet you wouldn't be interested in spending time out there, Safia? Although Jack's got an interesting story to tell.'

The girl shrugged, but there was a spark in her eyes. Finally they'd got her interested in something. 'Anything's got to be better than sitting around with you lot.'

Declan grinned. 'Feeling better already?'

'Maybe.'

Kara glanced to Safia's parents, who looked at each other and shook their heads. They murmured quietly in a language Kara didn't understand and finally Safia's mother sighed. 'Okay. If you think so. Do it.'

'Wait—' Sheikh El-Zayad tried to speak, but his wife stopped him, patting him on the knee.

She turned to Declan and winked, 'Don't worry. Leave him to me.'

It was very early days but Kara took the wins as they came. Safia needed to be stimulated and motivated— whatever it took. 'Okay, as soon as there's a bed free we'll move her in. Until that happens, how about we take a little stroll down through the main ward and see who's hanging out?'

Please be there, lightning boy.

'Yes.' Declan nodded his thanks to the Sheikh and Sheikha and bowed them through the door first, then followed with Safia. 'There's a games console over there. You fancy your chances against me?'

The Princess frowned. 'A video game?'

'Why not? It's great therapy for those thumbs.'

'Daddy would have a fit.'

She gave them her first real smile for weeks. But then surely anyone would have to smile with the offer of a few more minutes in Declan's company?

'You're on.'

It was late when Kara eventually managed to snatch time to write up her case notes for the day. Hiding out in Declan's offices at Kate's, she'd dodged the Sheikh's aides with their endless questions about maintaining Safia's dignity in the face of such intrusions as sharing the patients' TV room. Funny, what most people took for granted they'd had to fight for, for Safia—just some friends, a little hope...

Kara's feet ached—but then that was nothing new. Her head ached—but that was becoming a habit whenever Declan was around. Too much arousal could do that to a girl. The sooner she was home and out of the Declan Underwood temptation zone the better. Gathering her paperwork together and stuffing it in her bag she finished up.

The phone rang. *Damn.* She looked round for someone to answer it, but of course his secretary had left for the day, and Declan was consulting next door. Who the hell would ring his rooms so late?

Sighing, she picked up. 'Mr Underwood's phone.'

'Can I speak to Declan, please?' The voice was soft and sweet, unmistakably Irish. Niamh? Aoife? Briana? Roisin?

'I'm afraid he's consulting at the moment. Can I take a message?'

There was a frustrated sigh. 'Sure. But it won't make

a blind bit of notice. Tell him Niamh rang and he must call me back...*immediately*. It's very important.'

'You could try his mobile phone?'

'It's rung and rung to the voice mail a million times. The man's either got cloth ears or he's avoiding me. I'm resorting to underhand tactics and phoning him at work.' There was a smile in her voice. 'He hates that.'

The smile was catching, Declan's sister seemed warm and friendly—the kind of sister Kara would have liked if she'd been lucky enough to have one. 'Don't worry, I'll tell him. Oh, wait—he's just here.'

He'd come through the adjoining door.

'Still here? It's after five...'

He grinned and her heart melted. His eyes glittered, and the soft upward curve of his lips was like a promise.

'You know what that means.'

The five o'clock rule. Kissing was apparently allowed, according to him. Not her.

Dragging her heart back behind its steel barrier, she pointed to the receiver in her hand. 'Niamh's on the phone. She says it's important.'

'It's always important.' He threw some files onto his secretary's desk and shook his head. 'Tell her I'll call her later.'

Kara grinned. 'He's just coming, Niamh. He's—'

'Hey, I can wait all night. Just don't, for God's sake, try making excuses for him. He's a terrible liar. Tell him I've got more willpower than he'll ever have and I can keep ringing until he answers. And I will.'

Kara had no doubt that Niamh was just as willful as Declan.

They clearly all loved each other in a very definite sibling kind of way. Kara covered the speaker and held it out to Declan, shaking her head. 'She said she's had to resort to underhand tactics...'

She looked at the tired lines around his eyes, the tight clench of his jaw. Here he was, at way too late o'clock, still at work, planning his Theatre list for tomorrow, seeing clients after hours to make sure he could fit them into his schedule, attending to the needs of everyone but himself. And now this.

With a shock she realised how much she wanted to see him smile again. To feel the warmth of his smile on her, his breath, his touch. And soon.

'Do you always inspire such devious strategies in women?'

'Sadly only the ones I'm trying to avoid.' Glancing at the phone he let his eyebrows dip into a frown. Then he looked back at her.

She saw the mirrored need in his eyes—a raw need that fired something deep in her, something that shivered through each nerve-ending. Heat pooled in her gut, and lower, and then he was next to her, one hand in her hair, the other on her back. His mouth was on her neck.

'Declan.' She thrust the phone towards him. 'Your family loves you enough to be bothered. Talk to your sister. Be nice. That is all.'

'What is this? Secrets of the sour, sassy sisterhood?' He let out a contrite sigh. 'Ah, hell, give it here.'

Damn. Declan grabbed the phone, once again torn between the woman in front of him and his family's needs. He'd been too close to grabbing her and having her against that wall. To losing himself in her.

'Niamh. This had damn well better be important.'

'Hello to you too, Declan.' His sister lowered her voice. 'So, are you sleeping with her yet?'

'What?' His eyes popped as he strode across the room, out of Kara's earshot. 'No.'

'But you want to—she sounds nice. Won't take any crap from you, I wouldn't think.'

'Niamh, what do you want?'

'Apart from a big brother who shows his face every now and then? Sure, Declan, I can't remember what your ugly features look like these days.' She sighed. 'Is she pretty?'

He glanced at Kara, who now appeared to be nose-deep in a patient's notes. He looked at the soft golden shine on her hair, the way her lips twitched, that mouth that tasted of sunshine and sweetness.

'Yes. Very. Now, this is exactly why I live in London—to get away from all this…interrogation.'

'No, you live in London to get away from all those poor broken-hearted Dublin girls who wanted to make a decent man of you… And to avoid the truth.'

The truth that he would never be a decent man, because every time a woman had made those happy-ever-after kind of ministrations he'd run a mile. A sea. A country.

'Niamh. Leave it.'

'Will you come over for Mammy's birthday? Please? She won't be happy until she sees you again.'

'She won't be happy until I'm married off to the lowest bidder.' His heart squeezed. Poor Mammy…all she'd ever wanted was for him to be happy—but in her book that meant marriage.

He wasn't convinced. He'd seen the destruction marriage, and the end of it, had wreaked on *her*.

'I'll send her something. I can't—' Couldn't face going back. Couldn't look at her and know he'd failed her—in every way. He hadn't saved her from being hurt, and now he couldn't give her what she wanted most—hope. 'Yep. I'll send her something.'

'She doesn't need your flowers. She needs to see you. It's her sixtieth and she needs something to celebrate. When did you last come home? Can you even remember?'

No. Shame hit him in the gut. Working in London meant he could earn more cash than he ever would back home—which in turn meant he could support his family and have a life.

'I don't know—I can't face all those questions...' He turned his back and whispered, 'She's forever on my back.'

Niamh laughed. 'She just wants to know you're happy all the way over there. A bunch of flowers doesn't tell her that. Why don't you bring someone? That'd shut Mammy up. Hey, what about that girl? The one who answered the phone—?'

'Who? Kara?'

As he spoke Kara's head popped up. 'Yes?'

'Oh, sorry. Not you...' He pointed to the phone. 'It was...it's my sister.'

Niamh laughed again. 'Tongue-tied? You? Wow, you have it bad, big brother. Go on—ask her to come.'

Kara's eyes narrowed. She stood and picked up her handbag. 'What's she saying?'

Don't leave. Stuck in between two determined women, that was all he needed. But he wouldn't be taking her anywhere near his home.

'That...that the weather in Ireland's very warm...'

Kara waited, her eyes blinking innocently. 'The weather? Why—?'

'Coward!' Niamh hollered. 'Ask her. It'll get Mammy off your back.'

'Hmm…' He supposed his sister could be right. Having Kara there would be a delicious distraction. He could mix family with…a little pleasure. Would she? Could it work? How would it work? Hell, he didn't know, but it was a heck of a plan. Kara in his house… A man could think of worse ways to spend a couple of days.

Maybe it was time to go home.

He huffed out an exasperated breath. 'Niamh wants you to come visit Ireland.'

Kara stared, her hand on one hip. 'Your sister wants me to go to Ireland?'

'Just for a weekend. My mum's birthday. Sure, why not? You said you'd always wanted to visit the place.'

'No way.' Her hands were physically up in front of her. She didn't want this. She really didn't want this.

Niamh's voice crackled down the phone. 'Did she say yes?'

'Niamh, for heaven's sake leave us alone for a minute. She's thinking about it.'

Kara's cheeks reddened. 'Do you Underwoods always work in packs?'

'Believe me, my sisters could teach the army a thing or two about stealth operations.' But the more he thought about it, the more it became a perfect plan. '*They* want me to go back for her birthday. They said you should come too. *You* said I should be nice to my family. Bingo—everyone's happy. Say yes?'

'Emotional blackmail doesn't wear well on you, Declan.' She fiddled with her necklace.

'No ties, no strings.' At her frown he thought he'd better just be honest. 'Look, I just want to give Mammy some hope—to think that I'm off her hands. I…we… need her to stop worrying about us all and focus on her own life. There'll be the hassle of my sisters…but they're not so bad really.'

'No.'

But she'd released her grip on her bag. Was looking down at her magnificent shoes, out of the window, at the floor. She was wavering, he could tell.

Time to strike.

'I've tried my whole life to make her better—and the only thing she's ever said she needed was to see me settled and happy. She would love you, Kara. It's just a weekend. Two nights. Two. Nights.'

He held his fingers up just the way she had with her *Two kisses* quip. He saw the flash of recognition and the rush of desire on her face—not just in her eyes, but in the flush of her cheeks. And, goddamn it, in the ghost of a sexy smile.

He imagined what he could do to her—with her—in two nights. Hell, he'd settle for just two hours. Naked. Shoes optional. Actually, shoes definitely on.

'It's gorgeous at this time of year. The leaves turning golden, the rolling hills. Ireland…land of your ancestors.'

Then for a fleeting second he realised what a stupid plan it was. Because above the pretence and the joking he knew that he was actually falling for her. That some part of him wanted Kara in his chaotic life—and that was the maddest thing he'd ever thought. He wanted ties and that made him scared as hell.

Because after the weekend he couldn't offer her anything apart from a return to this—late-night meetings in his office, early mornings in surgery and the craziness of hospital life in between. Just colleagues. And then she'd be gone anyway, back to her team, and he'd be left with catching the scent of her in corridors, fleeting glimpses across the cafeteria…

His voice wavered a little as the reality of the plan sank in. 'But if—'

She smiled. 'Oh, okay, what the hell? Why not? I'm going to regret this, I know, but when you describe it like that how can I refuse?'

CHAPTER NINE

KARA STARED OUT of the hire car window as the Dublin countryside flew past. Pink clouds melted into rolling hills, ten shades of green, as the sun began to set around them. It was nothing...*nothing* like the endless red dry earth of her childhood, the heat, the bright, cloudless blue skies.

Here, lush fields carved by stone walls as ancient as the earth itself spilled out in front of them to the left and right as far as she could see. Cows grazed lazily, and ignored their momentous arrival in Declan's home county.

Momentous? Sure. What kind of far-side-of-madness idea was this? Panic rolled through her in waves.

This weekend was going to be sheer torment—not least because she would have Declan within the temptation zone for forty-eight exhausting hours. But then, she couldn't deny she wasn't a teensy bit intrigued to see where he'd grown up and what had made him the complex man he was today. Even if the reason she was here was to cajole his mother into believing he was happy and settled.

She wondered if Declan was having second thoughts too as he stared ahead with eyebrows furrowed, his jaw fixed. His mood was hard to read—but he definitely wasn't in his happy-go-lucky, carefree place. The silence between them since they'd checked in at the airport had stretched and stretched, interspersed by brief words and *über*-politeness.

As he drove he glanced over to her and she must have looked either a fright, or frightened, because he managed a smile.

'Hey, don't look so worried. It'll be fine.'

It was more a question than a statement, and she wondered just who he was trying to convince.

'I know. I know. I'm just a little nervous about meeting everyone.'

'Ah, they'll love you. How could they not?'

'Okay.' She wanted to run her hand along his leg and pat it and smile, tell him she was okay and looking forward to it all—do the kind of things you'd do to a friend or a lover. But she couldn't because, really, she was neither.

And the frightening truth was, deep down, that she didn't want to live something over the weekend and later want it to be true. But it was already too late.

He pulled up outside a large farmhouse and she could see, in the dimming light, a number of smaller outer buildings dotting the acreage. With walls the colour of thick clotted cream, wide picture windows edged by pink roses, the house took her breath away. She imagined Declan as a child, running around, up to his neck in mud, playing and working on the farm.

He opened the car door for her and she stepped out into a surprisingly warm gentle breeze.

'Wow. It's so gorgeous. It's like a dream house. You grew up here?'

'Well, on the farm, yes.' His eyes darkened. 'But there was the fire, obviously…and so we built this.'

And there her images of him morphed from innocent

to troubled. Her heart thudded. This place must bring back so many bleak memories for him. No wonder he barely wanted to visit.

'Ach, *Declan* built this.'

A thin, pretty woman with long dark hair stepped out through the front door, folded her flour-dusted arms and grinned.

'Not with his bare hands, you understand. Although he tried to in his weekends off from medical school. But he's a surgeon, not a builder—mighty fine with a knife, but we were deeply concerned about letting him loose with bricks and mortar. I'm Niamh. Pleased to meet you.' She stuck out her hand. 'Thank you for bringing him.'

'I…er…I didn't. He brought me, really. But nice to meet you too.' Kara shook Niamh's hand and immediately liked the warm, friendly welcome that put her a little more at ease.

'It was you on the phone, right?' At Kara's confusion Niamh explained, 'I recognise the accent. Australian? Kiwi?'

'Aussie.'

'I thought so. And I do get the feeling he wouldn't be here if you weren't. So you've done a grand job already.'

'Hello? I *can* hear you, you know.' Declan growled as he gave his sister's cheek a peck.

'Tosh, what do we care? And smile, Declan, it's only for a couple of days.' Niamh laughed. 'You certainly took your time getting here. And I don't mean the journey from the airport. Because that doesn't take a year and a half.'

Kara wondered what else Declan's sister thought behind those perceptive Underwood dark brown eyes. And, indeed, just what Declan had told her about the nature of her and Declan's relationship.

And then from behind Niamh came a roar, high-pitched squeals and a loud stamping along the wooden floor as four small children ran out and grabbed on to Declan's legs.

His face changed in an instant. His eyes lit up brightly and his smile stretched. 'Look at you all.' Swinging each one round in turn, he plastered a kiss on each plump cheek. 'Aine—pretty as a picture. Fiona—my, what a smile you've got. Saoirse—look at you.' Lastly he reached down between his legs and caught hold of a wee grinning boy. 'And Declan Junior—whoa, you've grown, my man. This is my friend, Kara. Say hi.'

'Hi, Kara,' they chorused, their curls bobbing in time with their words, and Kara's heart just about melted.

'Hi, everyone. Very pleased to meet you…er…Aine, Fiona, Saoirse and Declan.' If she repeated the names she might have a hope of remembering them.

She bent to shake their chubby hands and before she knew it was almost bowled over by sticky fists and warm bodies pressing close in a sort of clumsy, grubby scrum.

'You talk funny,' Aine whispered.

'So do you.' Kara gave the girl a big smile and tapped the end of her cute snub nose with her finger. 'And you're gorgeous.'

'Well, come in, come in. The others won't be long.' Niamh ushered the children back into the house and was just turning round herself when she glanced down to Kara's feet. Her hand went to her chest. 'Oh, my…'

Kara followed Niamh's line of vision and lifted her foot up, all the better to see her beautiful red suede ankle boots with black ribbon ties. 'Oh, yes. These. Totally impractical, I know. But just for the journey…'

'I think I just fell in love with your girlfriend. Clearly we're going to be great friends,' Niamh quipped to Declan as she led them into the house. 'You must tell me where you got them from.'

'Sure, I'd love to see you milking the cows in those,' Declan snapped, expertly avoiding the girlfriend comment.

But his eyes flickered towards Kara. She just couldn't read what he was thinking and once again she wondered what she was doing here—doing this.

'Come meet my mam.'

Kara's heart-rate trebled. Declan had explained that his mum was shy and very aware of her scarring, so it was important to put a lid on her loud-mouthed, out-there, army brat self.

But when Declan's hand fitted around hers and he walked her through the airy hallway to the large kitchen she stopped thinking and tried to just *be*. Which wasn't hard; being in his firm grip and the subject of his warm gaze made her lose track of her thought processes anyway.

The kitchen was everything Kara dreamt a family kitchen should be. Flour on the benchtop, creamy mounds of dough left to rise, a large wooden table covered in piles of pots and pans, and a warm, herby cooking smell that made her nervous stomach grumble.

Once again she felt out of her depth. She'd never had a home like this—one that felt so welcoming, that smelt of flowers and yeast and clear fresh air, that was busy and chaotic and so full of life. A lump thickened her throat. It was everything she'd ever hoped for growing up, pretty much alone—the career, the husband, the home life. She'd believed she could have it all.

Until hard reality had smacked her in the gut and she'd been left with little more than broken dreams.

Mary Underwood sat in the corner of the room, looking out of the window across the blackening night. As they approached she looked up and inhaled sharply. Tugging down one side of her long grey bob to cover a good part of her face, she stood and offered Kara a shaky smile. 'Goodness, I can't believe you've come home with our Declan. You're awful pretty, Kara. Nice to meet you.'

Kara could see the muted sadness in those dark brown eyes. The same eyes every member of the family had. But all of them shimmered with something different. With Declan it was wickedness, or heat, or cool restraint. Niamh's were tired and yet somehow content, and held a little of the wicked in them. Mary's were filled with an almost tangible love for her son but edged with pain.

The cause was right there on the woman's face. Melted skin pulled down her features into nasty ridges like old candlewax. Her hands too were scarred and lined.

Kara stepped forward, unsure whether to kiss her or shake hands…or what to say. Words felt inadequate. 'Nice to meet you. Thank you for letting me come—especially for your birthday. I'm really happy to be here.'

'You and me both. I never thought I'd see the day.' Mary nodded, relaxing a little with each softly spoken word, but still tugging at her hair. 'Now, Declan, take Kara to the cottage and settle her in. Be sure to be back by seven for your dinner.'

'Aye, Mam, will do. It's good to see you.'

He wrapped his arms round his mother but she batted him away with a friendly smile. 'Away with you, now. Can't you see I'm busy?'

They walked through the encroaching darkness to a small house across a field. Declan opened the front door and ushered her in, shutting out the four sets of Underwood eyes that hung around in the paved area out front. Cute they might be, but clearly his nieces and nephew hadn't got the hang of adult time. And he needed a good shot of that right now.

Actually, he needed a good shot of London right now... with Kara as a chaser.

Yet here he was, for the first time in many months, with a *girlfriend* in tow. What a crazy, mixed-up idea that had been.

She peered up at him through thick black eyelashes, her green eyes piercing. 'Wow. This is so different to the main house. So...stark. And so not the twee cottage I had in mind.'

He plonked their bags down on the whitewashed floor-boards and looked round at the clean lines. No frills, no mess. Masculine. His. 'Home sweet home.'

'This is yours?'

'Yes. When I could, I made it my priority to have some space. Sharing with that amount of oestrogen is way too dangerous for my health. So when I come home this is my space. No unwanted interruptions...' He nodded to the giggling coming from the other side of the door. 'Not too many anyway. Ach, they'll get bored soon enough. You can have the main bedroom. I'm just next door. In case... Well, in case you need me. For anything.'

Declan put Kara's bag on the master bedroom floor.

'Oh? And just what would I need you for?'

'You may need help changing for dinner. I'm all yours for unzipping...unbuttoning...unclipping...' He leaned in closer, inhaled the scent of outdoors and coconut shampoo. 'I think you'll find I'm pretty adept at it.'

'I don't doubt that for a second, but I can manage.' Kara gave him a strange half-smile, her hand clutching the hem of her cashmere cardigan. He'd never seen her quite so unsettled.

He liked that. Liked that she was such a mixed bag of emotions, but that she was determined to deal with it herself—not demanding anything from him, not clingy. Nor did she ask about a future for them, or push him into a corner, or cause a drama. That was how he liked things—uncomplicated.

So why the hell he'd invited her here to make things very complicated he didn't know. But he reminded himself they had only two days to do this. Then they would be free to go back to their uncomplicated lives in London.

Only now London didn't seem very uncomplicated either.

'Thanks for doing this. You being here means a lot to my mum. She was so pleased to see you.'

'I think it was you she was happy to see—seriously, I'm just icing.' Kara started to unpack her bag, but kept her voice low. 'Declan, why haven't you done reconstruction on her scars?'

'Don't you think I've tried? Don't you think I've offered to bring her to London and get her the best treatment available? She doesn't want to. She says she's come to terms with it and I just have to accept that. I became a plastic surgeon just so I could help her, but she's not interested.'

And even though he tried to bite down his frustration Kara noticed. Taking his hand in hers, she pulled him to sit on the bed.

'I understand—I do. But I guess you have to let it go. If she's come to terms with it, then so should you. She's not an invalid—she's a grown woman who clearly must know what she's doing if she's brought all you kids up.'

Kara didn't know the half of it.

'It's other things she's struggled with.' And he couldn't

bring himself to explain. He didn't want to even *think* about his father and the legacy he'd left.

Nothing about this place had any kind of reminder of his dad. Declan had made sure of that.

Kara's hand ran down his spine in soft strokes that almost undid him. 'I really hope your family like me. They seem lovely. All of them.'

'You haven't met all of them yet…that will be an experience. You did bring earplugs?'

'For sleeping?'

'No, for dinner. Don't say I didn't warn you.'

He grinned at her knotted brow and ached to smooth it over with his mouth. To wrap her in his arms and lie there surrounded by all the smells and sounds of home— the familiar, but with Kara, so exotic and different.

'It gets busy, but it's a family rule that we all eat together.'

'That's nice. I don't remember many meals like that growing up. It was usually just me and one of my parents, or a nanny, or a grandparent, and then as I got older, when I came home for the holidays, it was often just me and a TV dinner.'

At her words his stomach tightened—because although he'd made a space for himself far away he couldn't imagine growing up sitting at an empty dinner table in silence, or with only the TV for company. For him dinner had always meant chatter and good food and just the occasional argument. No wonder she'd grabbed the chance of marriage so young, to create a feeling of belonging.

She looked around the room, at the high ceiling and the intricate coving he'd designed. 'Did you really try to build this place?'

He laughed. 'Yes. I had a hand in all the buildings. This is a converted barn. It didn't get damaged much in the fire, so I just had it renovated to my specs. But I had more of a go at building the main house. Pretty naive, but when you're that young you think you can do everything.'

'And the great Declan Underwood *can't*? You do surprise me.'

It hadn't been for lack of trying. 'It soon became apparent that it was better for me to work as a doctor and pay someone else to do the physical work. As I earnt more we added more buildings—the barns, Niamh's house out back, the milking shed… But I did some labouring in my spare time.'

Dark memories slid through him. The smoke and the flames, the fear that had gripped his chest, the rough thick clutch at his throat as he'd tried to breathe in a furnace.

Then the days, months, years of dealing with scars, betrayal, grief. And finally restoration.

'Wow, that's some responsibility you carried here. Did you work with your dad?'

'No. He left.'

She frowned. 'So it really was just you? On your own?'

'Yep. Me and the builders, obviously…and the architects…' And the insurance. And the… Hell, there'd been a lot of professionals involved. Just not the one person he'd needed.

'But who did you ask for help? Who gave you advice?'

Would she not let it go? 'I didn't need any.'

'Everyone needs someone to talk things through with, Declan. Even you. Do you still have contact with your dad?'

'No.'

Once he'd been unable to leave his father's side, had looked to him for everything. To learn how to do the practical things for running a farm. How to be a decent farmer. A decent man. And then…

He swallowed back the bile rising in his throat. 'I wouldn't want anything from him now.'

'Why not?'

'Forget him, Kara. I have.'

He'd tried to erase the memories. The ones where his father had carried his boy high on his shoulders. The ones where they'd been fishing, hunting, laughing. Memories he didn't want because they weren't real. Oh, yes, he'd believed them then—but after his father had left he'd re-alised they were meaningless. Because love wasn't real—it was fleeting and flimsy and disposable. *That* was the one true thing he'd learnt from his father.

He looked at Kara, sitting there, not a memory. She was real, here, in front of him, and he grew hard just looking at that mouth, those eyes, that body. He wanted her, and that urgent feral response threatened to sub-sume him.

'So all that hard physical work explains these, then.'

Her hand slid to his biceps and a river of desire ran through him. When her hand slipped to his chest and her fingers brushed against his abs he was lost.

'And these too…'

That brief touch was like a spark to an ember. The next thing he knew he was leaning her back across the four-poster bed and planting kisses on her lips, on her cheeks and the sweet sun-blushed skin at her throat. And she was kissing him back—not hesitantly, not softly, but with all the intensity of a woman who needed kissing. Who wanted to be thoroughly kissed.

And that was what he told himself as he stroked his tongue in her mouth and felt her meld her body against his. *She wanted this.* As he peeled away the cardigan and dropped it to the floor, as he undid the tiny buttons on her blouse and unclipped the scrap of pure white lace that pretended to be a bra—because, by God, it was barely covering her straining breasts. *She wanted this.*

When he took her hardened nipple in his mouth and felt her moan into his hair. When she straddled him and rocked against his erection. When she kissed him hot and greedy and needy with her slick wet mouth.

Her hands were dragging his shirt away, her nails scraping along his back. Her mouth was kissing trails down his ribcage, her hair a mess of blonde against his chest. But it was her eyes that told him most, glittering dark like the most precious emeralds. *She wanted this.*

And, *God*, so did he. He wanted to be inside Kara right now—to ride her to the edge and back. To wipe away that half-smile and replace it with a sexy, satiated one. He wanted to watch her come, to taste her, to feel her clamp around him, to wake up with her in the morning. Because they had forty-eight hours to find each other before things were back on an even keel in a world where they didn't do complicated.

But in reality losing himself in Kara wasn't complicated at all. It was the simplest thing he'd ever done.

CHAPTER TEN

KISS ME. SHE was so on the edge of giving herself up to him.

And she didn't want it just to stop there.

But Kara heard the sound of footsteps and giggles outside the door and pulled away from Declan, naked from the waist up. Suddenly she felt cold—and not just physically naked but psychologically laid bare too. Because making love with him would confuse everything. Kissing him like this had already stirred enough chaos in her brain.

She rested her forehead against his and laughed. 'This sneaking around behind closed doors makes me feel like a teenager again.'

'Unfortunately that's the way it is here—no damned privacy. Even this far away from the house.'

He was still hard, she could feel him underneath her, but he didn't appear to mind. He just seemed content to stroke his fingers down the curve of her body.

'But I think it's dinnertime. We'd best get dressed and get down there. Hungry?'

Yes, but not for food. 'You bet.'

Fastening her bra and grabbing another top from her weekend bag, Kara made herself presentable. It was weird having him watch her do such an intimate thing that no one had seen her do since her marriage. Even weirder as he brushed by and kissed the top of her head, sheathing that gorgeous body back into his shirt. It all seemed so natural for him, this playing at being a couple. And for her it felt…strange. Connected and yet disconnected.

One thing was for sure: having seen him semi-naked, she was definitely going to miss that body when she went back to London and back to her old team.

'So, does your mum do the cooking for you all? That must be a mission.'

'Mostly. There was a time when she couldn't manage, so Niamh helped, but she's better now. Well…'

Once again something flickered behind his eyes and she wanted to ask Declan his story. Because while his mother might well be healed he still carried scars in his need to protect her.

'She seems just a little shy, Declan, that's all. But, hey, I don't know her, so I don't want to be talking out of turn.' She changed the subject, not wanting to start the visit off on the wrong footing. 'So, dinner…?'

'Can wait just a few more seconds. I have something much more interesting in mind…'

He pushed her against the door and kissed her again, this time gently, like a summer breeze against her lips, his hands cradling her face. And she kissed him back, determining to enjoy the next couple of days instead of analysing them. They both knew this couldn't go any further than a little flirtation, and she was big enough to deal with that.

The dining room was dominated by a large mahogany table and a selection of matching chairs, bright plastic highchairs and a long wooden bench. A glass chandelier gave off a subdued pearly glow. At one end of the room a large stone fireplace promised cosy winter nights, and all round the room on various dressers and bookcases were photos: a teenage Declan and his sisters, the babies, a selection of gruff-looking mongrel dogs, the farm, visitors.

As none of the pictures was of the siblings when very young, Kara suspected these had all been taken post-fire. 'Did you lose a lot of stuff in the fire?'

'Most everything. The house was pretty destroyed, but there were a few things we managed to save. No photos, though.'

'None of your mum? *Mam?*' Kara wanted to fit in, but the word didn't roll off her tongue just yet. She picked up a photo of Declan aged about sixteen, grinning wildly with a stack of bricks on a hod, then glanced at another of him in graduation gown and cap. 'My, my, how you've grown.'

'I damn well hope so. I was a wiry little whipper back then. And, no, she won't have any taken. She says she doesn't want to ruin the pictures.'

'But that's such a shame.' She bit back a question about Declan's father. No photos of him either.

'Dinner's ready,' Niamh announced, bounding in with a large casserole dish in her hands and a bottle of wine tucked under one arm.

Declan strode forward and took it from his sister. 'Careful.'

'Don't you love the macho? And the manners? Where did they come from? I think you've knocked some sense into my brother, Kara. It's about time someone did.' Niamh leaned towards her. 'So, the others are here. Take a deep breath and then let it out very slowly…oh, and take a big slug of wine to help calm your nerves. Let the chaos begin!'

And within a second Kara was enveloped in hugs and

hands and smiling faces, her ears filled with musical names and lyrical-sounding words. She was found a seat next to Declan, given a plate filled with steaming chunks of meat covered in a dark rich gravy, large mounds of creamy mashed potatoes and a glass of red. And she was smiling with Aoife, laughing at Roisin's tales of medical school, feeding one of the little ones in a highchair, and everything under the protective gaze of Declan. It was exhausting, but lovely.

'So, Declan's never brought a girl home before. Spill the beans…how did you two meet?'

It was Briana, the romantic of the family. She'd already told Kara about her dream wedding dress, the honeymoon, the number of babies she'd have. All she needed to do was find the right man. Kara didn't say anything about her own past, wanting Briana to hold on tight to her dreams, because every girl deserved them.

'At work—well, kind of…'

Declan grinned as his foot connected with Kara's under the table. His toes slid up her leg until she realised she must have been grinning like an…how did he say it? An *eejit*. An intense sexual need ran through her veins.

Then his hand shifted over to her lap and his fingers tiptoed towards her thigh. She squirmed in her seat.

'At a ball, no less. Kara wore a long gold gown and taught me a few Aussie swear words and a drinking game…a lot of tequila was involved. I knew immediately that she was the girl for me.'

And he grinned his goofy grin and made it sound, truly, as if they were made for each other. He never mentioned how she'd left him standing on the dance floor after a searing kiss that had turned her legs to jelly and her brain to mush. And heaven knew what they were doing here—doing this. Because she didn't have a clue.

Except that she wished his hands were running over every part of her.

'Ah, a ball…every girl's dream. So romantic.' Briana clapped her hands together. 'And the wedding?'

Whoa. Kara spluttered into her wine as she felt Declan's grip on her thigh tighten.

'Has not been discussed.'

'Leave it alone, Bri. They don't need you meddling in their business. Remember, Kara's our guest. Be polite.'

Declan's mother's voice soothed the conversation. Kara realised the older woman had been observing, but hadn't actually spoken until now. Everyone stilled and looked at her with surprise. Was it so unusual for her to contribute to a conversation?

'Kara, tell us, have you visited Ireland before?'

'No. Not at all, apparently I have ancestors here somewhere—County Wicklow, I think. I can't wait to have a sticky bea…a good look round tomorrow. Declan said he'd take me for a drive.'

'A drive?' Briana looked horrified. 'I thought he'd be teaching you how to milk cows. You know, in the cowshed…' Now she winked. 'Down and dirty…'

'Briana! You have a dirty mind,' Niamh interjected. 'Er…how about a spot of shopping? I could come with you.'

'We thought we'd take a look at the city on the way back to the airport on Sunday,' Kara answered, turning her head this way and that to speak to them all. 'He knows a good pub that sells great food.'

'Sure, Dec knows all the pubs with the best *craic*,' added Roisin with a wink. As the baby of the family, she clearly adored her big brother.

Uh-oh. Dictionary required. 'What's crack?'

'*Craic.*' Roisin laughed. 'It means fun. A laugh. There's

plenty of it in Dublin. And while you're there you could come have a look round the Trinity College campus. It's beautiful. Actually, you could give me a ride back there on Sunday.'

'What about a horse-ride? There's a trail over the hills that takes you down to the river—it's pretty special.' Aoife joined in, her hand never leaving that of her quiet fiancé, Ronan, and soon everyone had voiced their ideas of how to entertain an out-of-town guest.

Kara looked to Declan for an opinion, taking comfort in the fact that his hand was still on her lap and that the spotlight had moved on from their nuptials. His smile was slow and made her stomach flutter. She got the impression, with the smouldering heat in his eyes, that Declan's idea of entertaining his out-of-town guest was nothing at all to do with going out and everything to do with staying in.

'Whatever you want, Kara.'

I want you. She swallowed deeply, wondering just how much deeper she had to fall before she could harden herself to him completely. 'Wow, there are so many fabulous things to do here. I'll let you decide.'

When Declan squeezed her thigh…this time higher… much higher…Kara almost choked on her white chocolate and raspberry cheesecake.

Afterwards, when everyone was helping to clear up in the kitchen, Kara offered to help but was flatly refused. Irish hospitality, she supposed.

'Okay, but it's the party tomorrow, is that right? What do we do? What do I need to bring? Do you need help with anything?'

Niamh gently held her by the shoulders. 'No. Absolutely not. Now, we've a few things to do in here, but you go and sit down. Tomorrow you can do some sightseeing, and in the evening we'll have a cake.'

'Here, have another drink. It helps. Trust me, I know.'

Declan topped up Kara's glass while jiggling the small child sitting on his shoulders up and down. For all his self-imposed exile he'd managed to slip right back in and seemed, despite himself, to be enjoying his time here.

Because, whatever Declan said to the contrary, he was a family man through and through. She could see that from the pure joy in his eyes as he piggybacked each child in turn, as he lost himself deep in conversation with Roisin about her grades, as he watched his mother with a look in his eyes that spoke of his regret and a fierce love.

'Wait! Just wait a minute—let me get my camera. I so need to remember all of this.'

Kara dashed out to the barn and back and took a series of snaps of Declan with a variety of relatives and ankle-biters playing the fool, flicking each other with washing up foam. And then one with all the siblings looking reasonably decent and the children smiling. Mostly.

'Now, *that's* one for the album.'

Out of the corner of her eye she caught Mary watching, her eyes guarded, her shyness now morphing into embarrassment about being caught on camera. Kara raised her eyebrows in question...*do you want to join in*? But Mary turned away and shoved her hands in the soapy water.

So Kara got snap-happy with the rest of the family, clicking and laughing and showing the children all the photos she was taking—making them stick out their tongues, pull their best crazy faces, joining in with them to cries of, *'Again! Again!'* It seemed that she'd get tired of it long before they would.

A little later, when Declan approached his mum and she lifted her head to him and smiled, Kara clicked and caught a picture of them that, when she looked in the viewer, made her heart ache. From this angle, even though her face was in full view, the only thing that shone out was the deep love between the two of them. If only Mary could understand that everyone saw past her scars, and that the only person she was hiding from, really, was herself.

Suddenly Niamh grabbed the camera and Kara realised she was in the spotlight once again. 'Wait. Let's get one of the happy couple. Quick, Dec, get your arm around that lovely girl's shoulder. That's right. Great. Now smile.'

Happy couple. The idea thrilled inside Kara…and frightened her to death. Every instinct in her fought against being another half of something—something that might subsume her, something that would spiral out of control. And yet…

'Come here, then.'

Declan wrapped his arm round her and looked down into her eyes. And she could feel herself falling and falling into his gaze and his smile and his heat. She tried to smile too, but the whirl of emotions running through her stretched her too far. She wanted him. Wanted this. Wanted to have the dream, have everything.

But the harsh reality of it was that she'd fallen so hard for someone before…the wrong someone. And her dream had shattered into a million pieces along with her life. She couldn't do that again. Didn't know if she had the strength to pick herself up at the end.

Because how the hell did you ever know who the right someone was?

The walk back to the cottage was filled with things unsaid. The memory of his hand on her thigh lingered, turning from an ache to a need. He was close now—so close she could smell him again, that rich, earthy scent that was just him, mixed with a decent slug of red wine and white chocolate. Irresistible.

And maybe it was the wine, maybe it was the fresh Irish air, but her guard and her sense seemed to leech from her with every step closer to the cottage.

As they reached her bedroom door he looked down at her with eyes that held a zillion promises. 'You have everything you need?'

'Yes. Thanks.' *Except you.*

It was a pure physical ache. She wanted to pull him inside and drag him onto the bed again. But instead she demurely waited for him to invite himself in—it was his house after all. And she didn't know the rules. What would it cost her to be able to give a little of herself for two nights with him? She didn't want to think.

'Thanks for a lovely evening.'

His head was close to hers now, his hand against the door. But he didn't come in and close it as he had before. 'You certainly bowled them over.'

'Oh, you know…I have a gift.'

'So do I.'

He ran a finger down her cheek, making her insides melt. Hot and needy. How could one touch make her ache with so much want?

'Oh…' She spoke through a dry throat, her hand on his chest feeling the sharp erratic rise and fall of his breath. 'And what would that be?'

'You'll have to wait and see.'

'Spoilsport.'

He came into the room and closed the door. She inhaled sharply. Declan. The bed. Night. Reality hit her like a tornado. 'Are you…staying in here tonight?'

'You know, you ask way too many questions.'

His mouth was on her neck, sending ripples of need through her.

'Do you want me to?'

Yes. No. She didn't know. She was scared. Scared about what would happen if she gave herself to him. Scared about what would happen if she didn't.

'Oh, God, that feels so good.'

'You're very tense. Here, relax.' He sat her on the bed, knelt behind her and massaged her shoulders. Smoothly, slowly, rhythmically. Until she rocked under his hands, drifting from pleasure to some kind of daydream until she didn't know which was which.

His breath was on her neck. Heating her. 'I'm sorry, I know we can be a bit overwhelming. But the hard bit's over now—they've met you and you've survived.'

'It's not them. It's…this. I don't know what we're doing.' She went for her trademark forthright and hoped she didn't sound needy. She'd spent way too much time in her marriage trying to fathom out what was going on and never quite being able to work it out. From then on she'd determined never to be left in some kind of relationship darkness. 'Declan, why am I here?'

'Because you are very…very…lovely.' His mouth was on that soft spot of her shoulder that made her curl into him, and it would have been so easy to let him carry on. So, so easy.

She pulled away. 'No, really. That wasn't what I was asking. I don't want you to give me compliments. I want some truths. Really, why am I here?'

Declan's hands dropped to his sides. His eyes closed for a beat. Two. Good question. God knew why she was here, save for the fact he'd wanted something else to think about during the birthday weekend.

He could hear the *thud-thud* of his heart echoing in his ears. He searched for words. Found himself wanting.

But she deserved some kind of explanation. 'All my life I've worked to give them the things they want, that they deserve. The things my father didn't. Everything I did was to provide security and a future. And I'd do it all again in a heartbeat. But being back here always feels so…tying. So claustrophobic. I can't breathe.'

It wasn't just the people, but the memories. Dark emotions filled his chest.

'Sometimes London isn't far away enough…but I thought if I brought you along we could have some fun. Lighten things up a bit. I really do want to show you the place.'

And put some sort of distance between himself and his family.

Her eyes widened and he wanted to jump deep into them and never resurface.

'They're a handful, all right. But isn't that what families are like? Especially big ones like yours. Your mum deserves a medal to have had you all.'

'She deserves more than that. The things she went through…' It made his heart hurt and reinforced his determination never to get close to anyone.

So why he was sitting here, sharing this with Kara, he couldn't fathom. Part of him wanted to tell her everything. The other half wanted to run a mile—away from this proximity, from this feeling that somehow she might fit. Seeing his mother so betrayed by love had made him try to harden his heart. Hell, he hadn't had to try too hard. Watching his father walk away, refusing to turn to his wife's pleas and his son's desperate words, had cemented a block of ice in his chest.

He couldn't let it melt now. Talking to her, sharing things like this with her, would open him up to the risk of being hurt again.

'So tell me, Declan. What happened?'

Nonsensically, and the opposite of what he should have done, he silenced her with a kiss. The feel of her mouth underneath his sent spasms of need zipping through him. He wanted to erase the past, to create a new present that was just Kara and him. Wanted to fill his senses with her. She tasted sweet, like the cheesecake, hot as fire and soft. So soft beneath him. She smelt of freedom and heat and home and a foreign land he wanted to explore.

He pulled her close. When she opened her mouth he thought she was going to ask more questions. Whatever else happened, he was all out of talking. 'No. Not now, Kara.'

'Yes. Now.' Her hands were on his chest, fingers fisting the fabric of his shirt. And he realised, with a surge of heat in his gut, that she was not talking about the same thing he was.

CHAPTER ELEVEN

ALMOST REVERENTLY HE peeled Kara's clothes off. When she tried to unzip his jeans he stopped her hand. 'No. You first.'

And this time there was no embarrassment, no chill, as his hands stroked her from shoulder to waist or when he stood apart from her and looked. Just looked, with such pure intensity that she believed his words. The lump returned to her throat.

'My God, Kara, you are so beautiful. So, so beautiful.'

Then he was holding her close again, lips clamped to hers, and she feverishly tasted him, savoured him. She moaned when he dragged his mouth away. Moaned more when he pressed it against her neck. Her chest. Her nipple.

Silently he scooped her up into his arms and carried her to the bed. Whatever doubts she'd had until this moment were forgotten. She would have him. Because she couldn't not. This moment was meant to happen and she had no strength or desire to fight it. Her thoughts were muddled, but so clear. Bad idea. Good idea. All she knew was that she had to have him.

Her hands moved to his chest, ripping each button apart until she was feeling skin. Hot muscle under her fingers. She leant him back on the duvet and straddled him, relishing the hardness beneath her. Knowing that every single ache in her body was mirrored in his. Mirrored too in eyes that had lost their soulfulness, that were not teasing or playful but intense and dark and urgent.

'Kara, we don't have to—'

'Yes, we do.' She leant forward and kissed him again, arching against the hands now circling her bottom. Slowly, slowly his fingers trailed up and across her abdomen, making her catch her breath in short staggered gasps. Then his thumbs brushed her nipples, followed by his mouth. Hot and greedy, he licked as each bud hardened under his touch.

His jaw was stubbled and it burnt across her chest, and she enjoyed the raw feel of him, stoking a fierce need. Not listening any more to his resistance, she unzipped his jeans, shucked them to the floor and took him in her hand.

'Wait. Kara, wait.'

'I need you.'

She heard the words, heeded the emotion. Didn't care. Didn't care that she had opened herself to him in every way—to hurt, to pain. Because that would be some time in the future and this was now. *He* was now. And she didn't want to think about the past or some time not yet happened. She wanted to live this moment.

'God, Declan. I need you so much.'

Furious and fast, he sheathed, and then she was lowering herself onto him. His body was slick and hard. And she was ready for him. Had been ready for so long. As he entered her she gasped. Heat engulfed her, filled her.

Turning her onto her back, he murmured her name, thrusting deep and slow. Too slow. Too fast. Her mind was a chaotic whirl. Her body was responding to his scent, his touch. This was perfect. He was perfect.

And then he was harder, faster, and more perfect than she could even imagine, and she felt herself falling again. Falling deeper and deeper, and flying higher. Soaring. Until she was…he was…they were lost. Lost somewhere on the edge of forever. Somewhere deep in the core of her heart.

'Now, here's the gift I was telling you about last night.' Declan brought out the large parcel he'd hidden in the bottom of his luggage and handed it to Kara in the farm-yard.

The breeze had dropped and the early morning sun glinted off her hair, highlighting the gold. As she pulled her silver-grey cardigan around her and stamped her skinny-jean-wrapped legs he didn't think he'd seen any-thing so breathtaking.

And yet…

Her eyebrows rose. And was that a flicker of uncer-tainty behind those eyes?

Definitely. The smile she gave him was hesitant. She fiddled again with the hem of her cardigan, as she'd done the evening they'd arrived. Forthright Kara seemed to have developed a little more vulnerability, and she wore it in the dusky smudges beneath her eyes.

This was new ground. Complicated and unsteady. And if she felt anything like he did, then, man, they were in trouble. Because he didn't know the next step.

Friends? Lovers now? What? He'd never wanted any woman so deeply, or taken anyone with such need and intensity. Or wanted to stay and leave at the same time. No, he'd never wanted to stay before, and that was what spooked him the most. But he'd brought her here and he had to give her a good time for what was left of the weekend.

'Well, thank you, Declan. You mean you really do have a gift? I thought you were referring to…those other things.'

'Well, I know you have a passion for *these* kind of things, and I imagine you haven't got anything quite like them. But, believe me, you're going to need them.'

Confusion ran behind those green eyes as she ripped open the box and then tipped back her head and laughed. 'Gumboots? *Leprechaun* gumboots?' She held them up and turned them around and around as she took in the little grinning green men on the boots. 'Will I go all diddly-diddly now?'

'God forbid. The world is not ready for that. Please, stay a diddly-free zone.' He helped her take off her very unsuitable black patent pumps and steadied her as she slid her legs into her new rubber boots. 'Wellies. Top-boots. Waterboots. Not a gum in sight.'

'I love them. But for…?'

She gave him a twirl, kicked up one foot then the other. Pretty damned hot. And since when had he ever thought a woman in wellies could be hot?

'Milking. You don't get to come on a farm weekend for free, you know. There's something needed in return.'

Dark eyes blinked. 'You mean last night wasn't enough?'

'Last night was…more than enough.'

It had left something indelibly etched on his heart. Something he couldn't shake. Something he wanted to shake—because if he didn't he wasn't sure how he'd get out whole.

Without encouraging any more conversation along that line, he led her into a shed and climbed onto a dirt-splattered motorbike. The only way he knew how to clear his head. Then he pointed to the back, small as it was.

'Your chariot, my lady. I'll give you a backie down the field. We herd them up, bring them to the milking shed, then take them down again. Then we come back and hose the shed out.'

She looked at the bike, a little disappointed. 'This is nothing like the one in London. That is big and black and shiny and there's room for two. This is…shabby.'

'It is a bit grubby, I guess. But it's a nippy little fella. Come on—hold on tight.'

'There's no space.'

'Squeeze on. You'll be fine.' He pushed himself as far forward as he dared, and she slid right where he liked her best: hugging tight against his body, her legs wrapped round him, this time with no helmets, her hair flowing free in the wind.

With a roar he took her over the rough terrain, through divets and dips to the highest point of the hill and the deepest part of the valley. Fast. And he heard her squeal and screech, and he felt her arms tighten around his waist as the early morning chill bit into his cheeks.

When they reached the bottom of the hill she climbed off and dragged in a breath, pushing that silky blonde hair behind her ears. 'My God, that was wild.'

'You can drive on the way back if you like.'

'Oh, I don't know. I don't think so.'

'It's okay. I'll show you. It's not difficult.' Focus on something else. Anything to exorcise the confusion swirling in his gut right now. He took hold of the handlebar. 'Hop back on.'

Her eyes were sharp as she watched him. 'Maybe. I don't know. I think I might be better as a passenger.'

'I taught the girls before—you'll be fine. Give it a go.' He twisted the key and started the bike up. 'This side is the clutch and gears. The right side is brake and accelerator.'

He showed her a couple of times, until she got the hang of moving forward in first gear and quickly changing up to second.

'Go.'

Off she flew with a scream, stuttering and bunny-hopping, legs flapping out at the sides, then came to a juddering halt. 'Help!'

'Squeeze gently and slowly—there. See? You're getting the hang of it.'

He watched the flurry of hair, the cosmopolitan dressed form buzzing round the field—his life in London and his life in Ireland suddenly melding into one.

His heart jerked.

She had derailed him. Totally. His body knew how to react, but his brain was definitely, seriously spooked.

When she came back over the hill and drew to a halt her back wheel skidded in an arc. Mud churned like his thoughts, spraying him in dirt. 'Hey! Watch it.'

'Oops. Sorry!'

Not sorry at all, she clambered off, her hand over her laughing mouth, head tipped back. He watched the gentle curve of her neck, the movement of her delicate throat as she spoke.

'Told you I'd be rubbish.'

'No, you didn't. And you're not. You're a natural... Well, with a little practice.'

For a second their eyes caught, lost in the fun, lost in the moment. The urge to kiss her again was almost unbearable. He wanted to taste her, touch her. To put his mouth on those places he'd explored last night. To wake up with her again. But this time he wanted that waking to be joy-filled, not loaded with confusion.

As her laughter died on her lips questions formed in her eyes. Questions he couldn't answer. Questions he didn't want to be asked. And he knew that when they got back to real life nothing would be the same again.

'Okay.' He found his voice. 'So, let's get on with the milking. Everyone'll be waiting for us back at the house.'

Pushing all other thoughts aside, he instructed her in the best way to deal with the cows up close, but he was trying to keep a distance. Trying to keep a goddamned distance between friendship and something beyond intense.

'So this is the place where I grew up. Not much more than a village, really.'

Declan walked Kara along the cobbled main street of one of the prettiest places she'd ever visited.

The road was flanked with quaint shopfronts painted in pastels: pink, blue and white. Tiny flags wove across the road and back again; flowers adorned each windowsill. It was like something from a film, from the last century, from centuries ago.

'Gosh, it's so beautiful. How could you ever leave?'

'Because it's tiny and there's nothing here for me. At least not job-wise.'

'Well, maybe you should have built a hospital as well as your houses and barns.'

He laughed, a little more relaxed now, she noticed, as they'd put distance between themselves and the farm. But there was still an edge there, and she couldn't help thinking it had a lot to do with last night.

'Steady now, girl. I'm not Superman.'

'Well, really? That's a shame. There was me thinking…'

He looked at her quizzically and there was a warning in his voice not to mention last night. 'Thinking what?'

Actually, once again she hadn't been thinking at all.

Not thinking when she'd lain in his arms, when she'd taken him inside her and almost wept at the pleasure. Not thinking about tomorrow, or being back at work, or how she would extricate her heart from all of this when the time came.

Her heart. *Huh.* She tried to put everything into perspective. It was only sex. That was all. Natural and normal. The logical conclusion of attraction.

It wasn't…couldn't…be more than that.

'Ah, nothing.'

Heat flared in her chest at the realisation that it could be, might be, more than that, and she fished around for something to distract her—something that wasn't him and the thought of last night. Of how amazing he'd made her feel.

Glancing across the road, she saw a pharmacy. 'Hey, I've had a thought. Why don't we print off some of those photos I took last night and put them in a frame for your mum? I got some good pictures. I'm sure she'll like them.'

He looked bemused, but shrugged. 'You don't think the scarf you bought her is enough for a birthday present?'

'Well, it can be a thank-you-for-having-me gift instead, then. Or an extra present from you, if you like?' She hesitated to say *from us*. 'I don't want those lovely pictures to go to waste when all they'll do is stay on my laptop.'

She dragged him into the pharmacy and handed over the camera's memory card. Then they meandered through the shops along the main street while they waited for the photos to print.

Presently they came across an antiques shop. Inside was a cornucopia of old-style Ireland. Wicker baskets and old rusted irons, heavy wooden furniture and cloth embroidered in Celtic symbols. Nothing like Declan's place, but everything like his mum's.

Kara pointed to a silver picture frame with spaces for three photographs. 'Look, that's beautiful. Let's buy that.'

'Why?' he asked later as they sat in a café flicking through the prints. 'Why are you doing this?'

'Why not? Declan, you've got a lovely family here. I just want to celebrate it.' She showed him a picture of the little ones sticking out their tongues and laughed. 'How about this? Or this…?'

It was the photo of him and his mum in the kitchen.

'This. This one definitely.'

He shook his head, his mouth a grim line. 'I told you, she doesn't do photos.'

'Why? She looks beautiful in this. Look at it. You can't see her scars—all you can see is a very proud woman who has survived.' Kara's heart squeezed. 'Give it to her, Declan. I'm sure she'll love it. Would you give a decent photo to Niamh or Briana?'

'I guess.' Shaking his head, he hauled in oxygen. 'I just never really…'

'Really what?'

He didn't look at her. 'Could see past those damned scars.'

And if he felt almost responsible for them being there Kara could understand that. But if he was looking for absolution then she wasn't the one to give it. It had to come from within him.

She was beginning to understand just what made it difficult for Declan to get close to anyone. Responsibility wasn't just about giving things to people, it was about risking your heart with them…and he couldn't do that.

He'd been hurt badly, she thought, and he was all about protecting his family. But most of all himself.

'But if you can't see past them then how the hell will she?'

For a few moments he stared into his coffee cup. Kara couldn't read him. The day had been dotted with moments of reflection—him, her. She could see him building the barriers between them again.

'Okay, you're right. I'll give it to her. Thanks.'

She wanted to reach over and kiss a smile back on to his face. She'd lost count now of the kisses. 'So, what's on the agenda now?'

'Ah…' His eyes glittered and he shook off his mood. 'I'm torn between washing down the slurry pit or—'

'No way. You brought me here to do some sightseeing, not deal with cow poo.'

'You didn't let me finish…' Now his eyes positively sizzled with promise. '*Or* we could just go back to the cottage?'

He didn't need to explain any further. An afternoon in bed with Declan certainly appealed. Hell, she couldn't think of anything she'd rather do. There was only one night left, after all, before they went back to being colleagues.

Picking up the pictures, he secured three into the frame and went to put the rest back in the envelope. One dropped out onto the table between them.

The one Niamh had taken. *The happy couple.* Kara gasped. The way she looked up at Declan, her body turned into his, her arm secured around his waist, head tilted…the smile that laid open her heart. And the way his hand lay across her shoulder, possessive—but adoring.

God. Her heart felt as if it was rubbed raw. Was

that how they looked to everyone else? Truly, heart-stoppingly, gut-wrenchingly connected?

Panic rose from her stomach and tightened like a vice. This couldn't happen.

She couldn't feel like that—as if he was meant for her. As if this time—*this time*—things might work.

She couldn't allow her heart to be blown wide-open again.

She cleared her throat. 'I'm thinking horse-riding might be nice. Or we could babysit the kids while Niamh goes shopping.'

Anything. Anything that would stop her getting closer, falling deeper, losing herself further in Declan Underwood.

CHAPTER TWELVE

'MAM LOVES THE pictures. Thank you.' Declan found Kara sitting on a wooden bench in the garden, illuminated only by thick yellow moonlight.

He'd done his duty and given his mum more attention than she'd ever wanted, had helped around the farm and managed a horse-ride with Kara. Now the birthday cake had been cut and eaten and his family had settled down to watch a movie.

And he just needed a little distance from everyone. Except Kara. Seemed he couldn't keep distance from her no matter how much he tried.

Curling her wellie-clad feet underneath her bottom, she smiled. 'See. I told you she'd like them.'

'You know, I never realised just how much stronger she'd become over the years.'

'Well, Niamh would say it's because you don't get over to see her enough. But I'd say it's because you treat her the same way you always have. With respect, but pity too.' Kara shifted as he sat next to her. 'She doesn't need that now.'

'And you're always right?'

She nodded and her hair bobbed around her face. 'Obviously.'

'And smug too.'

'Takes one to know one.' She turned to look at him and wrinkled her nose as she smiled. 'I was meaning to ask you—why didn't you take over the family business, become a farmer like your dad?'

He cleared his throat as he tried to counteract the instinctive stiffening of his muscles at the mention of his father. 'No money in it. Not really. I needed something else, something more. Something…a long way from here.'

'You know, every time I mention your dad you close up just a little bit more.'

Busted. 'Bluntness just rolls off you, eh? You're not exactly one of those meek conformist women, are you?'

She shrugged. 'Believe me, I've tried and tried to fit my big cuboid persona into a round hole. And failed. Too many times to count.'

'Oh?'

She nibbled at her bottom lip and he could see her weighing up what to say. Silence stretched. He understood why she'd prefer to keep her secrets, but that didn't mean he didn't want to hear them.

'Too many times…?'

She sighed and peered straight ahead, her fingers gripped tightly together. 'Rob thought I should have been different… Well, let's just say I was a huge disappointment to him.'

'How could you ever be a disappointment?'

She shrugged. 'We started out wanting the same things, or at least I thought we did. But after he joined up he changed. He became more demanding, more possessive and authoritarian. It was his way or no way. He'd always said he was going to stay in the army for a few years, then get out…but that changed and he wanted to stay on for longer and longer. It was all about him and nothing about what I wanted or the dreams we'd made together. And I wasn't allowed to complain. Just comply.'

'So what? He wanted a divorce? Or...? Don't tell me he hurt you?' Acid rose in his stomach as he fought an intense primal anger at the thought of anyone laying a finger on Kara's perfect body.

She shook her head, her voice unsteady. 'Not physically. But the pressure was there always...to be the perfect wife, to do what was expected, not to ask for anything that I wanted, not to expect better...or more. God, I tried so hard to make it work. I wanted it all so badly. I wanted the dream. It was there, all I had to do was step into it, and yet...it wasn't a dream at all. I thought if I tried to love him more it would be enough love for both of us.'

Declan's gut contracted. The man had clearly been an idiot. 'You were so young, though. How did you even know what you were doing?'

'Yeah. Pretty tragic to realise at twenty-two years old that you've made the biggest mistake of your life and you're stuck. That you are way better at working than you are at loving.' She squeezed her hands together in her lap. 'I believed those vows, Declan. I loved him. I committed myself to him for life.' Her eyes glistened. 'Hard to admit it, but I was—plain and simple—married to the wrong man. It took me a long time to figure it out.'

Hell, he'd seen that before—right here in these damned fields, in what became a pile of smouldering ash. 'You didn't leave?'

Her brows came together. 'I didn't want to face the truth. I had enough trouble reconciling that sometimes love just isn't enough to keep two people together. I couldn't actually put voice to that fact.' She sighed. 'And when he died it all seemed such a waste—he could have been happier without me, with someone else.'

His stomach hit his boots. He imagined her as a teenager in a wedding dress, living a dream. The harsh reality she'd faced when it had crumbled around her despite how hard she'd worked to save it. So young. Too young.

Declan's heart jittered. He tipped up her chin and looked into her eyes. 'God, Kara, there are good men out there—men who will cherish and love you and who will willingly nurture you. But I do understand. I know enough about selfish men to write the goddamned book.'

'Your dad?' Her hand was at his cheek now.

Breathe. He nodded and stared out into the darkness. 'Yes, but let's just forget him too.'

She gave him a wobbly smile as she slid into his open arms and leaned her head against his chest. This was supposed to be about her...just about her. She looked to him for some kind of understanding or absolution.

'Good to know I'm not the only messed-up one.'

'We're all messed up somehow, Kara. You'll be fine. You are more than fine. You're marvellous.' He squeezed her against him, then stood up, pulling her with him. 'Come on, let's walk and clear our heads. Think about what we could do tomorrow.'

He needed to get away from the house he'd tried to build with his bare hands because of a dumb-ass man who'd pleased no one but himself. So he grasped her fist and wandered through the fading light towards the open fields. He'd moved to London to get away from all this... He never shared this stuff—not with Leo or any of the Hunter Clinic guys, not with his friends. Memories were best left alone as far as he was concerned. Until they threatened to overwhelm you.

'Talk to me, Declan. Tell me about your dad.'

'No. It won't make you feel any better.'

She squeezed his hand, her voice less shaky now. 'It can't make me feel much worse. Can it?'

How blissfully ignorant she was. And she should stay that way. 'Look at the stars, Kara. A bit different to the sky in Australia?'

She tipped her head back and stared upwards. 'A little. It's bigger and brighter in Australia, is all. And the constellations are in a different place. Now, stop avoiding it.'

And, yes, that was what he'd done for years. Buried everything deep and got on with making a better life. A life that was so damned full he didn't have time for this… sharing and sentiment and drama. Yes, she had some— as he'd suspected. But instead of being irritating it had cut him deep.

She stopped dead and hugged her arms around him until most of her pressed against a lot of him. 'It's only fair. I've told you my guilty secrets—now it's your turn. And I'm not moving until you do.'

'That's not much of a threat. I like it like this. Very much.'

He took the opportunity to smooth his hands down her back and press her against a lot more of him. And wondered whether getting hard in the middle of an intense personal conversation was against someone's rules. Clearly not against his. But then, he never had personal conversations like this, so he could put it down to rookie error.

She dropped her hold and took two steps back. 'Okay… so no hugs until you talk.'

'Would you ever grow up?'

'No. I don't want to. Growing up sucks. As I found out to my cost.' The smile slipped. 'But I guess I'm the only one big enough to open my heart.'

And even though he knew about this kind of game, because his sisters had played it too many times, and even though he knew not to rise to her challenge, that once he'd started he'd find it hard to lock his anger away again, he felt the words rising within him. Because Kara had that way about her that made you want to tell her the truth.

He looked back up the hill towards the house, saw the light in the kitchen. Remembered how the light had filled him with terror that night. The light and the thick smoke, the crackle, the orange sparks rising into the black sky. An acrid smell that had filled his lungs.

'Dad had gone out for a drink that night—nothing unusual. *"You're in charge, boy,"* he'd said as he'd left. He always did that. It was our…' his voice cracked at the irony '…in joke. I was in my room and heard screaming from the lounge. My mum was yelling at me there was a fire and to get the girls out. Thick black smoke was everywhere. Heat. The smell. But I managed to get to them in the back bedroom and fought my way down with them. One by one.'

Kara's hand cupped her mouth. 'I can't imagine the terror.'

'I thought Mum was outside. But I couldn't find her. I called and tried to go back in but I couldn't breathe. I couldn't get to her. I tried. *Tried.* But the more I tried the hotter the flames and the thicker the smoke became. I couldn't breathe. I thought she'd be dead. I thought…I'd let her die. Then suddenly Dad was there, taking control, running in to what looked like a furnace. And then I thought I'd lose them both.'

And, to his eternal shame, he'd hoped and prayed that if the worst thing happened and only one person got out alive it would be his father.

'Then he strode out with her in his arms.'

Kara stroked his back as they walked down towards the stream at the bottom of the hill. 'You must have been so scared.'

Desperate. But his hero father had saved the day. At that moment the thirteen-year-old Declan had thought he couldn't love his father more.

'Mum was in and out of hospital. She was in pain, grew depressed and withdrawn with her injuries. And Dad didn't help. He couldn't look at her. Wouldn't tolerate her black moods. He began staying out more and more. Left me to do more of the work around the place—stayed out overnight. I wanted to ask him what we'd done wrong, why he didn't want to be around us. But the look in his eyes was so cold. And then one day he took me to one side and told me he'd met someone else so he was leaving. That was the last time I saw him.'

Kara shook her head against his heart. 'After everything you'd already been through…'

'In sickness and in health. That's what he promised. To love her. To love us all. Mum took it badly. She believed he left her because of her scars and it sent her spiralling into a black depression. I thought…I thought at one point she'd never get better. She was damaged. Devastated. And she thought it was all because of how she looked.'

He managed to bite back the bitterness he'd felt for so long.

'You don't walk away from the people you love, no matter what happens. Not if love means anything.'

Declan had grown up loving that man with every cell in his body. There'd been a bond, he'd thought, sacred between father and son.

Something inside him had broken the day his dad had left. And he'd had no idea how to fix it.

So he had buried his anger and disappointment and

tried to turn it into something positive. Determined never to give anyone the chance to hurt him like that.

'But you know what? My mum didn't deserve that, and neither did the girls. If he wasn't prepared to provide for his family then I knew I had to man up and do it instead.'

And had done so every single day since.

The water babbled and gurgled, cutting through the thick silence of the night. His chest heaved as he fought back the memories, the fear and the anger.

Kara ran her fingers over his ribcage. 'I'm sure your dad was devastated too. I'm sure he did love you. Still does.'

'Funny way of showing it.'

Her palm flattened against his chest, her voice thick with sadness. 'I'm so sorry.'

So this was how distraction from his reality had panned out. Delving even deeper into his past. So not what he'd hoped for.

He tried to lighten the moment. 'Sure, it's fine, Kara.'

'It is now, yes. Look at what you've achieved. Just look at you, Declan. A career most people could never hope for. Sisters who are so, so proud of you—and you of them. A farm that provides food and an income, a beautiful house. More…so much more than many people have, and all because of you.'

She curled into him, hugging him close, and he felt the weight inside his chest begin to lift.

'It *is* fine—it's better than fine.'

He nuzzled his face into her hair and just for a few moments he let himself believe it could be.

They lay down on the grass, listening to the eerie night sounds, the fresh country air whispering over them. The familiar smells of his home mingled with Kara's scent. Her heat pressed against him; her hair tickled his chin.

Awareness prickled through his veins.

'You know what I think?' she whispered.

He doubted it was anything like what was running through *his* mind. But a man could hope. 'No.'

'I think we say to hell with them. To hell with everything they made us feel, the disappointment and the hate.' She rolled on to him, straddling him. 'We should let it all go. We deserve better. Much, much better. We need to forget it and take something for ourselves. What do you say?'

She made it sound so easy.

The air around them shimmered and suddenly her mouth was very close. Her breasts rubbed against his chest and he could feel them pebbling as she leaned closer. Her scent enveloped him and he grew hard again in an instant. Very hard. He wanted to kiss that mouth, those breasts, to take her to the edge of oblivion. To do it again and again until neither of them had any memories apart from this, here. Now.

'You have any ideas?'

'Oh, Declan, yes. Yes, I do.'

And then she was kissing him—hungry, hot kisses that obliterated the anger and filled his heart with something else. Something much better indeed.

CHAPTER THIRTEEN

KARA KISSED HIM because she had to get the cruel image of a boy trying to save his family out of her head. His eyes were filled with a lifetime of shadows, of hate and regret and sorrow, and she wanted to erase that too. To smooth down his edges, to change the blackness into light. She kissed him because she wanted to feel something, to be wanted.

And because she wanted him.

She wanted Declan more than anything she'd ever wanted before.

Meshing her hands into his hair, she kissed him with everything she had, told him with that kiss just how much he had touched her heart. And he kissed her back with the same longing, the same promises, the same damned wanting that had fizzed around them since that ball.

He rolled her onto her back and kissed hot trails down her neck, stripped off her top and bra and exposed her nipples to the cooling air. But his heat warmed her, made her dizzy, until she just wanted more of him. And more.

When his palm cupped her breast she arched against him, shocked by the moan coming from her throat, by how much she ached to have him inside her. When his mouth clamped her nipple and a shiver of desire rolled down her spine she thought she could now definitely die happy.

'God, Kara, I want you so much. It's killing me.'

His voice was deep and hoarse, more a growl than words. His eyes had darkened, were fierce and glittering with a need that she knew was mirrored in her own pupils.

'Have me. Take me.'

'Kiss me,' he whispered.

And she did. Again and again. Until her mind was almost numb and her lips were swollen and sore yet still hungry for more.

Her hands met his chest and she dragged off his shirt, buttons popping and flying who cared where. Then she pressed against him, slick skin on skin, and a primal, feral need shuddered through her. Grass tickled her back and the stream played a gentle backing track to his breathing, his words.

'Now these. Off.' He pushed off her wellies. No, he tried to push one off but it got stuck, so he tore himself away from her, knelt and tugged again at the first one, then the other, toppling backwards on the riverbank. His roar echoed through the trees. Somewhere an owl hooted.

She couldn't help the laugh. He looked magnificent, biceps bulging, muscled chest puffed out as he stood above her. All sexed-up because of her. 'But, Declan, I thought you wanted me to leave my shoes on?'

'Don't be ridiculous. Crazy, beautiful woman. How can I get to your jeans if you leave them on?'

He knelt and slid his hand to her jeans button, then he inched them down over her legs. Slowly. Too damned slowly.

'Besides, those leprechauns do nothing for me…but those ruby-red shoes…' He groaned. 'Man, next time…'

He pressed kisses down her abdomen, making her inhale sharply, sending spasms of need pulsing through her.

'Next time you put those on.'

Next time. He wanted a next time and they hadn't even finished this time. Had barely started. And, God, she definitely didn't want it to end. 'Whatever you want.'

'Everything. I want it all, Kara.'

And she could tell just how much he wanted her as he pressed against her. She unzipped his jeans, shrugged them off and took hold of his erection, felt him harden even more, felt the heat surge through him, the shift in his breathing. Until it was almost impossible to breathe herself for needing him inside her.

'Declan, now, please. I need you. *Now.*'

His fingers roamed her thighs, opened her legs and then he was sheathed and over her, entering her, pressing deep and hard. And there was nothing then except the sheer power of this man and this never-ending need.

'Kara. Kara. My God, you are so beautiful.'

Her name on his lips was like music. His mouth was against her cheek, against her ear, in her hair with every wonderful thrust. Hard at first, frantic, desperate until she was so close…so close. Then he slowed the rhythm and looked at her, holding back as the pressure inside her, outside her, over her, started to increase. Slowly, too slowly, not slowly enough, he kissed her with such need, such passion, that nothing else mattered. Nothing but this.

'Declan… I… I…'

'I know… I know…'

She was on the edge and that fired something urgent in him. Declan shifted her hips as he felt her clamp around him, drove deeper inside her, wanting to savour every moment, to ride sensation after sensation. Her hair pooled over the grass. Her body arched as he held her waist and rocked her.

But he held back. It would be too easy to let loose and put his own pleasure first. He wanted to show her that not all men were like her husband and his father—that there were good men too, who would put her needs first. This was for Kara—for everything she'd had to endure.

He put all thoughts of consequences to one side. He didn't know what would happen next—couldn't promise her more than this. Didn't know anything past this moment. He wanted it to last forever, but he was riding an edge and it wouldn't take much to plunge him over.

He slanted his mouth across hers, tasted her again, ran his hands along the smooth soft shape of her curves, gripped her bottom and pressed deeper.

'Declan…' She was panting now, her head rocking back. 'God, yes.'

And he tried to hold on just a moment longer, clasping her close, stroking her hair, looking into those deep emerald eyes misty with satisfaction. But when her hands gripped his back and she pulled him closer, moving her body in perfect rhythm as she moaned deep and long and loud, he was lost. And only Kara could show him the way back.

'So, will you give me a ride back to uni or not?' Roisin grabbed a rosy apple from the bowl on the kitchen bench-top and bit down hard. 'Only I can go with Ronan and he's leaving in a few minutes. Tell me now.'

'Don't be so rude. I'm sure Declan will offer when he's ready.' Niamh smiled at Kara and rolled her eyes. Then winced as she dodged a face full of porridge from Declan Junior's well-aimed spoon. It landed next to Kara on the table with a plop. 'Nice try, sonny. Next time see if you can get your evil Auntie Roisin square on the nose.'

The little boy grinned and loaded his spoon. Kara could see the glint in his eye. Like uncle, like nephew. It seemed the Underwood genes ran deep.

'Nah-ah. Only joking.' This time Niamh made sure the food went where it was supposed to. Then she lowered her voice. 'I can't thank you enough for bringing him over. The first time he brings home a girl…and, well, I'm so glad it was you. Don't be too long coming back again. Any nonsense from His Lordship over there and you get on to me, d'you hear? He might be my older brother but I'm not averse to kicking his bu—' She picked up a large bowl and smiled sweetly to the rest of the family. 'Now, who wants the rest of these eggs?'

Sunday morning and everyone had gathered for yet another meal. The scent of sausages and bacon had drawn Kara from the cottage, but she didn't feel hungry. After a sleepless night she didn't feel anything at all except numb, and yet at the same time overwhelmed.

She'd fooled herself into believing just for a few moments that making love with Declan wouldn't carve a piece of him onto her heart, wouldn't matter.

It did.

His story had touched her. His passion and determination had lit something deep in her. She hadn't just got a slice of him in her heart—she had a gaping hole filled with him.

This wasn't a juvenile infatuation or some kind of wishful thinking. She loved him. In such a short, intense space of time she'd fallen completely for a player who, underneath it all, wasn't a player at all.

He was a man trying hard to carve himself some space

in a life that was full, trying to squeeze some joy from a life that had been tarnished.

She loved him. The realisation hit her square in the chest as she heard his laughter and turned instinctively towards it with a leap in her heart.

She loved him, and instead of being the joyous thing Briana believed in it was terrifying. To lose control of her feelings—to put herself there again. The one thing Kara had tried so hard never to allow to happen.

Swallowing back the ache, she turned away.

'Are you ready?' Declan called to her from under a spaghetti of chubby arms and legs and a lot of giggling.

She wanted to run away, far away, and yet she'd never be ready to leave this. For the first time ever she felt as if she truly belonged somewhere, and knowing she'd never come back was breaking her in two. 'Give me a few minutes to get my things sorted. I won't be long.'

'Okay, well, I'll go with Ronan, then. Finally I get an answer I can understand.' Roisin sighed. 'Lovely to meet you, Kara. Please keep doing whatever it is you're doing to Declan…it suits him. He's actually nice.'

His sister wrapped her into a big warm hug and Kara squeezed her eyes shut.

'And come back soon.'

She couldn't keep doing this. 'Bye, Roisin. Keep up with those studies. If ever you get the chance to come over to London I'd love to show you around.'

'That would be great. I'd love to. You can count on it.'

And then she was gone, along with Ronan. A thick weight pressed in Kara's chest. Two down, another dozen or so goodbyes to go.

Somehow she managed to get a few moments alone in her bedroom to pack away her things and take stock. Although she'd been taking stock for hours—and it had got her precisely nowhere. No matter how much she tried to fill her lungs with fresh country air she still had trouble breathing.

She could not let Declan know her true feelings and she certainly didn't know his—couldn't guess. She couldn't turn a weekend into something more. Couldn't expect him to invest the same kind of emotion she'd foolishly invested.

And besides—they were colleagues. He was her boss and they'd crossed a line. What the hell had they been thinking? She couldn't love him. But she did.

'Time to go, Kara. Give me your bag and I'll put it in the car.'

He was standing in the doorway, but he didn't come in and kiss her as she'd thought he might. He just gave her a faint smile, then turned to wait for her, avoiding eye contact.

Last night they'd stumbled back up the hill satiated and exhilarated. Stopping to kiss every few steps until it had taken an age to get home. He'd cuddled against her in bed and they'd made love again. Then at some point in the night she'd fallen into a feverish sleep. And into regret.

Not regret that she'd slept with him, but that she couldn't…wouldn't…shouldn't do it again.

Now he was decidedly distant. Did he think it had been a mistake too? Was he struggling with *what next*?

It would be so easy to carry on as if everything would be fine. To pretend everything *could* be fine. But she was tired of pretending now. She just wanted to go home. Alone.

'Declan. We need to talk…about us.'

He put his finger against her lips and shook his head. 'Not here, Kara. Not now. We have to go. Everyone's waiting to say goodbye.'

Including him, it would seem.

'Okay. Then let's do it.' With a sigh she closed the door behind her and followed him to the leaving committee, that ache in her chest intensifying.

The hardest goodbye was Mary's. Surrounded by the little ones, Declan's mother wiped away a tear. 'So grand to have you here, Kara, my love. You must come back and visit us soon.'

'I'll try.'

'And I think I might come over to see you and that grand clinic you have.' She touched her damaged cheek. 'Who knows what you could do to make things a little better, right? I think it's time.'

Kara watched with a heavy heart as Mary hugged her son. How long would it be until he came back again? And who would he bring next time? No—she wouldn't allow herself to think that. Couldn't imagine standing back and letting someone else love him. This was, she knew, special...for them both. And very special for Mary. Two women loving one man.

But was it harder to be his mother and have him gone from her day-to-day life, but to be tied to him for ever? Or to be Kara—to have him gone from her life but to see him every day?

Fighting back tears, she settled into the car en route to Dublin. The grey road stretched out ahead and the sky was black with rain over fields that seemed to have changed from lush green to brown overnight. She didn't know what to say, even where to begin.

So she stuck to the mundane, her throat too full of goodbyes to start another. 'Looks like the weather's changed for the worse.'

'They say if you don't like the weather here, just wait five minutes. It's fickle like that.' He shrugged and looked ahead, retreating further and further into whatever black mood he'd created.

She couldn't bear the thought of this kind of pointless half-hearted small talk and shopping and sightseeing and more pretending for the next few hours. 'Declan, I don't think I can face shopping.'

'Okay.'

He glanced across to her, hands white on the steering wheel, his jaw tight. She wanted to hug him close, to look forward to a future with him in it—at work and at home. In a house like his. She wanted to rewind to last night, wanted him to kiss her again and tell her she was marvellous. But mostly, she wanted not to have fallen in love with him at all.

'Shall I see if we can get an earlier flight?'

'Yes. Yes, that would be good, I think. All things considered.' Not marvellous at all. Not even a bit.

His eyes narrowed—and was that a flicker of relief there too? Her heart began to break. There really was no going back.

'Okay. If that's what you want.'

'Yes. Yes, it is.'

So instead of finding the *craic* in Dublin's fair city and seeing the splendour of Trinity College they landed in a cold and dreary Heathrow in the early afternoon. The crowds pressed in as they jostled through Arrivals and all she wanted to do was get home to her apartment and pull her sheets over her head—like Safia had—and shut the world out.

As the underground train rattled towards the city Declan turned to her, his eyes clouded, voice flat. 'Thanks very much for helping me out this weekend. You were amazing. I hope you didn't hate it too much.'

Helping him out. Was that all it was, in the end? Yes.

It was. And she'd been under no illusions—apart from her own.

That damned lump was back in her throat again. 'No, it was wonderful. Thanks for inviting me.'

'You know…it was amazing. Really, the best.'

But… There was a but. There had to be a but.

He hesitated. His face closed in and she thought for a moment he was going to kiss her, but he played with a lock of her hair instead, running it through his fingers, back and forth. Judging by his frown a battle was being fought in his head. She didn't know what or who was going to be the winner but she had a bad feeling it wouldn't be her.

And it was so hard for her to stay quiet…because she always spoke first and regretted it afterwards—but this time, *this time*, she knew it was better to keep her mouth shut and her emotions hidden.

His mouth kicked up at one side. 'But we did agree… You know what it's like in London—so busy, work's full-on…neither of us has time for a relationship.'

He was right of course. She'd trodden that path before and all she'd achieved was misery and regret for all involved. Sometimes loving someone just wasn't enough. The pain in her chest tightened.

'I know what we agreed, Declan. No strings. And that's fine. Actually, that's great. Perfect. That suits me down to the ground. Because, as I said, I don't want anything to interfere with my job.' She forced a smile and fought the tears. She would not show him how she felt. 'Back to normal, then. I'll see you in the morning, bright and early.'

'Not quite.' He looked at his feet. 'I just got a text message from Leo. Karen's mum's well enough to be left, so

Karen's keen to get back to work. You've been reallocated back to your old team. From tomorrow.'

And he'd had to tell her this on a busy train? A sharp fist wedged under her ribcage. There really were no ties at all. Or the man was a damned sight better at acting than she was.

The train screeched to a halt. She glanced up. The next stop was hers. Biting down on her bottom lip, she tried to keep her voice light. 'Okay, well, this is it, then.'

'I'll see you back to your flat.' He picked up her bag.

'No. No, you won't.' She took her bag back from him, being careful not brush against him or inhale any of his scent that drove her wild. Better to say goodbye now, here on a busy train, than on her doorstep, watching him walk away and wishing him back.

At least this way she could be the one to leave and keep some semblance of dignity. Fighting tears, she forced her mouth into a smile. What she didn't want to do was rip open their...relationship...and tear it to shreds, into tiny heartbreaking pieces.

What she wanted to do was throttle him instead—and herself—for letting it get this far. For making love, for allowing herself to fall in love with him.

'I think I'm better going home on my own.'

His nostrils flared. 'I'm coming with you. No arguing. You could get mugged, or attacked, or anything.'

'And you think that risk bothers me?' She could deal with a mugger better than a broken heart any day. 'Declan, leave it. I'm not one of your sisters. You can't tell me what to do, and you can't dictate what happens in my life. I'm going home on my own.'

'But why?' He shook his head as if finally realising this was the end. 'Wait—'

'No, Declan. This is my stop. I have to go. I can't

spend the day going up and down the Central Line.' Or round and round in circles, getting nowhere.

A screech of brakes and a judder. The doors swished open and a rush of hot thick air entered the carriage.

His hand was on her shoulder. 'I'm sorry, Kara.'

'Look, we both knew this weekend was a one-off. What happens in Ireland stays in Ireland, right?'

Her fist tightened around her bag's strap and she concentrated on not letting her voice crack. She could not give in to her emotions. Later, maybe, when she was alone. But not now. Definitely not now.

'Really, there's nothing to be sorry about. We both knew what we were getting ourselves into.'

He lifted his eyes to hers and she saw someone struggling with a host of demons. And losing.

'Did we?'

Damn. Declan kicked the tube station wall and relished the pain emanating from his foot, let the hurt stoke his raging heartbeat. Then he kicked with the other one, just for the hell of it.

In the distance Kara walked down the platform to the escalator, back straight, shoulders taut, hair skimming her coat in a river of blonde curls. Curls he wanted to lose himself in. Hair he wanted to be pooling over the sheets on his bed. *Their bed.* In a future that was filled with her laughter and her sparkling eyes, her forthright honesty.

A few weeks ago he'd been satisfied with the life he'd carved for himself. Relationships that cost little more than his credit card bill. Work that he could invest as much of himself in as he physically and mentally was able. A job he loved. Now his life was brimful of complications every which way he turned. And he didn't know what the hell to do about it.

How could he let himself fall in love?

His heart twisted some more. *Did* he love her? *Could* he love her? The idea was so out there that he couldn't reconcile it. For a man who didn't believe in love the idea was laughable. But what else could describe the chaos in his heart?

Lust. He thought about how his body reacted to her. That was what it was. Lust.

And it was foolish even to want that. The way she'd been behaving all day—so closed-off and quiet—he'd got the message that she'd thought the whole weekend had been a stupid mistake. At least, making love had been a mistake—because that marked the point where everything had changed between them. Become harder, stronger, deeper.

Or was it that she was hiding her true feelings? Because the devastation in her eyes wasn't just at saying goodbye to his family, that much he knew.

He watched as she rose on the escalator, her red suede boots eventually disappearing out of view, and fought the urge to run after her. His heart splintered.

He'd managed just fine on his own until now—always setting the rules, always being the giver. He didn't know how to take something for himself, to rewrite the rulebook. He'd never allowed himself to get in so deep that he'd felt helpless, confused. So goddamn out of control.

Watching her leave was a million times worse than watching his father turn his back on his family. This time he didn't shout and plead. This time he let her go. Because, after all, that was the right thing to do. Before it got too deep and hurt too much.

She'd think he was mad enough having got off at her tube station just to watch her walk away, never mind chasing her down to have a conversation which started and ended with, *I can't. I don't know how. I don't want to love you.*

Because loving her would be too hard. Too easy. Too much.

But, God, he wanted her. The pain in his chest settled into a keen ache. As he picked up his bag and waited for the next train home he exhaled. Tried to shake the headache settling on his forehead. But it hung around, making his brain a hot mess of fuzz. He wanted her, but he couldn't take a risk on having her. He wasn't going to let anyone tread on his heart.

The harsh truth was, the weekend hadn't been a mistake. Falling for her had.

CHAPTER FOURTEEN

DRAKE'S WAS BUZZING. Sadly, Kara wasn't. But for the sake of the team she tried very hard to be. And apparently she was failing.

'Are you okay, Kara?' Angela, the surgical reg, put down a fresh glass of Pinot Noir and squeezed in next to her at the crowded dark wooden table. 'Only, you've been quiet for a long time. And that's just not normal. For you, anyway.'

'I'm fine. Really. Sorry, I've just had a lot on my mind recently.' Declan mainly. Well, Declan totally.

Kara laughed, wishing she'd managed to mask her feelings more successfully. Even during her brief social visits to Safia the girl had been asking awkward questions and raising those dark eyebrows, muttering something about losing the love of your life.

And she had.

Those few weeks with Declan had been the most precious and amazing time of her life. He'd fired something in her. Made her want things out of reach, want the impossible. Allowed her to dream. And now it was gone and she felt bereft all over again, as if something had been physically wrenched from her, and it hurt like hell.

She knew it would take time—but she would eventually heal. She just hadn't thought it would hurt so much. Working long hours on little sleep was stretching her to her limit, but whenever she closed her eyes she saw his face, heard his voice.

No longer. She was through with this. At least she was going to try to be through with it until she really was.

'You know what, Ange? I've decided to hell with it. I'm going to stop looking backwards and start again.'

Again. How many times was she going to start again?

This was definitely the last time. Over the past two weeks she'd fluctuated between *damn the man* and checking her phone to make sure it was still functioning as she prayed for a call from him. For anything. A glimpse of him—something. But he'd been strangely elusive.

So it turned out he didn't want her after all.

And so she'd consigned herself to being just another of his conquests.

Her stomach knotted at what they'd lost.

Inhaling deeply, she drained her wineglass and put it down. No point in wallowing in self-pity. She had a wonderful job, and so much to give to her patients and her career.

Despite everything she'd found a different place to belong—here, at work, doing surgery, saving lives. And while it didn't fulfil every need it kept her busy and re-warded enough not to dwell too much on what might have been. She had a great career path and a support-ive team.

'Well, thanks for the drink, everyone. I'm going to head off now. It's been a very long day.'

Tomorrow was the first day of the rest of her life, and she was going to make the most of every second. Declan Underwood be damned.

* * *

Declan assisted the Kate's emergency room staff to lift the badly burnt young man across from the paramedics' trolley to the department's one.

'Cause of the fire?' Declan always liked to know exactly what he was dealing with.

'Faulty electrics. They're living in a squat down on Crawford Crescent. Someone fiddled with the wires so they could have some free juice.' The paramedic shrugged. 'This one slept through a lot of it, so he was hurt the most. We've put an IV line in, started fluids and intubated. Blood pressure dropping. Pulse jogging along at ninety-seven and rising.'

Declan nodded and began a systematic assessment as he resecured the oxygen to the intubation tube. Starting with airway management.

'First off he has nasty laryngeal swelling due to smoke inhalation, so we need to monitor that IV input. I don't want to exacerbate the oedema. Okay, everyone, you know the drill. Cardiac monitoring, urine output, pulse oximetry. I need someone to cut off his damaged clothes and start burn-cooling and irrigation, but keep an eye on his core temp. I need an arterial line…crystalloid fluids.'

He turned to the paramedic again as his team began to carry out his instructions.

'Any signs of drug or alcohol use?'

'You name it, you've probably got it. There were empty vodka bottles around the house entrance and a couple of dodgy-looking packets of white powder in his pockets.'

'That will all impact on pain management. Cheers, mate.'

He watched the paramedic leave, then spoke to his reg, Karen, who was competent and capable. And not Kara.

His heart thudded with disappointment and regret as he met tired pale blue eyes, not vibrant sparkling green ones that could see into his soul.

'So, add in a comprehensive drug screen. Locate next of kin. Tetanus, probably too...'

As he worked on saving the man's life Declan relished every single second he was busy—because being busy meant he had to focus on something other than Kara and the burning hole she'd left in his heart.

'Today, mate, you have me. And there's no way you're going anywhere on my watch—except to the burns unit. Alive. And you're going to stay that way, so help me God.'

Yes, Declan liked to know exactly what he was dealing with. Which was why he'd watched like a useless pudding as Kara had walked away down the tube station platform. Why he hadn't contacted her for two weeks. Why he'd avoided looking for those emerald eyes and skyscraper heels in Drake's Bar or the staffroom or the hospital corridors. Why he hadn't listened out for her laugh. And why he'd been unable to sleep.

Because he had no idea what he was dealing with. But he had a nasty suspicion that it was a lot more than lust.

After settling the stable-for-now John Doe in the intensive care unit he made his way up to the private wing and went to see someone else it was going to be hard to say goodbye to. No matter how much he tried not to get involved, he couldn't help himself.

'Well, well. Look at you now. All ready to go?'

Safia stood in her home country's ornate dress, surrounded by packed suitcases, and smiled her regal smile. A genuine but nervous one. 'Yes. Thank you, Dec. But it feels a bit weird, going out there into the big wide world. Everyone wants to see the scarred Sheikha.'

'You will be fine. You *are* fine—just look at you.' He checked the reddened skin on her face, knowing that over time she would have minimal scarring. 'Give it a few months until everything has settled down and I'm sure you'll feel better about the results. And make sure you do the physio and attend all my follow-up appointments.' He gave her a pretend frown. 'Because I *will* growl if I have to.'

She waved a hand at him. 'You mean like you have for the past couple of weeks?'

'I have not.'

'Mr Underwood, you have been acting more like my dad than the chilled-out cool guy you were when I first came in here.'

She tapped her fingers on the bedside table and he marvelled at the flexibility she had there now, in such a short space of time.

'Missing someone?'

'No.'

'You forget that I might be a princess but I'm also a teenager. And I have to lie a lot to manage being both.' She shook her head and rolled her eyes. 'That looked a lot like lying.'

So what if he had been lying? There was no point discussing his private life—er…his non-existent private life—with a young girl. She was seventeen. What the heck did she know about life or love? But then at thirty years of age what did he? Absolutely nothing, it seemed.

He might as well be talking to one of his sisters. Hell, he was surrounded by women who thought they knew better about his love-life than he did.

'No, I'm just trying to do my job, Safia. Just getting on with things. I like to be busy.'

Her eyes glinted suspiciously. 'That's exactly what she said too.'

'You've seen her?' His heart did a clumsy jitter.

He didn't need to ask who Safia was talking about. He'd had ample opportunity to see Kara too, just hadn't taken it. He'd needed time and space.

And that hadn't worked either.

'She popped by yesterday to say goodbye and wish me well.' Safia frowned. 'She looked about as happy as you do. And she tried to pretend she was fine too, but she had all the classic symptoms.'

'Symptoms?' Now his heart did a double jitter. What was wrong with her? 'Symptoms of what?'

'In here.' Safia pointed to *BFF!* magazine's front page. '*"How to Know You're Falling In Love: 20 Classic Signs."*' She flicked open the mag and ran her finger down a page. '*"Loss of appetite."* She refused a chocolate when I offered it to her. And no doctor refuses chocolates. Ever. *"Sleeplessness."* She had big dark circles under her eyes. She looked exhausted and her hands were shaky. *"Lack of concentration."* She kept checking her phone and really didn't have a lot to say...'

'Okay—I don't want to be rude...'

Declan relaxed. The girl was talking about a little dream world she'd created to pass the time while she'd been in hospital. Fair play to her too—whatever helped the healing process was fine by him. But what he'd shared with Kara wasn't the stuff of teenage magazines. It had been very adult. Very intense. Amazing. Life-changing.

And he'd been a damned fool to let her go. But he just didn't know how to get her back. Or even if she would be interested.

'Perfect,' she'd said as he'd flailed around for words. *'What happens in Ireland stays in Ireland.'*

'But I don't think—'

Safia held up her hand. She was going to make a very fine wife to any sheikh brave enough to take her on.

'And when I asked her if she was missing someone, she lied too.'

'Safi…seriously….'

'I *am* being serious. Love is a serious matter—especially when you don't admit it. And it makes you grumpy.' She shrugged apologetically. 'Stop frowning. I'm just trying to be strong for you until you can be strong yourself. Everyone needs someone to help them along. Right?'

He hadn't seen that coming. Why were some people just so damned…*right*?

His heart did a little leap. 'And she lied too?'

'Yes. I think she loves you just as much as you love her. I didn't think you were that stupid, Mr Underwood.'

Stupid. Yes. *Eejit*. Yes. He resisted checking the magazine's list for the other signs of falling in love, because if he was honest he knew them well enough by now. He couldn't think of anything else but her. His mouth ached to talk to her, to kiss her. His arms cried out to hold her. His feet wanted to take off in their own direction to find her. His whole body had a physical withdrawal. And don't even ask about his brain…

So, yes. He'd fallen in love with her. And the only pain that love had caused was this—this not accepting it, this fighting it. Not being able to tell her. To cherish her. To hold her. See her. He'd been so scared to feel it. Admit it.

What the hell he was going to do about it, though, he couldn't fathom. He'd let something precious slip through his fingers while he'd been so damned focused on why they couldn't be together.

He missed Kara like he'd miss oxygen. He missed

her crazy attitude and her smile. He missed her scent and her heat. He missed that she knew what he needed even before he did.

And if he was going to manage living a life here in London he wanted her to be in it. Somehow. In fact he couldn't imagine another day without her. He just had to work out what to do about it.

Kara reached the top of the steps to her apartment and fitted the key into her lock. Looking back to the pavement below, she remembered the time Declan had dropped her off on his bike and the kiss they'd shared. Good times. Special times. Even now her skin prickled with awareness at the thought. Like some sort of sixth sense. He'd always had that effect on her—as if her body just knew when he was near.

In the distance she heard the distant purr of a motorbike. Her heart stalled as the awareness intensified.

Don't be silly. There are plenty of motorbikes in London. For goodness' sake, she couldn't keep having that reaction to every motorbike sound. She'd be exhausted.

Kick-starting her foolish heart again, she turned the key and put one foot inside her apartment. The purr turned into a deep, throaty roar. Louder and louder.

It was the kind of roar that only one type of bike made—the kind of roar you recognised. Her stomach clenched.

Could it be?

Sure enough, at the end of the road she watched a shiny black and chrome bike turn the corner, then pull up at the kerb, with a rider who would not look out of place on the cover of a magazine. Suddenly there didn't seem to be enough air to fill her lungs. When she did manage to inhale her breath was stuttering and sharp. Clutching her handbag strap, she felt her hand shake.

Dressed in black jeans and the old leather jacket that had definitely seen better days, but which she loved almost as much as the rider because it had saved his life, Declan looked dangerous and edgy. Far from his usual cool exterior. His eyes flashed with apprehension; a muscle twitched in his jaw. He didn't smile.

What was he here for? Her mouth dropped open. She put a hand to it and resisted the temptation to run down the steps and throw her arms round his neck.

Instead of speaking he climbed the steps, put a finger to her lips and shook his head, closing off all conversation. Then he walked her to the pavement, pulled out a helmet from the top box and fastened it under her chin. His eyes glanced to her legs, to her ruby-red shoes. A flicker of heat warmed the apprehension.

As she climbed onto the back of the bike he took her hand and steadied her as he'd done before. A flash of electricity buzzed between them, making the hairs on her arms stand upright. It would never diminish, it seemed, this attraction, this connection. Even when her heart was broken, when her head knew things could never work out, some parts of her body just would not give up on him.

She wanted to ask him where the hell they were going. What he was doing there so late at night. She wanted to believe this was what she hoped it might be. But as she slid her arms around the body she now knew so well and had ached so much to touch she reminded herself that this was not going to be what she wanted. That she must try to stay detached… But how could she when she was glued to him on a powerful motorbike?

There must be an emergency, a problem, something

serious to do with work, his family. Because why else would he be here?

Resting her head against his back, she clung on to that thought as they sped through the dark streets of London. Faster and faster they flew, the cool autumn wind blowing her hair around her face. And still she didn't know where they were headed, or why. But she knew that for these few minutes she would hold on to some kind of hope.

Soon enough they reached the riverbank. Now, in the dark, it had a different feel to it. Down in the houseboats someone was playing a slow soft tune as yellow lights danced across the water. Different, but equally beautiful. Like Declan. He'd changed. Thinner, maybe. His cheeks had hollowed out a little, making his cheekbones even more sleek and sharp. Guarded, but alert, his eyes danced along with the lights.

He lifted her off the bike and threw his helmet onto the grass. Then he pulled hers off too and his hands were cupping her face, in her hair, pulling her closer until his lips met hers and she couldn't help but melt into his kiss.

So it was indeed something serious. At his touch her body went into overdrive. She'd missed this so much. Missed this closeness, his smell. He tasted of fresh air. Of love. Of a future.

She'd been there before. It had failed spectacularly.

Her heart beat loud and slow against her ribcage. She put her hands on his chest and pulled away. 'Stop…stop. We can't do this. I'm sorry. I need to go. *We* need to go.'

'No…I have to tell you something.'

He walked her along the path where the scent of sweet aniseed herbs filled the air. Around them the breeze dropped, as did the music. And as they left the busyness

behind it felt as if they were the only two people in this
city of eight million.

He stopped and turned to face her. 'I've been a prize
idiot, Kara. I let you walk away from me and I know I
shouldn't have. I really should have told you how I felt.'

Her heart seized at his words. Part ecstasy, part regret.
'In what way? *Felt*?'

'Feel. How I *feel* about you. I was hurt badly when my
dad left, and I saw what love can do to a person when it
isn't returned. It can eat away at every part of you. Can
make you mistrust, make you question yourself, your
worth. It stripped away my ability to risk loving someone
else. So I tried hard not to care. I used it all as an excuse
not to get involved and give any part of myself away and
it worked fine for years.'

'I know.'

'But then I met you and everything changed. My life
changed. And the lives of those around me.'

He stepped back and gave her a cautious smile that
reached to the bottom of her heart and spread to every
corner.

'I love you, Kara. More than anything. And I want
some kind of a future with you—'

'Shh. Stop. I can't.' There—she'd said it. 'I just can't.'
Then she turned and stumbled across the grass, headed
who knew where, blinking back tears. Why had she let
him bring her here to say these things only to break her
heart a little more? 'Just go and find someone else to fall
in love with, okay? Because I can't do this.'

'Hey, we can do anything we want.' He tugged her arm
and pulled her round, seriousness etched across his face.
'I know you're scared. Hell, I am too. I've never done this
before…and I know I'm making a huge mess of it right
now. But it's from my heart, Kara. We can work things

out together. Just the two of us. We can carve our own space. We belong together.'

'No. I can't, Declan.' Her heart shattering, she dragged her wrists from his hands. *Belong?* How much had she ached for that all her life? And now she'd found it, it was beyond her grasp. 'I'm so scared things will change. That we'll get all wrapped up in this bit and not see the end hit us. I couldn't bear it if you fell out of love with me. If I'm not enough for you.'

'You don't think you're enough?' He tipped back his head and laughed. 'Kara, you're more than enough for any man. And certainly perfect for me.' He was reaching into his jacket pocket now. 'Is that why you retreated that day we left my mam's?'

'Because I fell in love with you, Declan. Despite how much I tried not to. You and your damned lovely family won me over. I didn't know what to do after we'd made love. I was so confused. It changed everything— it changed my heart.'

She touched her chest and felt her heart beating a crazy rhythm. Fast and shallow.

'But we'd both agreed there couldn't be more. And you didn't exactly make me feel like you *wanted* more. I don't want to say yes if it'll end in a few years. I can't take that risk. I can't do that again. Not with you. I love you too much.'

He palmed her cheek with his hand and looked deep into her eyes. Never had she seen such passion. True. Stark. Raw.

'Oh, my God, Kara, you think that if something doesn't work I'll chuck it aside? Get a replacement wife and family? If I promise you one thing it is this—I will be there for you, whatever happens. To love and cherish.

In sickness and health. Those vows mean something to me too. I am not my father.'

'No. No, you're not.'

When he hadn't contacted her she'd branded him with the same attributes her husband had had: shallow and selfish. But Declan wasn't like that. He'd shown loyalty and belief and strength to everyone around him. And now he was offering that to her too. It had taken him a bit longer than she'd hoped. But he'd done it. And she didn't doubt his sincerity now. Or his love. Because she could see that in his smile, in his eyes.

'Right now I have something to ask you.' He lowered one knee onto the grass and pulled out a small box, revealing a stunning emerald ring. 'Kara, I love you with all my heart. I don't want to imagine another day without you in my life. Would you do me the honour of being my wife?'

'Oh, my God. *Oh, my God.* That is beautiful.'

Tears pricked her eyes. She pressed her hand against her mouth to stop her lips from wobbling but she couldn't. Couldn't breathe or speak. He loved her. *Her.* And she loved him right back.

'It was my grandmother's. One of the only things we salvaged from the fire. I want you to have it. Mammy wants you to have it. Naimh says she'll kill you if you don't. The whole damned clan want— You get the picture. Please say yes. Or I'll be in a whole lot of bother.'

'Say it again.'

'What?'

'The whole proposal thing…' Her throat ached. 'I just love that accent. It makes my heart go diddly-diddly. Go on, say it again…please.'

He shook his head and rolled his eyes, but he wasn't

angry. He was happy. Very happy indeed. 'Kara, I love you with all my—'

Stamping her feet and clapping, she squeaked, tugging at his shoulder. It seemed that once the right someone came along you knew. You just *knew.* 'Yes! Yes! I will marry you. Yes! Now, get up and come here.'

'Aww. Give me a minute…'

His hand was on her ankle, his fingers running tiny circles around her foot, up her leg. Heat shot through her as he found that point…yes, *there*…that made her shiver with need.

'Now, these are very fine shoes. How about we take a very quick drive home so I can spend a little time getting to know them…?'

'You want me to definitely leave them on this time?'

'Hell, yes.'

She knelt down next to him, looking forward to getting to know him a lot better too. As he smiled at her she reached out and touched his beautiful face, ran her finger down his cheek until it met his mouth.

Then she leaned in close and whispered, *'Kiss me.'*

* * * * *

200 HARLEY STREET: THE TORTURED HERO

BY
AMY ANDREWS

MILLS &
BOON

All rights reserved including the right of reproduction in whole
or in part in any form. This edition is published by arrangement with
Harlequin Books S.A.

This is a work of fiction. Names, characters, places, locations and
incidents are purely fictional and bear no relationship to any real
life individuals, living or dead, or to any actual places, business
establishments, locations, events or incidents. Any resemblance is
entirely coincidental.

This book is sold subject to the condition that it shall not, by way of
trade or otherwise, be lent, resold, hired out or otherwise circulated
without the prior consent of the publisher in any form of binding or
cover other than that in which it is published and without a similar
condition including this condition being imposed on the subsequent
purchaser.

® and TM are trademarks owned and used by the trademark owner
and/or its licensee. Trademarks marked with ® are registered with the
United Kingdom Patent Office and/or the Office for Harmonisation in
the Internal Market and in other countries.

Published in Great Britain 2014
by Mills & Boon, an imprint of Harlequin (UK) Limited,
Eton House, 18-24 Paradise Road, Richmond, Surrey, TW9 1SR

© 2014 Harlequin Books S.A.

Special thanks and acknowledgement are given to Amy Andrews
for her contribution to the *200 Harley Street* series

ISBN: 978 0 263 90775 9

Harlequin (UK) Limited's policy is to use papers that are natural,
renewable and recyclable products and made from wood grown in
sustainable forests. The logging and manufacturing processes conform
to the legal environmental regulations of the country of origin.

Printed and bound in Spain
by Blackprint CPI, Barcelona

**Praise for
Amy Andrews:**

'There wasn't one part in this book
where I wanted to stop. Once I'd started it was hard
even to read the ending, but once I did it made everything
seem right. I am an avid fan of Ms Andrews, and once
any reader peruses this book they will be too.'
—*CataRomance.com* on
TOP-NOTCH SURGEON, PREGNANT NURSE

'A wonderfully poignant tale of old passions, second chances
and the healing power of love…an exceptionally realistic
romance that will touch your heart.'
—*Contemporary Romance Reviews* on
HOW TO MEND A BROKEN HEART

**These books are also available in eBook format
from www.millsandboon.co.uk**

Dedication

For Carol, Scarlet, Alison, Lynne, Kate, Annie and Louisa.

It was fun working with you ladies—
let's do it again some time!

200 HARLEY STREET

Glamour, intensity, desire—
the lives and loves of London's hottest team of surgeons!

Enter the world of London's elite surgeons as they transform the lives of their patients and find love amidst a sea of passions and tensions...!

In April, renowned plastic surgeon and legendary playboy Leo Hunter couldn't resist the challenge of unbuttoning the intriguing new head nurse, Lizzie Birch!
200 HARLEY STREET: SURGEON IN A TUX by *Carol Marinelli*

And glamorous Head of PR Lexi Robbins was determined to make gruff, grieving and super-sexy Scottish surgeon Iain MacKenzie her Hunter Clinic star!
200 HARLEY STREET: GIRL FROM THE RED CARPET
by *Scarlet Wilson*

In May, top-notch surgeons and estranged spouses Rafael and Abbie de Luca found being forced to work together again tough as their passion was as incendiary as ever!
200 HARLEY STREET: THE PROUD ITALIAN by *Alison Roberts*

And one night with his new colleague, surgeon Grace Turner, saw former Hollywood plastic surgeon Mitchell Cooper daring to live again…
200 HARLEY STREET: AMERICAN SURGEON IN LONDON
by *Lynne Marshall*

Then, in June, injured war hero Prince Marco met physical therapist Becca Anderson—the woman he once shared a magical *forbidden* summer romance with long ago…
200 HARLEY STREET: THE SOLDIER PRINCE by *Kate Hardy*

And when genius micro-surgeon Edward North met single mum Nurse Charlotte King she opened his eyes to a whole new world…
200 HARLEY STREET: THE ENIGMATIC SURGEON by *Annie Claydon*

Finally junior surgeon Kara must work with hot-shot Irish surgeon Declan Underwood—the man she kissed at the hospital ball!
200 HARLEY STREET: THE SHAMELESS MAVERICK by *Louisa George*

And brilliant charity surgeon Olivia Fairchild faces the man who once broke her heart—damaged ex-soldier Ethan Hunter. Yet she's unprepared for his haunted eyes and the shock of his sensual touch…!
200 HARLEY STREET: THE TORTURED HERO by *Amy Andrews*

Experience glamour, tension, heartbreak and emotion at 200 HARLEY STREET in this new eight-book continuity from Mills & Boon® Medical Romance™

These books are also available in eBook format and in two 200 HARLEY STREET collection bundles from www.millsandboon.co.uk

CHAPTER ONE

ETHAN HUNTER NEEDED a drink.

Bad.

After five hours of complicated surgery his legs ached like a bitch and finding the bottom of a bottle was the only sure-fire way to soothe the fiery path of hot talons tearing from thigh to calf.

It was that or painkillers, and Ethan refused to be dependent on drugs.

'We're heading to Drake's, Ethan,' a voice with a thick Scottish brogue said from behind. 'Why don't you join us?'

A sudden silence descended into the male change-room as Ethan turned around to find Jock, the anaesthetist from the surgery, addressing him. He looked around at the four others, who'd all been chatting merrily until now. Clearly none of them were keen on having Ethan join them.

Jock didn't look particularly enthused either.

Not that he could blame them. The longer the surgery had taken, the more his legs had ached, and the more tense and terse he'd become. Accidentally dropping an instrument had been the last straw, and kicking it child-ishly across the floor until it clanged against the metallic kickboard of the opposite wall hadn't exactly been his most professional moment.

He hated prima donna surgeons, but his simmering frustration at his shot concentration *and* the pain had bubbled over at that point.

Even so, he didn't need or want their *duty* invitation, no matter how much he craved some alcoholic fortification. Ethan was just fine with drinking alone.

In fact, he preferred it.

'No thanks, Jock,' he said. 'I've got to get back to the clinic.'

Which was true. There was an important case file he needed to familiarise himself with on Leo's desk. And some classy fine malt whisky to go with it.

He looked around at his colleagues. 'Thanks for your help in there, everyone. Good job.'

There was a general murmuring of goodnights and then Ethan was alone. He sank gratefully onto the bench seat just behind him, easing his legs, muscles screaming, out in front of him. He shut his eyes as the pain lessened considerably and sat there for long minutes as the rush of relief anaesthetised the lingering tension in the rest of his body.

It felt so damn good to be off them!

But he couldn't sit here forever. Work called. He reluctantly opened his eyes and reached for his clothes.

The black cab pulled up in front of the imposing white Victorian facade on Harley Street. Like the many clinics and physician's offices that called Harley Street home, the Hunter Clinic was as exclusive as the address implied.

Ethan's father, celebrated plastic surgeon James Hunter, had founded it over three decades ago, and it had gone on to become world-renowned as much for its humanitarian and charity work with civilian and military casualties of war as for its A-list clients.

Thanks largely to his brother Leo.

Certainly not thanks to their father and the scandal that had not only resulted in his premature death through a heart attack but had almost caused the closure of the clinic over a decade ago.

Again, thanks to Leo's drive and commitment, it had been avoided.

Not that Ethan gave a rat's about any of that right at this moment. Thinking about his father and his previously rocky relationship with his brother always got things churned up inside, and tonight he was barely coping with standing upright.

Ethan paid the driver and hauled himself out of the back through sheer willpower alone. The only thing that kept him putting one foot in front of the other was the lure of Leo's whisky.

Ethan grimaced as he limped through the corridors to his brother's office, holding on to the polished wooden handrails for added support. His badly mangled ankle and knee felt ready to give at any second, and the effort it took for his muscles to support them was bringing him out in a sweat.

Ethan wished he hadn't neglected his physio so much, or ignored Lizzie—Leo's wife and his ex-home visit nurse—when she'd scolded him about not using his stick. He hated the damn stick, and the questions it inevitably aroused, and he didn't have time in his busy schedule for the intensive physio required—but at this moment in time he was prepared to embrace both.

Not that it would help him now.

But what *would* help beckoned just beyond Leo's door, and Ethan had never been so glad to get to his brother's office. It had once belonged to his father, and he'd used to hate being summoned here by the *great man* himself, in a rage over some imagined slight or other, as his father had slowly spiralled downwards into alcoholic depression.

Thankfully those days were gone, but it was pleasing to know that a decanter of finest whisky could still be found within the walls of this office—even if it was rarely touched.

The last ten paces to the bookshelves behind Leo's desk were agony, but ultimately worth it as Ethan wrapped his hand around the satisfyingly full decanter. He splashed two fingers of amber liquid into a glass tumbler that sat nearby and threw it straight back.

Searing heat hit the back of his throat and almost instantly tentacles of warmth unfurled outwards from his belly. He poured himself another one and threw that back too, enjoying how the spread of heat pushed back the relentless creep of pain.

A third glass was poured, but before Ethan drank it he picked up both it and the decanter in one hand and reached for the back of the plush leather swivel chair with the other. Leaning heavily against the solid piece of furniture, he dragged it towards him, thankful for the wheels that made it easier, throwing himself down into it, groaning as the weight came off his legs.

He shut his eyes on a deep sigh as screamingly tense muscles found release. Nursing his drink and the decanter against his chest, he flopped his head back into the cushiony leather headrest, tilted the chair backwards and swivelled gently from side to side, enjoying the rush from the twin sensations of heat and relief.

Ethan wasn't sure how long he sat there, idly twisting from side to side, his eyes shut, his tired muscles almost jelly now they'd been given permission to relax. He just knew it felt good to be non-weight-bearing.

Bliss. Ecstasy. Paradise.

But he *was* here for a reason—apart from the damn good whisky. He dragged his eyes open, knowing he couldn't put it off any longer. Finally acknowledging that was exactly what he *was* doing.

On Leo's desk there was a chart. The chart of a child with a terribly disfiguring condition that Ethan could help.

He could change little Ama's life.

He *would* change her life.

But Ama's case was complicated in more ways than one. Her condition was complex and would require multiple surgeries to correct.

But that wasn't the issue. Ethan thrived on complex.

It was the strings attached to the case that were the problem. Big, fat strings involving someone from his past and the unholy mess he'd made in his selfish, juvenile need to hurt his brother.

Olivia Fairchild.

Olivia's charity Fair Go was sponsoring Ama and her mother and an interpreter to travel from sub-Sahara Africa to London and the Hunter Clinic, for surgery and rehabilitation.

And she would be here—tomorrow.

Olivia who'd loved him. And he'd thrown it in her face by using her to get back at Leo. Flaunting her in front of his brother, knowing how much Leo had fallen for her, taunting him with the woman he couldn't have.

Olivia had been heartbroken when she'd realised. The

look in her eyes that terrible, fateful day… He shuddered thinking about it now. The huge row he and Leo had got into, not knowing Olivia was listening to every ugly word. Him admitting that he was only interested in the sexy Aussie doc because Leo wanted her for himself.

It hadn't been true—not really. At the beginning, maybe, but not at that point. He'd enjoyed her company and there'd been something about her that had made him forget all his *stuff* when he was in her arms. The darkness that had been with him from his teenage years. The anguish over his mother's premature death. His dysfunctional relationship with his father. All had been lifted whenever she'd held him close.

But the damage had been done and his betrayal, his hurting her, had been unforgivable. *Toxic.* That was the word she'd used to describe his and Leo's relationship just before she'd fled back to Australia. And she'd been right. It had been toxic. And a lot of that had been on him.

But it wasn't any longer.

He'd been so angry and self-destructive back then. Angry at his mother for dying and the ensuing scandal over her infidelities, angry at his father for being weak and taking the easy, boozy way out after Francesca's death, and angrier at Leo for playing protector.

Protecting James from himself instead of confronting him over the inept drunk he'd become. And protecting Ethan from his father's wildly fluctuating mental state—from deep depression to manic rage—denying Ethan the opportunity to vent all his anger, frustration and loss.

Ethan cringed as he thought about what a bastard he'd been. He'd taken what he'd wanted with no regard for Olivia's feelings. Just stringing her along, thumbing his nose at her love, knowing how much Leo had had to grit his teeth every time he'd seen them together.

He'd thought himself so far above love back then—that he was immune to it. What a fool! It had taken a small, fierce, passionate firecracker of a woman from a foreign war-torn land to teach him how wrong he'd been. Maybe that was his punishment for Olivia?

Learning what love really meant and having it cruelly snatched away.

Ethan took a deep swallow of his drink, beating back memories of Aaliyah. He didn't need *that* guilt on top of his Olivia guilt tonight.

No whisky bottle would be safe.

Olivia…

Had she forgiven him? Did he even deserve her forgiveness?

He hoped so.

Or at least that they could put the past behind them. Because not only would he be seeing her tomorrow but he'd be working with her too. As a paediatric reconstructive surgeon, Olivia had been given clearance by Leo not only to assist in Ama's surgeries but to scrub in on any of the Hunter Clinic's cases during her stay in London.

The humanitarian side of the clinic, which was Ethan's baby, worked with charities from all round the world—Olivia's charity being just one. Consequently it had a reasonably robust operating schedule—many of the cases were kids. There would be plenty of opportunities for Olivia to keep her skills up to date while she juggled her hosting responsibilities for Ama.

And Ethan knew having another pair of hands—skilled hands—would allow them to do so much more.

But team work was critical.

He couldn't change what had happened in the past, and he was pretty damn sure she wouldn't want to re-hash it either, but he could treat her with the respect she deserved going forward.

He took another sip of his whisky as the questions circled round and round his brain. Questions he didn't have answers for. Questions that could drive him nuts.

That could drive him to the bottom of Leo's decanter.

But he'd come too close to being his father, to tak-ing the easy way out, a while back—he wasn't going there again.

He sighed and reached for the heavy walnut desk, grabbing hold and dragging the chair closer, trying to use his legs as little as possible. And there it was, right on the edge in the middle of the desk, Ama's chart.

Ethan placed the decanter and his glass on the table and pushed all thoughts of Olivia aside as he opened the chart and started to read.

Olivia Fairchild was late. She checked her watch for the hundredth time as she paid the taxi driver. The cool Oc-tober evening, a far cry from the heat of Africa, closed in around her as the taxi took off and she turned to face the familiar building on Harley Street.

Late or not, she took a moment to collect herself and clear her throat of the emotion that she'd been battling on the cab-ride. She blinked back stupid tears. Getting Ama and her mother settled into their room at the Lighthouse Children's Hospital had been more emotional than she'd expected. She felt flustered and off-kilter rather than cool and professional, which was what she'd hoped to be when she came face to face with her past.

But Ama had got to her tonight—just as she had from

day one. She'd been so apprehensive of her strange new world, and so distressed when her mother had left the room with the interpreter to attend to some paperwork, that Olivia had felt completely out of her depth.

For nine years Ama had known nothing other than a small village in sub-Sahara Africa where she'd been closeted away, not allowed to go to school or play with the other kids because of her disfiguring condition.

London must be terrifying.

Olivia, who had spent a lot of the past six weeks building a rapport with Ama, had tried her best to comfort the girl, but sometimes only mother-love would do and Ama had cried and cried until her mother returned.

And, oh, the way she'd clung had been gut-wrenching!

Olivia had been able to feel the frantic beat of Ama's heart through her painfully skinny ribs as the little girl had held onto her for dear life. And Olivia had clung right back, rocking her slightly, shushing her gently, feeling so inadequate in the face of the girl's anguish.

It had reminded her of the day she'd found Ama and her mother, both wailing and crying in the street, clinging to each other as two men engaged in a heated discussion had grabbed at them, trying to pull them apart. She hadn't been able to bear it.

A passing car hooted, bringing her back to the here and now, and Olivia shivered as the Hunter Clinic came back into focus. She took a deep breath, steeling herself to enter.

Her heart pounded as she mounted the stairs and pushed through the heavy doors. After-hours the clinic was hushed and deserted and she took a moment to absorb it all. Except for the stark whiteness of the updated décor, visible even in the darkened interior, it looked the same as she remembered—exclusive, luxurious, old money. It smelled the same. It *felt* the same.

And yet it didn't. It was familiar…yet not.

Maybe it was because *she* was different? Not the same starry-eyed Olivia who had trusted her heart to the Hunter boys only to be used in their toxic games and have it crushed into the dirt.

Older. Wiser.

Stronger.

It was warm inside and she undid the toggles on her duffle coat as her boot heels tapped on the exquisite grey and black marble floor on her way to Leo's office. It felt like a lifetime ago now since she'd walked these corridors on her frequent trips to see Ethan.

Ethan.

Olivia's heart skipped a beat as her stride faltered.

No. She would not think about him tonight. She wasn't here to see Ethan. She was here to see Leo.

Ethan would come tomorrow. And tomorrow would be soon enough.

Despite only the most subdued light, coming from lamps placed in discreet alcoves, her feet took her to Leo's office without any real direction from her brain. Once there she didn't stop to give herself time to think or doubt, she just reached up to knock on the door, surprised when it swung silently open under the weight of her closed hand.

For a moment, peering into the sumptuous darkened office, with just a desk lamp illuminating the room, she thought the man sitting at the desk, head bent over a chart, looked like Leo and she smiled.

'Leo,' she called from the doorway, her voice hushed

as seemed appropriate in the quietness of the deserted building.

Ethan, who'd been too intent to register the knock, looked up as his brother's name spilled from Olivia's lips, and even a decade down the track he still felt the impact of that mouth.

Wide and sexy, forming a natural pout that had always fascinated him. A mouth he'd kissed.

He'd *missed*.

It was a startling realisation for a man who'd felt dead inside for the past year. And he wasn't sure he liked it.

What the hell was she doing here? Didn't her flight arrive early tomorrow morning?

'Olivia,' he acknowledged, watching as her eyes, always two huge chocolate pools shimmering with emotional intensity, grew even rounder.

He should stand—innate good manners dictated that he should—but his legs felt about as supportive as wet noodles and he didn't trust them. Thankfully Olivia seemed too stunned to call him on it.

Olivia blinked as all the oxygen in the room was sucked right out. 'Oh…'

Ethan. Not Leo. *Ethan.* Her heart pounded in time to the drumming of his name through her brain.

Ethan. Ethan. Ethan.

'I'm sorry, I know I'm late, but…' She nervously checked her watch. 'I'm supposed to be meeting Leo here.'

Ethan hadn't been sure what they'd say to each other when he and Olivia came face to face again. They'd spoken twice on the phone about the case, which had been brisk and professional, but he'd thought it would be different when they were looking at each other. That old hurts might have fizzled out.

Evidently not, judging by the wariness in Olivia's startled gaze.

Her first words were not warm and welcoming. There was no *let bygones be bygones* about her demeanour. She hadn't smiled for *him* as she had when she'd mistaken him for Leo. And, perversely, it bugged him.

There was a wariness, a distance in her gaze. As if they were strangers instead of ex-lovers. And a part of him wanted to snatch her up, taste that pouty mouth again, remind her how good they'd been together.

If only he could get up without falling flat on his face!

'He's at home,' Ethan said abruptly, angry at the direction of his thoughts.

For God's sake, he was lucky she hadn't slapped him in the face. Clearly he wasn't thinking straight. *Clearly* he was just too damn tired to be facing ghosts tonight.

Olivia frowned. 'Oh…'

But…she'd called Leo the moment they'd landed and they'd arranged it. She delved around inside her bag for her mobile phone, pulling it out. Immediately she noticed two missed calls and a text—all from Leo.

Apologies. Something came up. Get Ethan up to speed and you can catch me up tomorrow.

'Something came up,' Olivia said, looking from the phone to Ethan as she relayed the text.

Ethan grunted as a rather unpleasant thought occurred to him. Leo had texted him during surgery, asking him to familiarise himself with Ama's chart—*on his desk*—before the morning. Had Leo set this up so he and

Olivia could get their first meeting over and done with in private—to give them room and privacy to clear the air?

His relationship with his brother was the best it had been in years, but he didn't appreciate being manipulated like this.

'I bet it did,' Ethan said dryly.

Olivia put her phone back in her bag. 'He wants me to get you up to speed.'

Ethan had sometimes forgotten, just looking at her, that Olivia was Australian. Her flawless peaches and cream complexion seemed eminently English, and it was only when she opened her mouth and the flat Aussie drawl came out that he remembered. That and the opal ring she still wore on the middle finger of her right hand—a gift from her parents for her eighteenth birthday.

'No time like the present,' he agreed grimly.

If Leo *had* set them up then it would be foolish not to use the time wisely.

'Come in.' He gestured, suddenly realising she was still standing just inside the doorframe. 'Take a seat.' He indicated with his head for her to take the one on the other side of Leo's desk.

Her movements seemed awkward and unsure as she drew closer. She certainly didn't seem to be in any hurry to reach her destination, and he waited impatiently for her to take her seat, his gaze drifting to the way the denim of her jeans clung to legs still as slender as he remembered.

As she drew level his gaze moved up. Her red turtlenecked skivvy was mostly hidden by the thick navy jacket she was wearing, but it did emphasise the length of her neck to perfection. A neck he'd explored in intimate detail.

Olivia was conscious of his gaze on her as she moved

into the room. Heat flared in her belly as she remembered the way he used to look at her—all intensity and wicked, wicked purpose.

Before he broke her heart.

She was thankful for the thick wool of her coat hiding nipples suddenly taking on a mind of their own.

She didn't have time for recalcitrant nipples.

They were two professionals, working together for the good of a patient. Yes, they had history, but if they kept things collegial, if they kept their focus on Ama, they'd be fine.

She was here to do a job and then get the hell out of Dodge.

She'd been burned by this man before. And fire had already claimed too much of what she'd loved.

Olivia sat, glancing briefly around at Leo's office. It didn't appear to have changed much since the days when it had belonged to his father. All dark and masculine—a stark contrast to the bright modern white outside.

Her gaze returned to Ethan and for long moments they just looked at each other. His lids were half shuttered; his gaze was totally guarded. He looked so…*distant* and she shivered.

He picked up the nearby whisky decanter and splashed some into a glass, silently asking her with a raising of his eyebrow if she wanted any. She shook her head, surprised to see him drinking, knowing how much he'd despised his father for his weakness where the amber liquid was concerned.

Keep it professional, Liv.

'You've changed,' she blurted out.

And it was nothing to do with the drinking. Ethan's eyes were the same deep brown as hers, but he had those amazing golden flecks in them that used to *glow* with fire and passion. He'd been so angry back then that they'd flashed and flared all the time as he'd struggled with his demons—his father's alcoholism, his mother's death and what he'd perceived as his brother's molly-coddling.

But she'd also seen them glow and flash at other times too. At work when he was totally absorbed in a surgery. And in bed…

There was no glow tonight. Just a dull glimpse of what had been. It was as if it had been snuffed out. Suffocated.

What had happened to turn those gorgeous flashing eyes so damn bleak? And his perfect chiselled face so damn gaunt? His severe haircut didn't help. Nor did the weary lines around his eyes. Not to mention that he needed a shave. His shaggy regrowth looked more salt than pepper at the grand old age of thirty-five.

Was he suffering some kind of PTSD from being blown half to hell during his last tour?

'You haven't,' he said, interrupting her reverie.

It was Olivia's turned to snort. 'Yes, I have.'

She'd been through more than her fair share of heartbreak these past ten years, and although she'd come through it stronger it had changed her utterly.

Ethan paused slightly, then acknowledged the truth of it with a nod. She was right. She was more reserved, less carefree. Her gaze was not as open, was more…*distant*.

Had that been his unforgivable actions or just getting older? Life in general?

Or had something else caused the coolness in her eyes?

'I just don't need to resort to whisky to prove it.'

Ethan felt the accusation hit him in the chest with all the power of a sledgehammer.

He threw back the contents of the glass and slammed

it down on the desktop. 'It's been a long day, Olivia,' he said, his jaw so tight it felt as if it was going to crumble from the pressure. 'Surgery is over and I'm off duty. A few glasses of Scotland's best isn't going to hurt.'

Olivia had never been one to beat around the bush and she wasn't about to start now. Clearly something was eating at Ethan—something had snuffed out the light. And, whilst she might not know what it was, she sure as hell knew whisky wasn't the answer.

'I'm sure that's exactly how your father started out.'

CHAPTER TWO

ETHAN'S HEART POUNDED a furious tattoo in his chest. Having his father shoved in his face was always a red rag to a bull, but pure overproof rage surged through his system at her matter-of-fact taunt. If anyone knew the location of his soft underbelly it was Olivia. And she'd never been afraid to call him on his crap.

It was the *Australian way*, she'd assured him all those years ago.

He gripped the edge of the desk and lurched to his feet, too angry even to register the limp protest of gelatinous muscles. 'Go to hell, Olivia,' he snapped.

Her words stung. They stung hard. Because they'd found their mark so accurately. After he'd been discharged from the hospital in Germany and returned to the UK to recuperate from his injuries he *had* drunk way too much.

Trying to block out the pain and the dreams and the guilt.

Leo's email had saved him. The offer to come back to the clinic and head up its humanitarian programme had been just the right bait to wave in front of him and he'd reached for it like a drowning man, knowing that he was treading the same slippery slope his father had trod before he'd slipped away altogether.

But he wasn't that guy any more. And it infuriated him to be pigeonholed after a few minutes' reacquaintance.

She had no freaking idea what he'd been through.

Olivia stood too, refusing to have him standing over her, trying to intimidate her with his height and breadth and sheer masculine presence—which he still had in spades despite his more mature looks.

So, she'd annoyed him—*good*!

Maybe it would make him realise that sitting alone in an office at nine o'clock at night with a decanter full of whisky wasn't the answer to whatever was eating him.

'I'll follow you down, shall I?' she enquired calmly.

Ethan pressed his closed fists into the hard wood of the desktop and prayed for patience. He didn't need her judgement—he could do that plenty on his own.

'I think you can bring me up to speed in the morning,' he said through clenched teeth. He was too tired for this crap. 'I'm going home. See yourself out.'

At least going home was his plan, but by the time he'd taken a few paces the adrenaline from his surge of anger had worn off and the message from his quad muscles that they were too fatigued to hold him upright had finally broken through the righteous indignation swamping his brain.

His legs buckled.

Olivia leapt forward in alarm as Ethan wobbled and then toppled sideways, reaching out for the desk wildly in an attempt to stop himself from falling on his butt. She grabbed hold of his arm and between her and the desk they saved him from being a rather inelegant crumpled heap on the expensive Turkish rug.

'What the hell, Ethan?' she said as he leaned heavily

against her, struggling for balance. 'How much *have* you had to drink?' she asked.

Ethan sucked air in and out between his teeth as his muscles protested. 'Not the booze,' he choked out, one hand reaching for a screaming thigh muscle. 'It's my damn legs.'

Olivia believed him. He definitely wasn't drunk. His words weren't slurred and he didn't stink of alcohol. In fact, with her nose damn near the vicinity of his throat, she could say for sure that he smelled the way he always had—of utter hedonism. Total crack for the olfactory system. It swamped over her now in a sweet pheromone cloud, and her body responded accordingly.

Honestly, the man was waging chemical warfare on her body and he didn't even know it, thanks to whatever was going on with his legs.

'Here, come on,' she said, staggering under the weight of him a little as she slung his arm over her shoulder. 'Over to the lounge.'

Ethan didn't have much of a choice. His thighs were trembling now from the effort of just standing and he felt as weak as a kitten. She led and he followed, and he felt about as potent and virile as a postage stamp.

'I'm fine,' he said as soon as they were near enough to the couch to reach for it. 'Let go.'

Olivia eased away as he flopped down onto the firm leather of the elegant Chesterfield and gave a relieved groan, his hands automatically reaching for his thigh muscles, his eyes shutting, his head flopping back as he kneaded up and down their length. She knelt down in front of him, his knees either side of her shoulders, resting back on her haunches, and waited for him to recover.

It took a few minutes for the creases in his face to start to iron out a little. 'What happened?' she asked quietly.

His hands stopped their massaging briefly before starting up again.

'Is it from when you were injured during your last tour?' she prompted, when it didn't look as if he was about to answer her any time soon.

His eyes flicked open and Olivia was struck again by how dull and lifeless they looked. No spark. No glitter.

'How did you know?'

She gave him a half-smile, trying to lighten the mood. 'We *do* have newspapers in Australia, you know. And this new-fangled thing called the worldwide web—which, you know, even goes all the way to Australia.' Her smile died on her lips when it was apparent he wasn't going to join her. 'You'll be amazed at what you can find on it,' she murmured.

Ethan pulled his head off the cushioned comfort of the lounge and pierced her with his gaze. Her honey-brown hair fell in wavy disorder around her face and he remembered vividly how it had felt spread out across his chest.

'You kept tabs on me?'

Olivia sucked in a breath as his low, gravelly voice swept hot fingers along the muscles deep inside her. And was that a flare bursting to life in those golden flecks?

'No,' she said, annoyed that even tired and in pain he could think such a thing.

Clearly his ego hadn't been injured.

'I haven't spent the past decade *pining* over you, Ethan Hunter, if that's what you think,' she clarified, her voice snippy even to her own ears. 'I researched the clinic on-line when I was looking at partnering with you guys. The newspaper articles about how you evacuated an entire hospital that was being heavily shelled showed up in the search.'

Ethan dropped his head back again and shut his eyes against the annoyance in hers and the echo of memories. He'd been meaning to check up on her over the years, but military life had been full-on and there'd always been an excuse not to.

And then he'd met Aaliyah.

Olivia watched him a little longer, the kneading of his long fingers hypnotic. Part of her wanted to take over— the Olivia of ten years ago would have.

This Olivia curled her hands into fists by her sides and said, 'What are your injuries?'

Ethan sighed, lifting his head off the lounge again. 'Legs shot to hell. Right knee and ankle torn up by shrapnel.'

'Have they been reconstructed?'

He nodded. 'As best they could. They're never going to be the same again, though.'

'Do you have some kind of physio regime, because your legs don't seem to be very strong. I'd have thought you'd need some kind of a walking aid—a stick or something?' She frowned, thinking back to the articles she'd read. 'It's been about a year, right?'

Ethan grunted. 'Yes,' he said tersely. 'And, yes, I have a regime.'

It took Olivia a second or two to realise she'd asked the wrong question. 'Do you *follow* it?' She folded her arms. 'Religiously?'

Ethan glared at her. God, she sounded like Lizzie. And Leo. And a lot of well-meaning other people who didn't have a freaking clue about the realities of his injuries.

'It's none of your damn business,' he growled.

'It *is* my damn business if you're going to collapse on the floor in the middle of operating on Ama.'

Ethan bristled at the implication, and at the unflinching demand he saw in her eyes. She was calling him on his professionalism and leaving him in no doubt that she was holding him to account. It rankled. But still, it was preferable to the pity he usually saw reflected in other people's eyes.

The *poor you* look that got under his skin like an army of marching ants.

She didn't seem to give a damn about the fact of his injuries or even how he'd got them—just that he could do his job. She was being a doctor. And it was in equal parts satisfying and irritating

'I'm not going to be collapsing on anyone,' he snapped. 'I just stood for an extraordinary amount of time today.'

'Which shouldn't matter if you'd been diligent with your physio,' Olivia said.

She knew Ethan. She knew he wouldn't respond to her empathy. God knew, the empathy and protection Leo had tried to force upon him all those years ago had driven a huge wedge between the brothers and she'd been just one of the casualties.

She knew he wouldn't let her massage his legs or talk about what had happened. But, having worked out in the field herself, in places no one should have to live, she did know that military men responded best to tough love.

'I've been a little busy trying to establish the humanitarian side of the clinic,' he snapped. 'I do what I can when I can.'

Olivia drummed her fingers against her biceps. 'Well, it looks like it's not enough. You should be stronger than this by now.'

Ethan knew she was right, but…it *had* been an unusual day. He let his head flop back again.

He needed to make time to get stronger in his legs. He'd gone from two months in hospital and multiple surgeries to home and feeling sorry for himself to throwing everything he had into his new role at the Hunter Clinic—none of which had been conducive to the hard yards he needed to do.

As Olivia watched he seemed to melt into the couch, exhaustion in every line of his body, and part of her wanted to lay her cheek on his nearby knee and just sit with him in silence. She was surprised to feel such tenderness for him after what had happened. But then the heat in her belly had been a surprise too, after all these years.

She nudged his knee with her shoulder. '*Have* you got a stick you should be using?'

Ethan lifted a hand off his thigh and massaged his forehead with it. He wished she'd just be quiet, already—she was like Jiminy freaking Cricket. 'Yes…' he said on a sigh.

'And the reason you don't appear to have it with you is…?'

Ethan lifted his head. 'I hate the damn thing,' he muttered.

Olivia raised an eyebrow. Did he realise how much he sounded like a petulant child? 'Does it affect your tough guy image, Ethan? I wouldn't have thought you so vain.'

Ethan snorted. Did she *really* think this was about vanity? 'No, it's just…' He shook his head, shut his eyes, rested his head back again as he realised he was about to admit the truth. 'It…invites conversations I just don't want to have.'

The heaviness in his voice reached right inside her gut and squeezed. *Hard.* She knew all too well how hard re-hashing things could be—talking about stuff that sometimes you just didn't want to talk about. Especially with people who had no connection to you.

So many people had wanted to talk to her after what had happened to her parents, had wanted to reminisce, lament, vent. And she'd spent an awful lot of time avoiding them.

Without thinking about it she slid a hand onto his knee. The fine wool of his trousers was soft against her palm, the contours of his knee hard.

'Ethan…'

Ethan lifted his head again as her touch caused a riot of sensations up his aching leg. *Good* sensations. She was barely touching him at all, but still it felt as if she'd injected pop rocks into his thigh. He looked at her neat fingernails and remembered how good they'd felt on other parts of his body. How *good* they'd been together. How much they'd sizzled.

How insatiable they'd been.

His reasons for being with Olivia might not have been exactly altruistic, but they'd been amazingly compatible in the bedroom.

Which reminded him how long it had been since he'd been with a woman. A year.

Not since Aaliyah.

He dragged his eyes off her hand and looked up. Their gazes locked. The worst thing about her touch was how familiar it felt. Here in this clinic, with this woman from his past looking at him with patience and compassion, it would be so easy to grab hold and travel back to a time when he'd been able to lose himself in her and have everything else fade to black.

But it felt…disloyal. To Aaliyah. And he despised himself just a little bit more.

'Just go, Olivia.'

Go before I kiss you. Before I haul you up on the couch beside me. Before I beg you to stay.

Before I use you one more time.

Olivia's belly clenched at the flare of heat that fired Ethan's dull gaze. She'd seen that look before. She knew what it meant. She knew what he wanted. Her breath grew thick in her throat as things south of her waistband stirred and strained, demanding she respond in the most primal way.

His nostrils flared as the silence stretched between them and she could feel the coiled intensity of his muscles. He wanted her. She could see that. Hell, half an hour in his company and she wanted him too.

But, unlike last time, she wanted *all* of him. She wanted his story and his sadness and his shadows. And she wasn't going to settle for scraps. For some quick roll in the hay while he made love to her with dead eyes. Because having sex with Ethan had never been a one-time thing for her and she needed to protect herself better than last time.

She was here for Ama. And then she was leaving.

She was not having sex with Ethan Hunter.

Olivia pushed herself shakily to her feet. She was standing between his knees now and an image of her straddling him played in glorious Technicolor inside her head.

She took a step back. 'Are you—?' She cleared her

throat of its sudden wobble. 'Are you heading home soon?'

Ethan shook his head. He probably hadn't been very capable of standing prior to Olivia touching him; he for damn sure wasn't now. 'I'll sleep here tonight.'

Olivia nodded. It seemed best, considering walking had been a monumental effort. 'Are you...will you be okay?'

'Dandy,' he said sarcastically, annoyed at her distant propriety—a far cry from the heat of the look they'd just exchanged.

Olivia ignored his terseness. 'What time do you want to meet in the morning?' she asked.

'Be here at nine.' His tone was dismissive and he hoped she got the message—*get the hell out*.

Olivia got the message. It rankled, but she didn't want to get into anything more with him tonight. It seemed their incendiary attraction still simmered and she didn't trust that the line between angry and passionate wouldn't blur and they wouldn't do something they'd *both* regret in the morning.

She turned on her heel and headed towards the desk, where her bag had been dumped when Ethan had fallen. She reached for it, her gaze falling on the decanter of whisky. She snatched it up. It could leave with her as well.

Out of sight, out of mind.

'You don't have to take it,' he said derisively from behind her. 'Even if I was capable of hauling my butt off this couch, I'm done with drinking tonight.'

Olivia turned, slinging the straps of her handbag over her shoulder. 'Consider this as my way of delivering you from temptation.' And with that she headed for the door.

Ethan tracked her progress, her clinging jeans, the

swish of her honey-brown hair down the back of her coat way too fascinating for his own peace of mind.

A surge of what felt like good old-fashioned lust swept through his system.

He didn't feel very delivered at all.

Ethan was woken by a hard shake to his shoulder who knew how many hours later? Except where there had been darkness there was now light. *Way too much light.*

Daylight streamed like glory from heaven through the open slats of the dark wooden blinds dressing the window under which the chesterfield sat, piercing like needles into his eyeballs.

'Ugh,' he groaned, shutting his eyes tight. 'Somebody turn down the sun.'

'What the hell are you doing here?' Leo demanded, ignoring his brother's protests as he yanked up the blind, causing a tsunami of sunlight.

Ethan groaned louder. 'It was late,' he said, shielding his eyes. 'I crashed here.'

'I should start charging you rent,' Leo muttered.

Ethan cracked an eyelid open to find his brother lounging against the far arm of the couch. He squinted at his watch. It was six-thirty in the morning. 'Lizzie kick you out of bed?'

Leo grinned, which was way too much for Ethan at this hour of the morning. 'She's not sleeping very well,— has to keep getting up to go to the bathroom. I'm trying to give her as much room as possible.'

Ethan was pleased his brother had found love, but such happiness was a bit hard to take—especially hard on the heels of his less than stellar reunion with Olivia. He sat and swung his legs over the edge of the couch, pleased to feel the strength back in his quads.

'You look like hell,' Leo said cheerfully.

'Gee…thanks.' Compared to last night he felt like a million dollars.

'You going to head home or shower here?'

Ethan ran his hands through his hair. 'I'll use your bathroom.' He always kept spare clothes in his office, and a private bathroom was one of the perks of being the director—or related to him anyway.

Ethan owned the clinic jointly with his brother, but had gladly ceded control to him when he'd decided to leave everything tainted with the Hunter name behind and put his medical degree to good use in the army. Leo had been angry that he was skipping out on his family responsibilities, especially with the clinic in such trouble after his father's scandal, and had spent the next ten years trying to involve his younger brother in the day-to-day running of the clinic.

But Ethan hadn't cared. He'd not wanted any part of lipo and boob jobs on a bunch of movie stars. He'd been doing *real* work and Leo could do whatever the hell he liked to salvage the professional and financial reputation of the once renowned Hunter Clinic.

And then he'd been blown all to hell and Leo had made him an offer he couldn't refuse. An offer he'd desperately needed to stop him from sliding into an abyss of self-pity.

Leo pushed up off the arm. 'When you're done I'll buy you breakfast.'

Three quarters of an hour later they were sitting inside a nearby café, tucking into a traditional English breakfast. They were both on their second cup of coffee.

'So. You saw Olivia last night, I take it?'

Ethan looked up from his plate. 'Yes. Nicely orchestrated,' he said with derision.

Completely unabashed, Leo said, 'How did that go?'

'How do you think it went?'

'Not as well as I'd hoped, by the sounds of it.'

'Let's just say I wasn't in the best shape when she arrived. She pretty much accused me of being one step away from the old man and then chewed my ear off about not doing my physio.'

Leo laughed. 'Still the same blunt old Olivia, huh?'

Ethan grunted, then took a sip of his coffee. 'She is and she isn't. There's a…reserve about her…she's not her usual vivacious self.'

'Maybe that's just being around you?'

Ethan contemplated his brother's observation. *Maybe it was.* 'Anyway…it didn't go well. She has your decanter of whisky too, by the way.'

Leo laughed harder. 'Did you discuss the case at all?'

Ethan shook his head. 'She's coming to your office at nine to brief us both.'

Leo quirked an eyebrow at his brother. 'Am I to be an intermediary?'

Ethan looked at his older brother. His tone was light but their history with Olivia Fairchild was complex. And, apart from one aborted attempt on the day of Leo's wedding, Ethan had never really apologised for his behaviour where that was concerned. He'd not only hurt Olivia but he'd also hurt Leo—deliberately.

Because he could.

He put his coffee cup down in its saucer. 'No. Of course not. About that…about Olivia…about what happened between all of us—'

'Don't worry about it,' Leo interrupted. 'Water under the bridge.'

'No.' Ethan shook his head. 'I was out of line.'

'Yes, you were.' Leo grinned. 'But…I knew deep down she never really liked me—not in that way. She certainly never gave me any reason to think there was anything other than friendship on her behalf. But…she was so gorgeous…my ego got in the way.'

Gorgeous. Yes, Leo was right. Olivia had been vivacious, sparkling, witty. Quick with a laugh and a snappy one-liner.

And utterly gorgeous.

'That doesn't make my behaviour any less reprehensible. You were right. I was using her to get at you and I'm sorry. I was pretty self-destructive there for a while, huh?'

Leo shrugged. 'Losing Mum was hard on you.'

'And not on you?'

'Ethan…we've made our peace. We *both* did things wrong and I don't expect you to spend the rest of your life apologising for something that happened a long time ago which we've put behind us.'

He paused and pierced his brother with a look that Ethan had come to know as his clinic director look.

'And I'm not the one you need to apologise to. That's what you were supposed to be doing last night.'

Ethan grimaced. 'Yeah. That didn't happen.' He glanced at his brother, who held his gaze with unwavering intensity. 'She refused to accept my apology last time. What makes you think she will now?'

'It's been a long time,' Leo said. 'And she's never struck me as being someone to hold a grudge.'

'It was pretty unforgivable.'

Leo nodded in agreement. 'You need to make it right,

though. You'll be working with her again over the next few months. You have to clear the air.'

Ethan knew Leo was right. Once upon a time that would have rankled, as everything about his brother's authority and over-protectiveness had rankled. But he'd done a lot of growing up and recognised good advice when he heard it. 'I know.'

There was silence for the next few minutes as they finished their breakfast. Leo put his utensils down on his plate and looked at his brother. 'I thought you and her might…'

Ethan glanced up from his breakfast. The possibility of he and Olivia glimmered for a moment. Her touch on his leg last night was almost tangible again, the way they'd been together settling around him in a fine mist he could almost taste.

But then memories of another woman—a woman he'd loved, a woman he'd left to die—pushed into the possibilities, beating them back, drowning them in a tide of guilt.

Aaliyah.

Ethan threw his napkin on his plate. 'Let's go.'

CHAPTER THREE

RUNNING EARLY THIS time, Olivia smiled at Leo as she walked into his office an hour later. She'd always had a soft spot for the incredibly hard-working elder Hunter brother and it hadn't been killed by time, distance or past wrongs. Yes, she'd told them their relationship was toxic but that hadn't really been Leo's fault.

Leo had been caught in the middle between his father and his brother and had practically killed himself to do right by both of them.

It was Ethan's bitterness that had been the true destructive force.

She thrust the whisky decanter she'd hauled all the way back in the taxi at him as she neared. 'I relieved Ethan of this last night.'

'Yes, he mentioned it.' Leo grinned taking it from her and then sweeping her into a huge hug.

'I can't believe it's been ten years,' he said as he pulled back. 'How have you been?'

Olivia gave her standard reply. 'Fine.' Because the truth was less than fine, and she refused to give it power over her. 'But now…what about you? Not only married but a baby on the way? I have to meet this girl!'

Easily deflected, Leo chatted for ten minutes about Lizzie and babies and their life together and Olivia was heartened to hear that Leo had found the happiness he'd always deserved. She'd valued and enjoyed his friendship and had been saddened by its becoming another casualty of Ethan's destructive streak.

If she'd only been smarter she would have chosen the older Hunter brother. But the heart wanted what the heart wanted, and from the moment she'd laid eyes on Ethan she'd been officially off the market!

She'd fallen hard for his good looks, charm and intelligence. Yes, he'd been angry, and hurting too, but he'd oozed undeniable potential from every cell in his being. She'd just known that one day he would do great things.

And that had been pretty damn irresistible.

But she would have resisted had she known she was going to cause an even bigger rift between the two brothers. She'd thought she'd be able to help them reconnect, to heal the cracks in their relationship that had been gutting to watch.

Her tender heart had been touched by the suffering they'd endured—their mother's death and the scandalous details of her life that had come to light after, and their father's messy slide into the bottle. Coming from a background that placed family above *everything*, she hadn't been able to bear the thought of what the Hunter boys must have been through growing up and she'd desperately wanted to help.

She'd wanted to show Ethan, and Leo by extension, how wonderful a loving relationship—like the one her parents had—could be. And to bring them back to each other.

But Ethan had been on a different page and she hadn't got the memo.

The light chatter stopped as soon as Ethan entered the room. Olivia was relieved to see him looking much more human this morning. Back to his usual level of *ooh la la* in a suit and tie. He'd hadn't shaved, but the lines around his eyes had disappeared. His gait was strong and sure even with the slight limp as he strode towards the desk.

She'd lain awake half the night thinking about their reunion and the state of his health. He seemed even more messed up than he had been a decade ago. Lucky for her, life had hardened her sappy little heart over the years, and the urge to fix Ethan Hunter had withered and died a long time ago. He was a big boy who could take care of himself.

Leo looked from one to the other as she and Ethan stood awkwardly in front of his desk. 'Let's get down to it, shall we?' he suggested.

'Yes,' they both said in unison, and then glanced guiltily at each other before simultaneously looking away.

Leo sighed. 'Take a seat,' he said, indicating the chairs opposite him, and Olivia wasn't sure whose butt was on whose respective chair faster—hers or Ethan's.

Clearly Ethan was keen to get this over with.

Good.

That made two of them.

Ethan strode into the Lighthouse Children's Hospital just prior to lunch. He'd walked from Harley Street. Last night the thought of walking any distance had been beyond him, but he usually walked from the clinic to the Lighthouse, and also to Princess Catherine's Hospital, time permitting.

The Hunter Clinic and its team of surgeons had operating privileges at both hospitals and neither was far to walk. Still, after Olivia's dressing-down last night he was using his stick, even if he did have plans to abandon it just prior to seeing his patients.

Olivia had accused him of vanity last night and he'd set her straight on that. Drawing attention to himself, to his injuries, wasn't something he was keen on. But it was more than that. A surgeon with a walking stick just sent the wrong kind of message. Especially in the world of plastics and reconstructive surgery. Patients wondered about a surgeon who couldn't heal himself.

Leaving his stick in one of the empty offices, he did his rounds. Being a visiting surgeon, he didn't have any junior doctors to accompany him but always made sure one of the nursing staff on each ward did. Nothing annoyed the nurses more than a doctor coming in and making changes to treatment and then leaving again without informing them.

And Ethan had learned a long time ago never to upset the nursing staff. That nurses were a vital part of the medical team—the interface between the doctor and the patient.

And you annoyed them at your own peril.

He prided himself on having good relationships with the nursing staff wherever he went, and at the Lighthouse particularly.

He left Ama to last. There was a lot that needed to be done before she went to Theatre next week and he wanted to have a clean plate today so he could focus solely on her. Plus Olivia was with her, and for some reason he was unaccountably nervous. It was obvious from her briefing this morning that this case was dear to her and he found himself not wanting to disappoint her.

He'd done that once already and was desperate to make amends.

He made his way to Ama's room by himself, assuring Ama's nurse, who was busy with another of her patients, that he would keep her up to date with the tests and procedures he was ordering. He heard laughter as he approached—Olivia's laughter. With her petite frame she looked as if she'd have one of those light and tinkly girly laughs, but it was surprisingly deep and throaty and it always came out at full roar—coming not just from her belly but from her heart.

He remembered it well from back when she used to smile at him, when she used to laugh.

It evoked powerful memories of a turbulent time in his life. A time when her laughter had helped ease a lot of his frustrations.

She had her back to the door when he pulled up and he lounged against the frame, observing her for long moments. She was sitting on the bed opposite a little girl who sat cross-legged in the lap of an older woman. Their skin was as dark and burnished as the finest ebony.

Ama and her mother, he assumed. Although he could only see them in profile and therefore the defect, which he knew to be quite significant, wasn't showing, given that it was the other side of Ama's face. He also noted the colourful headscarf that Ama wore draped over her affected side, obscuring it completely.

Looked at from this vantage point, Ama looked perfectly normal. But he'd seen the pictures—NOMA had ravaged the right side of her face, leaving her terribly disfigured.

A chequerboard sat between them and they were engrossed in a lively game. A third person—a young woman with skin more of a mocha colouring—sat on a chair beside the bed, also involved, switching between English and an unfamiliar language and laughing as Ama made a run of the board.

'Ama, you are getting much too good at this,' Olivia said, and laughed that full throaty laugh again.

The woman in the chair spoke to Ama in what he presumed was her own language and the girl giggled, her eyes sparkling in absolute delight.

Ethan was struck by how intimate the cosy little circle appeared. They all seemed very comfortable in each other's company. Ama's mother was looking at Olivia as if she was some kind of saint and Ama was smiling so big at Olivia, her eyes sparkling so brightly, it was like the sun shining.

Olivia passed over a red chequer piece to Ama and Ama laughed again, the whites of her eyes flashing as she held on to Olivia's hand for long moments before accepting the spoils and crowning her victorious piece.

Ama said something in her own tongue and the woman Ethan assumed was the translator said, 'Ama thinks she's winning.'

Olivia laughed again, and even with the distance between them, it whispered against his skin.

'Oh, does she, now?' Olivia said with mock indignation. 'We'll see how easy it is for her to win when I'm tickling her,' she announced, raising her hands and wiggling her fingers in Ama's direction before launching a tickle attack on a giggling, squealing Ama.

The chequerboard was upended, but nobody seemed to mind as general pandemonium ensued.

Ethan was struck by the genuine connection between Olivia and Ama and her mother. There was nothing forced or stilted—just an easy familiarity. But there was also an unspoken trust in their byplay, and Ethan knew how hard Olivia would have had to work to gain that trust. To take them out of their own country, away from everything they knew and trusted, and bring them to a strange place with strange people and strange customs.

But most of all it was just a joy to see the return of

the Olivia he'd once known. Last night she'd fluctuated from reserved to distant to tense, and this morning she'd been polite and professional. Hell, even when she'd been angry with him there'd been an aloofness that he'd never seen in her before.

But this was the Olivia of old. The one who got way too close to her patients. Who'd spend time at the end of a very long intern shift playing games or reading books to the kids in her charge, or stopping in at the shop to buy a favourite snack or a goofy toy for a child in her care.

Their bosses had frowned upon it, and he had teased her about it endlessly, but it was what made Olivia so good at what she did—she wasn't just their doctor, she was their friend.

That had, of course, led to tears on occasions. Every death or negative outcome she'd taken to heart. She'd considered herself a partner in a patient's journey and she'd felt it deeply when things went wrong.

Many a time he'd been a shoulder for her to cry on.

And he'd been worried last night, when she'd looked at him with such reserve and distance, that the old Olivia was gone forever. That maybe he'd been responsible for killing her off.

He was glad to see he hadn't.

She might have developed a harder shell, but it was good to know that she still had her gooey centre. It wasn't a particularly smart trait, or conducive to longevity in the profession, but as someone who also became a little too invested in the lives of the people he operated on Ethan recognised, on a subliminal level, that Olivia Fairchild was a kindred spirit.

It was why he'd chosen the army and humanitarian work over the more lucrative field of cosmetic surgery, unlike his father.

Because people mattered.

Ethan took a steadying breath and walked into the room. 'This looks like fun,' he said.

Olivia started at the sound of his voice and Ama, who took her cues in this strange new world from Olivia, shrank into her mother's arms, quickly pulling the head-scarf covering the right side of her face closer, patting it, checking its position.

'Ethan,' Olivia said, scrambling off the bed. 'I thought you weren't going to be here until after lunch.' She turned quickly to Ama and smiled at the girl, who was still a bundle of nerves. 'It's okay,' she assured her, and Dali, the interpreter, repeated the assurances to Ama and her mother in their own language. 'This is the doctor I was telling you about. Dr Ethan.'

Ethan smiled as Ama peeked out at him from her mother's shoulder. 'Very pleased to meet you, Ama,' he said, bowing slightly.

The girl's gaze darted to Olivia, and Olivia nodded and smiled again. She moved closer to Ethan, conscious of his tall breadth in her peripheral vision, trying to divorce herself from the sexual pull of him as she placed her hand on his forearm. 'We are old friends,' she said to Ama. 'We did our training together, here at this hospital.'

Ethan nodded. 'We sure did. Olivia used to tell us stories about having a pet kangaroo at home in Australia.'

That elicited a small smile from Ama and Olivia gave Ethan a grateful squeeze on the arm before she dropped her hand. Ethan's bedside manner had always been fantastic, but it had been a long time since she'd been familiar with his doctoring skills. A lot of surgeons tended not to be very good with their people skills.

Olivia introduced Ethan to Dali and to Ril, Ama's mother. He was at his charming best, but she was still nervous as to how he was going to go forward with Ama. Olivia knew he needed to see her face, but she also knew he needed to approach it very carefully.

'You like chequers?' Ethan said to Ama.

She gave a slight nod after Dali had translated.

'Do you mind if I watch while you and Olivia play?'

Ama looked at her mother, as the interpreter translated, and then at Olivia, who smiled. Very slightly she nodded her head.

'Excellent,' he said, smiling down at Ama.

Ethan drew up a chair opposite Dali on the same side of the bed. It was the side of Ama's defect and he was hoping that she'd become engrossed enough in the game to drop the fabric so he could get a good look. He was going to need a much closer examination before he operated, but for today he had to build some trust and he was happy to stay hands-off.

Two hours later Ethan knew a lot more than any photo could tell him about Ama's defect. Sure enough the girl had forgotten about trying to shield her face from him after about fifteen minutes, and he'd been able to get a much more thorough feel for the mechanics of what he was dealing with as the scarf slackened.

The extent of the destruction of her facial tissue and the functional impairment of her mouth and jaw were clinically challenging. He was going to need extensive imaging, but he was sure it was going to involve maxilla and palate losses as well.

It was shocking to look at. Ama essentially had a huge hole in the right side of her face, exposing the inside of her mouth, her jaw and nasal cavity. It was all the more shocking because it was a perfectly treatable condition caught early enough.

He knew from Olivia's briefing and studying Ama's chart that her NOMA had started the way it always did— with a simple mouth ulcer when she'd been four years old. But poor nutrition and poor oral hygiene had led to the ulcer developing quickly into full-blown NOMA. Her cheek had begun to swell and over the course of a few days it had developed blackish furrows as the gangrene set in. It had festered over weeks, forming horrible scabs. When the scabs had finally fallen away, she'd had a gaping hole in her face.

But Ama was one of the lucky ones—she'd survived. Ninety per cent of sufferers—usually children—didn't.

Just looking at Ama as she played chequers with Olivia swamped Ethan with a sense of hopelessness. NOMA *was* the face of poverty in poor, underdeveloped countries. And young children living in such extreme conditions where malnutrition was rife were at the highest risk.

He glanced at Olivia. The jacket she'd worn this morning to the debrief had long been discarded and her pencil skirt had rucked up her thighs slightly as she sat on the bed with her legs tucked up to one side. Her long-sleeved blouse fell softly against her breasts and was rolled up to the elbows. The top three buttons, which had been primly fastened all the way to the collar this morning, were now undone and gaping occasionally to reveal flashes of cleavage.

She looked perfectly at home and one hundred per cent unaffected by Ama's facial deformity as she played chequers. As if Ama was just another of her patients. But he knew Olivia's gooey centre well, and he knew she would be distressed by what this little girl had been through and the suffering she must face on a daily basis.

She glanced at him then and it was confirmed. Her gaze was a melted puddle of warm chocolate and it was begging him for help. To *do* something. To *fix* it.

And in that moment he'd have fixed it with his own bare hands if it had been within his power.

Instead he smiled at her and nodded.

He stood and smiled down at Ama and her mother. 'I'm going to get some tests organised,' he said, nodding reassuringly. 'They'll do them after lunch and Olivia will be with you the whole time, right?' he said, glancing at Olivia who had scrambled off the bed and was standing next to him.

'Right,' Olivia said, also smiling and nodding at Ama. 'I'm just going outside with Ethan for a moment,' she said. 'I won't be long.' She narrowed her eyes and wagged her finger playfully at Ama. 'Don't you cheat.'

Ama grinned.

Olivia was conscious of Ethan's big silent presence by her side as they walked out together. It was just like the old days—walking side by side through the Lighthouse.

Complete with the same old awareness. That delicious little frisson.

Which was pointless and useless and completely inappropriate!

'Thank you,' she said as they stepped into the corridor. 'You were very good with her.'

Ethan brushed off the compliment with a shrug. 'I think she'll be happy with the result.'

Ama was always going to have scarring and obvious skin grafting all her life, but he was confident they could close her oral and nasal cavities so she could swallow and eat properly and look more or less like other girls of her age.

Olivia smiled at him. 'I know she will.'

Ethan sucked in a breath at her full-wattage smile. It was the first one she'd given him in over a decade and he'd forgotten how deadly they were. 'I'll get the X-rays and MRI organised for this afternoon,' he said briskly, trying to dispel the strange tightness in his throat. 'We'll also need a full battery of blood tests.'

She put her hand on his arm as she'd done earlier. 'Again. Thank you. Will you ring me when you have the results?'

The fact that he hadn't yet apologised to her weighed on his conscience as she looked at him as if he'd discovered a cure for cancer. But as they stepped aside to let an orderly with a wheelchair pass Ethan knew that a hospital corridor wasn't the best place for it either.

'How about we go to Drake's for dinner and we can discuss it further there? I can bring my laptop and the images on a stick.'

Olivia blinked. 'Drake's is still around?' They'd been regulars at the bar during their time at the Lighthouse.

Ethan nodded. 'Drake's has been an institution around here for over a hundred years. There'd be a riot at the clinic if they shut down!'

Olivia laughed. Considering how many of Drake's clientele were hospital staff, Ethan was probably right. She hesitated, though. Being back with Ethan amongst so many familiar memories probably wasn't a good thing. Maybe she should try and limit that?

'Come on,' he persisted. 'You want to see the scans, and we've both gotta eat, right?'

Olivia couldn't fault his logic. 'That's true.'

'I'm seeing clients until six tonight, so how about I meet you there about six-thirty?'

She nodded before she changed her mind. 'Okay.'

Ethan waved to Olivia from the booth table he'd claimed when she arrived ten minutes late. He watched her wend her way through the early evening crowd. The cool night air had put some pink into her cheeks, reminding him of strawberries and cream.

He shook his head as the thought lodged in his brain. *Strawberries and cream?* For crying out loud—he'd be writing freaking poetry next!

'Sorry I'm late,' she said as she stopped in front of their booth and stripped her duffle coat and jacket off, revealing the blouse from earlier. His gaze drifted to her cleavage and those three little buttons, still undone.

'No worries,' he said as he forced his eyes upwards. 'I took the liberty of ordering you a glass of wine. You still like to drink Shiraz when it's cold outside?' he asked, indicating the glass of wine.

Olivia blinked at the glass, surprised he'd remembered. She probably shouldn't be—he'd always been a details man. But still, it had been ten years, and given the *true* nature of their previous relationship she was surprised he'd even bothered remembering in the first place.

'Oh, yes—thanks…' she said, settling into the booth opposite, pushing the bitterness aside. It was a long time ago and she was over him and the games he'd played.

Olivia took a sip and noticed the open laptop. 'That the scan?' she asked.

Ethan nodded. 'Yep.'

'Well, show us, then,' she said, placing her glass back

on the table. 'I've been dying to know how fully the NOMA has invaded and the true extent of the damage.'

Ethan looked over the rim of his beer glass at Olivia. The scans were very interesting, and he could only imagine how someone as invested as Olivia would be desperate to pore over them, but first things first.

He shut the laptop lid and took a steadying breath. 'In a moment,' he said. 'There's something I have to say first.'

Olivia glanced at him. His voice was deadly serious and her heart pounded like a gong in her chest. *What the...?*

'I owe you an apology.'

She opened her mouth to say something but Ethan cut her off with a slice of his hand through the air.

'Please, Olivia, I need to get this out.'

He'd been rehearsing it all afternoon and he was grateful that she closed her mouth and let him get on with it.

'I'm very sorry for what happened ten years ago. For my reprehensible behaviour. For the way I used you and hurt you. For involving you in something that I shouldn't have. Basically, I'm sorry for being a total...jerk. There is absolutely no excuse for my behaviour. And I'm not expecting your forgiveness. I don't blame you if you hate me. I just want to be able to clear the air so we can work together. With the budding partnership between Fair Go and the clinic we're going to be seeing each other quite a bit, and I don't want it to be awkward between us. At least not because I haven't apologised, anyway.'

Ethan's heart was pounding when he'd finished and he grabbed his beer for a deep, long swallow as Olivia sat like a stunned mullet in her seat.

CHAPTER FOUR

OLIVIA BLINKED AT the most comprehensive apology she'd ever received. Her fingers tightened around the stem of her wineglass as she was sucked back to the emotional tumult of that time.

He *had* acted reprehensibly. He *had* been a jerk. He'd hurt her. He'd broken her heart. Just…taken it and stomped all over it.

She'd never loved anyone as she'd loved Ethan Hunter.

He'd certainly made her wary of ever letting anyone in again. In fact she'd never really let anyone in since. Sure, she'd dated. She hadn't become some born again virgin. But she'd never given her heart to anyone else. And that was all because of Ethan. Mostly because he'd damaged it so badly, but also because, deep down, she'd measured every other guy against him.

And none of them had measured up.

Yes, the irony that a jerk had been her yardstick was not lost on her. But even though his motives for being with her had been grubby, his treatment of her had always been exemplary.

They'd had so much fun—being with him had been the best time of her life.

Ethan couldn't bear it as the silence stretched between

them and she just kept staring at him. What was going on inside her head?

'Olivia?'

Olivia dragged herself back from the past, her gaze focusing on *this* Ethan. The thirty-five-year-old version. He was seeking forgiveness. Seemed to *need* it, if the intensity of his gaze was any kind of indication. Was it purely about Ama and their having to work together or was there a more personal absolution he was seeking?

'I don't hate you,' she said, picking up the glass of wine and taking a sip.

Even when her heart had been haemorrhaging she hadn't hated him.

'Hate implies strong emotion and the truth is I don't feel anything for you, Ethan. Not any more. It was ten years ago. We're different people, a lot has happened, and I've been over you for a long time. But you're right—we do need to work together, so clearing the air is good and I appreciate your *very* comprehensive apology. Thank you.'

Ethan knew he should feel relieved, and he did. But her admission that she felt nothing for him was startling.

Nothing?

Seeing her again had aroused a whole host of feelings. Nostalgia, apprehension, uncertainty. Hope. Worry.

Guilt.

And when she'd touched him last night—need, desire, lust.

It certainly hadn't been *nothing*. After a decade apart and their turbulent history how was *nothing* even possible?

But she was looking at him with such assuredness. The same old Liv, but different. The emotion and the connection he'd witnessed at the hospital earlier, that she'd been known for, were nowhere to be seen.

Well…if that was the way she wanted to play it. She was, after all, the wronged party.

'No,' he said, reaching out to cover her hand with his. 'Thank you.'

Olivia looked down at their joined hands. She'd used to dream that they'd be this amazing his-and-hers medical team—just like her parents. Living and loving and sharing. Growing old together. She'd been such a fool.

And she wouldn't go there again.

She pulled her hand away. 'Don't,' she said.

Ethan frowned at her abrupt withdrawal. 'I'm sorry… I didn't mean… That wasn't…'

'Accepting your apology does not mean that we're going to pick up where we left off, Ethan.'

Ethan quirked an eyebrow. *Whoa.* 'I didn't think it did.'

Olivia didn't care how egotistical she sounded. She needed to put it out there. Ethan was still as handsome as he'd always been. Probably even more so now life and experience had given his good looks a devastating depth.

Not to mention those fascinating shadows in his eyes.

'I know you,' she said. 'I know how it starts. So just don't…'

Ethan blinked. Did she think he was using his apology as a segue into some kind of pass? He knew he didn't exactly hold the moral high ground with her, but her insinuation was pretty damn insulting. 'Well, surely,' he said, withdrawing his hand and wrapping it around his beer, 'for someone who feels *nothing* that won't be an issue.'

Olivia was surprised at the bitterness of his tone. Had she annoyed him by her deliberate choice of words?

Too bad.

She'd been lying about the nothing, of course. Her body had been in a complete jumble for the past twenty-four hours. She *wished* she felt nothing. The way she had after the tears and the anger and the heavy sense of loss had all passed and she'd gone through life on autopilot. *Nothing* felt far preferable to the other stuff. It hurt less.

She'd gone there too, after her parents had been so cruelly snatched away. She'd craved the pain-free bubble of *nothing* back then. And had spent way too long inside it.

'Just putting my cards on the table. You and I aren't going to happen. Not going there. Not going there ever again. *Never, ever.*'

Ethan had an absurd urge to laugh at her emphatic denials. But he didn't think that would be appreciated. 'Are you trying to convince me or yourself?'

Olivia shivered as the low, gravelly note in his voice slid along the muscle fibres deep inside her belly. Their gazes locked for a brief moment and in those seconds she saw the golden flecks in his eyes flare to life as if a match had been struck.

And she felt a corresponding flare in those muscle fibres as they smouldered, then flickered to life.

'Just promise me it won't happen,' she said, desperate as heat spread through her belly. 'Say it out loud. I need to hear you say it.'

Ethan wanted to reach across the table and yank her sexy mouth right on to his. Okay, she didn't want anything to happen between them, and after he'd screwed up so badly last time he owed her that at least.

But, damn—it was all he *could* think about now. *And he despised himself a little bit more.*

'I promise.' And he meant it. He raised his beer glass. 'Here's to *never, ever.*'

Olivia clinked her glass to his, feeling relieved and mollified. 'Good,' she said, taking a decent swallow of Shiraz. 'Now, show me the damn scan.'

They pored over the images for the next half-hour until their meals arrived. They talked about Ama's interesting facial anatomy, forever altered by the gangrenous infection. They talked about the staged repair and the different surgical approaches open to them. About anaesthetic options and the pros and cons of different types of grafting. About the potential complications.

During dinner they discussed timeframes and the team they'd need. They also touched on Ama's long-term recuperation and eventual follow-up. By the time their meals were finished they'd just about talked themselves through every aspect of Ama's care.

Olivia placed her cutlery on her empty plate and checked her watch—almost eight o'clock. If she left now she could be at the hospital before Ama went to sleep.

'You have somewhere to be?' Ethan asked as he drained the dregs of his second beer.

Olivia looked up. 'Sorry…yes… Do you mind? I've been reading some English books to Ama every night. She loves Dr Seuss, although I have no idea how much she understands.'

'I think Dr Seuss transcends language barriers,' Ethan said.

Olivia smiled. 'Yes, I think you might be right. It's just so good seeing her laugh, being a kid, you know?'

Ethan nodded. He'd been in a lot of places where children had to grow up too early. Where going to school

and kicking a ball around weren't options. Where the in-
nocence of childhood was usurped by the harsh realities
of war and poverty.

His mind wandered to Aaliyah. To how she'd de-
spaired about the children too.

So like Olivia in many ways.

'Yeah. I know.' He stood and grabbed his jacket,
shrugging off the memory, refusing to compare. 'Come
on, then, I'll walk with you.'

Olivia stood too. 'It's okay, it's not far. I'll be fine.'

'Liv,' Ethan said, 'I'm not going to let you walk the
streets of London at night by yourself—especially when
the Lighthouse is on my way home.'

Olivia's breath hitched as he reverted to the shortened
version of her name. Did he remember when he'd started
calling her that? Just after they'd first made love?

Had he even realised he'd done it?

'I've walked these streets many a time by myself, and
way later than eight o'clock.' During her year in London
she'd walked, bussed, tubed all over, at all hours of the
day and night.

'Not when I was around, you didn't.'

And it was true. Ethan always had been the perfect
gentleman. Well, except for that one time when he'd
dragged her into an alley on their way to her place and
had his wicked way with her because neither of them had
been able to wait.

She huffed out a little breath, annoyed at her brain
for dusting off that particular memory. 'Fine. Lead on.'

They were out on the street in under a minute. It was
chilly after the warmth of the bar and Olivia buttoned
up her duffle coat, pleased for its impenetrable warmth
as they turned in the direction of the hospital. Unlike the

thick wool of her tights, it *was* keeping out the cold. Her warm breath misted in the air and she set a brisk pace as icy fingers wrapped around her legs.

'So tell me about Fair Go,' Ethan said, leaning heavily on his stick to keep up with her.

Olivia stumbled a little at the unexpected question and felt his steadying hand briefly at her elbow before he removed it. 'I'm sure if you search for it online you'll find all you need to know.'

Ethan didn't care that she didn't want to talk. He needed to. Because all he could think about at the moment was a particularly steamy incident in an alley not far from here, and that wasn't conducive to a platonic walk.

'And why would I do that when I have the charity director at my disposal?'

Olivia shrugged. 'I started it a couple of years ago... I'd just finished my second stint with *Médecins Sans Frontières*—'

'Wait,' Ethan interrupted, placing a hand on her arm and urging her to stop. 'You worked for Doctors Without Borders?'

Olivia drew to a halt. 'Yes,' she said.

She remembered how Ethan had often talked about wanting to take his surgical skills into conflict zones. She had already been marinated in her parents' humanitarian works, and Ethan's fervour had easily infected Olivia. He'd hated—been embarrassed by—his father's lucrative cosmetic surgery clinic when there was so much suffering in the world, and had been determined to make a difference.

She'd hoped they'd do it together. Like her parents had. And then things had ended and she'd thrown herself instead into her parents' work in remote areas of Australia.

But when they'd been lost she'd needed something more. She'd needed to get away.

To be totally absorbed in something other than her own grief.

'What can I say...?' she said, pulling away. 'You inspired me.'

Ethan let her walk on for a bit, the belt on her royal blue coat pulled tight against the cold, emphasising her petite frame. He'd had no idea she'd followed through with their fledgling plans to join the famed international organisation. He'd assumed they'd fallen through when their relationship had ended.

He should have known—she'd always been strong-willed, her petite physicality belying the strength of her character.

'Where did you go?' he asked as he caught her up.

'Africa,' she said, keeping her gaze dead ahead. It was bad enough that he filled up her peripheral vision with all his sexy, haggard broadness.

'And that's where you got the idea for Fair Go?'

Olivia nodded. 'I saw a lot of kids with terrible conditions falling through the cracks because they weren't classed as *emergency* or *life-threatening*. But they did affect the quality of those kids' lives. And why should they have to suffer because they had the misfortune to be born into poverty? Why shouldn't they have the same expectations as kids in the western world?'

Ethan heard the husky note creep into Olivia's voice as they stopped at a red signal and waited to cross the road. 'I agree,' he murmured.

The Hunter Clinic was working with charities all over the world, trying to redress that balance.

'There are a lot of charity and aid organisations out

there that have a particular focus on certain regions or diseases or conditions or gender. And I get that—I do. There's just not enough charity dollars to go around.'

She turned to face him slightly.

'But it doesn't make it *fair*,' she said. 'I want to be able to give the children who fall through the cracks a chance at a better life too. They deserve a fair go too.'

Ethan nodded. Of course they did. So Olivia Fairchild was going to see to it. Good on her.

'I'm assuming your parents are the main benefactors?' he asked. 'They must be very proud of you.'

Like himself, Olivia came from a wealthy background. It had been one of the many things they'd had in common. Except Olivia's parents had turned their backs on lucrative practices and devoted their time to isolated communities as flying doctors.

Olivia was grateful that the light changed just then and they were able to cross the street as quick, hot tears welled in her eyes. She blinked them back. It wasn't Ethan's fault that he didn't know about her parents' tragic demise. She hadn't told him, and it was hardly as if their deaths had made international headlines.

She swallowed the lump in her throat. 'Yes. I got the money from my parents,' she said. 'And I have some good people I trust looking after the financial side of things.'

Ethan nodded. He knew how important it was to have trustworthy people involved in things like this. 'Well, Ama is very lucky to have someone looking out for her and willing to give *her* a fair go.'

Olivia suppressed a snort. He had no idea. Ama might be happy and bright now, but that was not how she'd been the day she'd first met the girl and her mother on a dirt street.

Ethan glanced at Olivia. Her brow was furrowed. 'You're frowning,' he said, shoving his hands in his pockets. 'Are you worried about Ama? Don't be. Everything's going to work out fine. Trust me.' He grinned as her frown continued. 'I'm a surgeon. And I'm *good*.'

Olivia looked up at him, his chiselled features filling her vision. His smile sucked the breath from her lungs. *Oh, he was good, all right.* They were probably a metre apart but he felt much closer—Ethan and his indomitable confidence had always managed to fill up the space between them.

She *was* worried about Ama. But not about the procedure or his ability to perform it. She had one hundred per cent faith in Ethan's capabilities and she knew Ama would be a very different girl by the time her multiple surgeries were done.

'I know,' she said. 'It's just…afterwards I'm worried about. When she heads back home again. You and I both know she's still not going to look like she did before NOMA, and that makes her…vulnerable.'

Ethan slowed a little. 'You're worried she'll still be ostracised?'

Olivia slowed too. 'Yes. And I'm worried that her uncle will still force her into marriage.'

Ethan blinked. 'What? She's *nine*, Olivia,' he snorted.

'That wasn't stopping him the day I found her.'

Ethan felt a cold fist close around his heart as Olivia's words sunk in. 'I beg your pardon?'

Olivia shuddered, thinking back to the horrible altercation she'd witnessed. She vividly recalled the taste of vomit in her mouth when the interpreter had finally sorted out what was happening.

'The day I found Ama her uncle, who was the head of

her household since Ama's father had died the year before, was giving her away to a man who looked at least forty. She was crying and clinging to her mother, and her mother was crying and begging her brother to reconsider.'

Another rush of emotion filled Olivia's chest. She shook her head against it, tried to push it back, but the memory was still so acute. How could anyone force a *nine*-year-old girl to *marry*? The thought was utterly vile.

Olivia wasn't naive—she knew awful stuff like that happened in places that the world didn't care to know about—but confronting it first-hand had been wrenching. Caught up in the rekindled horror of it, she turned to Ethan.

'You should have seen them,' she said. 'They were… clutching each other in the middle of this…street. It wasn't even a street, really—just this dirt…pathway. They were both so skinny and desperate and…wailing. Ril was wailing and holding on tight as this…disgusting old man with gnarled hands and three yellow teeth pulled at Ama's arm.'

Olivia halted, oblivious to the people walking behind her, caught up for a moment in the heat and utter despair that symbolised so much of Africa for her. It had been horrible. The consequences for Ama had she not intervened were still too much for her to bear.

Ethan gently took her elbow, moving her out of the path of other pedestrians who were bustling around them.

'It was terrible, Ethan,' she said, only vaguely aware that they were standing on the first step of the very grand entrance to one of the many clinics that populated the area. The Lighthouse was only two blocks away now.

'It's okay,' he murmured. The distress on Olivia's face squeezed his gut tight and he wanted to make it better.

Olivia shook her head. 'No, it's not,' she said.

'No,' he agreed. 'I'm sorry. It's not.'

She looked up at him. Muted light shone through the glass side panels of the grand doorway and fell over the planes and angles of his face. 'I couldn't leave her,' she said. 'I couldn't…'

Ethan nodded. 'Of course not.' His hand was still at her elbow and he gave it a gentle squeeze. 'What did you do?'

She shrugged helplessly. 'I gave him all the money I had on me and told him to get lost. And then I didn't let her out of my sight.'

Ethan smiled down at her. The light from inside lit her face and her eyes glittered with indignation. She looked fierce. Like a mother bear. He could just imagine her, furious and fearless, defending a child, standing up to a man in a hugely patriarchal society. Telling him to get lost.

'That was brave,' he murmured.

The compliment slid into all the places Olivia had forgotten about. Places that Ethan had always kept alive and humming. They were standing close on the step, closer than when they'd been walking, and she could smell the beer on his breath and the spice of his cologne.

'Dali called it stupid.'

Ethan chuckled. 'Well, it was probably a little of that as well.'

His low, sexy laugh was just the right timbre to produce an army of goose bumps and a funny little pull somewhere in the vicinity of her belly button. 'I was scared witless,' she admitted. 'But…what else could I do?'

Even now the thought of Ama's fate had Olivia just walked away was too distressing to think about.

Ethan shook his head. Her gaze was so raw and her question so earnest. 'You're a good woman, Olivia Fairchild. You always were.'

And he meant it. It buzzed through his veins, echoed around his head and filled up his chest. He was proud just to know her, to have a chance to know her again, and before he could stop himself he'd stepped in close, slid his hands onto her waist and dropped his mouth to hers.

And it felt good as she opened to him. Easy and sexy and right. Just as it always had. Her lips soft, her taste and her scent stirring old memories, urging him to go deeper, to pull her closer.

And he did.

Olivia temporarily lost her way as the taste and the touch and the smell of him wiped out all her common sense. It was as if she'd been transported back to their first kiss a decade ago. A kiss that had started out as a crazy, tired comfort thing, after a long, harrowing night shift together, and quickly became something quite different.

Something that had made absolute sense.

She slid her palms up the front of his jacket, smoothing and sculpting the muscles she knew lay beneath, clutching at his lapels as she tried to recapture that long-ago crazy/sane moment to take her away from the dirt and heat and poverty of Africa.

The tragedy of Ama and girls just like her.

The tragedy of her parents.

The tragedy of them.

Ethan groaned as Olivia deepened the kiss, opening her mouth wider, her tongue hot, dancing a wild tango with his.

'Liv…' His hands slid down to cup her bottom as his groin caught fire.

Olivia protested against his mouth as common sense wrenched her away from him.

One word.

Just one word and he'd yanked her back to reality.

'Damn it!' She pushed on his chest, stepping back, stepping out of his arms, sucking in air, breathing hard.

What was she doing? What the hell was she doing? Kissing Ethan again. Ethan, who was even more messed-up than he'd been a decade ago. Ethan with the shadows in his eyes.

Ethan whom she had to work with.

'You promised,' she hissed at him.

Ethan's head reeled from the abrupt disconnect. His head buzzed with the sexual high even as shame and guilt flooded over the top, smothering it very effectively.

He hadn't betrayed Aaliyah's memory in a year.

And here he was, kissing an ex-girlfriend on a public street like some grubby teenage boy.

Olivia glared at him, mad at herself but madder still at him. She'd be a bloody fool to get involved with Ethan Hunter again.

She pushed him hard in the chest. 'You promised *never, ever,*' she accused. 'We toasted it!'

'I'm…sorry,' he said, trying to pull himself together for Olivia as he battled his own demons. 'I…got carried away.'

Olivia knew the feeling.

But she was too angry to see his side right now. Too angry with herself. One touch of his lips and her resolve just disappeared.

She had to get away. She had to see Ama, for God's

sake. It was the whole reason they were out on the street together in the first place. Not for some public necking session.

'I have to get to the hospital,' she said tersely.

Ethan nodded. 'Of course. I'll see you in the morning,' he said, knowing the Lighthouse was close enough now for her to get there without his company.

But it didn't stop him watching her as she hurried away without a backward glance.

CHAPTER FIVE

By the time he entered his apartment ten minutes later Ethan had called himself every name under the sun. He'd kissed Olivia after expressly promising not to start anything. And even though she'd kissed him back it was unforgivable.

It seemed he was destined to behave unforgivably around Olivia.

And what about his vows to Aaliyah? Forgotten in one mad moment. What kind of a man did that make him?

Guilt chewed at his gut as he splashed whisky into a glass. Guilt over kissing Olivia. For *wanting* to kiss Olivia. For forgetting about the woman he'd loved—the woman he'd left behind in a Godforsaken part of the world, whom he'd promised he'd be back for.

Another broken promise.

Ethan's brain seethed and boiled like molten lava in a volcanic cauldron as he stared morosely into the depths of the amber liquid in the crystal tumbler. How could he have betrayed the memory of Aaliyah? Yes, she was gone. She was dead and he was alive. But it had only been a year.

One lousy year.

How could he have forgotten his promise to her the

day he'd asked her to marry him? That he would love her only, be faithful to her always?

And what about the silent pledge he'd taken the day he'd woken up in the hospital to the news of Aaliyah's death? That he was done with love. Done with relationships.

Done with emotion. With feeling. With passion.

Those things had died with Aaliyah and he'd literally felt the bands of cold steel wrapping around his heart as he'd sworn never to get involved again, never to love again. Hell, he'd welcomed them. They and the scars on his legs were his reminder that the women he loved tended to leave him.

His mother. Aaliyah.

He'd resigned himself to a solo life. Was he happy? No. But how could he be after what had happened to him? And where had happiness got him anyway? He was... content. He and Leo were in a good place, he was going to be an uncle soon, and he was doing good work. Important work that meant something to him.

And now Olivia had walked back into his life.

Ethan swirled the whisky in the glass. *Damn her.* Damn her for getting too close. Again. For making him remember what it felt like to be a man.

To want a woman. To want to feel her, taste her.

He hadn't needed that in his life. And he sure as hell hadn't missed it. The desire for physical affection had been non-existent.

Couldn't she just have stayed away? Left him with his ghosts and demons? He'd grown used to them for company and he'd been just fine here in his shell.

And yet with one look and that gut-wrenching shimmer of emotion in her expressive gaze he'd wanted more.

Just like that she'd wormed her way under his skin—just like ten years ago, when he'd only been supposed to be using her to throw in Leo's face but she'd come to mean more.

Even now he couldn't get her out of his head. Couldn't stop replaying their kiss over and over. He could still taste her, feel the curve of her waist embedded into his palm. Feel the tension in his belly and the tightness in his groin.

He shut his eyes, desperately trying to recall Aaliyah. Her bronzed skin, her midnight eyes, her calming touch. But all he saw was Olivia.

A surge of anger and frustration welled in his chest as Ethan fought another battle. The glass felt good in his hand—heavy. Reeking of money and class. As did the whisky. And he wanted nothing more than to knock it back. Have a second. A third. But Olivia was still in his head. As was her taunt from last night. Packing a bigger punch than it had already.

'I'm sure that's exactly how your father started out.'

Damn it!

He shook his head, letting the rage bubble up and out. Swinging wildly around, he threw the heavy crystal glass at the opposite wall. The crash was loud, as was the inevitable harsh shatter as shards of glass and liquid slid down the wall.

Ethan stood for long moments just staring at the mess, his heart pounding in his chest. He didn't feel any better. He still wanted a drink. He still wanted Olivia.

Damn it!

He stalked to the nearby gym set-up that Lizzie had organised for him back when she'd been his home visit nurse. She'd been determined not to just dress his wounds and check he was taking his medication but to bully him into doing his physio so he could strengthen his legs and stop brooding inside the house.

Ethan sat at the leg press machine. And took out his frustrations on it.

Olivia knew it was her turn to apologise this morning. After tossing and turning through another sleepless night she knew she was as much to blame for the kiss as Ethan.

No, she hadn't made the first move. But she hadn't immediately pushed him away either. She hadn't told him no or slapped his face. In fact she'd opened her mouth wider, invited him in, stepped in nearer, put her hands on him. For God's sake, she'd grabbed hold of his lapels and dragged him closer!

She might not have asked for it but she'd definitely encouraged its continuation. So *she* would be the one saying sorry, as soon as he walked through Ama's door this morning.

Thankfully he didn't make her wait too long, showing up at the room at eight-thirty in a set of blue Theatre scrubs.

And for a moment Olivia lost her breath.

She'd forgotten how damn good the man looked in blue. It was such a girly, sky-blue too, and yet somehow he oozed masculinity. Maybe it was the way he filled them out. The breadth of his shoulders, the narrowness of his hips… Or maybe it was the rough-looking salt and pepper whiskers at his jaw.

He shot her a hesitant smile and a quick nod before he turned his attention to Ama and her mother. She was watching something loud and animated on the overhead television, scarf firmly in place. There was no way she could possibly follow the plot—it didn't even make a whole lot of sense in English—but she seemed utterly engrossed nonetheless, even bursting out laughing occasionally.

Olivia watched as he pulled up a chair by Ama's bed and sat down facing the television, also taking in the cartoon.

'What's that dog doing?' he asked Ama, and Dali dutifully interpreted.

They chatted back and forth through Dali about the television show, as if he had all the time in the world instead of a Theatre list that probably started in thirty minutes. When an ad break came he took advantage, and Olivia listened as he explained to Ril and Ama, in clear simple terms, what the tests had shown and how they were going to proceed. It was pretty much an abbreviated layman's version of what she and Ethan had talked about last night in the bar.

Before they'd ruined the evening by letting their past rear its ugly head.

'I'm putting a team together now and we're going to do the first surgery on Wednesday next week,' he said, and waited for Dali to translate. 'The second one probably three or four weeks later.'

Ril, who was sitting on the bed next to her daughter, nodded and asked a question.

'Ril would like to know if Olivia will be one of the surgeons,' Dali said.

'Absolutely,' Olivia piped up. 'Let him just try and stop me!'

There was a lightness to her tone, but Ethan heard the undercurrent loud and clear. Did she think he'd try and block her after what had happened between them last night? He knew how much Olivia wanted to be involved—he would never do that.

He turned to reassure her. 'Of course Olivia will be there,' he said, smiling at her before turning back to Ama. 'I seem to remember she was an excellent surgeon and I have every faith she's only got better.'

Olivia, who'd been nervous of Ethan's answer, relaxed. 'I have,' she said with a smile for Ama's benefit.

She'd assured Ama she would be there with her the whole time, and even if Ama was asleep and not aware of her being there Olivia intended to honour her promise.

The questions went back and forth for a while longer and Olivia was impressed that Ethan was prepared to sit and answer every one—not hurrying, just being thorough, which was an exercise in patience when the whole process took twice as long with an interpreter.

When the questions seemed exhausted Ethan looked at the little girl and hoped he'd won her trust enough for his next request. He was conscious of what Olivia had told him last night—conscious that Ama's trust of men, particularly those in authority, must be very shaky.

But he really did need to examine the operative area a little more closely. He'd been careful not to leap into that too early, but he wanted to do some computer modelling over the weekend so it was important to be able to assess the current state of the oral cavity, the health of the mucosa and gums—something an MRI couldn't tell him.

He turned back to face Olivia. He needed her help now. 'I was hoping that Ama might let me have a look inside her mouth now?' he said. He looked at Ama. 'What do you say?'

Olivia took her cue as Dali spoke to Ama. She moved to the opposite side of the bed from Ethan, perched herself on the mattress and took Ama's hand with an encouraging smile for both her and her mother.

'Ethan's going to use a special light, like I was telling you,' Olivia said, 'to have a look inside your mouth so he gets the operation right.'

Ama started to look apprehensive and Olivia gave her hand a squeeze. 'It's okay. It won't hurt, and Mum and I and Dali will all be right here with you.'

Ama looked from Ethan to Olivia then back again, in that solemn way of hers with her big brown eyes. That look always broke Olivia's heart. Ama had eyes that had already seen too much heartache and suffering for one so young.

'See?' Ethan said, pulling a small pen torch out of his pocket and flicking it on, placing it in Ama's hand for her to get a feel for its harmlessness.

Ama looked down at the instrument. She turned it over in her hands and then turned it so the light shone directly in her eyes. She squinted and pulled the light away. She turned to look at her mother, then back at the torch, shining it in her face again. This time she squinted and gave a nervous giggle.

'This is what you'll look like,' Ethan said, taking the torch out of her hand, opening his mouth, placing the lit end against his cheek and then closing it again. His cheek glowed an eerie red and he waggled his eyebrows at her.

This time Ama laughed. As did Ril and Dali. Olivia's throat tightened at his ease with Ama, and for a moment she was transported back to the old days, when the torch-in-the-mouth thing had been one of their favourite games to play with the kids at the Lighthouse.

His bedside manner had always been second to none.

'See?' he said pulling it out, then wiping it over with an antiseptic wipe. 'It doesn't hurt at all.'

Ama pointed to Olivia and said something in her own language. Neither of them needed an interpreter to understand her meaning.

Olivia huffed out an exaggerated sigh, rolling her eyes as she held out her hand for the torch. 'If you insist,' she griped good-naturedly.

Ethan winked at her as he placed it in her open palm. His fingers brushed lightly against her and a little spark of heat ran up her arm. She glanced at him and wondered if he felt it too, but he was smiling at Ama.

Olivia flicked the torch on and popped it in her mouth. The acrid taste of antiseptic was bitter on her tongue but she ignored it, pushing the light into the mucosa of her cheek and closing her mouth around her. Her cheek dutifully glowed red and Ama laughed louder this time.

'Dali. Dali,' Ama said in her guttural accent, and Ethan laughed knowing there was going to be no quick way of doing this as both Dali and then Ril were also subjected to the trick, the torch being cleaned in between.

Consequently, when it came to the examination Ama submitted happily. Ethan was pleased to note that the oral mucosa looked relatively healthy and he took a few seconds to assess and familiarise himself with some of the landmarks he'd noted in the MRI.

But then the fun part came, when Olivia found a mirror and they spent ages flashing the light on and off inside Ama's unaffected cheek. Every time her cheek glowed red she laughed as if it was the funniest thing she'd ever seen. It was sobering to think that, sadly, in Ama's case it probably was.

'Okay, okay.' Ethan smiled. 'I've got to go but I'll be

in to see you…' he waggled his fingers at Ama and the girl giggled '…every day.'

Ama reluctantly surrendered the torch, holding it out to him, but Ethan shook his head. 'It's a gift for you. Enjoy.'

Ama's eyes widened as Dali relayed the message and Olivia felt a wave of goose bumps march over her skin as Ama hugged it to her chest.

Olivia followed Ethan out through the door as he departed. She wanted to get the apology off her chest straight away. A bit like he had last night.

'Thanks so much for that,' she said as they both watched Ama from the doorway, smiling as she flicked the light on and off and shone it on everything. 'Anyone would think you just gave her the sun.'

Ethan shrugged. Olivia was wearing a pair of snug jeans again today, and a fine woollen sweater that fell nicely against all the flesh beneath. It wasn't helping his resolve to keep his hands off. He'd thought about his re-kindling sexual attraction to her a lot last night, and probably limiting their alone time together was wise.

'Plenty more where that came from,' he said.

Olivia nodded. She knew that drug reps alone kept doctors endlessly supplied with such knick-knacks. 'Well, you made her day.'

Hell, given where Ama came from, he'd probably made her entire life! She doubted the girl had ever received too many gifts of such a magical calibre.

Ethan cleared his throat as they both watched Ama continue to play with her new toy. 'About last night—'

'Oh, no,' Olivia said, quickly cutting him off as she turned to face him. 'Let me.'

Ethan eyed her warily. 'Let you what?'

'Apologise,' she said.

Ethan folded his arms. 'Liv...*I* was the one who kissed *you*, remember? After I'd just promised I wouldn't go there.'

Olivia shook her head, trying to shrug off the way he said her name and how it heated all the old familiar places. Unfortunately the way the fabric of his scrubs pulled around his shoulders and biceps didn't help with the heat problem.

With her heart already fluttering, and her cheeks already flushed at the delicate subject matter, heat was the last thing she needed.

The memory of the kiss sat between them like a big guilty secret, and she'd rather crawl over an acre of glass than have to discuss the way they'd erred last night—like a couple of kids sent to the naughty corner by their parents to talk over their behaviour. She was a grown woman and it was an embarrassing discussion to be having.

But she couldn't let him take the fall for it either.

She needed to own her part in it.

'Yes, I know,' she said. 'But I didn't exactly stop you. I was as much to blame. Probably even more so if you consider my *never, ever* carry-on at the bar. I should have pulled back straight away. I should have...slapped your face,' she said, trying to make a joke to ease the awkwardness of the situation.

Much to her relief, Ethan eked out a half-smile. 'It's fine,' he dismissed. 'How about we both take equal responsibility and agree that being alone together is probably something we should avoid?'

Olivia let out a breath she hadn't been aware she was holding. She returned his half-smile with one of her own. 'That sounds like a good plan.'

Ethan nodded. 'Okay, then.'

'So… I take it I'm still okay to scrub in on some of your surgeries, though? I'm really keen to do what I can while I'm here, and now Ama and her mother are settled they're probably sick of the sight of me.'

Ethan grunted. He doubted that. Ama and Ril's faces lit up like a city skyline whenever Olivia entered the room. Given what she'd done for them, he didn't blame them.

He remembered a time when she'd made him light up too. When he'd felt more for her than he'd ever anticipated.

But he had to admit to being curious about how Olivia had developed as a surgeon. And they could always do with more help.

The clinic's humanitarian programme ran on a tight budget—it had to when billing charities was involved. Having a third surgeon in an op was sometimes necessary—as it would be with Ama and other big cases—but usually not.

It was certainly not a luxury they could afford.

And Ethan didn't believe in wasting money—too much of that went on in charity circles as it was. The Hunter Clinic was opulent and wealthy, and the programme was lucky to have the free use of it and all its associated services—including the pro bono time of any of its surgeons.

But the charities involved paid for all the extra stuff that the Hunter Clinic couldn't provide—including any outside surgeons—and Ethan didn't believe in running up their bills like that unless it was completely necessary.

But Olivia was free. And a free surgeon was a gift he wasn't about to knock back.

'I have a big burn contracture release tomorrow. I could use an extra pair of hands with it.'

A little trill of excitement ran through Olivia at the thought of being back at the table again. It had been a few months since she'd picked up a scalpel and she'd missed it.

'Sounds great.'

Ethan nodded. 'I'll be able to introduce you to some of the team that will be working on Ama's op next week as well. Kara Stephens is helping me out tomorrow. She's a junior surgeon—another Aussie who's a real go-getter and has wanted in on Ama's surgery ever since she heard the first whisper about it. And Jock McNamara is the anaesthetist on my list in the morning and I want him for Ama's surgery. He does a lot of anaesthetics for the facio-maxillary ops and really knows his stuff.'

'It'll be great to meet some of the team,' Olivia enthused.

'Good,' Ethan said. 'List starts at eight-thirty at Princess Catherine's.'

'I'll be there.'

There was an awkward moment when they both paused, waiting for the other to say something and then both realising simultaneously that the silence was growing.

'Right, then…' Ethan said. 'See you tomorrow, Liv.'

Olivia felt the emotional whammy again of what had been a very intimate connection between them. Liv had been the name he'd called her behind closed doors. The name he'd chanted in her ear as he moved deep inside her. The named he'd cried out as he came.

She couldn't be Olivia Fairchild if he reverted to Liv all the time. Olivia was a capable paediatric reconstructive surgeon. Olivia was a compassionate doctor who had put her skills and her heart on the line in Africa. Olivia was the director of Fair Go.

Liv was Ethan's friend. His confidante. His lover.

Liv was the woman who knew the depths of his pain and anger.

Liv was the woman who had loved him.

'Ethan.'

Her quiet call stopped him in his tracks and Ethan turned to face her. She hadn't moved from the spot in the hallway where he'd left her. 'Yeah?'

'Please don't call me Liv…' she murmured.

He was tall and dark and handsome and she wanted to run straight into his arms. Being here, in this hospital with him, stirred too many memories. Unfortunately none of the bad ones. None of the things that had broken her.

'It's too…hard…it's too…familiar.'

Ethan nodded slowly. A heat unfurled inside his gut and travelled south. He hadn't even realised he'd said it. The name—the endearment—had come from somewhere way back in the past. From memories rich with laughter. And spoiled by the callousness of his youth.

If he was going to cling to Aaliyah, to the welcome familiarity of his grief and guilt, then Liv *could not* exist.

'I'm sorry,' he said, rubbing the back of his neck. 'I didn't realise…'

Olivia nodded. 'I know.'

Ethan regarded her for a moment or two. 'I don't want this any more than you do, Olivia. I can't.'

She could tell from the dullness of his eyes that he was telling the truth. That his body was betraying him as much as hers was betraying her.

Remember that, stupid foolish heart—he doesn't want this. Neither do you.

'I know,' she said again.

They didn't say anything for a moment, and then Ethan said, 'See you in the morning,' and turned away.

Olivia watched him go, acutely aware of the contrast between a happy Ama to one side of her and the stoic set of Ethan's receding back to the other.

His choice of words intrigued her. *I can't.* 'Can't' implied more than a conflict of choice. 'Can't' implied something out of his control. Had he meant that? Or had it just been a slip of the tongue?

And if he had meant it, what exactly *did* it mean? Did it mean that he actually wasn't able to? Wasn't capable? Emotionally? Or had something happened to him physically on one of his tours? Maybe his injuries were more extensive than just his legs?

Could 'can't' mean that he wasn't able to perform sexually any more?

And why on earth would he think any woman worth her salt would give a damn about it?

Olivia gave herself a mental shake. What did it matter? She wasn't here to get involved in his life. To commiserate about any long-term effects of his war wounds or to kiss him better.

She was here for Fair Go. She was here for Ama.

And Ama was just one of the many kids she planned to bring to the UK for surgery. Several had already benefited, thanks to Fair Go and the generosity of the Hunter Clinic.

And that was what she needed to concentrate on.

Running a charity was a big freaking deal, involving serious money and financial responsibility, and she couldn't afford to drop the ball because some guy from a million years ago—who had, *by the way*, ground her heart into the dirt—looked at her with shadows in his eyes and called her Liv.

Ethan Hunter was a big boy who'd had his chance with her and blown it.

She wasn't his *Liv* any longer.

CHAPTER SIX

ETHAN WAS SCRUBBING up at the sinks in the scrub room the next morning when Olivia bustled through the door.

'God, I'm so sorry,' she said, barely acknowledging him as she pulled up beside him and reached over to remove a mask out of the nearby box, tying it on in record time. 'I underestimated the time it would take me to get here, and the streets…'

She shook her head as she wrenched off her opal ring and shoved it into the pocket of her scrub trousers.

'I don't remember them being this busy ten years ago.'

She opened a sterile packaged scrub brush and flicked on the taps, wetting her arms from the fingertips to the elbows. She turned to look at him as her right hand attacked the nails on her left hand with the brush. She knew the scrub routine back to front and could do it blindfolded.

'When did it get so busy?'

Ethan blinked. Olivia had always been a chatter. Her ability to fill up a silence or engage a total stranger with her intelligent observations on any subject was one of the things that had drawn them together in the first place. She'd always blamed it on her single child status, remarking that chatter had been her defence against loneliness.

Certainly their stilted, awkward conversations over the past few days had been well out of character.

But she was in fine form this morning.

'It's London,' he said, smiling beneath his mask. 'The streets have always been busy.'

Olivia conceded his point as she turned back to inspect her work. A large window in front of them gave them direct visual access to the Theatre and Olivia noted that the patient was already on the table and was being draped.

She switched the scrubbing brush to the other hand. 'Well, it's a far cry from Africa, that's for sure.'

'True. Not a lot of giraffes in London,' he remarked dryly.

To his surprise she laughed. A laugh that came straight from her soul and ruffled the edges of a hundred different memories. Having her beside him like this again, in scrubs and a mask, her expressive eyes dominating—it was as if they'd never been apart.

It felt comfortable. Like old times.

As it could have always been if he hadn't been so angry and vengeful, so damn determined to lash out.

So he did the only thing he could do to distract himself from futile games of *what if*. He started talking about the case.

'Our patient today, Daleel, is a twenty-eight-year-old Somali man who suffered burns five years ago to over forty per cent of his body. Frankly, how he survived I'll never know, because he only had the most rudimentary of medical care.'

Olivia nodded. It was something she'd seen over and over during her time on the front line and working with various aid organisations in conjunction with Fair Go. Men, women and children who survived against all the odds—like Ama—but who were left permanently and hideously disfigured with absolutely no hope of leading a normal life.

'His right arm is fused to his torso, his right hand is badly contractured, and the severe scarring of his face and neck have led to a contracture that's pulling his whole head into a downward flexion.'

Ethan, at the end of his scrub, held his bent soapy arms out in front of him, hands up, elbows down, and dunked them under the spray tap. He watched as the water sluiced from his fingertips down his arms and dripped suds off his elbows into the sink.

'Think you can handle it?' he asked. The soap was all gone now, and he flicked the tap off with an elbow, then held his arms over the sink a little longer, waiting for his elbows to stop dripping.

'I think so,' Olivia said.

He glanced at her and for a moment their gazes met over the top of their masks and the sense of familiarity returned. Ethan straightened. 'See you in there,' he murmured.

Olivia was conscious of him in her peripheral vision, his sterile arms out in front of him, using his back to push open the swing doors. Then through the glass window she saw him emerge into the Theatre, hands still up and out from his body, striding towards the scrub nurse who was already masked, gowned and gloved and holding out a sterile towel for him to dry his hands.

She continued her scrub, watching Ethan go through the familiar routine of gowning and gloving. She'd never known a man to look so damn good in what was essentially a no-frills dress. The plainness of it just seemed to emphasise the broadness of his chest and the length of his frame. Some women got off on men who wore Armani suits. But she much preferred a man in Theatre garb.

And *damn* if Ethan didn't rock a pair of scrubs.

He chose that moment to glance up from checking the tray of instruments that had been placed near the patient, and their gazes locked as he looked directly at her. Olivia blushed, grateful for the camouflage of the mask. Had he been able to read her less than professional thoughts?

Was he remembering her fetish for a man in scrubs?

Did he remember that time she'd admitted to the erotic dream she'd had about him, involving an examination table, some handcuffs, a pair of scrubs and the very inventive use of a scalpel for removing said scrubs from his otherwise naked body?

They never did get round to enacting that particular fantasy...

The other surgeon—what had Ethan said her name was?—leaned in obliviously, asking him a question, and Olivia quickly dropped her gaze.

What the hell was she doing?

She was here to help give a man his life back. Not to have completely inappropriate, unprofessional and *graphic* thoughts about a highly respected surgeon.

Olivia dunked her arms under the water, watching the soapy residue disappear down the drain, and hoped to God her erotic thoughts would follow.

Ethan entered Drake's the following Tuesday night with a spring in his step—not exactly easy to do with his limp. Tomorrow was Ama's operation and everyone at the clinic was psyched about it. The team was in place and raring to go, Kara could talk about nothing else, and he knew Olivia—although she was more subdued than the excitable junior surgeon—was also eager to get underway.

He knew how close she was to Ama's case.

Maybe she shouldn't be. Maybe it wasn't the professional thing to do. If something went wrong... But some cases just got to you—he knew that.

And nothing was going to go wrong.

The surgery tomorrow was complex, but they all knew what they were doing. And Ama's new life was just around the corner.

'Ethan!'

Ethan looked up to find Leo waving at him across the reasonably full bar. He was at a table with Olivia, Kara, and her fiancé, Declan Underwood—a plastic surgeon who also worked at the Hunter Clinic.

He made his way over to the group. He was supposed to be meeting Leo here for an after-work drink and a general catch-up. There'd been a fairly full surgical list the past five days and Ethan had only been into 200 Harley Street for a few hours on the weekend, to do the computer modelling for Ama's surgery.

But Leo liked to have a meeting once a week to discuss general Hunter Clinic business and Ethan had bunked out on the past two. He appreciated his brother wanting him involved now he was an active partner in the business, but Ethan had no doubt that Leo could and did run the clinic perfectly well without his input.

Hell, the man had dragged the sinking clinic out of the scandalous mire it had sunk into after their father's headline-grabbing drunken scene and subsequent death. He'd worked day and night not only to put it back into the red but into the hearts, minds and chequebooks of every A-lister in Europe and beyond.

The only decisions Ethan wanted to be consulted over were those that involved the humanitarian programme. Then he was all ears.

'I hope you don't mind us crashing your party.' Declan grinned, half standing and holding out his hand as Ethan pulled up at the table.

The man's Irish brogue seemed more pronounced tonight, and Ethan assumed it was due to the almost empty pint of Guinness sitting in front of him.

Ethan shook Declan's hand, nodding a welcome at Kara and Olivia, who returned it with a cool smile. 'Not at all. Leo just wants to chew my ear about figures anyway. You've saved me.'

'Hmph,' Leo said good-naturedly. 'As if that would get me anywhere.'

There was general laughter as Ethan sat in the spare chair. It was between Leo and Kara and opposite Olivia, and he glanced at her as he sat down.

'Looking forward to tomorrow, Kara?' Ethan asked.

'You betcha.' She grinned.

Hearing her Aussie accent, Ethan realised the Brits were outnumbered at their table tonight.

'I don't think I'll be able to sleep. I feel like a kid on Christmas Eve.'

Leo laughed. 'That's what I like to see,' he said. 'Enthusiasm.'

Ethan smiled as he glanced at Declan, who was looking at Kara as if she was a tasty little Christmas treat waiting under the tree and he was Santa. Ethan felt a pang in the centre of his chest. He'd known that feeling.

He'd *loved* that feeling.

The feeling that you never wanted to be anywhere

else, with anyone else, just wrapped up in a bubble, just the two of you.

'Don't worry, darlin',' Declan said, exaggerating his accent. 'I have just the thing for insomnia.'

Everyone laughed, but still Ethan felt the pang throb a little harder. Leo had the same look as Declan and they were both clearly very contented men. Satisfaction oozed from their pores.

He glanced at Olivia again. Had she ever had anyone special? He realised he'd been so busy these past five days keeping his distance that he hadn't bothered to find out much about her life that didn't relate to work. There was ten years lost between them—maybe the wariness he saw in her expression now was to do with a man?

Conversation naturally flowed onto the case for a while, and it was good seeing Olivia relax again. She was in her comfort zone and the old spark came back. The passion and the fervour she obviously had for what she was doing sent a little buzz around the group and it was hard not to get a little high off it.

Ethan knew that feeling well. He'd got the same kick from the work he'd done these past ten years. Sure, initially when he'd first joined the army it had been the pressure and the danger he'd thrived on. The risks of front line work had made him feel more alive than he'd ever felt back home, with a drunken father and a stiflingly over-protective brother.

But he'd learned the hard way the downside of front line work. That you couldn't save everyone and that innocent people too often paid the price.

Leo had thought Ethan had joined up to spite him, and in some ways he had. But he'd caught the bug—

the thrill of transforming somebody's life. And that was why he did it.

'You're sticking around for the hospital ball?' Kara asked Olivia, dragging Ethan back into the conversation.

Olivia shrugged. 'Oh… I…I didn't know there *was* a ball.'

Kara frowned at Ethan and Leo. 'What's the matter with you two?' She tsked with a smile on her face. 'You're really not very good hosts, are you?' She looked back at Olivia. 'It's the Lighthouse Ball—it's the highlight of the year. It's on in two weeks. *Everyone* goes.'

Olivia stilled with what she hoped was a smile on her face. Oh. *That* ball. Memories swamped her. A fabulous red dress. An exquisite set of matching lingerie. She'd been to *that* ball a decade ago—on Ethan's arm.

'You will come, right?' Kara said. 'Don't make me be the only Aussie there.'

Olivia shook her head. *Been there, done that.* 'I don't know how Ama will be by then.'

'No, Kara's right. It was remiss of me not to mention it,' Leo interjected. 'You should definitely go.' He looked at his watch. 'You should get Ethan to take you. You remember how much Ethan loves to dance, right?'

Leo grinned at his brother, and if Olivia hadn't been so annoyed at Leo she'd have been heartened by how much closer the two men were now, compared to their toxic relationship a decade ago.

'Funny,' Ethan said to his brother. 'You're hysterical.' He looked at Kara. 'I don't dance,' he said.

Olivia nearly snorted at the understatement. He could manage a waltz/shuffle and that was about it. He much preferred to mingle and be charming and to look dashing in a tux and turn every woman's head.

The last thing she wanted to do was go to a damn hospital ball with Ethan.

Ethan in a tux.

She'd had a fantasy about him in a tux involving a scalpel as well.

'Sorry—got to go, guys,' Leo said. 'Lizzie can barely stay up past nine these days.'

'And to think,' Ethan quipped, 'he used to party with princesses till dawn.'

Leo grinned at his brother. 'Totally overrated,' he said, then departed quickly.

Olivia saw Leo's departure as a perfect opportunity to effect her own, but before she could get her goodbyes out Kara was back onto the subject of the ball.

'Are you sure about the ball?'

Olivia nodded quickly. 'I don't have a dress anyway,' she said, hoping that another woman would understand such a conundrum even if it was hogwash.

'Oh, good grief, that's not a problem,' Kara dismissed with a wave of her hand. 'Have you *been* to Oxford Street? With your figure we could find you something in a jiffy. Plenty of places in London to shop for ballgowns. Actually, I even know this great place where you can get some Australian designer stuff.' She paused for a second and narrowed her eyes as she stared at a spot just above Olivia's head. 'You're from Sydney, you said, right?'

Olivia nodded. 'Ah…yes. But my parents were flying doctors so I mainly grew up in the Outback. Not many ball frocks out there,' she said, trying to make a joke.

But Kara was clearly enthused about the idea.

Ethan could see Olivia's lack of enthusiasm a mile away. 'Kara,' he said with mock sternness, 'you're badgering.'

'Sorry,' Kara said, but her grin didn't look very contrite to Ethan and his spine prickled—in a bad way—when she looked speculatively from him to Olivia and then back to him again.

'You just never know, right?' Kara said. 'The craziest things happen at balls,' she murmured, and she slid her hand onto Declan's and they smiled at each other.

Ethan suppressed an eye-roll. He'd already heard from Lizzie about how Declan and Kara had set tongues wagging at the Princess Catherine's ball because of a saucy stolen kiss. Why was it that people in love thought everyone else should be in love too?

They were worse than reformed smokers.

'Come on, love,' Declan said, standing. 'I think it's time we go before you're whipping out the tape measure. And you've got a big day tomorrow.'

Olivia was relieved when Kara took the bait. With them gone she'd have the perfect excuse to be gone too.

'Well, let me know if you change your mind about the ball,' Kara said as she shrugged into the jacket that had been slung around the back of her chair. 'Or the dress shopping.'

Olivia nodded, relieved that talk of the ball would soon be over. 'I will,' she said with absolutely no intention of following through.

The couple turned to leave, but at the last moment Kara stopped and turned back mid-collar-straightening.

'Oh, God,' she said, looking at Olivia. 'I just realised… *Olivia Fairchild*… Your parents were the flying doctors that were killed a few years back in that terrible bushfire, right? I'm so, *so* sorry…that was such a tragedy.'

Olivia blinked as a hot spike of pain cleaved her right through the middle. So far away from home and five years down the track she hadn't expected anyone to get the association, and even though Kara was an Australian it was completely unexpected.

'Oh…yes,' she said, forcing the words out around a throat that felt as if it was collapsing in on itself. 'Thank you,' she stammered. 'It was a…shock.'

'It was awful,' Kara agreed. 'Just awful.'

'Yes,' Olivia said, nodding automatically, her head roaring with a tsunami of suppressed emotions.

Ethan looked from Olivia to Kara and then back to Olivia again. Olivia looked like she'd been struck, her peaches and cream complexion almost waxy now it was so pale. He frowned. *What the hell…?*

Olivia's parents were dead?

Ethan glanced at Kara, who clearly realised she'd spoken without thinking and didn't know what to say next. She looked at him, lost, and then shrugged, a panicked *help me* look on her face.

He nodded his head at her. 'It's okay,' he murmured. 'Go home and get some sleep. We need your A Game tomorrow.'

Declan nodded at Ethan over Kara's head. 'C'mon, darlin',' he said, and Ethan was relieved when the couple quietly withdrew.

Olivia sat staring at the glass of wine she'd barely touched and Ethan wished he knew where—*how*—to start. Olivia had been so close to her parents. He remembered what a foreign concept that had been for him and how they'd both struggled to understand the dynamics of each other's families when they were used to different upbringings.

'I'm sorry,' he said.

Olivia shut her eyes. She didn't want to hear his

condolences. She didn't want to share such a terrible gut-wrenching part of her life with him. It was too… *significant*—something lovers shared—and at the moment she could barely breathe from the sense of loss weighing down her lungs and settling in her bones.

She'd forgotten how much it hurt. How much she missed them. Being overseas, being away from it all, it was easy to forget it had happened. Easy to pretend she'd go home and they'd be waiting for her.

Sometimes the stark reality that she'd *never* see them again—which played like a soft chant in the back of her head anyway—roared out at her and hit her like a blast wave to the chest.

'It's fine,' she said, her thumb rubbing absently over the cool fiery opal in her ring, remembering the day her parents had given it to her.

'It's *not* fine, Olivia,' he dismissed tersely, then frowned at her, trying to understand. 'Why didn't you tell me?'

Olivia glared at him. 'Oh, you're annoyed because I didn't *tell* you?'

Ethan sighed. 'No, Olivia. No. I just…I wish I'd known.'

Olivia clung to the slow burn of anger in her chest. It was easier to be mad at him than at two dead people, than at an act of nature that had killed fifteen others that day.

She sucked in a breath as a wave of pain crested in her throat. 'You could have *asked*.'

Ethan blinked at the low accusation in her voice, trying to think back to the conversations they'd had since she'd returned. It was true they hadn't really talked about anything personal—hadn't he only just thought that tonight?—but…

'You said your parents had given you the money for your charity.'

Olivia snorted. 'They did,' she said bitterly. 'In their will.'

Ethan was silenced by the depth of her grief. He'd lost his father a decade ago, his mother ten years before that. And despite finding out about his mother's infidelities after her death, and his contentious relationship with his father—or maybe because of them—his loss and grief had been compounded.

But that had been a long time ago.

Aaliyah's death, on the other hand, had not. And, whether Olivia knew it or not, he understood the rawness of grief. He also understood now that *this* was what her reserve was about.

She was hurting.

She was grieving.

'What happened?'

Olivia felt a hot tear well in her eye and fall down her cheek and she brushed it savagely away. She knew he wasn't going to let it go—best to just get it out there as quickly and painlessly as possible.

'Five years ago…a massive bushfire…it swept through Outback Queensland. We were all there. Mum and Dad were pitching in with the authorities, out driving a rusty old four-wheel drive somebody had commandeered for them, helping to evacuate all the outlying properties, giving first aid, et cetera.'

Olivia could still smell the thick smoke blanketing the air, feel the sting of her eyes and the irritation of her airways, hear the almighty roar of the fire as the wind swept it along at a horrifying pace.

She picked up her glass of wine and stared at the fluid level as she absently swirled it. 'I was in the rural hospital, dealing with the casualties as they came in. I'd wanted to go with them but they said I was needed at the hospital. And I was, of course.'

Another tear fell and she dashed it away too.

'I'd just finished organising an evac for my third escharotomy of the day when the police came. The wind had changed…they'd been cut off…surrounded…'

Olivia shut her eyes, trying to block out the demons that had dogged her for so long.

'I dreamt about how they must have died for months afterwards. How *terrifying* it must have been. How terrified *they* must have been… I know they would have been thinking about me…worried about me…'

Ethan sucked in a slow ragged breath. He could tell her the smoke would have rendered them unconscious first. He could say it would have been quick—so quick. Those fires moved at a horrendous pace.

But she knew all that. She was a doctor. Except when she shut her eyes.

Then she was a daughter.

'I'm sorry,' he said again.

Olivia opened her eyes. She didn't want him to be sorry. She wanted them back. But Ethan couldn't do that. Nobody could. And she was damned if she was going to vent her spleen to a guy with shadows in his eyes who had rebutted every effort she'd ever made to get him to open up to her.

She shrugged, clawing back her composure. Reaching for the reserve she wore now like an armour against the things that threatened to cut her off at the knees.

'I guess that goes in the *bad luck* basket, huh?' she said, her voice still husky with emotion as she raised her glass in his direction.

Ethan's gut clenched at her faux flippancy. 'Olivia…
Don't… You can talk to me…'

'No, Ethan. You and I…we *don't* talk.'

'Maybe we should.'

Olivia snorted. *Like that's going to be a two-way
street.* 'Okay, then,' she said, her voice heavy with sar-
casm. 'You go first. Tell me, Ethan…' she leaned in closer
to him '…what happened to you while you were in the
military that made you even more screwed up than before you left?'

Ethan shook his head. 'Olivia—'

'Bum-*bah*!' Olivia hoped that sounded like a game
show buzzer. 'Wrong answer.'

'Olivia.'

She ignored the note of warning in his voice. She was
riding a surge of anger that she thought had been resolved
a long time ago.

Obviously not.

'Oh, no, Ethan. *No, no, no.* You don't get to hear *my*
sob story and then just stay all stoic and clammed up. You
don't get to have all of *me* and keep all of *you* to yourself like last time. That got me burned bad.' Olivia gave
an hysterical little laugh at the irony of her word-choice.

Burned.

'You want me to talk to you? Well, that's a two-way
street and we both know…' she paused and threw back
her wine in three long swallows '…that's not the way
you play the game.'

Then she placed the glass on the table and stood. 'I'm
going to check in on Ama before I go home. I'll see you
tomorrow.'

Ethan stood too. 'I'll come with you.'

Olivia glared at him. 'No,' she said. 'You will *not*.'

CHAPTER SEVEN

ETHAN STOOD IN the corridor just outside Theatre Nine the next morning, watching Kara and Olivia scrubbing up through the glass window in the swing door that led into the scrub room from outside.

They were chatting—not that he could hear what they were talking about. He wondered if it was about Kara's revelation last night. About Olivia's parents. Or maybe about the ball again.

Although he doubted it. If he knew Olivia it would be about Ama, about the surgery. She liked to go over the game plan as she scrubbed. He'd forgotten that about her, but working with her on his recent surgeries had brought it all back. She'd want to be focused on today, on the surgery. She'd be going over and over the plan in her head.

The last thing she'd want was to be in a bad emotional place. She was going to need all her concentration for today and she wouldn't want to have any distractions.

He admired that about her, and working side by side with her these past few days he'd been impressed by what a first-class surgeon Olivia had become. He'd always known she would be—she'd been impressive a decade ago, when her surgical skills were in their infancy—but he was pleased to see that his predictions had come to fruition.

Pleased that he'd had the opportunity to see her in action again.

Pleased that nothing seemed to faze her.

Her front line experience had shaped her into a mighty fine surgical all-rounder, as it had him, and no matter what surgery he was doing she'd scrubbed up and joined the fray, Ama's schedule permitting.

'Excuse me,' someone said from behind him.

'Sorry,' Ethan said, stepping aside as one of the scout nurses carrying a sterile tray of instruments pushed open the swing door and entered.

Ethan felt his muscles ache slightly at the sudden movement. After Olivia's news he hadn't got much sleep last night, and he'd hit his home gym around midnight, hoping to cause enough exhaustion to cure his insomnia.

It had been that or the bottle.

He'd been working on his physio every night since he'd begun spending his days working side by side with Olivia. He'd been suffering from a restless energy when he got home each night and it helped.

He'd always welcomed the quiet of his apartment, but it seemed oppressively so after a day with chatty Olivia. She seemed always to be in his head, and alone with his own thoughts—thoughts that usually involved Aaliyah— he'd been desperate for something to drive her out.

So he'd been exercising. Hard to think of anything other than pain when he had to push himself through. Still, he was already feeling the benefits in the strength and stamina of his quads.

And it was a much better option than what he would have chosen not that long ago—liquid denial.

Kara and Olivia finished up their scrub and headed for the Theatre, arms out in front of them. Ethan quickly pushed open the door and stepped into the scrub room.

'Olivia,' he said, and both women stopped and turned around to look at him. 'Can I have a moment, please?'

Olivia stifled a sigh. She'd thought it would be too much to ask to just get through this day without some kind of post-mortem over last night. Kara had already apologised three times during their scrub.

Olivia turned her head and smiled at Kara. 'Go on ahead,' she assured the junior surgeon. 'I won't be a moment.' When Kara was gone she turned back to Ethan. 'I don't want to do this now, okay?'

Ethan nodded. He'd suspected as much, but he didn't want her going in there with any kind of unspoken stuff between them—they needed to be a team. Best to clear the air now. 'I just wanted to—'

'I know what you "just wanted to," Ethan,' Olivia interrupted impatiently. 'But not now, okay? Can we just get through Ama's surgery? Can today please just be about Ama?'

Ethan shoved his hands on his hips. Clearly she was in the zone and *did not* want to be yanked out of it. 'Okay.'

Olivia nodded. 'Good. See you in there.'

The surgery was involved. They began with removing the protruding teeth that had been warped and buckled by disease, then they cut away all the old scar tissue. Bone was harvested from Ama's hip to replace the missing section of maxilla and plated and screwed into place. Then a thick piece of skin was removed from her arm and used as a graft to cover the gaping hole in Ama's face.

Such a large piece of grafted skin required a blood

supply, so they used a small artery and vein from the neck to provide this. Lastly they were able to rebuild the mouth, using what Ama already had and reshaping it to the way it had been before she'd fallen victim to NOMA.

Five hours later Ama's face was finally whole again. The surgery was done and she was on her way to the High Dependency ward, where she would be closely monitored for the first twenty-four to forty-eight hours.

'That was incredible,' Kara said, her eyes sparkling as she degowned and tossed it in the bin.

Olivia nodded, relieved and very happy with the result. 'Yes.' She grinned. 'It was.'

Ama's face would always be different from everyone else's. Her cheek would look a different colour and consistency to the rest of her face, with an obvious demarcation around the graft, and her lip line would always be just a little bit deviated.

But she'd be able to swallow, eat, chew and talk properly. And, more important, she'd have a more socially acceptable face. She could go to school. She could make friends and play with the other children.

She could be a *child*.

'You guys were awesome,' Kara continued as she and Olivia headed to the change-room.

Olivia wanted to get up to the HDU as soon as possible—Ethan had gone with Ama.

'You didn't even really talk to each other but you both seemed to know what each other needed. It was like you'd been operating together for years!'

Olivia had been so engrossed, so in the zone, she hadn't really noticed. But, looking back, she realised Kara was right. She and Ethan had worked together like a well-oiled machine. But then they'd always been very compatible—in *every* way.

'It's just practice,' Olivia dismissed. 'You do this for long enough and it becomes second nature.'

'Well, you call it what you want,' Kara said as she pushed open the change-room doors. 'I call it synchronicity. And it was pure magic to be a part of it, so thank you.'

Olivia didn't know what to say to that. Everything had gone very smoothly—no rabbits out of hats required. 'You weren't so shabby yourself,' she said.

Kara blushed and looked at Olivia, her face glowing from the compliment. 'Really?'

Olivia laughed. 'Yes, really. Now, stop fishing for compliments and let me get dressed so I can go see our patient.'

Kara gave a cheeky salute. 'Yes, ma'am.'

But she left Olivia in peace and Olivia was dressed and heading to the HDU in ten minutes.

The first couple of hours post-op Ama was pretty out of it. Olivia, Ril and Dali sat quietly by her side, talking occasionally but essentially maintaining a silent vigil. Ethan checked on her a couple of times, with Olivia assuring him that she'd page him when Ama woke or if any complications occurred.

It was in the third hour that things started to go wrong. Ama awoke in a great deal of distress and pain. She was clearly frightened and thrashing around the bed, pulling off her oxygen mask, calling for her mother.

She was given a bolus of painkiller intravenously and her morphine infusion rate was increased. It worked temporarily, but she became more agitated and distressed again over the next hour—crying and at one stage, before

Olivia leapt up to stop her, clawing at her face, blindly beating at it.

Ril was becoming distressed by her daughter's condition as more pain relief was given, the infusion increased further and some sedation added in on top. And both Ethan and Olivia were worried she would damage some of the reconstructive work they'd done with all her thrashing around. They were particularly worried about the viability of the graft. They checked beneath the dressings, but whilst it was oozing there didn't seem to be any excessive blood and the graft still appeared intact.

Nonetheless neither of them wanted to take a chance, and Ethan ordered arm restraints which wouldn't allow Ama to bend her elbows. A nurse wrapped them around her arms and Olivia felt better knowing that Ama wouldn't be able to reach her face any more if she remained unsettled.

When next Ama woke she was talking gibberish.

'I don't know what she's saying,' Dali said to Olivia, and there was fear in her eyes for her young charge. 'They're just words that don't make sense and then she talks crazy stuff about spiders on the ceiling.'

Both Ethan and Olivia looked at each other. 'It's the morphine,' she said.

Ethan nodded. Of course he should have thought about the possibility of Ama reacting badly to the morphine—the spider hallucinations were a clear sign of that—but the language barrier made everything so much harder.

'We'll change it to another opioid.'

A different infusion was started, and a bolus of it given, but Ama was in a significant state so was started on an infusion of a drug to keep her sedated, which fi-

nally managed to settle her completely after another half
an hour.

By early evening she was sleeping heavily, although
responding briskly to stimuli, and everyone was exhausted. Ril had fallen asleep in a hard plastic chair beside the bed, holding her daughter's hand, her head on
the mattress at an awkward angle. Dali was also dozing.

Olivia looked at the monitor. All Ama's vitals looked
in good shape and the oxygen mask was firmly in situ.
The figures blurred before her eyes as she felt her eyelids
drooping. It had been a long and exhausting day. After the
smoothness and success of the surgery none of them had
planned for this kind of stormy post-op course, although
things like reactions to opioids weren't uncommon.

It had been draining. And awful to see such genuine
distress and terror in Ama, who was usually so bright and
sunny despite all the reasons for her not to be.

Add to that the tumultuous events of last night that
had led to very little sleep, and Olivia was finding it hard
to keep her eyes open. The room was so quiet and the
steady *beep, beep, beep* of Ama's monitor was strangely
hypnotic. Despite the hard plastic of the chair she was
sitting in, it was bliss to shut her eyes. Just for a moment.

Olivia wasn't sure how long had elapsed when the trill-
ing of Ama's monitor woke her. She was disorientated at
first as she looked at her watch—almost 10:00 p.m. Her
back and neck protested as she squinted to focus on the
monitor and identify the alarm in the darkened cubicle.

The oxygen saturations had fallen into the eighties.
She also noted there was some tachycardia, and Ama's
blood pressure was a little on the lower end—but it had
been anyway, since the sedation had begun.

Olivia stood up and went over to Ama's bedside. The oxygen mask had slipped off. She went to place it back on but her hand stilled when she noticed the pallor of Ama's lips and the gurgly sound of her breathing.

'Ama?' Olivia said, reaching for the girl's hand to give it a squeeze. The hand was cold and clammy. Olivia frowned as she placed the mask and called, 'Ama!' again, giving her the firm shake of the shoulder to which she'd responded briskly just over an hour ago—nothing.

Ama's nurse arrived. 'The ICU registrar is a couple of minutes away,' she said. 'Ama's been getting increasingly tachycardic the past fifteen minutes, and her sats are starting to drift, so I want him to check her out.'

Olivia nodded, pleased the nurse was on the ball. 'Can you page Ethan too, please?' she asked.

The nurse went off to do Olivia's bidding. Ama's saturations had barely improved, so Olivia turned the oxygen up.

'Ama?' Olivia said, applying a painful stimulus to the girl's sternum, using the knuckle of her index finger and rubbing hard. Still nothing. Olivia reached over and paused the infusion of sedation, which she noticed had been decreased significantly since she'd drifted off to sleep.

Ama should be responding.

The tone of the saturation trace dropped and Olivia glanced up to see they were only eighty per cent now, despite the extra oxygen.

She also noticed the respiratory trace was slowing right down. A very bad feeling welled in the pit of Olivia's stomach as she flicked on the light and assessed the movement of Ama's chest. It seemed to be barely moving at all.

Ril woke up, blinking as bright light flooded the cubicle. So did Dali. They were speaking to each other in their language, and Dali was asking Olivia questions, but Olivia was back at the ABCs of medicine.

Airway.

That was always priority number one in medicine, and Olivia was beginning to think Ama's was compromised. The gurgling she could hear was a concern, and Olivia leaned down, her ear to Ama's mouth, as she used her index finger to give Ama some jaw-thrust. Blood welled out of Ama's mouth and Ril looked horrified, pointing and crying and talking rapidly to Dali.

'What is wrong, Olivia?' Dali asked. 'What is wrong?'

Now Olivia was certain Ama was bleeding, but had no idea to what extent.

The feeling of foreboding increased.

'I'm not sure,' she said, reaching for the Yankaeur sucker jammed under the pillow, 'but Ethan's coming and we're going to take good care of her—do you hear? Please take Ril along to the parents' lounge and I'll come and explain everything as soon as I can.'

Olivia had a feeling this was going to get messy. And the thick blood slurping noisily into the tubing from Ama's mouth confirmed it.

Olivia was aware on a peripheral level that Dali and Ril were having a heated exchange but she shut it out. Ama was her concern.

Come on, little girl. Don't do this.

Do not do this.

'Dali,' Olivia said as the blood kept coming and Ama remained unresponsive, despite the very potent stimulus of a large plastic sucker hitting the back of her throat, 'get her out of here *now*!'

The nurse returned as Dali led a wailing Ril away. 'She needs a twenty mil per kilo bolus of whatever you have running,' Olivia said. 'And get some of her blood from the fridge.'

They'd cross-matched six units for surgery but had only used one during the operation because the blood loss had been so minimal.

Ama was making up for it now.

Two more nurses entered the cubicle area as the registrar arrived. And Ethan about thirty seconds later. She'd never been more pleased to see him. She was aware that she was quaking on the inside but her training was taking over. Later she'd probably throw up, but right now she was in the zone.

'She's bleeding,' Olivia said, not looking up from Ama.

Ethan felt the same surge of adrenaline he always felt when an emergency evolved. He used it to his advantage to focus himself, to hone his intuition.

'Let me look,' he said, striding over to where Olivia stood. 'Pull the bed out.'

One of the nurses released the brakes on the bed and moved the bed down so Ethan could slip in at the head of the bed. He angled an unresponsive Ama's jaw open and could see nothing for the blood.

The alarm behind him trilled again as Ama's heart-rate started to fall.

'Get the resus trolley,' Olivia told one of the nurses as she watched the alarming drop of Ama's heart-rate on the monitor.

'I need a laryngoscope,' Ethan said,

Within seconds they had both. Ethan tried to look

down her throat using the laryngoscope but his view was totally obscured by congealed blood. He pulled out.

'Get me a trache kit,' he said.

One of the nurses scurried off to get one as the other two busied themselves drawing up resus drugs. When Ama's heart-rate hit fifty Olivia started external compressions and asked for atropine to be administered.

The nurse who had fetched the sterile trache pack opened it for Ethan and opened a sterile pair of gloves for him.

'Page Jock,' Ethan said as he plunged his left hand into the left glove, preparing to do a down-and-dirty emergency tracheostomy. Securing Ama's airway was vital. 'Tell him to get his butt back in here. As soon as this trache is done we're going back to Theatre to get the bleeder.'

The nurse squirted Betadine over Ama's throat as someone else laid the back of the bed flat, then raised the bed higher to accommodate Ethan's six-foot-two frame. The atropine had done the trick and Olivia had stopped compressions for the moment. She also asked for a pair of gloves, knowing that Ethan might need a hand, leaving the registrar to monitor everything else.

Ethan made a quick incision into Ama's throat, his plan being to secure the airway by the insertion of a tracheostomy tube and get to Theatre ASAP. But when he opened the neck there was so much blood it took him longer than he'd hoped, and he and Olivia literally had to scoop out the congealed blood to identify where he was going to stick the tube, all the while conscious of the screaming alarms and the ticking of the clock.

He finally placed it after two fraught minutes, and it was a relief when Olivia squeezed in the first breath via the bloodied Laerdel bag and there was immediate chest movement and improvement of the oxygen saturations.

Ethan glanced at Olivia. She had blood on her clothes but her look of sheer relief was exactly the way he felt—as if they were back in the field and they'd executed a major save together. For a moment he'd never felt closer to her.

'Let's get her to Theatre,' Ethan said.

Olivia nodded. 'I'll have a quick chat to Ril and join you.'

By midnight Ama was out of Theatre and had been taken to ICU this time. They'd identified the bleeding—most probably caused by Ama's initial thrashing around—and she was going to be kept ventilated and sedated overnight and hopefully have the tracheostomy removed in the next few days.

By the time they'd seen her settled in the unit and spoken to Ril and Dali it was close to one in the morning and Olivia was dead on her feet.

'C'mon,' Ethan said to her as she hovered around Ama's bedside. 'Home for you.'

Olivia shook her head. 'I want to stay.'

'You're exhausted,' Ethan said, pulling her to one side. 'You need a break.'

'I'll catch some sleep in a spare office somewhere later,' she dismissed.

'Olivia.'

'I'm fine,' she reiterated, looking over his shoulder at the monitor.

'Olivia...' Ethan said again.

Olivia dragged her gaze off the monitor to look at him—his tone had brooked no argument. *'I'm fine.'*

'You are not fine,' he said. 'You are running on empty. You need to get out of those clothes, which have blood on them. You need a shower. When did you last eat? You need food. And you need to sleep—a *decent* sleep on a decent bed, not some awful office examination couch.'

Olivia looked down at her clothes, realising for the first time that they had a patch of dried blood which looked as if someone had dabbed her with a large paint-brush dipped in red paint. Ethan was still in his Theatre garb.

'I'll get some scrubs,' she murmured.

'Liv…' Ethan shut his eyes, cursing to himself as the word he shouldn't use slipped out. *Damn it.* He was too tired to care. 'She's stable now, and sedated. At least go home, have a shower, change your clothes, have something to eat.'

Olivia didn't even register that he'd called her Liv. At least not on a conscious level. Having a shower and something to eat sounded like bliss—she was starving. All she'd had to eat since breakfast was a packet of crisps from the vending machine. But she was staying a twenty-minute cab-ride away from the hospital and she wanted to be close while Ama was still in ICU.

Olivia shook her head. 'I can't,' she said.

Now the drama was over she was starting to feel a little shaky. She'd been so terrified they were going to lose Ama at one stage.

'I talked them into this. I told them we could fix her. I promised Ril she would be okay…'

'Olivia, she *is* okay.' Ethan put his hands on her shoulders and waited until she was looking at him. 'Listen to me,' he said. 'This isn't your fault. This isn't my fault. Bad things happen sometimes and post-op haemorrhage is always a risk—you know that. And there was a combination of factors here. But she's fine. You did good.'

Olivia saw the flecks in his eyes flare to life with the conviction of his words. She knew he was right, but a combination of adrenaline overload and low blood sugar were clouding her judgement. '*We* did good,' she said.

Ethan smiled. 'Yes. We did. Now…' He squeezed her shoulders gently before dropping his hands. 'Go home.'

Olivia shook her head. 'I'll just go to the Theatre change-rooms and have a shower. I'll get something from a vending machine.'

'No, Olivia. You need to get out of here for a while. Clear your head. Get some distance. This case has taken up your whole life for weeks and weeks now.'

'I'll be too far away,' Olivia said, starting to get a little fed up with his persistence now. 'I don't want to go too far.'

Ethan stared in exasperation at her. 'Fine—come to my place, then. I'm heading there and it's only a five-minute walk. You can shower, change, eat and then if you really insist on coming back I'll walk you.'

Olivia chewed her lip, undecided. She desperately wanted a shower and something to eat. Sleep she could live without. It was tempting. 'You're still in the same place?'

Ethan nodded. 'Yep. And Il Conte is still just down the road, and I have a takeaway container of their best spaghetti in my fridge.'

Olivia felt the flutter of her belly as a hundred great memories rushed out at her. How many more would be waiting for her at Ethan's place? She doubted there was a square inch, certainly not a single horizontal surface, they hadn't made love on.

But it *was* the perfect solution—a place close by for a quick pit stop and then off again.

In and out—no time for the memories to cling and hold.

And there was a time she would have killed for Il Conte's spaghetti.

'Okay,' she conceded. 'But I'm coming straight back.'

'Of course.'

'Let me just check on her one last time.'

'Okay. I'll get out of these and grab some fresh scrubs for you and meet you at the entrance in ten?'

Olivia nodded. And hoped to God she hadn't just made the biggest mistake of her life.

CHAPTER EIGHT

IT TOOK OLIVIA ten seconds to realise she *had* just made the biggest mistake of her life. Stepping into Ethan's apartment was like entering a time warp where nothing had changed. The upstairs apartment of the old Victorian terrace was exactly the same and it was as if they were coming home from work together as they so often had, chatting about their day, anticipating a long session of lovemaking.

Even just standing inside the entranceway old memories floated around her, dizzying her with their potency.

She really needed to eat something.

Hell, she could recall a time when they'd fallen to the floor right where she was standing, so eager to get their hands on each other they hadn't been able to wait. The door had barely clicked shut, for crying out loud.

And…oh, God…the door—Ethan had pressed her against that once and brought her to a screaming orgasm in under a minute.

'Go have a shower,' Ethan said, brushing past her. 'I'll heat up the spaghetti.'

Olivia doubted her legs would carry her that far, afflicted as they were suddenly by a bad case of the shakes. Her head spun a little. 'Actually, do you mind if I eat first?' she asked. 'I think my blood sugar is bottoming out.'

Ethan turned. She looked pale and washed out. She swayed a little as he watched and he took a step towards her.

'Don't,' Olivia said as she reached for the nearby wall for stability.

If he touched her she'd melt right into him, and God alone knew where *that* would lead in this place where she'd spent about seventy-five per cent of her time in his bed. Or on his couch, or his table, or against his walls or his door...

'You look like you're about to fall over.'

'I won't,' she assured him, waving him back. 'As long as you feed me pronto.'

Ethan nodded. 'On it.'

Olivia followed him into the gleaming steel and granite kitchen at a slower pace and sat down at the big central black marble counter that hosted four bar stools. Her stomach grumbled and her hands shook as she placed them against the cool surface.

Somewhere else they'd made love.

Her brain shut down that memory before it even got out of the starting gate and she concentrated instead on Ethan, clattering around, putting a bowl in the microwave, piling another one with spaghetti, waiting to put it in. She noted the familiar Il Conte container, and how amazing the food smelled even cold, and she almost told him not to bother to heat it up she was *that* hungry.

'You want a coffee?' he asked. 'Probably be handy if you're going back.'

Olivia nodded. It was going to be a long night, and she was going to need all the help she could get. He turned to a fancy coffee machine that *was* new, placed a pod in the top and a cup under the spout and pressed a button. The microwave beeped and he pulled the bowl out, giving the spaghetti a stir with a fork. She watched steam rise off it and her mouth watered.

He went to return it to the microwave. 'It'll be fine like that,' she assured him.

Ethan frowned. 'It's not heated all the way through. It's only just warm, really.'

Olivia shook her head. 'Don't care,' she dismissed, holding her hand out for the bowl. 'Near enough is good enough.'

He chuckled as he passed it over. Her belly growled again and she wasn't entirely sure it was anything to do with food. His sexy stubble was even more so as he stood in his kitchen, serving her spaghetti and coffee as he'd done a hundred times before.

Olivia demolished the bowl in two minutes flat. She didn't lift her head, she didn't converse, she didn't notice when Ethan placed her coffee on the bench. She just ate, barely registering the aroma of basil and the sweet taste of fresh tomatoes.

When she was done she looked up, finding Ethan's amused gaze. 'Sorry.' She grimaced.

Ethan laughed as he cradled his coffee cup in his hand. 'I always did enjoy watching you eat,' he murmured.

Olivia remembered all the other things he'd enjoyed watching her do. Laughing at a joke, slipping on a pair of high heels, shaving her legs.

Getting undressed.

Coming as if the world was going to end.

Her stomach growled again, and for damn sure this time it was *nothing* to do with food. He was watching her mouth and, nervous, she licked her lips, finding some stray sauce and removing it with her tongue.

Ethan almost groaned out loud as her nervous licking still managed to miss a bit of sauce. Once upon a time, standing here in his kitchen, with her sitting opposite in that chair, he'd have just leaned across the bench and licked it off. And the desire to do so now thrummed through his veins like a siren call.

He'd *never* wanted to taste her this badly.

Instead, exercising the control he'd perfected in the military, he ground his feet into the marble tiles, reached for a serviette from the counter behind him and passed it to her. 'You missed some.'

Olivia took it and dabbed at her mouth, excruciatingly aware of his intent stare. Of the way he'd paused, coffee cup halfway to his mouth, and just looked at her, taking in every movement. She knew that stare. It was stirring memories and stroking along her pelvic floor, causing the muscles there to preen in an utterly Pavlovian response.

Shower.

Shower, shower, shower.

Her brain was doing its best to drag her back from the edge. To remember how he'd used her, hurt her. She'd *made love* to him a hundred times in this apartment, fallen *in love* with him, and all the while he'd just been *having sex* with the woman his brother had wanted.

'I think you're done,' he murmured.

His voice blew over her, soft as feathers. Caressing her skin and tickling a memory of the past out of hiding.

The time he'd tied her wrists and ankles to his bed and spent hours taunting her, touching her spread-eagled body, tracing his tongue all over her. Backing off every time she built, refusing to let her come, gorging himself instead on his tactile feast and driving her mad with lust until finally he'd relented.

'I think you're done,' he'd said.

And when he'd put his mouth to her she'd had an orgasm that had gone on for an eternity.

Her blood flowed slow and thick through her veins as the memory played out. It pounded through her head and washed through her ears. Her breath felt like syrup in her lungs. Her abdominals had turned to goo, like flaming marshmallow, melting her to the chair.

Olivia saw Ethan's knuckles whiten as his grip on the cup increased. Was he thinking about it too?

Ethan wasn't sure which memory Olivia was caught up in, but she needed to stop now if she wanted to leave here unmolested. Today had been intense—very intense. It would be bad to do something neither of them should just because they were reacting to the pressure of the day and a bunch of memories.

Even if they *were* really great memories.

She was looking at him as if she wanted to hurdle the bench and drag him to the ground. But she wouldn't thank him for it in the morning. He knew her too well.

'Olivia.'

Olivia blinked at the warning in his voice, the memory receding as awareness of the present filtered back in. A well of loathing rose in her chest and burned hard and high in her throat.

Ama.

She had to get back to Ama.

Olivia reached for her coffee cup and took a fortifying sip, too embarrassed even to look at Ethan. She took another and, as it wasn't too hot, blew on it and took a bigger swig. Then she placed it on the bench and stood.

'I'll have a shower and get out of your hair,' she said, still not looking at him.

Ethan didn't want her to go. Actually…he did. He wasn't sure he could last a night with her here in his apartment again and not just give in to what his body wanted. He'd felt dead inside for a year, but ten days back in her company and certain parts of him were very definitely coming back to life.

But she needed to sleep and that was more important. Maybe he could convince her after her shower?

'Scrubs on the back of the couch,' he said.

She didn't answer, didn't even acknowledge his words, just grabbed the scrubs on her way past and disappeared from his sight.

It was bliss under the hard, hot spray and Olivia wanted nothing more than to slide down the wall, hug her legs to her chest and nod off under the steady cleansing heat, until the tension in her muscles had eased and the squall inside her stomach had settled.

But she was afraid to shut her eyes. The whole shower smelled like him, smelled so male—soap and shampoo and aftershave—and she was reminded of how often they'd made love in here too.

A lot.

And Olivia knew the second she allowed her eyelids to shut she'd be there again, her back to the tiles, Ethan buried inside her, groaning *'Liv…'* into her ear as he came.

Or going down on her, looking totally in control despite his position of supplication on his knees in front of her, his hands holding onto the backs of her thighs, holding her up, as her world splintered around her.

Olivia ruthlessly shut off the taps as steam built in the

cubicle, heating the mix of male aromas to a wild liquid cloud, painting her body, marinating her in memories. Drifting her into dangerous territory.

Ama.

She had to get back to Ama.

She towelled off quickly, throwing on her scrubs *sans* underwear—she'd sling her duffle coat on over the top and no one would ever know she was going commando. The aroma of fresh laundry and Ethan's spicy soap surrounded her, reminding her of clean sheets and him, and she yawned, her eyes gritty despite the shower.

She turned off the heating lamps and stepped out of the en-suite bathroom into Ethan's darkened bedroom. A shaft of light from the hallway penetrated into the gloom, lifting the visibility level a little. Enough to make out objects like his big soft bed—still in the same spot—beckoning her like a fluffy freaking cloud, with its blizzard-white duvet and matching pillows—something that had always seemed so out of place in this overwhelmingly male bachelor pad.

It whispered to her. *Rest. Sleep. Dream.*

And the thought of getting just a couple of hours' shut-eye was utterly, utterly seductive. But she dragged herself back from it, padding through his bedroom in her bare feet, the thick rug luxurious on her soles as she headed for her bag and coat and a brisk walk in the cold London night.

Then an object sitting on a shelf near the door caught her eye and she stopped. It looked eerily familiar, and despite her brain telling her she needed to get the hell out of his room she was drawn to it by the insistent tug of ancient strings.

Its shape became more distinct as she neared and Olivia's heart beat a solid tattoo in her chest as she reached for it. The bronze was cool as she wrapped her fingers around the miniature figurine, but the spark of memory soon heated the object, sending warm tingles up her arm.

He'd kept it.

Stupid tears needled at her eyeballs as she looked down at the nude young woman reclined in a pensive pose and she blinked them back. He probably didn't realise he still had it. Which fitted right in with the rest of the decade-old stuff in this apartment that time forgot.

He'd bought it at Portobello Road market because he'd said the woman's secretive smile reminded him of her just after she came. As if she'd touched the stars and knew all their secrets. That had been two days before she'd found out about his dastardly behaviour. Two blissful days when she'd floated on cloud nine because this exquisite, dainty, perfectly detailed piece of eighteenth-century sculpture had reminded him of her and the magic they made together.

Olivia ran her thumb over that Mona Lisa smile, remembering that day. It was probably the last time she'd ever been deep-down-in-her-bones happy.

'She's still beautiful, isn't she?'

Olivia's thumb stilled. She was aware suddenly of the heat of him at her back. Of his overwhelming presence enveloping her in a cloud of old memories and new desires. It fluttered in her pulse and prickled along her nerve-endings, peaking her nipples and fanning along the bare skin of her nape—her hair was up to avoid getting wet.

'Yes,' Olivia said, placing her gently back.

Ethan wanted to bury his nose in the exposed stretch of skin in front of him, right where her nape joined her shoulder, which the square neckline of the scrub shirt left beautifully exposed. He wanted to sniff her there. Inhale deeply. Smell his soap on her.

Remember back to the days when his smell used to be stamped all over her.

He itched to pull her hair out of its rough and ready up-do. The wet ends of the tendrils that had half fallen down taunted him more.

'I *am* sorry about what I did, Olivia.'

Olivia shut her eyes briefly. 'I know,' she said.

'It wasn't all mercenary. I did care for you too.'

'I know,' she repeated, then she took a deep steady breath and opened her eyes she turned to face him.

But he was close, so much closer than she'd realised, and his scent was intoxicating, and his neck was just there, its fat pulse bordering the hard ridge of his trachea, pounding right in front of her even through the thick growth of stubble.

She shut her eyes again as a wave of longing rolled through her, sweet and hot, like sherbet and crack cocaine.

She remembered how hard he'd fought for Ama tonight. How he'd taken over, securing her airway, fighting for the little girl's life. Scooping out blood, never giving up as he'd raced against the clock and the hazards of prolonged hypoxia.

'Thank you,' she said, her voice husky even to her own ears, thick and lumpy in her throat. 'For Ama.'

Ethan shook his head. She was looking at him with *those* eyes. Eyes frank with professional admiration and personal gratitude. A truly deadly combination. *Oh, crap.*

'Liv…'

And that was it for Olivia. A husky entreaty so masculine but so needy. She couldn't fight it any more. She couldn't deny it any more. She and Ethan had been on a slow trajectory towards each other since coming back in contact again and tonight he had sling-shotted into her orbit in a most spectacular fashion.

She was lost. Heat and lust clouded her senses until her head was full of him. Every breath filled her up a little bit more until she was drowning in the essence of him. The intelligence of what she was about to do was so far out of her reach her brain might as well have been residing in Australia.

'Oh, God…Ethan,' she muttered as she slid her arm up to his neck and yanked him closer until her body was flush with his, going up on tippy-toe, shoulder to shoulder, hip to hip, feeling the hard press of him against her belly.

The golden flecks in his eyes were glowing the way they used to, with passion and life, and she had no hope now of resisting him now the shadows that had warned her to keep away were gone.

'I can't not do this.'

And then she pressed her mouth to his and she was lost in a vortex of arousal so strong there was no room for thought or for second-guessing. It was just him and his lips and his coffee taste and the rapid dissolution of all those years pretending she was over him.

Ethan devoured her mouth on a surge of longing so all-consuming his knees almost buckled. But he felt her give against him and he held on to her tight, holding them both up in the maelstrom that descended.

He was lost in a heady cloud of want that he hadn't experienced in a long time. Ama and the near disaster they'd avoided was forgotten, the Hunter Clinic was forgotten, Fair Go was forgotten, even Aaliyah was forgotten as an all-consuming surrender stormed his body.

Olivia had got under his skin and ploughed through his defences. Her mouth was as sweet as he remembered—sweeter—like a revelation, like a homecoming. Her breathing was heavy—like a rough panting in his head. And when his tongue entered her mouth she made a soft whimpering noise at the back of her throat that took him way back to the beginning, to when she hadn't been able to keep her hands off him.

Back to when he could have had her any time, anywhere, anyhow.

And nothing else had mattered.

He didn't stop to think about consequences or regrets or common sense. The need to have her, to reacquaint himself with *every* delectable inch of her, swamped *every* cell in a dire imperative to mate and he followed where it led, hopeless to resist.

He moved according to the dictates of his body. He kissed and he touched and he felt, his senses filling with her, intoxicating him with desire, his head humming with the need to be skin on skin, to feel her under him, to move deep inside her.

Before he knew it her scrub top was up and off and his hands were full of the soft mounds of her breasts, her nipples hard and ready in his palms. Then he was moving his hands down, pushing under the waistband of her scrubs, cupping her naked bottom, pushing them down her hips and off, conscious on some level that she was kicking out of them.

And then she was naked and he needed just to look at her, to remember every naked inch of her. To take her in and familiarise himself with the pure visual delight of her.

She didn't protest as he picked her up, his mouth still joined to hers, their tongues duelling and clashing, their mouths trying to suck up as much of the other as they could.

He laid her on the bed and she looked just as he remembered: long and lean and utterly lovely. Lust had honed his night vision and he could see her nipples were pale and puckered tight. Her hair had escaped its messy up-do and was now spread out around her head like a cloud. Her half-closed eyes and pouty full lips were so damn sexy he almost lost it right then and there.

Olivia's head spun. She was so alive with the touch and taste of him she was practically levitating off the bed.

'Ethan…' she half sighed, half moaned, and held her arms out to him.

Ethan didn't need any further encouragement. He was suddenly awake, bursting with life and passion, and Olivia was his Princess Charming. She'd kissed him and woken him from a long sleep. A wellspring of desire he'd thought long dead was grabbing fiery possession of his groin and tugging hard.

He was out of his clothes in seconds, his erection, hard and urgent, springing gratefully free of the confines of his trousers, and as he joined her on the bed, his mouth lowering to rejoin hers again, her hand slipped along the length of him.

'Oh…' He groaned into her mouth as she gripped his girth just the way he liked it—good and firm.

Olivia revelled in the harsh scratch of his whiskers and in his guttural groan. And the way he filled her palm… *Dear Lord.* He'd always been big and solid, but feeling him again was like coming home, and when she stroked him she remembered just the way he liked it—as if it had been imprinted into her memory banks forever.

But he remembered about her as well, and she arched her back, gasping into his mouth as one hand slid to a breast and the other found its way to the slick folds at the juncture of her legs, stroking her just right too. Just the way she liked it—good and firm.

Olivia's head buzzed with the overload of sensations. But it wasn't enough. She wanted him inside her. Pounding hard and deep. Panting in her ear. Wanted to listen to him coming undone.

To come undone with him.

'Now, Ethan,' she said. *'Now.'*

Ethan heard and understood her demand for what it was—a call of the wild. The irrevocable need to mate, to be one. And maybe he should have been strong enough to resist it, to make this long and slow, to tease and taunt, to bring her to orgasm first before succumbing to his own overriding desire to be part of her.

But all the wasted years battered against him and he didn't want to waste another second.

'Ethan!' she called again.

He knew a sexual demand when he heard it, and he knew she needed him to be inside her as much as he needed to be there too.

He didn't think about anything other than her as she wrapped her legs around his waist, inhaling the smell of his soap on the skin of her neck as he buried his face there and thrust into her, sliding home, deep and sure, on a groan that seemed to echo up from the mists of time.

He didn't think about their history. He didn't think about Ama or the emergency trache he'd had to perform. He didn't think about his injuries.

He didn't think about Aaliyah.

He didn't even think about a condom.

He just let the sound of her gasp fill his head and the dig of her nails ground him to the bed and the frantic rhythm of their bodies take him away.

This was Olivia, and it was as if they'd never been apart.

'Yes,' she said. 'Oh, God…please, yes…don't stop…'

Ethan had no intention of stopping. He just held her tight and thrust over and over, her gasps pushing him higher and higher, urging him on, his heart-rate ratcheting up with each erotic slide of flesh into flesh.

Hard, hot, delicious tension coiled in his shoulders, buttocks and the backs of his thighs. Fire raged out of control in his loins and spread to his belly. It built to an inferno until every muscle burned and shook from the unbearable tautness.

'Let go, Ethan,' she whispered. 'Let go.'

And he did. In a shocking jolt everything snapped and he fell headlong into ecstasy, slipping his hand between them into all her slick heat, finding just the right spot and stroking her there as his world came apart, aware of her muscles clamping down tight around him and the sharp keening of her cry as she joined him.

And he kept rocking and thrusting, riding it out, keeping it going, until the last shudder had undulated through him and the last cry had been wrung from her mouth.

Until they were both spent and lying on their backs, gasping for breath and reaching for sanity, fighting and losing the battle to keep heavy lids open.

CHAPTER NINE

OLIVIA DIDN'T KNOW where she was when she first woke. It was dark and everything was unfamiliar. She was used to that, travelling so much, but this felt different.

It took several more seconds for the warm pillow beneath her head to register as human. Warm, male, human.

Holy crap!

She sat up as everything came crashing back. Ethan's apartment. Il Conte's spaghetti. A warm shower. A bronze figurine. Urgent, need-you-now sex.

Really great, need-you-now sex.

Ethan stirred, shifted, mumbled something and rolled on his side but didn't wake. He'd always been a heavy sleeper—something that apparently the military hadn't cured him of. But given how exhausted they'd both been it wasn't surprising.

But *she* was wide-awake. Panic skittered along her veins and edged up her heart-rate.

Crap! She'd slept with Ethan-freaking-Hunter. The one man on this earth she'd vowed she'd never, ever sleep with again! *Good going, Olivia. Really smart move. Nothing like taking a giant leap backwards in your evolution as a human being. Why not just give the man your heart*

*on a platter and a great big knife to stab right through
the centre of it?*

Did you learn nothing?

But then another thought came crashing through her
self-loathing. *Ama.*

Oh, hell! She leapt from the bed, her heart-rate ratcheting up another notch—what was the time? She had to
get back to the hospital.

Olivia could barely think straight as she dashed
around, trying to find her scrubs and get dressed in the
dark, trying and failing to leave the bedroom without a
backward glance and annoyed at herself when the broad
sweep of a naked shoulder made the muscles deep inside
her belly twist—in a good way.

A really good way.

Damn it!

She forced herself out into the still lit hallway and the
even brighter open-plan lounge/kitchen. She found her
shoes near the lounge and shoved her feet in. Grabbed her
coat discarded on a kitchen stool and shoved her arms in.
Then she shoved fingers through her hair and hoped to
hell it didn't look as if she'd just rolled out of bed with a
man who was a very bad bet.

She snagged her bag as she hurried past the counter
heading for the door, digging around in it for her phone,
finding it as she reached the knob, and yanked the door
open, clicking it shut behind her as she scrolled through,
looking for any missed calls or messages.

None.

Her shoulders sagged in relief as she hit the stairs.
But it wasn't enough—she needed to know more. Olivia
speed-dialled the ICU as she scurried down the stairs. A
nurse answered as her foot hit the bottom step and by the

time she was out of the apartment and striding towards the hospital she'd ascertained that Ama was stable, sedated and doing well.

'I'll be there in five minutes,' Olivia informed the nurse, then hit the end button.

Only then did she notice other things. Like her frantic breath misting into the air, the cold slapping into her face as she all but burst into a jog on the footpath, the sting in her thighs as needles of frosty air penetrated the cotton of her scrubs.

Olivia pulled the collar up on her duffle coat and tightened the belt, hunching into its thick layers for added warmth. *It was freezing.* She'd forgotten how cold London was in November.

It had been warm in Africa.

It had been even warmer in Ethan's bed.

What *had* she been thinking? *The man feeds her spaghetti and keeps a dumb memento from their time together and she just opens her legs for him?*

The slight ache there mocked her for her stupidity, as did the dampness slicking her inner thighs. They hadn't even used a damn condom. Two *doctors* who should *know* better and they hadn't even stopped to be responsible!

She hadn't thought. Or cared. She'd just needed him inside her.

Her brisk footfalls were loud on the deserted pavement and each one formed the rhythm to her self-loathing.

Stupid. Stupid. Stupid.

Idiot. Idiot. Idiot.

Fool. Fool. Fool.

Olivia was grateful when she rounded the corner and the lights of the hospital were just there—close enough to reach out and touch. Like a beacon of hope, saving her from a bitchy internal dialogue and a series of thoughts that could only get more ugly.

She couldn't worry about any of the Ethan stuff right now.

They *were* going to need to talk, but for tonight—until Ama was out of the woods—she didn't want to think about anything else. She certainly didn't want to have a *conversation* with him when their sex was still on her skin and his kisses still imprinted on her mouth.

And, if she knew Ethan at all, he wouldn't be cherishing the idea of talking either. Hell, they'd spent months together a decade ago and he clearly hadn't spoken to her at all—not about anything of import. About what was going on with him, about his pain and anger. Clamming up and being all brooding and silent seemed to be his speciality.

And, for once, Olivia was glad of it.

Ethan woke with a start. Aaliyah's laughter was a faint echo in his head, teasing him somewhere in the distance, fluttering elusively just out of his reach, like a ribbon in the breeze.

But in his mind's eyes he tried anyway, his hand extending, grabbing nothing but air.

Same as always.

Aaliyah. I'm so sorry, Aaliyah.

Gloomy daylight bled in around the heavy curtains at his window, matching his mood to perfection. The low hum of London traffic was a fitting background to the mumbled recriminations of his thoughts.

He rolled his head to the side, where his arm was flung out on the mattress. The empty space was cold: no hint of bodily warmth, no dent in the pillow beside him to indicate anyone had been there.

Same as always. *But not.*

Olivia was long gone and he was...*relieved.*

He sat up in bed on a groan, his nudity mocking him. The smell of Olivia, of their joining, infused his senses, refusing to let it be just another bad dream. He ploughed his fingers into the cropped hair covering his bowed head.

'Aaliyah,' he whispered.

Hell. He'd promised her he'd love her only. *I'm so sorry, my love.*

And now he'd betrayed two women. Aaliyah *and* Olivia.

Olivia, who deserved better than some half-man, physically *and* emotionally crippled.

But, damn it! She'd got under his skin. Like she had last time. Sneaked in under his defences. And for a little while last night he'd felt alive again. He'd been relying on his work to do that for him this past six months. And it had been working.

But last night...

'Damn it!'

Ethan swung his legs over the bed. Work had been *more* than fulfilling for him. He'd felt accomplished. He'd felt as if he was making a difference—especially when he'd thought his days of making a difference were over.

When he'd been medically discharged from the military he'd doubted he would ever be fulfilled again. But Leo had given him a way and Ethan had been proud of the Hunter Clinic's humanitarian programme, developed and nurtured under his leadership.

And after Aaliyah that was all he'd needed. He was

done with everything else. Emotions, relationships. And resigned to it.

And then along came Olivia.

And he'd screwed it up a second time. Done something completely unforgivable. Not only betraying the memory of the woman he'd been going to marry but by reaching for Olivia again, whom he'd promised to leave alone.

Goddamn it!

Ethan rose from the bed, a slow burn of anger replacing his gloom and disappointment. How could he have done it? Where was his iron-clad self-control? Where was his single-minded focus? Where was *his word*, damn it?

He'd promised Aaliyah he'd love her only. Then he'd promised her he'd come back for her. And just last week he'd promised Olivia he'd keep his hands off.

All broken.

It seemed he was destined in this life to let everyone down, to destroy all that he held dear. People he loved got hurt, went away. His mother had died and he'd never stopped missing her, even when the truth about her had come to light. And Aaliyah. So passionate and dedicated. Gone too.

But Olivia, who'd had enough heartache of her own, was still alive, and after nearly destroying her once he *wouldn't* do that again. He operated best alone, where he couldn't hurt anyone.

He stalked into the bathroom, with a slow simmer of anger in his belly and a skinful of self-loathing for company. He flicked the cold tap on and stepped straight under the spray, hoping to hose them off enough to be able to function today.

Hoping he could hose Olivia away as easily.

* * *

Olivia was at Ama's bedside when Ethan arrived half an hour later. Ril and Dali had ducked out to get some breakfast. She looked up as he swept into the isolation room. He was in a dark suit with a russet tie and if anything he looked more haggard than ever. The lines she'd first noted around his eyes at their reunion were back with a vengeance and his stubble was now almost a soft beard.

But the flecks in his eyes flared briefly as his gaze roved over her—checking her for signs of damage, she assumed—and her heart gave a funny lurch in her chest.

And then she remembered how stupid she'd been. How those golden flecks had made her lose her head. *And her clothes.*

And how her focus had to be Ama.

Ethan watched her expression cool and followed her lead. 'Olivia.' He nodded.

Olivia felt absurdly close to tears at the formality in his voice and the stiffness of his expression. *What the...?* Clearly some recalcitrant part of her had been hoping that he'd tear down all her well-reasoned objections and whisk her up in his arms. But, like her, he'd obviously decided to focus on Ama and keep things strictly professional between them.

And that was a *good* thing.

'Ethan.' She nodded too, then turned back to Ama.

Ethan hadn't been sure what he was going to say or how he was going to act this morning but her coolness helped him decide. Mutual professional respect was the only way forward. They had to see each other and they had to work together, both now and in the future. And to do that they had to forget what had come before. Forget their baggage. Maintain a strictly collegial relationship.

And keep the hell away from each other in between times.

Hadn't they already agreed to that anyway?

And failed.

Ethan pushed it all away, slipping into a skin he knew well—*Mr Hunter.* 'How is she this morning?' he asked.

They had a ten-minute conversation about Ama's progress and the plan for the next few days, which involved removing the tracheostomy and getting her out of ICU. Ril and Dali returned then, and Ethan and Olivia had a long talk with them about the previous night and what the next days and the next steps were for Ama.

Ril was worried about her daughter still, but encouraged by her progress, and Olivia assured her again that she would be with them all until Ama was well enough to go home and she would be the one taking them back to Africa.

Ril smiled as Dali translated, patting and rubbing Olivia's arm, nodding and speaking words of gratitude in her own tongue as tears shone in her eyes. Olivia was extraordinarily moved by Ril's faith.

When Ril was satisfied she returned to the chair by her daughter's bed and Ethan turned to Olivia and said, 'They want us to sit in on the ICU round—you want to join me?'

Olivia nodded. She did want to be able to co-ordinate Ama's care with the ICU doctors.

'It's starting now. Shall we?' he said, and indicated for her to precede him out of the room.

Olivia told Dali where they were going and then walked ahead of Ethan, conscious of his gaze on her back. Conscious that only a handful of hours ago she'd been in his bed. Conscious that, under her coat, she was wearing the same clothes he'd stripped her out off. That his smell clung to her skin. That the evidence of her arousal and their unprotected sex had mingled to feel all hot and slick between her legs.

'Whereabouts?' she asked, her head slightly turned.

Ethan fell into step beside her. 'End of the corridor, turn right, third door on the left.'

She didn't acknowledge him, just followed along silently beside him, and he took a breath and broached the subject of the elephant stomping along beside them.

'About last night…' he said.

'No.' Olivia shook her head vigorously, not breaking stride as her heart did a crazy leap in her chest. She'd been sure he'd be in ostrich mode. 'Let's not do this, okay?'

Ethan tried to keep it casual as they walked down the very public corridor. He wanted to get this thing between them on to an even keel as fast as possible, and the only way to do that was to clear the air about what had happened at his place last night.

They couldn't just pretend it hadn't happened. That was a sure-fire way to breed resentment.

'We *do* need to talk about it, Olivia. Hell,' he said lowering his voice, 'I didn't even use a condom.'

That particular little gem had come to him in the shower.

The fact that it hadn't even crossed his mind at the appropriate time had been shocking. He wished it had—not least of all because he didn't have a condom anywhere in his apartment and that would definitely have brought them both to their senses. There'd certainly be no need for this awkward morning-after conversation, walking down a busy corridor in a *children's hospital*, whispering about unprotected sex as if they were teenagers!

'You think I don't know that?' Olivia demanded. 'I'm not wearing any underwear. Trust me, I know. And I know we need to talk about this, and we will,' she said. 'Just *not now*. Not while Ama's still in ICU, okay?'

Ethan nodded, clamping down hard on the leap in his pulse and the hitch in his breath at the thought of her going commando. Things stirred and he battered them down with all the authority of a dictator crushing a revolt.

He cleared his throat. 'Okay, sure,' he agreed.

'Thank you,' she said.

And they both continued in silence.

That was pretty much the pattern for the next few days. Quick, professional meetings involving stilted conversations about Ama and her progress. Nothing personal, just medical.

Day two post-op Ama's tracheostomy was removed and she was moved to HDU. They had none of the opiate problems that had been the catalyst for her post-op bleed and Ama, although quiet and exhausted from her unexpected complications, improved every day.

Two days later she was back on the ward and Olivia was finally starting to feel that they had turned a corner. Ama wasn't back to her full cheeky, happy self, but she was showing interest in the world around her again and even asked for the television to be put on.

Olivia thought that was real progress, and for the first time since the operation actually allowed herself to think about other things.

Naturally her thoughts turned to Ethan.

* * *

Ethan, on the other hand, whilst exceedingly pleased with Ama's progress too, was increasingly crotchety and frustrated.

He hadn't been able to sleep since Olivia had slept in his bed. At first he'd thought it was just her scent keeping him up, but he'd changed the sheets to no avail.

He lay awake for hours, his brain circling around what he'd done, his gut heavy, and when he slept it was with strange dreams of Aaliyah and Olivia. He was chasing them both as they ran from him, teasing him with their laughter, only to catch one and watch as her face blended into the other. Changing back and forth until he didn't know whether he was holding Aaliyah or Olivia.

It took him two sleepless nights to realise that the feeling of a lead weight in his belly was his guilt flaring to life again. This bed had belonged to Aaliyah, even though she'd never slept in it. She'd come to him in his dreams here, and as much as they'd tortured him with their heartbreaking clarity they'd also kept him close to her.

He'd used to welcome the night and sleep, when he could be with her again.

But now Olivia was in the bed too. In his head. And the guilt was eating him up.

After that realisation the dreams changed. They became bloody and disturbing. They became nightmares. Slices of that awful day when all hell had broken loose magnified tenfold in his head.

The heat and the smoke. The noise of bombs and gunfire. The blood. The carnage.

Aaliyah's, *'Go, Ethan, I'll be fine,'* played like a broken record, waking him in a cold sweat.

Driving him out of the bed. *Their* bed. But not any more. Because Olivia was in it too. In his head again.

The empty bed mocked him. He was alive and getting naked with Olivia when Aaliyah was dead. Dead because he hadn't got back to her in time.

A few weeks ago he would have poured himself a drink or twelve. But something had changed—he didn't seem to crave it as he had. As his father had.

Ethan had worried that there was some genetic component and he would turn out like his old man, become the type of person he'd despised in his father.

It was a relief to realise he didn't *need* it.

He headed for his home gym instead and pounded it out on the leg press and treadmill. Filling his head with Aaliyah, trying not to think about Olivia. Trying to exercise—exorcise—his guilt into oblivion. Trying to exhaust himself.

He needed to sleep.

A tired surgeon made mistakes!

On the morning of day five Olivia was going slightly stir-crazy from spending all day cooped up in the hospital. She hadn't had any form of exercise in weeks now and she was beginning to feel it. As a jogger, she usually pounded the pavements wherever she was, but going out in a freezing London morning was not something she welcomed.

Instead she decided to take up Leo on his offer of using the Hunter Clinic pool in the basement next to the gym. It was heated, and she could slip in there early, while no one was around, do some laps and be dressed and at the hospital by eight.

She needed to do *something*. Dali had texted her to say

that Ama wanted to see her new face. They'd all seen it and were very happy with how it looked—Ril had even cried—but Ama hadn't been interested. Olivia had been concerned about her reaction but Ethan had put it down to her extended recovery time and assured her it was fine, that Ama would get to it in her own time. That she needed to be ready.

And she was ready today.

Olivia was both nervous and excited, with butterflies dancing in her stomach whenever she thought about how Ama might react. She hoped she would be pleased. She hoped the old cheeky Ama would be back.

But in the interim she had to do something to rid herself of her nervous energy and, lucky for her, she always packed a swimsuit wherever she went!

Ethan increased the speed on the treadmill, trying to outrun the thoughts pounding through his head. He was using the clinic gym because his whole apartment, not just his bed, seemed to remind him of Olivia now. After being away from it for a decade and coming back to it again with Aaliyah's death still so fresh, it, along with his head space, had felt exclusively hers.

The place they would have lived. The kitchen they would have cooked in. The couch they would have snuggled on.

The bed they would have slept in.

But now Olivia was there too.

Sure, she'd been there before. Had spent a lot of time at his place. But that had been a long time ago—in a different lifetime practically. When he'd been spoiled and angry and unworthy of her love. Of anyone's love.

When he'd thought he'd been as injured as he could possibly be. *Man—had he been mistaken!*

Because a lot had happened since then. Aaliyah. His injuries. And now Olivia.

Who was everywhere in his apartment.

He'd had to get out.

Olivia heard a machine's noise and some grunting as she headed to the pool/gym area and hesitated for a second. She'd thought this early she'd be here by herself. But all she wanted to do was swim. A little bit of splashing surely wouldn't disturb anyone doing a workout. Especially not if they were making that much noise.

And maybe it was Leo. She needed to give him an Ama update anyway.

But as she walked closer she realised it wasn't Leo. It was Ethan. He wasn't wearing a shirt, exposing his broad back and shoulders completely to her view. A back and shoulders she'd know anywhere. The same back and shoulders she'd clung to the other night as he'd pounded into her like a man possessed.

Sweat beaded on his nape and in the furrow of his spine as his traps, rhomboids and lats bunched and re-laxed with each yank on the rowing machine handle. He was gliding frantically back and forth on the seat as if he was rowing for gold—or trying to outrun his demons.

Olivia almost turned and walked away and left him to his punishing exercise. There was no way he could have heard her above the noise of the machine and his own significant exertion. But they still hadn't talked, and she figured now Ama was better and they were alone it was as good a time as any.

She took a breath and continued towards him, leaning her butt against a nearby bench press apparatus.

Ethan started as the woman he'd been trying to row out of his head appeared beside him in a white fluffy robe tied loosely at the waist.

He almost groaned out loud. Did she *have* to be everywhere?

He turned back to concentrate on his workout, zoning her out of his peripheral vision as he regained his rhythm and rowed harder.

Olivia watched him ignoring her for a few moments, his eyes locked on the screen in front of him, where his programmed workout was ticking down. Her gaze dropped to his chest. She hadn't meant it to—it just did. The light smattering of hair across his pecs and bisecting his belly was so familiar to her, yet she didn't recall being conscious of it the other night.

Nothing but his mouth on hers and his hardness inside her had registered.

Annoyed at the direction of her thoughts, she folded her arms and asked in a raised voice, 'So, are there any sexually transmitted diseases I should know about?'

CHAPTER TEN

OLIVIA WAS SORRY that she got no discernible reaction from Ethan save for a tightening of his jaw. He just continued to pull on the handle of the rower and glide back and forth with powerful precision.

She wasn't actually worried about it. She was on the pill and Ethan, for all he could have been with his looks and his money, had never been a man whore. Or casual with contraception. They'd had a *lot* of sex and never *not* used a condom, despite her already being protected against pregnancy.

But it *had* been ten years, and in lots of ways the man before her was more of a stranger now than he'd ever been.

And weren't men in uniform supposed to have women throwing themselves in their paths?

Her gaze dropped to the bunching of muscles in his arms as they bent and straightened, bent and straightened. Ethan must have been a sight to behold in combat gear. All tall and broad, his tight butt emphasised by his long-legged stride. What girl could have resisted that when combined with his charming smile and his penchant for going all shaggy with his stubble?

She could imagine him right at home in some rocky

barren landscape in the middle of nowhere, doing what he did best—saving lives.

A minute later the machine beeped and Ethan, his thighs screaming, eased back on the pace, gliding up and down the rower more sedately now as he allowed his muscles and his temper time to cool down.

Olivia had been in his head and his dreams for the past five nights and now she was here, busting his balls. He refused to look at her, to answer her, until he was totally chilled.

When the cool-down period ended he finally pushed the seat back into the starting position, took his feet out of the foot plates and grounded them on the floor. He picked up his towel from beside the machine and dried off his head, nape and chest, then looped it around his neck and hung onto the tails.

'You're joking, right?' he said as he finally turned his head to look at her.

His eyes had gone from dull to downright chilly and Olivia suppressed a shiver. He seemed even further away than ever. 'I don't know you any more, Ethan.'

Ethan returned her gaze unflinchingly. 'You know me.'

God, if anyone knew him it was her. Not even Aaliyah had known him so warts and all. She'd only seen the good side of him, working side by side with him in a remote civilian hospital, swept up in the life and death of it all.

Easy to be heroic.

It was Olivia who had seen all the ugly stuff too.

Olivia looked away from the intensity of his eyes, her gaze dropping to the floor. She didn't want to think about the truth of his words. She shrugged. 'Maybe you had a girl in every port?'

Ethan's hands gripped the towel harder. There'd been very few women since Olivia and no one serious. Not until he'd totally lost his heart to Aaliyah anyway. 'I wasn't in the freaking navy, Olivia.'

Olivia toed the thin floor-covering. 'So you're clean?'

Ethan nodded. 'Yes. And I take it you are also—and still on the pill?'

It was Olivia's turn to nod. 'Good,' she said, prising her eyes off the ground. 'I guess we've had our talk, then.'

But they didn't get all the way to his face. Her gaze snagged on the bulk of an exposed quad. A quad deeply furrowed by the criss-cross of pink scar tissue, each deep fissure naked of the dark blond hair covering the rest of his thigh.

'Oh, God, Ethan…' she gasped, looking up at him and then back down at his legs, seeking the other exposed quad too, shocked at the state of them. 'Bloody hell…'

Ethan quickly whipped the towel off his neck and threw it across his lap. 'It's nothing,' he dismissed, cursing himself for not thinking. His gym shorts came to just below his knee—more than adequate cover—but he hadn't counted on the hem riding up to expose his injuries.

Or for her to be here.

The only person who had ever seen his scars apart from the myriad doctors and nurses who had treated him in hospital was Lizzie, who'd had the unenviable job of dressing his stubborn wounds as his home care nurse.

Olivia felt hot tears spike at her eyes. This was not *nothing*! No wonder his legs had almost given out on him that first time they'd seen each other again. She felt awful. They'd both been naked together the other night and she'd been more interested in having him inside her than worrying about his wounds or checking out his body.

Before she knew what she was doing she'd dropped to her knees beside him, pushing the towel aside. 'Ethan,' she whispered, looking up at him and then looking back down, one tentative finger following a deep ridge from one side of his thigh to the other.

She remembered that he'd said gunfire had caused his injuries and looking at them objectively, as a doctor, she knew it to be true. She'd seen too many bullet wounds in Africa.

Dear God, the pain he must have gone through.

And then without conscious thought she was lowering her mouth to where her finger had been. Kissing him better. Knowing that it was too little too late. Hating that he'd been so terribly wounded. That she'd judged him so harshly.

Ethan looked at her downcast head. The brush of her lips against the numb edges of his wounds and the caress of her honey-brown hair was strangely erotic.

He wasn't strong enough for this.

He'd just spent an hour trying to exorcise the memory of her. Trying to recapture the essence of Aaliyah. Her stoic, haunted beauty. Her steady, calming presence.

'Olivia…' he murmured, shutting his eyes, touched by her empathy, aroused by the visual of her bent head over his legs, the feel of her mouth hot against his thigh. Hating that something so obviously emotional, that gouged at his gut, also yanked at his groin. How could something so innocent be so sexual?

She had to stop. Or he was going to do something he regretted. The loathing he felt for himself cranked up another notch.

'Olivia!'

Olivia raised her head and looked at him as she sat back on her haunches. He looked torn, and the flecks in his eyes were glowing again, like the flash of fire in her opal ring. 'I hate that this happened to you,' she said. 'I just want to be able to…take it all away. To go back…'

Go back to the beginning. To stay and fight for him rather than storming out in a fit of pique. Even if he had deserved it. Maybe he wouldn't have joined up. Maybe she could have helped mend the rift between him and Leo.

Ethan shook his head. 'You can't,' he said, fighting against the compassion he saw in her eyes.

'How did this happen?' she whispered.

Ethan shook his head. His heart was clinging desperately to Aaliyah, to the promises he'd made her, but other parts of him wanted to scoop Olivia up, press her into the hard floor of the gym and fill the entire cavernous room with her cries.

To forget about how it had happened.

But he'd hurt her once before and he wasn't going to screw up his life—or her life—again with the mess that was in his head. There'd been enough loss in his life and he wasn't going to spread any collateral damage.

He wasn't a good bet. He knew that.

But she needed to know that.

He didn't want her to see him like this—as some man crippled by what had happened to him. As an object of sympathy. He didn't want her sympathy. She needed to stop thinking of him as some wounded man and remember how he'd crushed her heart into the dust.

Pulling himself together, looking down at the ugly

ridges that marred his skin, he was glad now though that she *had* seen them.

They were his constant reminder that he'd let Aaliyah down. That he didn't deserve a woman's love.

A tsunami of anger rolled inside him. She wanted to know how it had happened? *Fine.*

'There was this woman,' he said, glancing at her. 'Another doctor. Aaliyah. Aaliyah Hassan.'

Olivia swallowed at the way he said her name. There was a softness there—an affection. He'd sure as hell never said *her* name that way.

'I was working with her in a remote hospital in the south,' Ethan said. He paused and took a swig of water from the bottle on the ground beside the rower. 'They got a lot of civilian and military wounded through there,' he said, staring into the bottle. 'I was kind of…seconded there with some other medical personnel for quite some time. She was…amazing.'

Olivia didn't need him to say it. The truth of it was in the melting of his eyes and the way her stomach fell. 'You loved her.'

Ethan looked at Olivia. 'Yes. We were engaged to be married.'

Olivia was surprised how much it hurt and immediately castigated herself. Had she thought a decade later he'd be pining away for *her* somewhere, regretting his actions?

They'd both got on with their lives.

'What happened?'

'The area where the hospital was situated came under attack one day. We had to evacuate. It was…carnage.' Ethan shuddered at the memory. 'Aaliyah and I and a team from the base worked for hours on the evac, with shells landing all round us. It was almost done—we just had two criticals and another six patients to get to safety—and I told Aaliyah to go with them, that I'd wait behind. But they'd been her patients and she didn't want to leave them. She told me to go. There were some of my guys there for her protection, so I left.'

Olivia shut her eyes. She knew how this was going to end even before he finished—even before she looked down to see him kneading the scarred flesh of his thighs as if he was trying to pull it off his bones.

'I told her I'd be back for her in thirty minutes.' He looked up from his legs at her. 'They only had to wait another thirty minutes.'

Olivia nodded as she opened her eyes. 'You didn't get back in time?'

Ethan raked a hand through his sweaty hair. 'I did. We did. Two ambulances got back within thirty minutes. I was pushing one of the gurneys across to the entrance. Then this gunfire came out of nowhere, slamming into my legs, and I was falling to the ground. And then a shell slammed into the building and it just blew…it was… *flattened*. And I don't remember anything after that… not until I woke up in a field hospital.'

Olivia didn't need him to say the words. It was obvious that his fiancée had died in the building. 'And you feel guilty?'

He glared at her. 'You think I shouldn't?' He snorted.

Olivia knew a lot about this kind of guilt. *Survivor guilt.* 'You think you should have been in that building instead of her?'

'Yes. I wanted her out. I'd been trying to get her to evac with the others all day.'

'So…you'd be dead instead of her?'

'Yes,' he snapped.

Olivia tried not to flinch at his answer. She for one was pleased he hadn't been in the hospital when it had been flattened.

Ethan sighed. 'I don't know,' he said. 'Maybe things would have been different, would have gone down differently.'

Olivia nodded, knowing intimately how that question had haunted her. 'Do you think me being with my parents that day would have made a difference?'

Ethan felt the question slice like a stiletto between his ribs. The thought of Olivia burning to death with her parents was too horrific to contemplate. 'That's not the same thing, Olivia.'

Olivia cocked an eyebrow at him. They both knew it was *exactly* the same thing. 'Do you think I should feel guilty about that?'

Ethan looked at the floor. 'Of course not.' He looked up at her. 'Do you?'

She shrugged. 'I did. For a long time.'

'And how did you get past it?' In the beginning his guilt had been paralysing. And even now, particularly since Olivia, it was too much for Ethan to bear.

'I realised I wasn't living.' Olivia drew in a shaky breath. It had taken her a long time to come to terms with that. 'And my parents wouldn't have wanted that any more than they'd have wanted me there with them in the vehicle that day.'

Ethan stared at the woman in front of him. She'd been through a harrowing time a few years back. Had made the same kind of choice that he'd had to make. But she'd grown up in a stable, warm, loving environment and had always been well-adjusted.

He hadn't. He didn't have those kind of emotional

building blocks. For all that he'd loved his mother, the truth was that she'd been a vain socialite who had rarely been at home and his father had been first a bombastic, domineering taskmaster who'd thrived on the rivalry he'd whipped up between his sons, then later a morose drunk.

Olivia waited for him to say something but his dull brown eyes seemed lost somewhere in the past. 'Do you think Aaliyah would blame you?' she pushed. 'Would want you to be blaming yourself?'

Ethan looked down at his legs, at the scars that reminded him every day of Aaliyah. Of how he'd let her down. *Of how he'd failed.*

He stood abruptly, the towel slipping off his shoulders. 'Don't say her name,' he said.

He couldn't bear to hear Aaliyah's name coming from Olivia's mouth. They were so mixed up in his head he couldn't deal with another variation.

Olivia blinked at the vehemence in his voice, striking right into her heart. She pushed out of her leaning position, standing up straight. 'Ethan?'

'What do you want?' he demanded, glaring down at her.

'To help you. I understand what you're going through.'

Yes, keeping out of his way would be wiser, but she couldn't walk away from him right now.

Not when he looked so gutted.

Ethan's lips curled. 'You don't understand,' he said contemptuously, aware he wasn't acting or sounding rational but unable to stop himself. She was looking at him with those eyes, all warm, gooey and compassionate, as if he deserved her empathy, and it made him even more incensed.

Because he didn't.

'Whatever it is you think I deserve, I don't,' he said.

'I loved her and I left her to *die*. Hell, Olivia, I *used* you to make my brother jealous. You once said that my relationship with Leo was toxic, but you know what? I think maybe it's just me that's toxic. Me that destroys everything good in my life. Maybe I'm just my father's son? On the path to self-destruction. I'm damaged goods, sweetheart.'

Olivia couldn't bear the raw pain in his voice but she knew Ethan needed to get this stuff off his chest. 'Were,' she said.

'No, don't do that, Olivia.' He shook his head vehemently. 'I know that look. Even when I was destroying you ten years ago, when you realised what I'd done, you looked at me with those disbelieving eyes. Like I *really* wasn't a bad person. Next you'll be dropping by to check on me and cooking me dinner. Don't build castles in the air over me. *I don't deserve it.* What I did to you, what I did to Aaliyah, they're imprinted in my brain. I can't just forget.'

Olivia blinked. Was that what she was doing? Was she building castles? Was she falling in love with him again? A man whose heart was buried in a foreign land with the woman he loved? A woman he couldn't forget?

She shut her eyes against the truth of it. *No. Please, no.*

It had been bad enough the first time around. Loving a man who hadn't loved her in return. Only this time she'd be competing with a ghost.

She was a fool of the highest order.

'What if I can make you forget?'

Olivia blinked as the words spilled into the tense space between them. She had no idea where they'd come from or even what she was offering. A relationship where he used her again? Or something more platonic, where she helped him work through his guilt?

And lost a bit of herself every day? Loving him with nothing in return?

Oh, hell, she was a first class idiot.

Ethan looked down at her, at the slice of cleavage he could see where the robe gaped. He had no doubt she could make him forget everything in a hundred different ways—she already had.

But it always came back.

And he'd just hate himself a little bit more. And so would she—eventually.

He lifted his left leg and placed his foot on the apparatus beside her, the pink scars stretching as he leaned forward onto the leg. She looked down at them and then looked back up at him, her gaze killing him with her empathy.

'I have these to remind me,' he said bitterly.

Then he pushed off the machine, picked up his towel and water bottle from the floor and limped away without looking back.

Olivia swam up and down the twenty-five-metre pool non-stop for half an hour after that, her brain churning as she followed the black line.

I love him. I love him. I love him.

She was in love with Ethan Hunter. Again.

Still.

Had she ever really stopped? Sure, she'd despised him for a long time, and she'd buried herself in her work until it didn't hurt any more. But that wasn't the same as not *loving* him any more.

She hauled herself out of the pool, water sluicing off her, sitting on the edge in a puddle.

Stupid.

Stupid, crazy idiot.

Even more stupid now, given that Ethan was in love with someone else. *A dead woman.* A woman whose death had trapped him in a cast-iron cage of guilt and penance where he didn't think he was deserving of love.

The mere thought both broke her heart and expanded the love in her chest even more.

Prime, numero uno *idiot*!

He'd made it clear that he wasn't going to let her in, that his heart belonged elsewhere, and she knew she couldn't go down that track with him again. She wasn't going to beat her head against the same brick wall she hadn't even realised she'd been beating her head against last time.

She had to have more self-respect than that, no matter how much Ethan's story tugged at her excessively sappy heartstrings!

He was right. No castles in the air for Ethan Hunter. Not this time.

Olivia's heavy thoughts dogged her all the way up to the clinic after she'd showered and changed. And she was still mired deep in the question of her sanity when she almost ran smack-bang into Lizzie, Leo's wife and the nurse in charge at the Hunter Clinic, as she stepped into the main section of the building from the basement stairs.

'Oh, sorry,' Olivia apologised, taking a moment or two to gather her thoughts.

Lizzie was in early. It was still barely seven-thirty. She'd crossed paths with the impressive head nurse a couple of times over the past few weeks and had been invited to their place next week for dinner.

'It's fine,' Lizzie dismissed with a quick smile. 'You look a little distracted.'

'What?' Olivia asked. 'Oh…no, sorry, just…' She

shook her head. *Just what?* Inventing new and imaginative ways to murder your brother-in-law?

'Ah,' Lizzie said. 'I know that look. It's a man, yes?'

Olivia blinked. She was so stunned by the question she heard herself saying, 'Yes.'

'Come on,' Lizzie said. 'I have just the thing for that.'

Olivia glanced at her watch. She still had time, so she followed Lizzie to Leo's office. Lizzie headed for Leo's desk and Olivia hoped Lizzie wasn't going to offer her some medicinal whisky at seven-thirty in the morning.

Lizzie sat in Leo's chair, then reached down and to the side. Olivia heard a drawer opening and some riffling before Lizzie produced an intriguing flat box with beautifully embossed gold letters she couldn't quite make out.

Not that she needed to. Chocolate boxes looked pretty much the same the world over.

Lizzie opened the lid and inhaled appreciatively. She offered the box to Olivia who, despite not being a huge chocoholic, took one anyway.

'Leo always keeps a stash here for me. The baby has made this old sweet tooth even sweeter, and God alone knows I ate truckloads of the stuff when Leo and I were dancing around each other.'

Olivia unwrapped the golden foil and bit into the sweet treat. It melted on her tongue and fizzed seductively against her tastebuds. She shut her eyes as it rushed through her system. 'Mmm,' she said, opening her eyes. '*This* is good chocolate.'

Lizzie nodded enthusiastically as she picked a second out of the box. 'They're from the kingdom of Sirmontane. Marco—or I should say *Prince* Marco of Sirmontane, who Ethan patched up after being wounded in battle and who is engaged to Becca, our hand therapist—keeps me in constant supply. I've never been to a royal wedding before—I'm very excited.'

Olivia had tried not to flinch when Ethan's name was mentioned but it had been unexpected. She was pleased that Lizzie seemed too engrossed in reaching for a third chocolate to notice.

'Sirmontane is known for its excellence in chocolate,' Lizzie said, offering Olivia another, which she took without hesitation. 'Better than anything you'll get from Switzerland.'

Olivia nodded. It *was* exceptional chocolate. She'd heard about Prince Marco, and had met the lucky Becca once, but she hadn't known that Ethan had been his surgeon. Just the mention of his name took some of the sweetness out of the experience.

Lizzie nodded. 'The perfect antidote for what ails you, don't you think?'

Olivia nodded non-committally as she savoured the smooth rich flavour on her tongue. It really was quite spectacular, and had made her temporarily forget her man problems, but ever since Lizzie had said his name Ethan had become front and centre again.

Why did she have to love *him*?

Lizzie narrowed her gaze. 'I'm going to take a punt and guess that you're not thinking about the marvels of European chocolate?' she asked.

The sweetness coating her tongue turned to dust in her mouth and Olivia shrugged. 'No.'

'Are you thinking about Ethan?'

Olivia blinked. She liked Lizzie from what little she knew about her, but Olivia wasn't sure if she wanted to get into *this* with Lizzie, given the whole love triangle history she'd shared with Leo and Ethan.

'I do know, you know…about what happened ten years ago. Between you and Leo and Ethan.'

Olivia wasn't sure what she should say to that. Was Lizzie angry? Was she going to call her names or want pistols at dawn? 'Oh.'

'Leo thinks there might be a chance for you and Ethan this time around. A real chance. Do you love him?'

Okay. Now Olivia really didn't know what to say. Lizzie sure didn't beat around the bush. 'I… I…' What was the point in admitting it when it was a futile thing to feel anyway?

'Do you know what happened to him on his last tour?'

'Yes.' Olivia nodded, pleased to be able to answer one question at least. 'I read it in the paper and he and I… we've talked about it since.'

Lizzie sat back in Leo's chair. 'He's been through a lot. His injuries were horrific.'

'I know,' Olivia agreed. 'Not to mention Aaliyah.'

Lizzie frowned. 'Aaliyah? Oh, you mean Dr Hassan? The doctor that was killed when the hospital was bombed? Yes. He hasn't really said much about her, but I think he feels a degree of guilt over that too. I think everything about that day feeds into a significant case of PTSD.'

It was then Olivia realised that Lizzie didn't know about Aaliyah. Didn't know that Ethan had lost the woman he loved that day. Which probably meant that Leo didn't know either.

He hadn't told anybody.

Except her.

What the hell did that mean?

'Look,' Lizzie said, leaning a little closer and offering Olivia another chocolate. 'I know this is none of my business, but Ethan is kind of lost, and he needs someone to stick with him, and I think, by the way you flinched when I mentioned his name before, that you're probably the one to do it.'

Olivia shook her head. Lizzie might be well intentioned but there was a lot she clearly didn't know.

Lizzie raised her hand at Olivia's objection. 'I know these Hunter men. I know how they push you away. But I also know that they didn't exactly have warm and fuzzy upbringings and that they're hurting deep down inside—Ethan probably more so than Leo.'

Olivia admired how Lizzie was on Team Hunter. A wife should be. But… 'I don't think you know the full story,' she said tentatively.

'I know Ethan behaved reprehensibly,' Lizzie said. 'But if you love him, please, *please* don't give up on him.'

Olivia watched as Lizzie's hand fell to her belly, to a baby that wasn't even on show yet. 'The Hunter men are worth the fight.'

Olivia felt absurdly like crying. If only it were that simple.

She knew how great it felt to be Ethan's woman. Even if he had been with her for all the wrong reasons he'd always been very attentive. Made her feel as if she *was* special. And she believed a lot of that had been genuine for him.

But there was another person now in their already complicated relationship. A woman he'd made it clear was his one and only love. How was she supposed to compete with Aaliyah?

Was she destined always to love a man who didn't love her back?

'Another?' Lizzie asked.

Olivia nodded. Why not? Chocolate was simpler than the problems that whizzed and clashed in her brain.

And it might be the closest she'd ever come to gratification again.

She found the biggest one and sank her teeth into it.

CHAPTER ELEVEN

THREE DAYS LATER Ethan stood in the doorway of Ama's hospital room and watched as Ama admired herself—actually, *preened* was probably a better word—in front of a small hand-held mirror. She angled her head from side to side and brought the mirror closer for a moment or two, before taking it back to appreciate a wider frame.

She'd been looking at herself in the mirror practically non-stop since she'd first seen her new face a few days ago, and he never got tired of seeing her reaction. She still had the staples in her graft, and there was residual swelling around the operative area, but her face was now 'whole' and it was obvious Ama was thrilled with the result.

Yes, they had more work to do in the next couple of months, and the dressing over Ama's trachea from her healing stoma was a constant reminder that not everything had gone smoothly. But the aesthetic part of the reconstructive surgery had been an outstanding success.

Olivia was clearly ecstatic with the result. He watched her as she sat on the bed in front of Ama, and even though Ethan could only see her in profile he knew she was grinning broadly at Ama's mirror antics. He enjoyed the sight for long moments, because the minute she saw him it would all change.

She'd been cool towards him the past few days. Not that he could blame her. He'd pushed her away in his need to cling to Aaliyah and this was the result. But still, he hated to see the distance in her gaze, hated the walls between them even though he was responsible for them.

Even though he knew it was the best way forward.

As he watched, Olivia gave Ama the pen torch and he could see the girl's eyes shining from way across the other side of the room. Ethan remembered how Olivia had talked about having children one day. He thought about all the kids at the Lighthouse he'd seen her with too. She was a natural and, watching her with Ama, he knew she'd make a great mother.

Something stirred in his chest at the thought of what her babies might look like—stirred, tugged, kicked—but he quashed it. Whatever mini-Olivias looked like it was none of his damn concern.

Ama giggled and dragged his attention back to the room. She popped the pen torch into the side of her mouth that hadn't been operated on and, with her mouth closed, flicked it on. Ama watched as her cheek glowed red in the mirror and she laughed so hard Ethan thought she was going to fall off the bed. It was so infectious, so joyous, so innocent—as it should be—he couldn't help joining in.

He saw Olivia's back stiffen slightly as he entered the room but she turned and gave him a small smile, and even if her eyes were cool her demeanour was one hundred per cent professional as she stood politely.

Ethan sat on the bed where Olivia had been and there was some more playing with the torch, and Ama, who'd really come out of the shell she'd been in post-op, chat-

ted as if she'd been mute all her life and had just found
her voice. Dali was scrambling to keep up with her and
Ethan laughed at her enthusiasm.

He glanced at Olivia, who was looking down at Ama
with affection in her gaze. Was she thinking the same
as he was? Would Ama have been this carefree—this
animated, this happy—if she'd been married off at such
a young age?

Was she thinking about the potential Ama had now?

Olivia had literally given this lucky little girl her life
back.

'Well, I think you are way too well to be in hospital,
Little Miss,' Ethan said, looking back at Ama. 'I think
it's time you went and stayed with your host family until
your next operation.'

Olivia watched Ril and Ama's face as Dali translated. They were so rapturously happy she could feel
tears scalding the backs of her eyes. Fair Go had sourced
an African family to host Ril and Ama in between surgeries, and she knew how much they were both looking
forward to some familiarity.

There was a flurry of excitement in the room and
it was hard for Olivia not to get caught up in it. She'd
been keeping herself in check around Ethan, but when he
smiled at her with a *how-great-is-this?* look in his eyes
she found herself smiling back.

It *was* great. Apart from a hiccup or two, Ama's surgery had been successful and that was something to celebrate. There was no reason to be churlish because their
personal baggage sat like a loaded luggage carousel between them.

But when he cocked his head to indicate he wanted
to talk to her outside she felt the barriers going up. The

man was rocking a pair of scrubs again and she really wasn't strong enough for this.

Now Ama was being discharged there was no need to see Ethan on a regular basis until Ama came back in for her next scheduled op. And once Ama was back in Africa Olivia would be gone also. Sure, she'd be coming back and forth to London on charity business, and she'd also be in phone and email contact with him, but that would be so much easier than this.

Having to face him so soon after their talk in the gym, after realising she still loved him, was too hard. She could accept that she loved him, and that he'd never return that love, but not if he was parading around in her deepest secret fantasy garb, taunting her with what would never be hers.

Olivia took steadying breaths as she stepped into the corridor with him, hoping this wasn't anything personal. He'd made his position clear and she was fine to walk the line he'd drawn.

'Tell me again where Ama's staying?' he asked, folding his arms across his chest.

Olivia tried not to notice the way the scrubs pulled tight against his biceps and to concentrate on what he'd asked, relieved it was all business. They had a brief conversation revolving around Ama's discharge planning and her living arrangements in between ops.

'I'll get Helen to make an appointment for Ama in my rooms on day ten,' he said, making a mental note to tell the very efficient Hunter Clinic senior receptionist when he got back there this afternoon. 'The staples have to come out then, so it might as well be the first follow-up.'

Olivia nodded. 'I'll see that she gets there.'

Ethan studied Olivia for a moment. It sounded as if

she wasn't going to be attending herself and he wondered just how much he was going to be seeing of her now. He knew it was a good thing, to get some distance from each other, but perversely he didn't want *not* to see her either.

Talking to her the other day had been harrowing, and he'd been harsh and awful, but he'd felt as if a weight had been lifted from his shoulders.

Hell, he'd slept through three nights in a row.

Olivia turned to go—clearly they were done here. But his 'I need to thank you for the other day,' pulled her up.

She turned and arched an eyebrow.

'I know I was…harsh, and I pushed you away, but… it really helped being able to talk to you…about what happened. About…' he dropped his voice '…Aaliyah. I feel…better. I'm sleeping better.'

Olivia couldn't believe what she was hearing. She shut her eyes against it, wishing it was as easy to shut her ears. She didn't want to know how much *better* Ethan felt. Did he have any clue how much *worse* she felt?

A wave of anger and frustration welled in her at his obliviousness. 'I shouldn't be the only one who knows this, Ethan,' she said, lowering her voice to a scathing whisper as she folded her arms. 'Hell, I can't believe you've never *told* anyone. Don't you think that Leo should at least know?'

Ethan was taken aback by her contemptuous disbelief. He'd never thought to tell Leo. It had all been too big, too horrible even to contemplate. He'd just been hanging on, getting through each day and then Olivia had come back. He and Leo might be closer now, but he doubted they'd ever be *that* close. 'Why?'

Olivia shook her head. 'Dear Lord…why do you *think*, Ethan? Because he's your brother, you idiot. He *loves* you. You've taken all this time to mend your fences and work on your relationship and yet you keep this big... *huge* thing that's been weighing you down and screwing you up for over a year all to yourself? *He's your family*, Ethan, and I know you don't really know how that works, but trust me on this—you share this kind of stuff with each other.'

Ethan frowned. She was really ticked. 'Okay...maybe you're right...maybe it *is* time I told Leo. But I don't understand why you're so angry about it.'

Olivia all but rolled her eyes. *Because I love you too, you idiot.*

'Hey, Olivia, just checking you're—' Kara stopped when she realised that Olivia wasn't alone in the corridor and that things were a little intense between her and Ethan. 'Oh, sorry,' she apologised.

'Don't be,' Olivia said stiffly, glaring at Ethan. 'Perfect timing.'

She turned and gave Kara a strained smile. Kara looked from Olivia to Ethan and then back to Olivia. The look on her face said she wasn't sure at all about the timing.

'You wanted something?' Olivia prompted tersely.

Kara put up her hands in a placatory manner. 'I was just seeing if we were still on to go dress shopping this arvo.'

Olivia groaned inwardly. Damn it. The hospital ball. She'd forgotten that Kara had finally harangued her into going. But with Ama being discharged and spare time on her hands she was going to need something to fill it.

'Sure,' she said, softening her smile and nodding reassuringly at Kara. 'Looking forward to it.' *Like a scalpel to the jugular.*

Kara nodded and scooted away with what Ethan could only describe as indecent haste. 'So…you're going to the ball, then?' he asked.

Ethan had thought she'd resisted all Kara's entreaties to let her hair down and have a night of fun.

Olivia felt tension lock her jaw at the surprise in his voice. Right at this moment she resented the hell out of how well he *thought* he knew her. 'Yes, I am,' she said, her voice not so much of a whisper any more. 'And I'm going to dance with *every* available man there. *And* I will be making it my mission to not go home alone,' she lied. 'You got a problem with that?'

Ethan felt her angry challenge kick him right between the eyes. As it happened, he had *big* problems with it. He knew he had no say over who she did or didn't sleep with, and that she was a free agent, but the thought grabbed at his gut and squeezed hard.

He was aware of the curious gazes of the staff passing by them in the corridor. 'Why don't you say it a little louder?' he said, keeping his tone low.

Olivia saw red. *Patronising bastard.* She opened her mouth to refute his statement about the volume of her voice when a male nurse winked at her as he passed by. 'Put *me* on your dance card, darlin',' he said in a thick Irish accent.

Olivia blinked, startled by the offer, heat flushing her cheeks. 'You got it,' she said, and then smiled as the Irish charmer grinned and clutched his heart, all without missing a step.

Ethan clenched his fists by his sides and made a mental note to talk to the guy about *boundaries.* 'Olivia…' He shook his head. 'This isn't you.'

Olivia returned her gaze to Ethan's face. He did look

less tired than she'd seen him. 'Oh, yes it is,' she said testily, lowering her voice again. 'This is who I am now.'

Now he'd made it clear his heart was taken.

Ethan took a step towards her. 'Olivia.'

It was like a punch to his solar plexus when she took a step back, her eyes frosty. It had never been his intention to hurt her. *Again.* He'd laid his cards on the table to *avoid* hurting her. But right now she looked as if she'd never hated him more. Not even that day she'd overheard the argument between him and Leo and called them toxic.

Olivia wanted to step closer so badly she had to grind her feet into the floor to stop herself. Ethan was right—it wasn't her. But she had to break his hold over her.

He was damaged and, damn it, she deserved someone whole.

Someone who had their whole heart to give.

He was waiting for her to say something; she could tell. But there were no words, just a heart that was crumbling in her chest. So she turned and walked away.

There was a knock at Ethan's door at six o'clock the next night. He'd been prowling around his living area nonstop since he'd walked in half an hour ago, and a bottle of whisky was sitting on the kitchen bench.

He felt restless and edgy, but every time he stopped to pour himself a drink he realised he didn't want it. He wished he did—he wished he could drink the whole damn thing and forget about Olivia dancing with every man at the ball.

He didn't know why this was making him so crazy, but he knew whisky wasn't going to make it better.

Right now all he wanted to do was go to Olivia's place,

drag her into his arms and kiss her senseless. That was what he craved more than whisky.

But he didn't have the right. He couldn't offer her what she needed. What she deserved.

Leo was standing on his doorstep in a tux when Ethan opened to the second knock. As if he needed another reminder of the ball. 'You really didn't have to dress to come see me,' Ethan said derisively.

'I didn't wear this for *you*, brother dear. My wife usually lasts an hour with me in a tux before she wants me out of it. My motives are purely ulterior.'

Ethan screwed up his face. 'Too much information,' he said, standing aside, indicating for his brother to come in and following Leo's broad shoulders down the short hallway into the living area. 'Did Lizzie send you?'

It had been a clinic day for him today, and Lizzie had been relentless in her campaign to have both Hunter men in tuxes representing the Hunter Clinic at the ball.

'Yes.'

Ethan gave a half laugh, half snort at the bald admission. 'I'm not going to the damn ball.'

Leo folded his arms and didn't look as if he was going to be moving any time soon. Not without Ethan anyway. 'She's going to be annoyed with me if I don't show up with you.'

'Well, only for an hour, by the sounds of it. I'm sure you can tough it out. Flirt with her a little. You might be able to get her out of there in under an hour.'

Leo chuckled and Ethan felt a pang at how obviously happy his brother was to be under the thumb. Ethan watched him stroll towards the kitchen bench, hands in his pockets.

'Good to see you actually have your own whisky instead of always relying on my stash,' he said as he took his hands out and lifted the bottle, inspecting the label. 'You planning on drinking all of this tonight?'

Ethan looked at Leo. He read the unspoken thoughts in his brother's eyes as the spectre of their father rose between them. 'No.' Although a few weeks back he would have given it a good shake.

Leo nodded. He put the bottle down, then perched himself on one of the bar stools. 'Okay. So what's going on with you?' He held up a hand as Ethan started to interrupt. 'I know you and I don't really do this…*talking* stuff…but I do hope you know you *can* talk to me?'

Ethan regarded his brother steadily. He looked uncomfortable, and Ethan knew it couldn't have been easy for Leo to initiate this. They'd had some frank discussions in the last six months. Got a lot of things out in the open. Told some home truths. But those had eventuated from tense, heated conversations. None of them had started out as a simple, *'What's going on with you?'*

And then a thought struck him and he narrowed his eyes. 'Has Olivia been talking to you?' *She wouldn't say anything, surely?*

Leo frowned. 'No.' He looked at his brother speculatively. 'What about?' He sat up straighter. 'Is everything okay?'

Olivia's voice played through Ethan's head.

'Don't you think that Leo should at least know?'

'He's your family, Ethan.'

'You share this kind of stuff with each other.'

'No…she's fine… We had a talk yesterday, that's all. She kind of told me off.'

Leo chuckled. 'She's pretty good at that from what I

remember. I don't think anyone can say the word *toxic* with quite as much disgust dripping from it as Olivia.'

Ethan gave a half-smile. She had given them both a right dressing-down that day. 'She reckons I should tell you about what happened to me on tour.'

Leo shook his head. 'I know what happened, Ethan. The papers gave a pretty good rundown of it and your injuries speak for themselves. I think I can fill in the gaps. I don't want you to rehash it if you don't want to.'

'Not about that,' Ethan said. He headed to the kitchen and grabbed two crystal tumblers from one of the overhead cupboards—this *was* going to require some alcoholic fortification.

He cracked the lid on the bottle of whisky and splashed a couple of fingers in each glass. His hand shook. He couldn't believe he was about to open up to Leo. Prior to three days ago no one had known about Aaliyah, and now not only did Olivia know, he was about to tell Leo also.

But Olivia was right—they were brothers, and if he wanted their relationship to continue, to thrive and grow instead of always being stilted…

And he did want that, he realised.

He pushed a glass towards Leo before swallowing half of his down. 'There was a woman…' he said.

Leo looked at Ethan. 'Oh,' he said, and swallowed half of his whisky down too.

CHAPTER TWELVE

FOR THE NEXT fifteen minutes Ethan talked and Leo listened. Ethan was grateful for his silence. It enabled him to tell the story of him and Aaliyah in his own words and it all just tumbled out.

'I'm sorry,' Leo said, when Ethan seemed to have talked himself dry.

'Thank you.'

'I wish you'd told me earlier.'

'Yeah,' Ethan acknowledged as he stared into the depths of the whisky he was swirling in his glass. 'Sorry...'

Leo shrugged it off. 'And Olivia knows?'

Ethan nodded grimly. 'She does now.'

'She loves you, you know?'

Ethan glanced up sharply at his brother, pleased he didn't have a mouthful of drink. His heart leapt painfully in his chest at the possibilities. *At the impossibilities.*

'She *told* you that?'

Leo shook his head. 'No. Of course not. But I've seen Olivia in love with you once before, remember? I know what that looks like.'

Ethan shut his eyes. If anybody knew after their love triangle debacle, it was Leo. *This was bad.* He'd seen the other day how her compassion for what he'd been through had melted her heart. Hardly surprising—Olivia always had been one of the most empathetic people he'd ever known. She'd told him ten years ago that his big wounded eyes were what had attracted him to her.

And he'd been aware of the slippery slope. That was why he'd warned her about building castles in the sky.

But if he'd known…if he'd suspected…

What? He'd have been more direct? More direct than *I'm damaged goods* and *Steer clear*? The truth was his biggest fear was that he wouldn't have. That he would have ruthlessly taken advantage of her like he had a decade ago. For some reason she'd got back under his skin and he was beginning to crave her more than he'd ever craved whisky.

Ethan shook his head, pushing away the thought, clinging to the memory of the woman he loved. 'I love Aaliyah.'

Leo quirked an eyebrow. 'Are you telling me or yourself?'

Ethan glared at his brother as thunderclouds gathered in his gut. 'I would be very careful what you say next.'

Leo didn't look remotely concerned. 'You think you can only ever love one person, Ethan? Just stop for a moment and think about how *crazy* that is. That means I'd still be hung up on Olivia and have no room for Lizzie.'

Ethan's hand tightened around his glass. The idea of Leo and Olivia clawed at his gut with about the same ferocity as the shame he felt at his actions a decade ago. 'You didn't love Olivia.'

'No. But I could have. If she hadn't been so gung-ho about you.'

Ethan looked down into his drink. 'I'm sorry about that. She really deserved you more than me.'

Leo nodded. 'That's very true.'

Ethan glanced up, startled, then saw the smile on his brother's face and returned it with a grudging one of his own.

'Look, Ethan, if this Aaliyah was as amazing and compassionate as she sounds do you think she would have wanted you to *never* love again? To never *be* loved? Would you have wanted that for her if, God forbid, it had been you that had stayed behind in the hospital that day?'

Ethan held his brother's gaze, the truth of what he was saying looming large in his brain. Of course Aaliyah wouldn't have wanted that. And nor would he. She'd been a wonderful, passionate, beautiful woman. For her never to have found someone else to share that with would have been a travesty.

'No,' he conceded.

'I think she'd be pretty annoyed about it, don't you?'

Ethan looked into his heart. Aaliyah had been very passionate and opinionated—*annoyed* was probably a mild descriptor.

But still he couldn't let go. 'I can't… I feel like I'm betraying her.'

'Why is it a betrayal?' Leo demanded. 'Loving again after death and heartache and your whole world going to hell? That's resurrection, Ethan. That's affirmation that the love you felt for Aaliyah wasn't something wasted and lost forever. It honours her memory. It says that loving Aaliyah was so amazing it was worth all the heartache. That love is worth it.'

Ethan's head buzzed at his brother's reasoning.

'And can you look at me—*really* look at me,' Leo said, 'and tell me you don't feel *anything* for Olivia.'

Ethan knew he couldn't do that. His feelings for Olivia had been churning inside him for weeks now, and were becoming more and more muddled since they'd ended up all over each other in his bed. He'd been pushing them away, holding them back, because of the guilt he felt about Aaliyah.

But what if Leo was right? What if there was more than one person for everyone? What if loving again honoured his love for Aaliyah instead of betraying it.

What if he could love Olivia *without* betraying Aaliyah?

'Tell me what you've been feeling since you told Olivia about Aaliyah.'

Ethan dragged in a breath, still trying to wrap his head around the revelations of the night. 'I feel…lighter… better. Like a weight's been lifted. I've carried it around so long it felt like a block around my neck. I've been sleeping so much better. And I haven't had a drop to drink since I told her until now.'

'I think that's called catharsis. Interesting choice of who you chose to tell first, don't you think?'

Ethan shrugged. 'I guess.'

Leo looked at his brother and Ethan felt as if he was being weighed up. 'A little while back you pretty much told me I'd be a fool to let Lizzie out of my life, and so now I'm here, telling you the same thing. I think you love Olivia, but you're too screwed up by your past—not just what happened on tour, but before, way before that, with Mum and Dad—and too frightened of the future to admit it. But make no mistake: you are a fool if you let her get away a second time. Life's short, Ethan. *You* know that more intimately than anyone. Don't blow it by clinging to somebody who you know, deep down, wouldn't ask you for that sacrifice.'

Ethan felt a heat spreading in his chest as possibilities bloomed. Was Leo right? Did he love Olivia? He'd studiously avoided any deep emotional attachment to her last time because his agenda with her had had nothing to do with love.

But there'd been no agenda this time.

He tried to push the spreading heat, the possibilities back—he'd really screwed up with Olivia again. 'I think I may have blown any chance with her, Leo.'

'Yeah, knowing you, you've been a complete idiot,' Leo agreed. 'But love forgives, Ethan. Above all, love forgives.'

Leo was looking straight into his eyes and Ethan felt as if his brother wasn't just referring to the situation between him and Olivia. 'You should write for Hallmark,' he joked, because the enormity of what he was contemplating was too, too much.

Leo rolled his eyes. 'Yeah, yeah.'

But then suddenly it seemed right. As if something that had been holding impossibly tight in his gut had just twanged free.

'I love her,' Ethan said, and it came out on such a pent-up rush of emotion he felt as if he'd just breathed his heart up and it was lying on the marble benchtop between them.

He felt panicked and afraid, but also…hopeful.

It took a few moments but Leo smiled at him. Slowly at first, and then bigger, almost in time with the love blooming inside Ethan's chest.

'Well, let's go and get her, then.' Leo grinned, swallowing the dregs of his drink in one hit. 'Come on, Cinderella, you *shall* go to the ball. Where's your tuxedo?'

Olivia had never felt this alone in a room full of people in her life. She could see her reflection in the French doors of the opulent room, and even sipping champagne in a group of people she looked so damn forlorn not even she could bear to look at herself.

Kara had picked out the perfect frock for her—a purple frothy gown with shoestring straps that crisscrossed at her cleavage and spilled down into a full gauzy skirt with thousands of diamantés sewn into it. They shone like stars in the light from the expensive crystal chandeliers. It sat low on her back, making a bra impossible, and brushed against the floor.

She'd twisted her hair up into a hasty knot because she'd been too despondent to wash it, and the only accessories she'd indulged in were a touch of lip gloss and her opal ring.

Kara had exclaimed at how stunning she'd looked when Olivia had made her entrance, and every available man in the room, and a lot of the not so available ones, most certainly agreed. Her dance card was full. Olivia hoped that was just from opportunity rather than from word getting around that she was auditioning men to take home.

She wasn't going home with anyone.

In fact she was counting down the minutes until it might seem respectable enough for her to leave. Alone. When would it be okay to plead a headache and slip out through the door?

She hated that she felt so down. The ballroom was lit by thousands of tiny lights, like a fairy kingdom, and the band that was playing soft melodic jazz would at any other time have delighted her. Hell, the whole room was a visual feast, with the lights and the decorations from something out of *A Midsummer's Night Dream* not to mention the beautiful array of colourful fabrics swirling around.

Gorgeous women sparkled and dashing men dazzled in their elegant tuxedoes. Normally she would have been in her element.

But tonight, despite no shortage of men to dance with, she could barely raise a smile.

Her reflection mocked her. *What did you expect?* And it was right. She shouldn't have expected anything. But a part of her had, deep, *deep* down, hoped that Ethan would swing by and pick her up. That he would gallantly announce that he was her date and the only man she would be going home with.

God! She was such a sucker for a happy ending. And there was nothing like a grand ball to stir that old chestnut.

The man was damaged beyond repair, for crying out loud. And his heart was buried in an ancient arid landscape with a woman she could never compete with.

Stupid. Stupid. Stupid.

The lights blurred and formed stars before her eyes as she rapidly blinked back even more stupid tears. This had to stop. She was lucky—things were going well. Ama's surgery had been a success, she and Ril were settled with their host family and Fair Go was thriving.

So many more people in the world had it so much worse—Ama was a classic example of that. She should be deliriously happy.

And she was. But there was an emptiness inside her as well. And there was only one thing that could fill it.

Ethan.

Ethan *freaking* Hunter.

'I do believe you promised me a dance.'

Olivia was dragged from her introspection by a sexy Irish accent. She smiled at the familiar face—a nice-looking man, with kind, flirty eyes.

Far better than dull, lifeless eyes. This man looked as if he knew how to laugh and show a girl a good time.

'I do believe you're right,' she said.

He told her his name was Aidan as he led her to the floor, and when they found some available space he took her in his arms and held her at a comfortable distance. They made some polite chit-chat for a few moments.

'So,' Aidan said. 'You and Ethan, huh?'

Olivia almost tripped over his feet. It was on the tip of her tongue to deny it, but he was so open and honest-looking, so undemanding, she found herself smiling. 'Guilty.'

Aidan sighed dramatically. 'Surgeons get all the hot women. You know, you really should give a male nurse a go. We're *very* good with anatomy and we have a much better bedside manner. Plus—although I can't speak for anyone else—we're always exceedingly grateful.'

Olivia laughed, finally relaxing and enjoying the man's company. 'I'm afraid my heart was a done deal a long time ago.'

'Clearly the man's an A-grade fool.'

Olivia smiled. 'Yes. He's the top of his class.'

'Well, you know, having drunken sex with a lowly male nurse is a great revenge tactic.'

Olivia supposed she should have been shocked or affronted by Aidan's forthright conversation but she wasn't either. His tone was light and his gaze was flirty. She didn't feel threatened or unsafe. Just amused—and God knew she needed a laugh about now.

Aidan was good and kind—it shone from his soul. Not to mention smart—laughing a woman into bed was a very good ploy.

'Thanks. I'll keep it in mind.'

Aidan nodded and they danced for a few moments in silence. 'I'm just saying,' he said, pulling back to look into her face, 'I'd volunteer for the job 'cos that's just the kind of guy I am.'

Olivia laughed. 'You're a trooper. And I appreciate it.'

He sighed again. 'Not going to work, huh?'

Olivia shook her head. 'Sorry. If it's any consolation, I would if…'

Aidan nodded. 'If you weren't head over heels in love with the man who is now pushing his way through a crowded dance floor looking like he wants to make mincemeat of my face.'

Olivia frowned at him. 'What?'

But then an imperious voice, so English compared to the soft burr of Aidan's accent, said, 'May I cut in?'

Aidan looked at a tense-jawed Ethan, then at Olivia. 'It's up to you, darlin',' he said. 'You can dance with him or I can take him outside and beat him up.'

Olivia blinked at Aidan's joviality in the face of what was a fairly hostile situation. Ethan might be dressed in a tux but that was the only civilised thing about him right now as he glared down at the Irishman in stony silence.

'Just say the word,' Aidan chirped.

Olivia did a quick calculation of the body mass difference between the two men and her respect for Aidan trebled. He was going to make some girl an amazing partner one day.

'Thanks.' She smiled at him and squeezed his arm. 'You've been fabulous, but I think I can take it from here.'

Ethan relaxed slightly when the Irish nurse bowed gallantly and melted away. 'May I?' he asked.

Olivia's heart was thrumming against her ribs so loudly she could barely hear him. 'I didn't think you danced,' she said waspishly.

Ethan grabbed her by the waist and pulled her close. 'I do tonight.'

Olivia's arms went around his neck automatically, for stability, and then just because he looked so damn good and smelled a thousand per cent better. He swayed against her, and for someone who battled a limp and maintained he couldn't dance he managed to get to the end of the song without stepping on her feet or crashing into anyone.

They pulled apart as everyone else did, and clapped politely, but the whole time he was looking at her with lust and heat and sex in his eyes and Olivia's belly turned to mush and her legs to jelly. She felt as if they were the only two people in the room.

'Let's get out of here,' he said as the band started a new song, taking her hand and leading her to the French doors.

By the time they'd stepped out onto a terrace that was lit with enough tiny lights to power an entire fairytale castle Olivia was grateful for the cold air on her heated flesh. Her dress was not suitable for a November night in London, but she was so hot and bothered it was a blessing.

'Ethan, what do you—?'

It was as far as she got before he turned and cut her

off with a kiss that was so deep and hard and hungry all she could do was shut her eyes and hang on.

When he pulled away they were both panting, and Olivia was annoyed at herself for being swept away by the lights and the dancing and his dashing frame filling out a tuxedo as well as he did a pair of scrubs.

Hell, the man had even shaved.

'What do you think you're doing?' she demanded.

Ethan had been rehearsing his speech on the way over in a taxi with Leo, but then he'd seen her dancing with Irish and it had wiped everything other than the urge to break fingers from his brain. And then he'd been holding her, and she looked so damn good and so incredibly sexy there was no way he was ever going to remember the impassioned entreaty he'd worked on with Leo.

'I've been incredibly stupid,' he said.

Olivia blinked. 'You have?'

Ethan nodded. 'Yes. I have. I love you. I'm in love with you. But I couldn't admit it to myself. I felt bad even feeling it, and then Leo said—'

'Leo?' Olivia interrupted as her heart started to beat a little bit faster at the possibilities he was presenting.

'Yes, he came over and we talked, and I told him about Aaliyah, and he made me see that she would never have wanted me to bury my heart and my life with her.'

'Oh,' she said faintly, noting the bright glow in his eyes as the golden flecks outshone the fairy lights. Did this mean what she thought it meant? Dared she hope? Her pulse tripped at the thought.

Ethan pushed his fingers into her hair, cradling her cheeks, itching to pull it out of the knot and see it cascade down her shoulders, feel the heavy warmth of it sifting over his fingers.

'I've just been so…lost, Olivia. After Aaliyah I felt like I'd lost *everything*, and I was just existing in this dark, cold, barren place. And then you came back and brought the warmth and the light, and you got under my skin, just like you had the first time, and I tried to ignore that, tried to not want it, but I couldn't.'

Olivia fought against the urge to throw herself into his arms. She wanted him to be sure. 'Because you love me?'

Ethan nodded. 'Yes. You were right when you said Aaliyah wouldn't want me to blame myself for her death, and Leo was right about how Aaliyah would want me to love and *be loved* again. I guess I needed to open up to the people who love me and let them help me through, because when I did…it suddenly made sense. But you know us Hunters—not big on emotional declarations.'

Olivia could feel a block of emotion rising in her throat. Why hadn't the stubborn man had this kind of revelation a bit earlier? 'Oh, Ethan.'

Ethan was encouraged by the husky quality of her voice. 'I know I don't deserve a second chance. That all I ever seem to do is hurt you, Liv. But—'

Olivia cut him off with her mouth, raising herself up on her tippy-toes and throwing her arms around his neck. She didn't care about that. There'd been a decade of hurt between them, but he loved her and they had a lot of decades ahead.

'Yes, you do,' she said, pulling back after long breathless moments. 'We both do. So we screwed it up in the past? This is now, and we *both* deserve this. We're good people who have had crappy things happen to them— you bet your ass we deserve this. And you'd better be in this forever, Ethan Hunter, because I love you too, and *together forever* is the only second chance I'm interested in.'

Ethan smiled, and then he laughed, lifting her off her feet and swirling her around and around, her diamantés dazzling and sparkling. He felt as light as the air he was swirling her in, and more alive than he'd been in a very long time.

He eased her back to the floor and placed his forehead against hers. 'For ever and ever, Liv, I promise.'

And then he kissed her. He kissed her with everything he had, showing her all their tomorrows.

And it was good.

EPILOGUE

IT HAD BEEN a perfect day for a wedding. Not even a frosty October day had stopped the bride from wearing her mother's immaculately restored wedding dress. The vintage piece from 1950 fell only to the knee, and the cap sleeves bared her arms, but inside the opulent function room of one of London's swankiest hotels it was warm and cosy.

The tinkling of glasses caused a hush around the room and the occupants all turned to face the bridal table, draped in filmy white and decorated with sprigs of fluffy yellow wattle to match the touches of the Australian wild flower in the bride's hair and bouquet.

Leo Hunter stood up in his place and announced, 'It's been a hell of a year.'

A murmur of agreement ran around the wedding guests. Some laughed. Everyone smiled. Lizzie especially, who slipped her free hand into her husband's and squeezed. In her other she cradled their sleeping three-month-old baby girl. Little Francesca was the spitting image of her father and the light of their lives.

'It took a decade to get these two—' he turned to Ethan, sitting beside him, and Olivia, sitting on the other side of her new husband '—together, and another year for them to finally tie the knot amidst their busy schedules, but I think we can all agree it's been worth the wait.'

More general agreement and smiles.

'I'm not going to go on. I think everyone here knows that the Hunter men aren't big on all that mushy, emotional stuff.'

General laughter now at the understatement. Everyone present knew the Hunter siblings were great at terse exchanges and loaded silences and only reasonably new to the whole brotherly love thing.

'I just wish Ethan and Olivia all the love and happiness I know they both deserve. I also wish them luck in their new endeavour as they set off to Africa to train up local teams at the new facility the Hunter Clinic and Fair Go have jointly funded.' Leo raised his glass and turned slightly to face the bride and groom. 'To Ethan and Olivia. Good things always.'

Ethan and Olivia rose from their seats as people toasted them. Ethan held his hand out to Leo and they shook. 'Thank you,' he murmured as myriad glasses clinked together. 'It means a lot to me to have you by my side today.'

Olivia watched as Ethan and Leo embraced, tears pricking the backs of her eyes. She looked at Lizzie, who smiled and winked at her through suspiciously bright eyes.

Ethan waited for his brother to take his seat, clearing his throat from a rush of unexpected emotion, then turned to Olivia, who was glowing for more reasons than one. A surge of pure male pride flooded him at knowing that *he* was responsible for that look on her face, that *he* was the one going home with her tonight and every night.

He squeezed her hand as he turned to address the room and said, 'I think we can all agree that I'm the luckiest man in this room tonight.' Then he turned back to Olivia, dipped his head and kissed her very thoroughly to a re-sounding chorus of applause, cheers and hoots.

When he finally released her it was gratifying to see the way her dark brown eyes had melted into two thick, sludgy pools of sticky-sweet lust more desirous than any chocolate from Sirmontane.

Collecting himself from his own libido spike, he turned to speak again.

'As Leo said, we're not known for our emotional monologues, so I'm going to keep this brief too. I'd like to thank everyone for coming and helping us to celebrate our day. It *has* been a hell of a year, and it's great to look out at you all and see how many of us from the Hunter Clinic family have found happiness in that time. There must be something in the water.'

Everyone laughed and he waited for them to quiet down before he continued.

'For a long time I'd resigned myself to not ever being happy. Truly happy. And then along came Olivia… again…and she has made me happier than I ever knew I could be.'

He looked down at her and smiled as the room filled with coos and wolf-whistles.

Ethan faced their guests again. 'Up until last night I didn't think it could get any better than this—which just goes to prove you *can* get to thirty-six and know noth-ing, because now it appears I'm going to be a daddy and I'm no longer *just* happy, I'm whole.'

For a moment there was stunned silence, and then the room erupted in wild applause as the grinning parents-to-be were treated to a standing ovation.

'And now, if no one objects,' Ethan said as he hushed

their guests with a raising of his hands, 'I'm going to dance with my pregnant wife.'

Hoots and hollers met his proclamation as he took Olivia's hand and gestured for her to accompany him.

Olivia looked at her brand-new tuxedoed husband. 'We don't have to dance, Ethan,' she said over the din.

Ethan smiled. 'Yes, we do. I've been taking lessons.'

'Lessons?'

'Trust me,' he said, kissing her again. 'I'm a doctor.'

But their path to the dance floor was littered with well-wishers and it was a slow trip.

Lizzie and Leo were the first to embrace them.

'Welcome to the club, Ethan,' Leo said, and both Lizzie and Olivia were surprised when the brothers embraced again.

Iain and Lexi were next in line. Little Bonnie, recently adopted from China, was alert in her father's arms and smiled at the newlyweds in a way that melted Olivia's heart.

'She's such a cutie,' Olivia said.

Lexi smiled. 'Just like her father.'

Kara and Declan stopped them next, Kara giving Olivia a huge hug. They were both brown and relaxed, having not long returned from their honeymoon on the Great Barrier Reef.

'You know I'm taking total credit for this, right?' Kara said. 'If I hadn't badgered you to go to the ball…'

Ethan laughed. 'Okay, you can take the credit for the wedding, but *I'm* taking credit for the baby.'

Declan laughed. 'I'm sure Kara will give you that one.'

Marco and Becca were the last ones to catch them before they got to the dance floor.

'Zorro,' Ethan said, offering his hand to the other man, not remotely concerned to be addressing the second in line to the royal throne of Sirmontane so casually. 'So glad you could come and add a touch of royalty to our humble wedding. Not quite as spectacular as *your* marvellous celebration last year.'

Marco grinned at the familiar jovial banter. 'Nowhere near as many people to potentially offend either,' he said good-naturedly. 'Weddings, my friend, are just the icing. The cake,' he said, smiling down at Becca, 'is always the best bit.'

Becca rolled her eyes and clutched playfully at her heart. 'Such poetry, my darling.'

'Are you going to be okay, Clavo, with your limp and your two left feet?' Marco teased. 'If you need me to do the honours…?'

Marco, known for his ability to tango, had been Ethan's go-to man when he'd considered taking some dance lessons so he could wow Olivia in their first dance as husband and wife. The royal Prince and fellow war veteran had set him up with some exclusive lessons from a friend who ran a Latin dance club in Soho.

'You take care of your own wife.' Ethan winked. 'I'll take care of mine.'

And with that Olivia was finally alone with her husband on the dance floor. The strains of something soft and sweet filled the room as he swept her along in a dance that was slow and simple and sexy and all she had to do was follow his lead.

They didn't talk, because clearly the world's most competent surgeon was concentrating too hard on not screwing up, but Olivia's heart almost exploded in her chest at his willingness to go so far out of his comfort zone for her.

His limp was barely discernible these days, due to his strict adherence to regular physio—something which he demonstrated ably as the song came to an end and he dipped her dramatically, following through with a searing kiss to cat-calls, applause and wolf-whistles.

Another song struck up as Ethan righted Olivia and other couples joined them on the dance floor. Ethan moved into a slow shuffle. The scent of wattle and happiness suffused his senses as he pulled her closer.

'You look very sexy, Mrs Hunter,' Ethan murmured in Olivia's ear, even though he knew his independent wife was not changing her name.

'You're not bad yourself, Mr Hunter,' she murmured. 'Of course scrubs would have worked just as well for me.'

Ethan chuckled. 'I have some in the hotel suite.'

Olivia pulled her head off his shoulder swiftly, looking up at him. His cheeky grin let her know he was teasing. She shook her head at him.

'Oh, look, Ethan,' she murmured as the cutest sight caught her attention over his shoulder.

She danced them around slightly so they could both witness it. Their two flower girls were dancing with the page boy, holding hands in a circle. Mia, the eldest, was six and was Mitch Cooper's daughter. As they watched Mitch and Grace cut in. Mitch picked up Mia and all three of them danced together, their arms around each other. Olivia even heard Mia call Grace *Mummy* and her heart swelled in her chest. She knew how much Grace had wanted to hear that word from the little girl she loved like her own.

That just left Ella and Isaac dancing together. At two and a half, Ella looked the picture of health after her risky experimental cancer treatment in the US over a year ago had been more than successful.

Olivia glanced over at Rafael and Abbie, whose marriage had almost disintegrated under the strain of their daughter's illness. They were watching Ella like the two proudest people on earth, and their four-month-old son, Stefano, with dark curls just like his sister's, was proof that things were very good between them.

Isaac, who was five, was dancing with Ella a bit like the way Ethan had danced with her, his little tongue stuck out in concentration as if he was trying to be all grown up and not step on her toes. Olivia located Charlotte and Edward up amongst the band. She'd hired the band on Edward's recommendation and watching him now, seated at the baby grand piano, his fingers tinkling the ivories, she was glad she had. Edward was obviously familiar with the guys and they were happy to have him up with them, playing the piano like a professional musician instead of a microsurgeon.

Charlotte was sitting beside him, enjoying the show, but Olivia noticed her glancing frequently over at Isaac, keeping a watchful eye on him. As a single mum to Isaac for so long, Olivia knew that Charlotte found it hard not to hover, but Edward's love and commitment had made her more secure. Charlotte looked blissfully happy. They both did.

Seemed it was the night for it.

'How long do you think,' Ethan asked, nuzzling her neck, bringing her attention back to the tight circle between them and the heat that was building with every rock and sway, 'until we can leave?'

Olivia smiled into his shoulder. 'Well, I *am* pregnant. And pregnant women *do* get very tired.'

Ethan grinned, his lips just below her ear. 'I like the way you think.'

'Good,' she said. 'Give me your jacket and get me out of here.'

Ethan grabbed her hand and pushed her out into a twirl before pulling her back in and dipping her.

'Yes, ma'am,' he muttered against her mouth.

* * * * *

A sneaky peek at next month…

MEDICAL
ROMANCE™

THE ULTIMATE IN ROMANTIC MEDICAL DRAMA

My wish list for next month's titles…

In stores from 1st August 2014:

❑ Tempted by Her Boss – Scarlet Wilson

& His Girl From Nowhere – Tina Beckett

❑ Falling For Dr Dimitriou – Anne Fraser

& Return of Dr Irresistible – Amalie Berlin

❑ Daring to Date Her Boss – Joanna Neil

& A Doctor to Heal Her Heart – Annie Claydon

Available at WHSmith, Tesco, Asda, Eason, Amazon and Apple

Just can't wait?

Visit us Online

You can buy our books online a month before they hit the shops! **www.millsandboon.co.uk**

0714/03

Join our *EXCLUSIVE* eBook club

FROM JUST £1.99 A MONTH!

Never miss a book again with our hassle-free eBook subscription.

★ Pick how many titles you want from each series with our flexible subscription

★ Your titles are delivered to your device on the first of every month

★ Zero risk, zero obligation!

There really is nothing standing in the way of you and your favourite books!

Start your eBook subscription today at www.millsandboon.co.uk/subscribe

EBOOK_SUBS

Join the Mills & Boon Book Club

Subscribe to **Medical** today for 3, 6 or 12 months and you could **save over £40!**

We'll also treat you to these fabulous extras:

- FREE L'Occitane gift set worth £10

- FREE home delivery

- Rewards scheme, exclusive offers…and much more!

Subscribe now and save over £40
www.millsandboon.co.uk/subscribeme

SUBS/OFFER/M1